Colin Forbes (1923-2006) was the prin
thriller writer Raymond Harold Sawkins. S
mostly as Colin Forbes. He was most famo
of thrillers in which the principal character is Tweed, a
of the Secret Intelligence Service. Forbes started out working as a sub-
editor for a publishing company before serving with the British Army
in North Africa and the Middle East during the Second World War.
When he went back to civilian life, he worked for a publishing and print
company, eventually becoming a novelist on a full-time basis. Forbes
made his debut as a published author in 1966 using his real name of
Raymond Sawkins for the novel *Snow on High Ground*. His debut
under his preferred pen name (Colin Forbes) came in 1969 with *Tramp
in Armour*.

TERMINAL

Colin Forbes

SILVERTAIL BOOKS ◇ London

First published by William Collins Sons & Co. Ltd in 1984

This edition published by Silvertail Books in 2023

www.silvertailbooks.com

Copyright © Colin Forbes 1984

This edition is published with the permission of International Literary Properties UK Limited

978-1-913727-28-4

For Jane – who holds the fort

Author's Note

Swiss clinics are among the finest and most advanced medical establishments in the world. They provide a standard of care without equal. The Berne Clinic, which plays a prominent part in this novel, does not exist. All characters are creatures of the author's imagination.

terminal – most concise form of an expression; fatal illness; point of connection in electric circuit; railway or airway terminus...
The Concise Oxford Dictionary

Prologue

No night should have been as cold as this one. No woman should have to endure what Hannah Stuart endured. She ran screaming down the snowbound slope – screaming when she wasn't choking and coughing her lungs out. Behind her she heard the snarling and barking of the ferocious Doberman dogs coming closer.

Wearing only a nightdress, over which she had thrown her fur coat, her feet shod in rubber-heeled sensible shoes which gripped the treacherous ground, she stumbled on towards the wire fence surrounding the place. As she ran, she tore the 'thing' off her face and head, dropping it as she took in great gulps of icy air.

The night was dark but the whiteness of the snow showed her where she was going. Another few hundred yards and she would reach the fence which bordered the highway, the outside world – freedom. Now she could breathe the night air she wondered if it were even worse than the 'thing' she had discarded. With the temperature below zero it was like breathing in liquid ice.

'Oh, my God, no!' she gasped.

Something had landed just ahead of her, a shell-like projectile which quietly burst with a hissing sound. Desperately she tried to hold her breath while she ran through what billowed ahead. It was impossible. She absorbed more lungfuls of the filthy stuff and started choking again.

Behind the dogs they had released ran men in military-style uniforms, their heads and faces hideously disfigured by weird apparatus. Hannah Stuart didn't look back, didn't see them – she just knew they were coming for her.

At the point she was heading for a large wire gate bisected the fence. It was closed but she knew that under her feet lay the snow-covered road leading to that gate. It made her progress faster – such as it was.

Still choking, she reached the gate, her hands clawing at the wire as she struggled to haul it open.

If only a car would come up the highway, if only the driver saw her. If only she could get this goddamned gate to open she might even survive. So many 'if's...' The panic she fought to hold in check was welling up. Frantically, she stared up and down the deserted road for sight of a pair of headlights. In the dark nothing moved. Except the dogs which were nearly on top of her and the men who, fanned out in an arc military fashion, came up behind the animals.

She gave one last choking gulp. Her hands, bleeding now as she went on clawing at the gate, lost their grip. Smears of red blood coated the ice-encrusted gate as she slipped down, and then fell the last few feet. The iron-hard ground smashed her face a savage blow.

She was dead when they reached her, eyes sightless, her complexion already showing signs of cyanosis poisoning. Two men with a stretcher took her back up the slope. The dogs were leashed. One man took out a piece of surgical gauze to remove all traces of blood from the gate, then followed his companions.

This was in Switzerland in the year 1984. On the gate a metal plate carried an engraved legend. *KLINIK BERN. Wachthund!* BERNE CLINIC. Guard Dog!

One

Tucson, Arizona. 10 February 1984. 75°. A sizzling tremor of heat haze. In the shimmer the harsh, jagged Tucson Mountains seemed to vibrate. Behind the wheel of her Jaguar, newly imported from England, Dr Nancy Kennedy let her frustration rip, ramming down on the accelerator.

Expertly, she corrected a rear wheel skid as she swung off Interstate Highway 10 and headed up the hairpin bends towards Gates Pass. Her passenger alongside her, Bob Newman, did not appreciate the experience. Clouds of dust from the road enveloped them and he began choking. He felt like yelling – even screaming.

'Do you have to drive your latest toy as though you're racing at Brands Hatch?' he enquired.

'Typical British understatement?' she asked.

'Typical American way of handling a new car. You're supposed to run it in,' he commented.

'That's what I'm doing...'

'What you're doing is ripping the guts out of it. Just because you're worried about your grandfather in that Swiss clinic you don't have to kill us...'

'I sometimes wonder why I got engaged to an Englishman,' Nancy snapped.

'You couldn't resist me. Christ, it's hot...'

Newman, forty years old, had thick, sandy-coloured hair, cynical blue eyes of a man who has seen too much of the seamy side of the world, a strong nose and jaw and a firm mouth with a droll, humorous expression. He knew it was 75°: he had seen the temperature register on a digital sign outside a bank as they left Tucson. He wore fawn slacks, an open-necked white shirt and his jacket with a small check

I

design was folded in his lap. He was already sweating profusely. The dust was adhering to the sweat. It was eleven o'clock in the morning and they had just finished one row. Maybe it was time for another. He risked it.

'Nancy, if you want to check on why your grandfather was rushed off by air to that place in Switzerland you're going the wrong way. This road does *not* lead to the Berne Clinic...'

'Oh, shit!'

She rammed her foot on the brake and he would have gone through the windscreen but for the fact they both wore safety belts. A second earlier she had swung off the road into a lay-by. Flinging open the door, she stormed out of the car and stood with her back to him, arms folded, standing by a low wall.

He sighed. She had, of course, left the engine running. Turning off the ignition, he pocketed the keys and joined her, his jacket over one arm. He studied her out of the corner of his eye.

Twenty-nine years old, Nancy Kennedy was at her most attractive in a rage. Her smooth skin was flushed, her raven hair falling to her shoulders. He loved exploring that dense mane of hair, soothing the back of her neck, and then nothing could stop them.

Five feet eight, four inches shorter than Newman, she had legs your fingers itched to stroke and a figure which caused all men's eyes to stare when they walked into a restaurant. Angry, she tilted her head, emphasizing her superb bone structure, high cheekbones and pointed chin expressing self-will.

It constantly amazed him. He had seen her in a white coat practising her profession, supremely competent and self-controlled – but in her private life Nancy had the temper of a she-devil. Often he suspected it was the contrast which attracted him – apart from her physical assets.

'What does the famous foreign correspondent have in mind?' she enquired bitingly.

'Looking for facts – evidence – instead of flying off into the wild blue yonder...' He looked at the staggering view and corrected his description. 'The dirty grey yonder...'

Beyond the wall the road began to descend again in an even more terrifying series of twists and bends. Beyond that it looked like the mountains of Hell – a pile of gigantic cinder cones without a trace of green vegetation on the scarred rock faces.

'We were going to have a lovely day at the Desert Museum,' she pouted. 'They have a beaver lodge underground. You can go down a staircase and see the beavers nestled in the lodge...'

'And all the time you'll be worrying and talking about Jesse Kennedy...'

'He raised me after my mother and father were killed in a car crash. I don't like the way Linda secretly had him moved to Switzerland while I was at St Thomas's in London. There's an odd smell about the whole business...'

'I don't like Linda,' he remarked.

'You like her legs – you never stop looking at them...'

'I'm a connoisseur of good legs. Yours are almost as good...'

She thumped him, turned round and leaned against the wall, her expression serious. 'Bob, I really am worried. Linda could have phoned me when they diagnosed leukaemia. She had my number. I'm not happy at all. She may be my older sister but she's no right to take the law into her own hands. Then there's her husband, Harvey...'

'Don't like Harvey either,' he said easily, twirling an unlit cigarette in his mouth. 'You realize the only way to check this? Not that I think for a moment there's anything wrong – but you won't settle until I convince you...'

'So, convince me, Mr World Foreign Correspondent who speaks five languages fluently.'

'We proceed systematically as though I was checking out a big story. You're a doctor and a close relative of the man we're enquiring about – so the right people will have to talk to me as long as you're present. The family doctor is on my list – but first we interview the specialist who took the blood tests that showed it was leukaemia. Where do we find him?'

'A man called Buhler at Tucson Medical Center. It's in the city. I insisted on Linda telling me all the details – I say *insisted* because I had to drag the information out of her...'

'Doesn't prove a thing,' Newman commented. 'Knowing you're a doctor she might have been worried she hadn't done it your way: She might also have resented your questioning

'We seem to be doing it backwards,' she objected. 'I can't see why you don't talk to Linda first, then our doctor, then the specialist at the Center...'

'Deliberately backwards. That way we get testimony and check what the others say later. It's the only technique which will show up any discrepancies. I still think it's a wild goose chase but...' He spread his hands. '...I just want to settle your mind and then we can get on with living.'

'It's queer – Linda not phoning me while I was doing my post-graduate work at St Thomas's...'

'You said that before. Let's get some action. Specifically, let's get to the Center before Buhler goes to lunch. And no argument – I'm driving. Hop in the passenger seat...'

'Didn't you know, Nancy? No, of course not – you were away in London when Buhler was killed...'

They were at the Center talking to a slim man of fifty wearing a sweatshirt and slacks. Dr Rosen had taken them to his private office and Newman sat watching him and drinking coffee. Rosen had an alert, professional manner and was clearly glad to help Nancy in any way he could.

'How was he killed?' Newman asked casually.

'*Killed* was perhaps the wrong word...'

'But it was the word you used,' Newman pointed out. 'Maybe you could fill us in on the details. I'm sure Nancy would appreciate that...'

Dr Rosen hesitated. He stroked his thinning hair with his right hand as though searching for the right words to express himself. Newman frowned at Nancy who was about to say something and she remained silent.

4

'It was *very* tragic. He went off the road near Gates Pass in his new Mercedes. He was DOA when we got him back here...'

'He must have earned a lot of money to afford a Mercedes,' Newman remarked.

'He told me he got lucky during the one trip he made to Vegas. He was that kind of man, Mr Newman – if he made a killing... I'm using that word again – don't read any significance into it. What I'm saying is, if Buhler came into a lot of money he would hang on to it.'

'You said "very tragic" and I noticed you emphasized the first word. He had a family?'

Rosen swivelled in his chair, gazed out of the window and then turned back to face Newman who had the impression Rosen was uncomfortable about the subject of their conversation. Clasping his hands, he leaned forward across his desk and looked at both his visitors.

'Buhler went off that road at speed because he was drunk. It was a shock to all of us because we'd never suspected he was an alcoholic...'

'Driving off a road when you've had one too many doesn't make you an alcoholic,' Newman pressed. 'Why not complete the story?'

'Buhler had no family, wasn't married – except to his job. He had no relatives we were able to trace. When the police checked his home they found cupboards stacked with empty bottles of whisky. The evidence was conclusive – he'd been a secret drinker. That's why I said very tragic...'

'And he *was* the specialist who checked my grandfather's blood sample and diagnosed leukaemia?' Nancy interjected.

'That's correct. Young Dr Chase brought them in himself for Buhler to check. Unfortunately, there was no doubt about it – if that's what you're wondering, Nancy.'

'I wasn't wondering that – why this Dr Chase? For years our doctor has been Bellman...'

'All this has to be in confidence, Nancy. Some of it I'm only telling you because of our long acquaintance – and to put your mind at rest about Jesse being sent to that clinic in Switzerland. Mrs Wayne changed your doctor – she never liked Bellman. Said she preferred someone younger...'

'Linda chose this Dr Chase!' Nancy's tone expressed near amazement. 'Someone entirely new – and young – advised her to shuttle Jesse off to Europe?'

'Well...' Rosen hesitated again, glancing at Newman, who gazed back with no particular expression. 'Frank Chase has gone up like a rocket – he's very popular. My guess is he'll soon have a string of wealthy patients. He has a way with... people.'

The records,' Nancy persisted, 'the blood samples Buhler took to check my grandfather. They're here at the hospital?'

'They were destroyed...'

'That's not right,' Nancy protested.

'Wait a minute. Please!' Rosen held up a placating hand. 'Let me finish. Buhler was an eccentric. As I told you, he lived for his work. He had a habit of carrying his files round with him so he could study them whenever he felt like it. They were inside the car when he went over the edge. There was a partial fire – all his records were incinerated...'

'How young is this Dr Frank Chase?' Newman enquired.

'Thirty-two. He still has a long way to go to get to the top of the tree, if that's what you were wondering. But he's climbing.'

'Could we have Dr Chase's address?' Newman asked.

'Sure. He's out on Sabino Canyon Road.'

'Very nice, too,' Nancy commented. 'Skyline Country Club territory. Linda is practically his neighbour if he's far enough out.'

Rosen said nothing as he took a pad and wrote carefully in a fine Italian script. Newman read the address upside down and for a member of the medical profession it was surprisingly legible. Something in Rosen's attitude puzzled him: the doctor had given Newman several close scrutinies as though trying to make up his mind about something, an aspect which was bothering him. He tore off the sheet, folded it neatly and handed it to Newman – which caused Nancy to raise her eyebrows.

He stood up and came round his desk to shake hands and escort them to the door, opening it to let Nancy leave first. His handclasp was warm and reassuring.

6

'I really don't think you have anything to worry about,' he told her. 'The Swiss are very good...'

He waited until Newman was halfway along the corridor leading to the exit before he called him back. Newman told Nancy he would be with her in a minute and to wait in the car. Rosen closed the door once the Englishman was inside his office. He handed him a visiting card.

'That has my phone number here and at home. Could I meet with you this evening? Just the two of us over a drink for half an hour? Do you know the Tack Room?'

'Nancy took me there.' He slipped the card inside his wallet. 'It's a nice place...'

'MOBIL give it a five-star rating. Seven o'clock? Good. Maybe considerate not to mention this to Nancy. A few weeks before Jesse was shunted out of Tucson, we had an eminent Swiss medical personality here on a tour of the States. Linda, Nancy's sister, attended one of his lectures.'

'Any significance in that?'

'He happens to be head of the Berne Clinic...'

Two

'Where the hell have you been, Nancy?' Newman demanded. 'I've sat here roasting in your Jag. for exactly forty-three minutes. At least I've got the smell of that place out of my system...'

'And how long were *you* with Rosen?' she flared. 'I might have sat here waiting forty-three minutes for you...'

'Three minutes,' snapped Newman.

'Well, how was I to know? I popped into another department to see an old friend and she had a lot to tell me. I've been away at St Thomas's for a year in case you've forgotten. And do you mind getting out of the driving seat?'

'I'm driving...'

He inserted the ignition keys and switched on the engine. She said something under her breath and her classic, pleated skirt swept high up her long legs as she sat in the passenger seat and slammed the door. She asked the question as he drove smoothly out of the Medical Center.

'What smell were you referring to – the one you got out of your system?'

'Disinfectant. Hospital disinfectant...'

'You hate anything medical, don't you? I can't imagine what you ever saw in me the night we first met in that place in Walton Street. Bewick's, wasn't it?'

'My favourite London restaurant. And I saw your lovely legs. You display them frequently...'

'*Bastard!*' She thumped his shoulder. 'What did Rosen want to tell you that was too spicy for my delicate ears?'

'With my not being a doctor, being British, he wanted to emphasize the conversation had been strictly confidential. He's a careful type, very ethical and all that. Now, guide me to the mansion of Dr Frank Chase...'

Holding the slip of paper Rosen had given Newman in her hands and staring straight ahead, Nancy spoke only to give directions. Sabino Canyon Road starts in a well-populated area on the north-east outskirts of Tucson heading for the Catalina Mountains. It starts as a district for the well-off and progresses up the canyon into an oasis for the wealthy.

Newman noted the houses were getting bigger, the grounds more extensive, and again ahead the mountains danced in the heat dazzle. But the Tucson range was like a series of gigantic, broken-backed dinosaurs turned into rock. Like the Skyline Country Club, the Catalinas were opulent, welcoming and had vegetation.

He accelerated past the Wayne property in case Linda happened to be looking out of a window. Nancy glanced at him with a hint of amusement.

'Why the sudden burst of enthusiasm?'

'So Linda can't phone Chase and warn him we're coming.'

'Robert, you never miss a trick,' she needled him.

She always called him Robert when she was either annoyed or wanted to get under his skin, knowing he disliked his Christian name. He parried the thrust by grinning and not replying. The Jag went on climbing and behind them the city of Tucson spread out in the bowl formed by three separate mountain ranges.

'Slow down, Bob,' she warned, 'we're close now. That place on the left must be Chase...'

A split rail fence enclosed the property, a large, L-shaped house with two storeys and a green pantile roof. Newman drove through the open gateway and along the drive which divided – one arm leading to the front porch, the second to the double garage at the side of the house. The wheels crunched as they pulled up.

In front of the house the 'garden' was a generous stretch of gravel out of which grew evil-looking saguaro cacti. Shaped like trees, they had a main trunk from which sprouted prickly branches stretching up towards the sky as though trying to claw it down. A man standing by the double garage pressed a button and Newman, who had switched off the engine, heard the purr of power-operated doors closing over the garage. In the wing mirror he watched the man approaching with a wary tread.

Thirty-two, Rosen had said. The man wore tight blue jeans and an open-necked shirt with a large check design. His face was bony, the skin tanned under a mop of thick brown hair. Seeing only that much in the mirror, Newman took an instant dislike to him. He looked up as the man put a long-fingered hand on the door top. Manicured nails and a strong whiff of after-shave lotion.

'Dr Frank Chase?'

'Yes.'

The word hung in the hot air like a challenge and the brown eyes which stared down at Newman measured him for the operating table. Newman smiled amiably and said the one thing which he thought would throw Chase off balance.

'I don't think you've met Dr Nancy Kennedy. Sister of Linda Wayne. Grand-daughter of Jesse Kennedy. She's about to launch an investigation into why her grandfather was hustled off five-and-a-half thousand miles away without consulting her. This is a lovely place you've got here, Dr Chase.'

'Miss Kennedy, I'm afraid there was no question your grandfather was suffering from leukaemia...' Dr Chase laid a thin, bony hand on the arm of the reclining chair Nancy sat in at the rear of the house by the side of the oyster-shell-shaped swimming pool. His smile was sympathetic but Newman observed the smile did not reach the brown eyes which studied her. 'You see,' Chase continued, 'we had the top specialist in the state examine him. Dr Buhler...'

'Who conveniently died in a car accident,' Nancy interrupted him coldly. 'And even more conveniently had the records of those tests with him so they now no longer exist. The only real evidence, when you get to the bottom line, that he has this disease.'

'*Conveniently?*' Chase's smile became a little tight. 'I don't quite follow.' His hand clasped Nancy's gently. Here we go with the famous bedside manner, Newman thought as he stretched in his own chair and

10

sipped his glass of bourbon. 'Dr Kennedy,' Chase continued more formally, 'I do realize you must be overwrought. You were fond of your grandfather...'

'I *am* fond of my grandfather...'

She pulled her hand free and swallowed a large gulp of her own drink. Newman stood up and eased his shoulders as though stiff from sitting. He grinned as Chase glanced up at him sharply.

'Mind if I just wander round your place?' he suggested. 'I'll leave you and Nancy to talk this thing out alone.'

'That might be a very good idea,' Chase agreed. 'Feel free...'

The obligatory swimming pool and its surrounding patio were tiled with marble. The walls of the house were plaster painted a dark sludge green. The picture windows looking down on Tucson were huge and triple plate glass doors slid open on to the patio. As he wandered towards the side of the house Newman peered inside.

The largest hi-fi system he had ever seen occupied the end wall of the sitting-room. The rest of the furniture reeked of money. He looked back before he disappeared round the garage end of the house and Chase had his back to him, crouched forward as he spoke earnestly to Nancy, whose expression was blank as she listened.

It intrigued Newman that Chase's first action on seeing them arrive had been to close the garage. He may well have recognized Nancy – the Wayne house was full of photographs of her with Linda. His shirt stuck to his back as he shuffled quietly over the gravel which had a gritty feel that seemed to compound the heat.

Holding his glass in one hand, he lifted the lid of the control box attached to the wall. Two buttons, one green, one red. He pressed green. The same purring sound of highly-efficient – and expensive – hydraulics as the doors elevated. He stood staring at the occupants. One red Ferrari. One red Maserati. Blood-red. Very new. A small fortune on eight wheels.

'You're interested in cars, Mr Newman?'

'I'm a car buff, Chase. So, apparently, are you,' Newman said easily.

The doctor had come after him silent as a cat. Even the sneakers he wore should have made some sound on the gravel. He stood looking at Newman and the smile was gone. His right hand held a refilled glass of bourbon. He swallowed half the contents in one gulp and wiped his mouth with the back of his other hand.

'You usually go creeping round people's homes, prying? That's the foreign correspondent coming out, I guess. Incidentally, I understood you and Nancy were engaged – but I notice no ring on the third finger of her left hand...'

Newman grinned amiably. He made a throwaway gesture with his hand. Chase did not respond. His mouth twisted in a faint sneer, he waited, his head tilted forward. Newman put a cigarette in his mouth before replying.

'Let's take that lot in sequence, shall we? You have something to hide because you can afford a couple of brand new sports jobs?'

'I don't like your tone...'

'I'm not crazy about yours, but as long as enough rich patients continue to love you what does it matter? As to Nancy, we have a trial engagement...'

'I'd just as soon you didn't light that cigarette, Newman. You should read the statistics...'

'You think I'll pollute the atmosphere out here?' Newman lit the cigarette. 'Did you know that in Britain a lot of doctors have given up smoking and preach the gospel? Did you also know that the graph showing the degree of alcoholism among British doctors shows a steady climb.' Newman glanced at Chase's glass. 'You should read the statistics.'

'I've heard of trial marriages...' Chase's sneer became more pronounced. 'But a trial engagement is a new sexual exercise...'

'So, I've broadened your experience. Hello, Nancy. I think we ought to leave now – unless you have more questions for your friendly family doctor...'

Tight-lipped, Nancy waited until they were driving back along Sabino Canyon Road before she spoke. Extracting the cigarette from Newman's mouth, she took a few puffs and handed it back to him. He knew then she was in a towering rage.

'The condescending bastard! God knows what Linda sees in a man like that. Our previous doctor, Bellman, is a nice man.'

'I've nothing against Frank Chase,' Newman remarked airily as he swung round a bend. 'He's a hyena – scooping up red meat wherever he can find it, holding rich old ladies by the hand as they tell him about their imaginary ailments. That doesn't make him a conspirator. Your sister's place next? I'd like to talk to her on her home ground rather than at the Smugglers Inn. In people's homes you see them as they really are. The other night when she brought Harvey over for dinner at my hotel she put on an act. Her public image.'

'Do you know the one thing Chase didn't suggest when we were out by the pool – the one thing he should have suggested if he had really wanted me reassured about Jesse?'

'Oddly enough, as I wasn't there all the time, I don't know.'

'He never suggested that we visit the Berne Clinic so I could see Jesse for myself. And yes, I think you should talk to Linda. I'll leave you alone. Mind she doesn't seduce you...'

'It all started when Jesse – we all called him that – had a bad fall from his horse, Bob...' The large dark eyes stared at Newman, the long lashes half-closed demurely over them. 'You do prefer to be called Bob, don't you? Nancy calls you Robert when she wants to make you mad. My kid sister is full of little tricks like that. Is that the way you like your tea? Have I got it right?'

Linda Wayne sat beside Newman on the couch, her long legs sheathed in the sheerest black nylon and crossed with her skirt just above her shapely knees. She wore a high-necked cashmere sweater which emphasized her full figure. When she had shown him into the vast living-room her right breast had briefly touched his forearm. He had felt the firmness under the cashmere, a material quite unsuited to the temperature outside but perfect for the stark coolness of the air-conditioning.

Her hair was jet black, thick and shoulder-length like Nancy's. Thick, dark eyebrows made her slow-moving eyes seem even larger. Her voice was husky and she exuded sexuality like a heavy perfume. Newman stopped himself gazing at the sweep of her legs and tried to recall what she had just said.

'Your tea,' she repeated, 'is it the right colour?'

'Perfect...'

'It's Earl Grey. I bought it in San Francisco. I just love your English teas. We drink a lot of tea in the States now...'

'But you don't ride horses much down here any more.' He swallowed a gulp of the tea quickly. He hated Earl Grey. 'So what was Jesse doing on a horse?'

'He rode every day like they used to years ago, Bob. We put him to bed upstairs and called the doctor...'

'Frank Chase?'

'That's right...' She had paused briefly before she replied. She began talking more quickly. 'Bellman, our previous doctor, was getting out of touch with modern developments. I thought a younger man would be more likely to move with the times. It's a good job I took that decision – he gave Jesse a thorough examination, including blood tests. That's how we found out Jesse was suffering from leukaemia. You can imagine the shock...' She moved closer to him and clasped his free hand. She looked very soulful.

'It was a very big jump,' he said.

She looked puzzled, wary. 'Bob, I'm not following you...'

'From Tucson, Arizona to Berne, Switzerland.'

'Oh, I see what you mean.' She relaxed, gave him a warm smile. 'Jesse was a mountaineer. He liked Switzerland. He discussed it with Frank – Dr Chase. He simply acceded to my grandfather's expressed wish, bearing in mind the patient's best interests...'

'Come again? No, forget it. No thanks, no more tea.'

He simply acceded to my grandfather's expressed wish, bearing in mind the patient's best interests.

Linda's dialogue had suddenly gone wrong – she would normally never talk like that. But Frank Chase would. It confirmed what Newman had expected to happen. During the time between driving away from

Chase's place down Sabino Canyon Road to Linda's home the hyena had called Linda to report their visit – to instruct her.

She squeezed his hand gently to get his full attention and began talking again in her soft, soothing voice. 'Bob, I'd like you to do everything you can to settle my kid sister's mind. There's nothing she can do about Jesse except worry...'

'The kid sister can fly to Berne to find out what the hell is really going on...' Nancy stood in the open doorway, her manner curt, her tone biting. 'And when you've finished with it you might give Bob back his hand – he's only got two of them...'

'Nancy, there's simply nothing to go on,' Newman said emphatically. 'As a professional newspaper man I look for *facts* when I'm after a story – *evidence*! There isn't any showing something's wrong...'

It was mid-afternoon and they were eating a late lunch at the Smugglers Inn where he had insisted on staying. If gave him independence and kept Linda Wayne at arm's length. Nancy slammed down her fork beside her half-eaten steak.

'Fact One. Nobody asked for a second opinion...'

'Buhler, who did the blood tests, was tops according to Rosen. I gather you respect Rosen?'

'Yes, I do. Let that one slide, for the moment. Fact Two. I never heard Jesse say a word about he wished he could live in Switzerland. Visit it, yes! But God, he was always so glad to get back home.'

'When a man is ill, he dreams, to blot out reality...'

'Fact Three!' Nancy drummed on. 'At the very moment Jesse is ill because he falls off his horse Linda calls in an entirely new doctor. Fact Four! The only man who can confirm this diagnosis of leukaemia, Buhler, is dead. And his records go up in smoke with him! So everything rests on Dr Chase's word, a man you called a hyena...'

'I didn't like him. That doesn't make him Genghis Khan. Look, I'm seeing Rosen this evening. If nothing comes of that, can we drop the subject? I have to decide whether to accept this pretty lucrative offer from CBS to act as their European correspondent. They won't wait forever for a decision...'

'You want the job?' she interjected.

'It's the only way we can get married – unless you agree that we both live in London or somewhere in Europe...'

'I've given up years of my life to practise medicine and I want to live in the States. I'd feel lost and marooned anywhere else. And, Bob, I am going to Berne. The question is – are you coming with me? There might even be a big story in it...'

'Look, Nancy, I write about espionage, foreign affairs. Where in God's name is there that kind of story in this Berne business?'

'You've been there. You've done your job there. You speak all the languages – French, German, Italian, plus Spanish. You told me you have friends there. The bottom line is, are you going to help me?'

'I'll decide after I've seen Rosen...'

'Bob, what does a woman take off first? Her earrings, isn't it?' She divested herself of each gold earring slowly, watching him with a certain expression. 'Let's go to your room...'

'I haven't finished my steak.' He pushed his plate away and grinned. 'It's underdone, anyway. I've just lost my appetite.'

'You ordered your steak rare. The experience I'm offering is rare too...'

Three

New York, Kennedy Airport. 10 February 1984. 0°. The slim, attractive Swissair stewardess in her pale blue uniform noticed this passenger the moment he came aboard Flight SR 111, bound for Geneva and Zurich. She escorted the man, over six feet tall and heavily-built, to his reserved first-class window seat and tried to help him take off his shaggy sheepskin jacket.

'I can do it myself...'

His voice was gravelly, the tone curt. He handed her the jacket, settled himself in his seat and fastened the belt. He inserted a cigarette between his wide, thick lips and stared out into the darkness. The flight was due to depart at 18.55.

As the stewardess arranged his jacket carefully on a hanger she studied him. In his early fifties, she estimated. A dense thatch of white hair streaked with black, heavy, dark eyebrows and a craggy face. Clean-shaven, his complexion was flushed with the bitter wind which sheared the streets of New York. His large, left hand clutched a briefcase perched on the adjoining seat. She straightened her trim jacket before approaching him.

'I'm very sorry, sir, but no smoking is permitted...'

'I haven't lit the damned thing, have I! I am very familiar with the regulations. No smoking before the words up there say so...'

'I'm sorry, sir...'

She retreated, carrying on with her duties automatically as the Jumbo 747 took off and headed out across the Atlantic, her mind full of the tall American passenger. It was the blue eyes which worried her, she decided. They reminded her of that very special glacial blue you only saw in mountain lakes.

'Thinking about your boyfriend?' one of her companion stewardesses enquired while they sorted out the drink orders.

17

'The passenger in Seat Five. He fascinates me. Have you noticed his eyes? They're chilling...'

The white-haired man was sipping bitter lemon, staring out of the porthole window, when a hand lifted the briefcase off the seat next to him and dumped it in his lap. He glanced sideways as a small, bird-like man with restless eyes settled into the seat and began talking chirpily, keeping his voice low.

'Well, if it isn't my old pal, Lee Foley. Off to Zurich on more Company business?'

'Ed Schulz, go back to your own seat.'

'It's a free country, a free aircraft – just so long as you've paid. And I've paid. You didn't answer my question. The senior roving foreign affairs correspondent for *Time* magazine always gets answers to his questions. You should know that by now, Lee...'

'I quit the CIA and you know it. I'm with one of the top international detective agencies in New York. You know that, too. End of conversation.'

'Let's develop this thing a bit...'

'Let's not.' Foley leaned across Schulz. 'Stewardess, could I have a word?' He produced two airline tickets from his breast pocket as the girl bent forward attentively. 'I've reserved both these seats. These tickets say so. Could you kindly have this intruder removed? He's trying to sell me something.'

He settled back in his seat, slipped the tickets she had looked at into his pocket and resumed his gaze out into the night. His whole manner indicated *the matter is settled, no more to say.*

'I'm afraid this seat is reserved,' the girl told Schulz. 'If you could return to your own seat maybe I could bring you something more to drink?'

'Another large whisky.' Schulz, his normal chirpiness deserting him, stood up and glanced at the back of Foley's head. 'See you in Zurich. *Pal!*' He walked off down the gangway.

'I hope that man didn't disturb you, sir,' the stewardess who had originally shown him to his seat said to Foley.

'You did the job,' he said without looking at her.

Shaken, Schulz sagged into his aisle seat and realized he was sweating. Ice-cold bastard! He mopped his damp forehead, adjusted his tie and glanced at the blonde creature alongside him. She gave him the same warm, welcoming smile he had experienced when he first sat down.

Forty years old, he guessed. Wedding ring on her finger. The right age – Schulz was forty-five. Once they got away from their husbands they were ready for a little dalliance. He hoped she was going all the way to Zurich. He hoped she'd go all the way with him! The unspoken joke felt a little sour. It was the encounter with Foley. He thanked the stewardess for the fresh drink and memories drifted through his mind.

Lee Foley. Executioner for the CIA. They shied away from that word. Special operative was the euphemism. The rumoured body count down to Foley's expertise was as high as twenty-five men – and women. Now the story was he had quit the CIA and was working for CIDA – the Continental International Detective Agency. Schulz thought he might radio a cryptic signal to the Zurich office to have a man waiting to follow Foley. He'd think about it when his nerves settled. He turned to the blonde woman.

'Going on to Zurich, I hope? I'm Ed Schulz of *Time* Magazine. I know a nice little restaurant in Zurich, the Veltliner Keller...'

No memories drifted through the mind of Lee Foley. He refused dinner and ordered more bitter lemon. Not from virtue, he seldom touched alcohol – it clouded the mind, slowed down the reflexes. How many people who used it as a pick-me-up realized it was a depressant? Cigarettes and the occasional woman were his relaxations. They had to be classy women and definitely not professionals. This thought triggered off another one.

'When I have to buy it I'll hang up my boots...'

Some Brit had used that phrase when they were passing a brothel on the Reeperbahn in Hamburg. Bob Newman, foreign correspondent. The guy who had recently broken the Kruger case in Germany and earned himself another cluster of laurels. Now Ed Schulz could never have come within a mile of cracking that espionage classic. He wondered where Newman was tonight – and immediately pushed the irrelevant thought out of his head.

'Maximize your concentration,' was one of Foley's favourite phrases. 'And *wait* – forever if need be – until the conditions are right...'

Foley was waiting now, eyes half-closed in an apparent doze as he observed the progress of dinner round Ed Schulz's seat. The conditions were right now he decided as coffee was served. He felt inside the little pocket he had unzipped earlier and squeezed a single soluble capsule from the polythene envelope.

Standing up, he strolled along the corridor to where two stewards cluttered the aisle next to Schulz whose head was turned away as he talked to his travelling companion. He held a balloon glass of Remy Martin in the accepted manner, fingers splayed, and in front of him was a cup of black coffee which had just been poured.

Foley nudged the nearest steward's elbow with his left hand. As the man turned Foley flicked the capsule neatly into Schulz's cup. Alcoholic fumes drifted in the air, no one noticed a thing. Foley shook his head apologetically at the steward and went back to his seat.

He checked his watch. Another six hours to Geneva. After he'd drunk his coffee laced with the special barbiturate Schulz would sleep for eight hours. He'd stagger off the plane at its ultimate destination, Zurich. He wouldn't even notice an unfamiliar taste. And many times in his apartment Foley had practised the quick flip with his thumbnail, spinning capsule into empty cup.

Foley had bamboozled Schulz earlier when he had displayed two tickets for Zurich in front of him to the stewardess. At the check-in counter he'd told the girl to put Geneva tickets on his baggage. Whenever he was travelling, Foley always booked ahead of his real destination – or followed a devious route, changing aircraft. He glanced round before extracting the documents from his briefcase. He wouldn't be disturbed again tonight.

The night flight had reached the stage he knew so well. All the passengers were sleepy – or asleep, lulled by the monotonous and steady vibrations of the machine's great engines. He refused a pillow offered by a stewardess and opened the briefcase.

In the last few hours since the surprise phone call to CIDA his feet had hardly touched the ground. He had the typed record of his long phone conversation with Fordham at the American Embassy in Berne. It was headed, *Case of Hannah Stuart, deceased, patient at Berne Clinic, Thun.*

Nothing in the typed record indicated that Fordham was military attaché at the American Embassy. His eyes dropped to the comment at the end of the record.

We are extremely worried about the possible implications on the international situation about rumoured events and situation at this medical establishment.

Foley opened a large-scale map of Switzerland and concentrated on the Berne canton. His finger traced the motorway from the city of Berne running south-east to the town of Thun. In either Geneva or Berne he'd have to hire a car. He was certain he was going to need wheels for this job.

Four

Gmund, Austria. 10 February 1984. 1°. For Manfred Seidler, thousands of miles east of Tucson and New York, the day dawned far more grimly. The Renault station wagon was still inside Czechoslovakia as it moved swiftly towards the lonely frontier crossing point into Austria at Gmund – now less than two kilometres ahead. He glanced at the driver beside him, sixty-year-old Franz Oswald who, with his lined, leathery face and bushy moustache, looked seventy.

Seidler checked his watch. 6.25 a.m. Outside it was night and the deserted, snowbound fields stretched away into nothing. Despite the car heater it was cold but Seidler was used to cold. It was Oswald's nerve which bothered him.

'Slow down,' he snapped, 'we're nearly there. We don't want them to think we're trying to crash the border – to wake them up...'

'We mustn't be late.' Oswald reduced speed and then confirmed Seidler's anxiety. 'Let's pull up for a second. I could do with a nip of Schnapps from my flask to get us through...'

'No! They mustn't smell drink on your breath. Any little delay and they may make a thorough search. And leave all the talking to me...'

'Supposing they have changed the guard earlier, Seidler? If fresh men are on duty...'

They never change their routine.'

He replied curtly, forced himself to sound confident. He glanced again at Old Franz – he always thought of him as old. Oswald's chin was grizzled and unshaven. But Seidler needed him on these trips because Oswald carried frequent *legal* supplies over the border. To the men at the frontier post he was *familiar*. Just as the vehicle was a familiar sight. Now they could see the distant guard-post.

'Headlights full on,' Seidler ordered. The old boy was losing his grip – he had forgotten the signal to Jan. 'Dip them,' he snapped.

The stench of fear polluted the chilly atmosphere inside the Renault. Seidler could smell the driver's armpit sweat, a sour odour. Beads of perspiration began to form on the old man's forehead. Seidler wished to God Franz hadn't made that remark that they might have changed the guard earlier.

If the car was searched he could end up in Siberia. No! It wouldn't be Siberia. If he were tortured he knew he would tell them about the previous consignments. They would be crazy with rage. He'd face a firing squad. It was at that moment that Manfred Seidler decided that – if they got through this time – this would be the last run. God knew he had enough money in his Swiss numbered bank account.

Taking out a silk handkerchief, he told Franz to sit still and he gently mopped the moisture from the old man's brow. The car stopped. By the light shining through the open door of the guard hut Seidler saw the heavy swing-pole which was lowered and barred their way into Austria.

'Stop!' he hissed. The old fool had nearly switched off the engine. Leaving the motor running was *familiar*, creating in the minds of the guards a reflex feeling that after a perfunctory check they would raise the barrier and wave the Renault on. A uniformed figure with an automatic rifle looped over his shoulder approached Seidler's side of the car.

Seidler tried to open the door and found the damned thing had frozen. Quickly, he wound down the window. Icy air flooded in, freezing the exposed skin of his face above the heavy scarf. The soldier bent down and peered inside. It was Jan.

'Sorry,' apologized Seidler, 'the handle's frozen.' He spoke in fluent Czech. 'I should check the wooden crate in the back. The *wooden crate*,' he emphasized. 'I'm not sure I'm permitted to take the contents out. Just take it and dump it if it's not allowed...'

Jan nodded understanding and his boots crunched in the crusted snow as he walked with painful slowness to the rear of the hatchback. Seidler lit a cigarette to quiet his nerves. They were so close to safety he dared not glance at Franz. He knew he had committed a psychological error in emphasizing the *wooden crate*. But as on earlier trips he was taking a gigantic risk on the assumption that people are never suspicious of something under their noses. It was the much larger *cardboard* container alongside the crate Jan must not investigate.

Compelling himself not to look back, forgetting that his window was still open, he took a deep drag on his cigarette as he heard Jan turn the handle and raise the hatchback. Thank God that handle wasn't frozen! There was a scrape as Jan hauled out the crate – followed by the divine sound of the hatchback being closed.

A light flashed to his left through the open window. Someone with a torch must have emerged from the guard hut. He continued staring steadily ahead. The only sounds in the early morning dark were the ticking over of the motor, the swish of the windscreen wipers maintaining two fan-shapes of clear glass in the gently falling snow.

A returning crunch of boots breaking the hard snow. At the window Jan, his high cheekbones burnished by the wind, reappeared. The rifle still looped on one shoulder, the crate expertly balanced on the other. His expression was blank as he bent down and spoke.

'Until next time...'

'The same arrangement,' replied Seidler and smiled, stubbing out his cigarette in the ashtray. A small gesture to indicate that this transaction was completed.

Jan vanished inside the hut as Seidler wound up the window – God he was frozen stiff. With the feeble heater he'd be lucky to thaw out by the time they reached Vienna. The barrier pole remained obstinately lowered across their path. Franz reached for the brake and Seidler stopped him.

'For Christ's sake, wait! No sign of impatience...'

'It's not going as it usually does. We'd be away by now. I can feel it – something's wrong...'

'Shut up! Didn't you see Jan yawn? They're half-asleep at this hour. They've been on duty all night. Nothing ever happens at this Godforsaken spot. They're bored stiff. They've slipped into a state of permanent inertia...'

Seidler realized he was talking too much. He began to wonder whether he was trying to convince himself. He stared hypnotized by the horizontal pole. It began to wobble. Christ! The tension was beginning to get to him.

The pole wasn't wobbling. It was *ascending*. Franz released the brake. The Renault slid forward. They were across! They paused briefly again while an Austrian official glanced without interest at Seidler's German passport, and then they were driving through the streets of the small town of Gmund.

'You realize you were photographed back at the frontier post?' Franz remarked as he accelerated along the highway beyond Gmund towards distant Vienna.

'What the hell are you talking about?'

'You were photographed by a man in civilian clothes. Didn't you see the flash-bulb go off? He had a funny camera with a big lens...'

'A civilian?' Seidler was startled. 'Are you sure? Someone with a torch came out of the guard hut...'

'No torch. A flash-bulb. I watched him out of the corner of my eye. You were looking straight ahead.'

Seidler, a man in his late forties with a thatch of dark brown hair, slimly built, a bony face, a long, inquisitive nose and wary eyes, thought about it. It was the reference to a *civilian* which worried him. Always before there had been no one there except uniformed guards. Yes, this was definitely the last run. He had just relaxed with this comforting thought when Franz said something else which disturbed him.

'I'm not helping you again,' the old man rasped.

Suits me to the ground, Seidler thought, and then glanced to his left sharply. Franz was staring straight ahead but there was a smug, conniving look in his expression. Seidler knew that look: Franz was congratulating himself on some trick he was going to pull.

'I'm sorry to hear that,' Seidler replied.

'That business back at the frontier post,' Franz went on. 'I felt certain they'd changed the guard. It's only a matter of time before they *do* change the guard. Jan won't be there to collect his Schnapps and wave you through. They'll search the car...'

He was repeating himself, talking too much, over-emphasizing the reasons for his decision. That plus the satisfied smirk. Seidler's devious and shrewd mind began searching for the real reason. His right hand thrust deep inside his coat pocket for warmth felt the flick knife he always carried in the special compartment he had had sewn into the pocket.

Money! Franz worshipped the stuff. But from what source could he obtain more money than the generous amount Seidler had always paid? The road to Vienna passes through some of the loneliest and bleakest countryside west of Siberia. Flat as a billiard table – a monotonous snow-covered billiard table – the bare fields stretched away on both sides, treeless.

It was still dark when they drove through one of the few inhabited places between Gmund and the Austrian capital. Horn is a single street walled by ancient, solid farmhouse-like buildings. Giant wooden double doors seal off entrances to courtyards beyond, entrances large enough to admit wagons piled high with hay and drawn by oxen.

What the devil could Franz be up to? Seidler, an opportunist par excellence, a man whose background and character dictated that he would always live by his wits, probed the problem from every angle. A *Mittel-European,* his father had been a Sudeten German in Czechoslovakia before the war, his mother a Czech.

Seidler spoke five languages – Czech, German, English, French, Italian. The Czechs – and Seidler was mostly Czech – have a gift for languages. It was this facility, plus the network of contacts he had built up across Europe – allied with a natural Czech talent for unscrupulousness – which had enabled him to make a good living.

Six feet tall, he sported a small moustache and had the gift of the gab in all five languages. As they approached Vienna he was still wrestling with the problem of Franz. He also had another problem: he had a tight schedule for the consignment inside the cardboard container resting at the tail of the Renault. The aircraft waiting for him at Schwechat

Airport. His employers were sticklers for promptness. Should he risk a little time checking out Franz when they reached Vienna?

The first streaks of a mournful, pallid daylight filtered from the heavy overcast down on Vienna as Franz stopped the Renault in front of the Westbahnhof, the main station to the West. Here Seidler always transferred to his own car parked waiting for him. It wouldn't do to let Franz drive him to the airport – the less he knew about the consignment's ultimate destination the better.

'Here's your money. Don't waste it on drink and wild, wild women,' Seidler said with deliberate flippancy.

The remark was really very funny – the idea of Franz Oswald spending good money on girls instead of at the tavern. The old man took the fat envelope and shoved it into his inside pocket. His hands tapped the wheel impatiently, a gesture out of character Seidler noted as he went to the rear of the car, lifted the hatchback and grasped the large cardboard container by the strong rope handle. Slamming down the hatchback, he walked back to the front passenger window and spoke.

'I may have a different sort of job. No risk involved. A job inside Austria,' he lied. 'I'll get in touch...'

'You are the boss.' Franz released the brake without looking at his employer and the car slid past. Seidler only saw it by pure chance. On the rear seat a rumpled, plaid travelling rug had slipped half on to the floor, exposing what it had hidden. Seidler froze. Franz had stolen one of the samples from the consignment.

Early morning workers trailed out of the station exits below the huge glass end wall and down the steps as Seidler moved very fast. There was a jam-up of traffic just at the point where you drove out of the concourse and Franz's Renault was trapped.

Running to his parked Opel, Seidler unlocked the car, thrust the cardboard container onto the rear seat and settled himself behind the wheel. He was careful not to panic. He inserted the ignition keys first time, switched on the motor and pulled out at the moment Franz left

27

the concourse, turning on to Mariahilferstrasse. Dreary grey buildings loomed in the semi-dark as Seidler followed. It looked as though Franz was heading into the centre of the city – away from his home.

Seidler was in a state of cold fury and, driving with one hand, he felt again the flick knife in the secret pocket. The smirk on Franz's face was now explained. He was selling one of the samples. The only question in Seidler's mind now was who could be the buyer?

Stunned, Seidler sat in his parked Opel while he absorbed what he had just observed. A spare, brisk-looking man with a military-style moustache had been waiting for Franz. Outside the British Embassy!

Seidler had watched while Franz got out of his Renault, carrying the small cardboard container as he joined the Englishman. The latter had taken Franz by the arm, hustling him inside the building. Now it was Seidler who tapped his fingers on the wheel, checking his watch, thinking of the aircraft waiting at Schwechat, knowing he had to wait for Franz to emerge.

Ten minutes later Franz did emerge – without the container. He climbed in behind the wheel of the Renault without a glance in the direction of Seidler who sat slumped behind his own wheel, wearing a black beret Franz had never seen. Something in the way he had walked suggested to Seidler Franz was very satisfied with his visit to the British Embassy. The Renault moved off.

Seidler made his move when Franz turned down a narrow, deserted side street lined with tall old apartment buildings. Flights of steps led down to basement areas. Checking his rear view mirror, Seidler speeded up, squeezed past the slow-moving Renault and swung diagonally into the kerb. Franz jammed on his brakes and stopped within inches of the Opel. Jumping out of his car, he ran along the pavement in the opposite direction with a shuffling trot.

Seidler caught up with him in less than a hundred metres opposite a flight of steps leading into one of the basement areas. His left hand grasped Franz by the shoulder and spun him round. He smiled and spoke rapidly.

'There's nothing to be frightened about... All I want to know is who you gave the box to... Then you can go to hell as far as I'm concerned... Remember, I said this was the last run...'

He was talking when he rammed the knife blade upwards into Franz's chest with all his strength. He was surprised at the ease with which the knife entered a man's body. Franz gulped, coughed once, his eyes rolled and he began to sag. Seidler gave him a savage push with his gloved hand and Franz, the hilt of the knife protruding from his chest, fell backwards down the stone steps. Seidler was surprised also at the lack of noise: the loudest sound was when Franz, half-way down the steps, cracked the back of his skull on the stonework. He ended up on his back on the basement paving stones.

Seidler glanced round, ran swiftly down the steps and felt inside Franz's jacket, extracting his wallet which bulged, although the envelope of Austrian banknotes Seidler had passed to him was still inside the same pocket. He pulled out a folded wad of Swiss banknotes – five-hundred-franc denomination. At a guess there were twenty. Ten thousand Swiss francs. A large fortune for Franz.

The distant approach of a car's engine warned Seidler it was time to go. His gloved hand thrust the notes in his pocket and he ran back up the steps to his car. He was just driving away when he saw the sidelights of the approaching car in his wing mirror. He accelerated round a curve and forgot about the car, all his thoughts now concentrated on reaching Schwechat Airport.

Captain 'Tommy' Mason, officially designated as military attaché to the British Embassy in Vienna, frowned as he saw the driverless Renault parked at an angle to the kerb, the gaping entrance to the basement area. He was just able to drive past the vehicle, then he stopped and switched off his own engine.

The sound of the Renault's motor ticking over came to him in the otherwise silent street. With considerable agility he nipped out of his Ford Escort, ran to peer down into the basement, ran back to the Ford, started up the motor again and drove off at speed.

He was just in time to see the rear lights of the Opel turn on to a main highway. He caught up with it quickly and then settled down to follow at a decent interval. No point in alarming the other party. First thing in the morning and all that.

Mason had first noticed the Opel parked outside the Embassy when he was interviewing Franz Oswald. Peering casually from behind the curtains of the second floor window he had seen the car, the slumped driver wearing one of those funny, Frog-style berets. At least, the Frogs had favoured them at one time. Didn't see them much these days.

He had seen no reason to alarm his visitor who, much to his surprise, had actually kept their appointment. More surprising still – even a trifle alarming – had been the contents of the cardboard box. When his visitor had left Mason had thought there might be no harm in following the chap – especially since Black Beret appeared also to be in the following business. You could never tell where these things might lead. Tweed, back in London, had said something to this effect once. Odd how things Tweed said, remarks casually tossed off, stuck in the mind.

Mason, thirty-three, five feet ten, sleepy-eyed, trimly-moustached, drawly-voiced, crisply-spoken, using as few words as possible, was a near-walking caricature of his official position. At a party shortly after his arrival in Waltz City, the Ambassador had indulged in his dry humour at the new arrival's expense.

'You know, Mason, if I was asked to show someone a picture of the typical British military attaché I'd take a photo of you...'

'Sir,' Mason had replied.

Mason was soon pretty sure that the Opel chap was heading for the airport – unless he continued on to the Czech border and Bratislava, God forbid! But any man who left bodies in basements at this hour was worth a little attention. A quarter of an hour later he knew his first guess had been spot on. Curiouser and curiouser. What flight could he be catching before most people had downed their breakfast?

Seidler drove beyond the speed limit, checking his watch at frequent intervals. Franz Oswald was only the second man he had ever killed – the first had been an accident – and the reaction was setting in. He was shaken, his mind taken up with one thing. Getting safely aboard the aircraft.

Customs would be no problem. Here again, timing was vital – the chief officer on duty had already been paid a substantial sum. When it came to essentials his employer, so careful with money, never hesitated to produce the requisite funds. Turning into the airport, he drove past the main buildings and continued towards the tarmac. Josef, who didn't know anything, was waiting to take the hired car back to Vienna.

Seidler jumped out of the car, nodded to Josef, lifted the large container from the back of the Opel and walked rapidly towards the waiting executive jet. The ladder was already in position. A man he had never seen stood by the ladder, asking the question in French.

'Classification of the consignment?'

'Terminal.'

Five

London. 10 February 1984. 8°. Tweed, short and plump-faced, middle-aged, was gazing out of the window of his office at SIS headquarters in Park Crescent when Mason called from Vienna.

Through his horn-rimmed glasses he looked out towards Regent's Park across the Crescent gardens. Small clusters of gold sprouted amid the green in the watery morning sunlight. Early spring crocuses. It was something – promising the ultimate end of winter. The phone on his desk rang.

'Long distance from Vienna,' the internal switchboard operator informed him. Tweed wondered when Vienna was a short distance. He told her to put the call through and settled himself in his swivel chair. They exchanged the normal preliminaries identifying each other. Mason sounded rushed, which was unusual.

'I've got something for you. Won't specify on the phone...'

'Mason, where are you speaking from?' Tweed asked sharply.

'A booth in the General Post Office, middle of Vienna. The Embassy phone goes through the switchboard. I've just hurtled back from Schwechat Airport – that's...'

'I know where it is. Get to the point...'

Tweed was uncharacteristically sharp again. But he sensed a terrible urgency in his caller's voice. Mason was the SIS man in Vienna under the cloak of military attaché. The British were at last learning from their Soviet colleagues – who were never who they seemed at embassies.

'I've got something for you, something rather frightening. I won't specify over this line – I'll bring it with me when I come to London. Main thing is a Lear jet with Swiss markings left Schwechat half an hour ago. Destination Switzerland is my educated guess...'

Tweed listened without interrupting. Mason was his normal concise self now. Short, terse sentences. Not a wasted word. As he listened Tweed made no notes on the pad lying in front of him. When Mason had finished Tweed asked him just one question before breaking the connection.

'What is the flight time Vienna to Switzerland?'

'One hour and ten minutes. So you have less than forty minutes if I've guessed right. Oh, there's a body involved...'

'See you in London.'

Tweed waited a moment after replacing the receiver and then he lifted it again and asked for an open line. He dialled 010 41, the code for Switzerland, followed by 31, the code for Berne, followed by six more digits. He got through to Wiley, commercial attaché at the British Embassy in Berne, in less than a minute. He spoke rapidly, explaining what he wanted.

'... so alert our man in Geneva and the chap in Zurich...'

'The time element is against anyone getting to the airports to set up surveillance,' Wiley protested.

'No, it isn't. Cointrin is ten minutes from the centre of Geneva. Twenty minutes in a fast car gets you from Zurich to Kloten now they've finished the new road. And *you* can check Belp...'

'I'll have to put my skates on...'

'Do that,' Tweed told him and broke the connection again.

Sighing, he got up and walked over to the wall-map of Western Europe. Mason could run rings round Wiley. Maybe he ought to switch them when Mason arrived home. Vienna was a backwater – but Berne was beginning to smoulder. And why did everyone forget Belp? Even Howard probably had no idea Berne had its own airport fifteen minutes down the four-lane motorway to Thun and Lucerne. Plus a thrice-weekly service from Belp to Gatwick. He was studying the map when his chief, Howard, burst into the office. Without knocking, of course.

'Anything interesting cooking?' he asked breezily.

Howard had all the right connections, had gone to all the useful schools and university, which completed the circle, giving him all the right connections. An able admin, man, he was short on imagination and not a risk-taker. Tweed had been known – in a bad mood – to refer to him privately as Woodentop.

'Possibly Berne,' Tweed replied and left it at that.

'Berne?' Howard perked up. 'That's the *Terminal* thing you latched on to. What the hell does the word mean – if anything?'

'No idea – that it means anything. Just that we keep getting rumours from a variety of sources.' He decided not to mention to Howard the reference Mason had made to 'a body involved'. It was too early to excite Howard.

'I hope you're not employing too much manpower on this,' Howard commented. '*Terminal*,' he repeated. 'Might be an idea to watch the airports. That would link up – airport, terminal...'

'I've just done that.'

'Good man. Keep me informed...'

Wiley phoned Park Crescent at exactly 4 p.m. He apologized for not calling earlier. The lines from the Embassy had been jammed up most of the day. Tweed guessed he had really waited until nearly everyone – including the Ambassador – had gone home. It was now 5 p.m. in Berne since Switzerland was one hour ahead of London in time.

'I got lucky,' he informed Tweed. 'At least I think so. If this was the plane you're interested in...' He described the machine and Tweed grunted and told him to go on. 'A passenger disembarked and carried a large cardboard container to a waiting truck. A canvas-covered job. Stencilled on the side were the words *Chemiekonzern Grange AG*...'

'Let me write that down. Now, go on...'

'It's a weird story. I followed the truck – the passenger travelled in the cab beside the driver – back along the motorway towards Berne. It turned off on to a road I knew was a cul-de-sac, so I waited. Pretended my car had broken down and stood in the freezing cold with my head under the bonnet. God, it was cold...'

Mason would have left that bit out. Patiently this time, Tweed waited. At four in the afternoon he had the lights on. It was near-darkness outside and cars passing along the main road had their lights on also.

Tweed felt a little disappointed in the report so far. He couldn't have said why.

'About a quarter of an hour later a small van appeared down the same side road. I nearly missed it – then I spotted the same passenger sitting beside the van driver. I followed the van which headed towards the city. Lost it in the traffic on the outskirts. Funny thing is, I could have sworn it passed me later driving down the opposite lane – *away* from the city...'

'So, that's that?'

'Hold on a minute. I did notice the name painted on the side of the van. I'm damned sure it was the same one both times...'

Tweed was writing down the name when Howard came into the office, again without knocking. Tweed scribbled out the second name as Howard came round the desk to peer over his shoulder, another irritating habit. He thanked Wiley and put the phone down.

Tweed had no doubt Howard had paid one of his frequent visits to the switchboard room – to see if anything was going on. He also knew that Howard often stayed back late at night so he could poke around his staff's offices after they had gone home. Which was why Tweed locked away anything of interest and only left trivia on his desk.

'Any developments?' Howard enquired.

'I'm not sure. I haven't decided yet but I may have to go to Berne myself. As you know, we're fully stretched. Keith Martel is away on a job and it's all hands to the pumps...'

'Any excuse,' Howard commented drily and rattled loose change in his pocket. 'You like Berne. Any developments?' he repeated.

'This morning Mason reported he had something for me – *something rather frightening* were the exact words he used. I think it was delivered to him at the Embassy. He's bringing it to us within a few days, so it has to be serious – maybe very serious...'

'Oh, Christ! You're building up another crisis.'

'Crises build themselves up,' Tweed pointed out. 'And that was Wiley on the phone...' As if you didn't know, he thought. 'From Vienna Mason reported to me this morning he followed a man – who may be an assassin – to Schwechat Airport outside the city. He saw this man board a private Swiss jet. I put tags on three Swiss airports – although there are plenty of others. Wiley has just told me a similar aircraft landed at Belp...'

'Belp? Where the hell is Belp? Funny name...'

'Look at the pin sticking in the wall map. It's the airport for Berne.'

'Didn't know there was one.' Tweed said nothing but peered over his glasses as Howard scrutinized the map. 'So it was an airport,' Howard said with satisfaction. 'A terminal! This is getting interesting...'

With Howard it always helped to get him on your side – or at best in a neutral status – if he thought he had contributed an idea himself. Tweed continued talking in his level tone.

'Wiley saw the aircraft disembark one passenger carrying a large container. Eventually he was driven away in a small van. Wiley noted the name on the side of the van. At the moment I have several disconnected pieces which may eventually build into a pattern.'

'Or a crisis...' It was the nearest Howard ever came to cracking a joke. He swung round on one heel, flicked an imaginary speck of dust off his regulation pin-striped suit. Howard was a trendy dresser; always wore a camel overcoat of the length which was the latest vogue. 'Well, what was the name on the van?' he asked.

'Klinik Bern...'

Six

Tucson, Arizona. 10 February 1984. 55°. The sun had sunk behind the mountains and Tucson was bathed in the purple glow of dusk as the temperature also sank. Newman raised his glass to Dr Rosen in the Tack Room, probably the most luxurious eating establishment in the state. The tables were illuminated by candlelight.

'Cheers!' said Newman. 'I've seen Frank Chase, I've talked with Linda Wayne – and got nowhere. No evidence of anything odd about Jesse Kennedy being sent to the Berne Clinic...'

'You know Jesse was flown direct to Berne by executive jet?'

'Linda didn't say that...'

'Have you ever heard of Professor Armand Grange, eminent Swiss specialist?'

'No. Should I?'

'Surprising Linda didn't mention him. Grange was on a lecture tour of the States – drumming up business was my impression. And from the moment Linda met him she treated him as her *guru*.'

'*Guru*?' Newman looked at the kindly but shrewd face of Rosen. 'I thought you used that word for some Indian fakir who offers salvation – provided you obey the gospel...'

'That's right,' agreed Rosen. 'Grange is into cellular rejuvenation – something the Swiss have practised for years. We're still not convinced. Maybe we're old-fashioned. But Grange certainly gathered in some disciples on that tour – always rich, of course.'

Newman turned sideways to study his guest. 'I'm sorry, I'm not sure I'm following this. You're trying to tell me something, is that it?'

'I suppose so.' Rosen accepted a refill. He seemed to mellow outside the Medical Center. Maybe it was the relaxing atmosphere of the Tack Room, Newman thought. Rosen went on. 'Some of what I'm saying may not be strictly ethical – could even be taken for criticism of a professional colleague – but we are talking about a foreigner. I suspect Grange's clinic is full of wealthy patients he attracted during his tour. Two carrots – one for relatives, one for the seriously ill patient.' He smiled ruefully. 'You know something, Newman? I think I'm talking too much...'

'I'm still listening. Sometimes it's good to get things off your chest.'

Newman watched Rosen with an attentive expression. It was part of his stock-in-trade as foreign correspondent – people often opened out to him when they wouldn't say the same things to their wives or colleagues – especially their wives.

'Linda Wayne,' Rosen continued, 'went overboard with Professor Grange the way a drowning woman grasps at a floating spar. He was the answer to her prayer – to get Jesse Kennedy far away, as far away as possible. The carrot Grange offers is to take sick relatives off the hands of their nearest and dearest. The price is high, but like I said, he deals only with the very wealthy. The carrot to the sick patient is the hope of cellular rejuvenation, a new chance at life. I suppose it's a brilliant formula.'

'The carrot worked with a man like Jesse Kennedy?'

'There you put your finger on the key, what's worrying me.' Rosen sipped at his drink and Newman carefully remained silent. 'If Jesse had leukaemia he'd face up to it – but no way would he be into cellular rejuvenation. Did you know he once did a job for the CIA? It was over ten years ago when we had German pilots being trained by our people at a secret air base out in the desert. A very tough CIA operative came down to cooperate with Jesse. Can't recall his name. Linda Wayne fooled around with him. Now I *am* talking too much...'

'What exactly did Jesse do?'

'He used to ride his horse for miles by himself in the desert every day. They gave him a camera. One morning he spotted a German pilot handing an envelope to a stranger who stopped his car on 110 – Interstate Highway 10 which runs all the way from LA to Florida. The stranger came after Jesse with a gun...' Rosen smiled, a dreamy look on his face. 'That was very foolish of him. Jesse rode him down with his horse, the CIA man turned up and one German pilot disappeared for ever. The CIA man shot the stranger. Jesse told me about it years later...'

'You said "*If* Jesse had leukaemia..."'

'Slip of the tongue. You think a man like Jesse would crawl off to Switzerland when he loved the desert? A man who started from nothing and parleyed a bank loan into twelve million dollars?'

'Just *how* did he do it?'

'Vision. He was a crystal ball gazer – he looked into the future. When he came to Tucson from Texas over twenty years ago he guessed Tucson would expand one day. He bought options on land outside the city limits – and when that increased in value he used the extra collateral to buy more and more land further and further out...'

'So,' Newman commented, 'Linda is worth eight million dollars when Jesse goes and Nancy gets four million?'

'His will is common knowledge. He made no secret of it. And if anything happened to Nancy first, then Linda collects the whole twelve million. Maybe you see why it worries me – that kind of money at stake.' Rosen played with his empty glass. 'No thanks. Two is my limit. You know, Newman, I thought you'd be just the man to check out this mystery. You cracked the Kruger espionage case in Germany – I read the book you wrote afterwards. That must have made you a pile...'

'Not four million dollars,' Newman said shortly.

'Oh! Now I get it – I sensed you couldn't make up your mind about marrying Nancy. The money worries you, which is to your credit. I still think you ought to go to Berne...'

'Now you sound like Nancy. She never stops...'

'Argue against her and it will just make her more determined.' Rosen smiled again. 'Or maybe you've found that out?'

'We've had our moments. Jesus, look what just walked in...'

'Harvey Wayne, Linda's husband. He's into electronics, as you doubtless know. He's another one greedy for a dollar...'

Rosen stopped talking as a fat, pasty-faced man in his early forties came over to them. He was wearing a cream-coloured dinner jacket, dark trousers and the oily smile Newman found so distasteful. He put an arm round the Englishman's shoulder.

'Hi, pal! Hear you and that cute sister-in-law of mine will soon be in Berne. Give my regards to that old coot, Jesse...'

'You heard what?'

Newman's tone was cold. He glanced at his shoulder and Harvey reluctantly moved his hand. He gave Rosen a throwaway gesture of resignation with his hand, then shrugged.

'Did I say something I ought not to have?'

'You haven't answered my question,' Newman replied.

'You're not rousting Dr Rosen the way you did Frank Chase, I hope.' Harvey looked towards the entrance and smiled again. 'We have company. You have the opportunity of getting a direct answer to your question...'

Linda, wearing an off-the-shoulder cocktail dress and a come-hither smile, had entered the Tack Room and was heading towards them, her innocent eyes staring straight at Newman. Beside her walked Nancy, a few inches shorter, dressed in a cream blouse and a midnight blue skirt. Heads turned as the two women progressed across the room. Newman stood up, his expression bleak.

'Let's go somewhere quiet,' he said to Nancy. 'We have to talk and I do mean now...'

The blazing row took place in the lobby, carried on in low tones so the receptionist couldn't hear them. Newman opened the conversation, treading warily at first.

'I'm sure that creep, Harvey, has got it wrong. He's just told me we're going to Berne...'

'I have the tickets, Bob.' Nancy produced two folders from her handbag and handed them to him. 'It's a very direct route. An American Airlines 727 from Tucson to Dallas. One hour stopover in Dallas. Then an eight-hour flight – again American Airlines – to Gatwick in England from Dallas. The last lap is by Dan-Air from Gatwick to Belp. That's the airport just outside Berne...'

'I have actually heard of Belp,' Newman replied with deceptive calm.

'We take off on tomorrow's flight...'

'I can actually read an airline ticket...'

'Somebody had to take a decision.' She looked pleased with herself. 'And I've just got out of Linda that Jesse didn't go that route. He was flown to Belp by private jet...'

'So?'

'Jesse was careful with money. *If* he'd agreed to go he'd have travelled in a wheelchair on a scheduled flight rather than hire a jet. Don't you think I've done rather well?'

'You'd have done a bloody sight better to consult me first. How do you think I felt when your louse of a brother-in-law comes up to me in front of Rosen to give me this news?'

'Really? Linda must have phoned him at the office. He was working late. She's planned a farewell dinner for us here...'

'Count me out...'

'Robert! It's all fixed.' Her temper began to flare. 'I'm all packed. You said you could pack anytime in ten minutes even to go to Tokyo...'

'That's when *I* want to go to Tokyo. Look, Nancy – and don't interrupt. There's not a shred of evidence that there's anything wrong about Jesse being flown to the Berne Clinic. I've talked to Dr Chase. I've had two conversations with Rosen. I've stared at Linda's legs while she talked to me...'

'Is that what you're so anxious not to leave – Linda's legs?'

'Now you're getting nasty. Nancy, you can't just push me around like this. It's no basis for any kind of relationship – let alone marriage.'

'Oh, shit, Bob...'

'Look, Nancy, this argument has been going on practically since we first met in London three months ago...'

'That was when I tried to phone Jesse and heard from Linda that he'd been sent to Switzerland. I really do feel something's very wrong. Remember, I am a doctor...'

'And I'm a foreign correspondent who looks for evidence. I haven't

41

found anything to justify your anxiety. Now you present me with this *fait accompli*, this package deal all wrapped up in pink ribbon.'

He waved the ticket folders under her shapely nose. She took both his wrists in her hands, leaned up to him and nestled her face alongside his, whispering in his ear.

'Bob, would you please come with me to Berne to quiet my fears. For my sake?'

'That's a better approach...'

'It's the approach I should have used first. You're right – I should never have bought those tickets without consulting you. I'm sorry. Truly.'

He freed one hand and reached under her hair to stroke her neck. The receptionist was putting on quite a performance at not noticing them. She nestled her head against his chest and purred contentedly. He freed his other hand, grasped her chin and lifted it up to kiss her full on the lips.

'Nancy, I have to go back to Dr Rosen to ask him one more question. We leave for Berne tomorrow...'

Harvey Wayne had just left Rosen when Newman sat down opposite the doctor. Rosen nodded towards Harvey's retreating back with a grimace.

'He's been pumping me, trying to find out what we were talking about. How did the argument go?'

'The way I expected it to.' Newman's manner had changed. He was crisp, decisive. 'Have you any idea where the majority of patients in the Berne Clinic come from?'

'My impression – it was no more than that – was they mostly come from the States. Plus a few from South America where they can still afford the fees. Is it significant?'

'It could be the key to the whole operation.'

Seven

11 February 1984. The DC10 flew at 35,000 feet above the invisible Atlantic as the machine proceeded at 500 mph in a north-easterly direction for Europe. In her first-class seat Nancy was fast asleep, her head flopped on Newman's shoulder. He moved her carefully so he could leave his seat. No risk she would wake up: when Nancy fell asleep she went out cold.

Taking a pad from his pocket, Newman wrote the signal in capital letters so there could be no error in transmission. Standing up, he summoned a stewardess, put a finger to his lips and nodded towards Nancy. Taking the girl by the arm he guided her towards the pilot's cabin and spoke only when they were inside the galley.

'I'd like this message radioed immediately to London. Find out the cost while I wait here...'

The stewardess returned in less than a minute. An attractive girl, she studied Newman frankly. You weren't supposed to fraternize with passengers but... She found Newman's droll, easy manner irresistible. And her flat wasn't far from Gatwick. And he was English. *And* the female passenger he was travelling with wore no ring. A girl had to make the most of her opportunities. She told him the cost of the message and he took his time paying her in dollars.

'The radio operator is already transmitting, Mr Newman...'

'You're a helpful girl to have around...'

'I have two days off at Gatwick...'

'Give me the phone number?'

'I'm not supposed to...'

'But you will...'

He loaned her his pad and ballpoint pen, tucked a cigarette in the corner of his mouth, and watched her while she wrote the figures on

43

the pad. She added a name and upside down he read *Susan*. He took the pad off her and slipped out of sight as the curtain moved and a steward appeared. He gave her a little salute.

'Thank you for dealing with that for me,' he said for the benefit of the steward who was unnecessarily polishing glasses. 'When should it reach London?'

'Within a matter of minutes, sir...'

'Thank you again.'

He winked at her, pushed aside the curtain and went back to his seat. Nancy was awake, stretching her arms, thrusting out her well-rounded breasts against her tight cashmere sweater. He gave her a look of amiable resignation as he settled himself beside her.

'You're a dog,' she said. 'You've been chatting up that stewardess.' She wrapped a proprietary arm round his. 'You know, sometimes I think I should grab you for good while I can. You're not safe to leave roaming around loose.'

'What stewardess?'

'The one with the superb legs who showed us to our seats, the one you couldn't take your eyes off, the one whose eyes ate you up. Discreetly, of course...'

'Change of plan,' he said abruptly.

'Which means?'

'You'd better have some coffee to get you properly awake before I tell you.' He summoned the steward who had finished polishing glasses and gave the order. Then he relapsed into silence until she had drunk half the cup.

'I've been a good girl,' she said. 'What change of plan?'

'We don't take the Dan-Air flight from Gatwick to Belp. We take the bus from Gatwick to Heathrow. Then we catch a Swissair flight to Geneva. Going in via Geneva disguises our real destination.'

'Bob!' She straightened up so abruptly she almost spilt her coffee. 'You're taking this thing seriously. You do think there's something peculiar going on. God, you're a dark horse. Sometimes I feel I'll never really know you. Your whole manner has changed...'

44

'If we have to do the job we might as well do it professionally...'

'That isn't the reason,' she pounced. 'Rosen told you something which changed your whole attitude. So why the hell did we have to have that embarrassing row in the lobby of the Tack Room?'

'Rosen told me nothing. We're just doing it my way. You might call it a *fait accompli*,' he replied airily.

'I asked for that one,' she conceded. 'And I still don't believe you. Well, isn't that nice?'

She looked at him and Newman's head was rested against the back of the seat. His eyes were closed and he had apparently fallen into a catnap, something he was able to do anywhere at any time.

In the pilot's cabin the radio operator crumpled up the note from Newman's pad he had transmitted. The signal seemed innocuous enough and he didn't give it a second thought.

Addressed to Riverdale Trust Ltd with a PO Box number in London it was brief and to the point.

Aboard American Airlines Flight... ETA Gatwick... Proceeding to Heathrow to board Swissair flight to Geneva, repeat Geneva. Newman.

Manfred Seidler was running for his life. He used every devious means to throw a smokescreen in the eyes of those who would try to track him. Using a fake set of identity papers, he hired a car from the Hertz agency next door to the Bellevue Palace in Berne.

He drove only as far as Solothurn where he handed in the car. From the station he caught a train to Basle. If anyone *did* manage to trace him so far they would – with luck – think he had gone on to Zurich. He fostered this fiction by buying two separate one-way tickets – to Zurich and to Basle. He bought them at ten-minute intervals, using two different ticket windows. As the express slowed down and slid into the main station at Basle he was standing by the exit door, clutching his suitcase.

He phoned Erika Stahel from a booth in the huge station. He found himself staring at every passenger who lingered anywhere near the booth. He knew his nerves were in a bad way. Which was when a man made mistakes. Christ! Would the cow never answer? Her voice came on the line as if in response to his plea.

'It's Manfred...'

'Well, well, stranger. Isn't life full of surprises?'

Erika didn't sound welcoming, certainly not enthusiastic, he thought savagely. Women needed careful handling. He forced himself to sound confident, pleasant, firm. Any trace of the jitters and she wouldn't cooperate. She knew a little of what he did for a living.

'I need a place to rest, to relax...'

'In bed? Of course?'

Her melodious voice sounded sarcastic. He wondered if she had a man with her. That would be a disaster area. It was a few months since he'd last contacted her.

'I *need* you,' he said. 'As company. Forget bed...'

'This *is* Manfred Seidler I'm talking to?' But her voice had softened. 'Where have you come from?'

'Zurich,' he lied easily.

'And where are you now?'

'Tired and hungry – inside a phone booth at the Hauptbahnhof. You don't have to cook. I'll take you out. Best place in town.'

'You counted on me being here – just waiting for your call?'

'Erika,' he said firmly, 'this is Saturday. I know you don't work Saturdays. I just hoped...'

'Better come on over, Manfred...'

Erika Stahel lived in a small, second-storey apartment near the Munsterplatz. Seidler lugged his suitcase through the falling snow, ignoring the cab rank outside the station. He could easily have afforded transport but cab-drivers had good memories. And often they were the first source the Swiss police approached for information.

It was ten o'clock in the morning when he pressed the bell alongside the name *E. Stahel*. Her voice, oddly recognizable despite the distortion of the speakphone, answered as though she had been waiting.

46

'Who is it?'

'Manfred. I'm freezing...'

'Come!'

The buzzer zizzed, indicating she had released the front door which he pressed open as he glanced up and down the street. Inside he climbed the steps, ignoring the lift. You could get trapped inside a lift if someone was waiting for you. Seidler had reached that state of acute nervousness and alertness when he trusted no one.

Her apartment door was open a few inches and he had reached out to push it when he paused, wondering what might be on the far side. The door opened inward and she stood looking at him without any particular expression. Only five feet four tall, she was a trim brunette of twenty-eight with a high forehead and large, black steady eyes.

'What are you waiting for? You look cold and frightened – and hungry. Breakfast is on the table. A jug of steaming coffee. Give me your case and eat...'

She said it all in her calm, competent voice as she closed the door and held out her hand for the case. He shook his head, decided he was being too curt and smiled, conscious of a sense of relief. He was under cover.

'I'll put the case in the bedroom if you don't mind. A couple of minutes and I'll be myself...'

'You know where the bedroom is. You should by now.' Her manner was matter-of-fact but she watched him closely.

Inside the bedroom with the door closed, he dropped the case on one of the two single beds and looked round quickly. He needed a hiding-place and only had minutes to find a safe one.

Moving a chair quietly against a tall cupboard, he stood on it and ran a finger along the top. His fingers came away with a thin film of dust. The rest of the place was spotless – but small women often overlooked the tops of tall cupboards. He stepped down and opened his suitcase.

The smaller, slim executive case was concealed beneath his shirts. He raised the catches quietly and took out several envelopes. All of them contained large sums of money – he had emptied his bank account in Berne on Friday just before the bank closed. Another envelope held the twenty five-hundred-franc notes he had extracted from the dead Franz Oswald's wallet in the Vienna basement.

Clutching the envelopes, he climbed back on the chair and distributed them across the top of the cupboard which was recessed. His final touch was to put two shirts into the executive case – to explain its presence – and then he closed the larger case, locked it and shoved it under the bed nearest the window.

'One ravenous lodger gasping for that steaming coffee and your lovely croissants,' he told Erika cheerfully as he emerged into the comfortably and well-furnished living-room which served also for a dining-room.

'My!' Her dark eyes searched his. 'Aren't we suddenly the bright, suave man-about-town. Good to get off the streets, Manfred?'

He swallowed the cup of coffee she poured even though it almost scalded him. Then he sat down and devoured three croissants while she sat facing him, studying him. Like Seidler, her parents were dead and she had no close relatives. Erika had worked her way up to the post of personal assistant to the chief executive of the bank she worked for. And her background was modest. Probably only in Switzerland could she have risen so high on sheer hard work and application.

'I'm quite happy on my own,' she had once confided to a girlfriend. 'I have a good job I like, a lover' (she meant Manfred, although she didn't identify him). 'So what more do I need? I can certainly do without being tied down at home, touring the supermarkets with some yelling brat – and a husband who, after three years, starts noticing the attractive secretaries in his office...'

'You were glad to get in off the streets, Manfred?' she repeated.

'Look outside the window! It's snowing cats and dogs. And I have been working very hard. I feel like holing up – some place no one knows where I am. Where the telephone won't ring,' he added quickly.

For once Seidler was telling the truth. He had cleverly chosen Basle to go to ground; Basle where three frontiers meet – Swiss, French and German. In case of emergency, the need for swift flight, he only had to board a train at the main station and the next stop – minutes away – was in Germany. Or, from the same station he could walk through a barrier to the other section and he was already on *French* soil. Yes, Basle was a good place to wait until he decided on his next move – until something turned up. Because for Manfred Seidler something always did turn up.

Then there was Erika. Seidler, a man who spent most of his time making money engaging in illegal, near-criminal activity – and who was now a murderer – appreciated that Erika was a *nice* girl. It was such a pleasant change to have her for company. He woke up from his reverie, aware she had said something.

'Sorry, I was dreaming...'

'Since you were last here I've been promoted...'

'Higher still? You were already PA to a director...'

'Now I'm PA to the president of the bank.' She leaned across the table and he stared at the inviting twin bulges against her flowered blouse. 'Manfred,' she went on, 'have you – you get around a lot, I know – have you ever heard anyone refer to the word *terminal*?'

Seidler's sense of well-being – brought on by a full stomach, the apartment's warmth (Erika could afford to turn up the central heating) and the proximity of Erika – vanished. One word and the nightmare was back on his doorstep. He struggled to hide the shock she had given him.

'I might have,' he teased her, 'if you tell me where you heard it.'

She hesitated, her curiosity fighting her integrity. Curiosity won. She took a deep breath and stretched out her small hand to grasp his.

'I was taking coffee into a board meeting. My boss said to the others "Has anyone found out anymore about this *terminal* business, what it means, or is it just another rumour about the Gold Club?"'

'Gold Club? What's that?'

'Well, it doesn't really exist officially. I gather that it comprises a group of bankers who have certain views on national policy. The group is known as the Gold Club...'

'And your boss belongs to it?'

'On the contrary. He doesn't agree with their views, whatever they may be. The Gold Club is based in Zurich...'

49

'Zurich? Not Berne?' he probed.

'Definitely Zurich...'

'Who is your boss?' he enquired casually.

'I'm talking too much about my job...'

'I could find out so easily,' he pointed out. 'I'd only have to phone you at work and you'd say, "Office of..." There are other ways. You know that.'

'I suppose you're right,' she agreed. 'In any case, it really doesn't matter. I work for Dr Max Nagel. Now, does *terminal* mean a railway station? That's the current thinking...'

'They got it right first time. More than that I don't know.'

'A railway station – not an *airport!*' she persisted. 'We do have an airport at Basle.'

'Positively nothing to do with airports,' he assured her.

He stood up and wiped his mouth with his napkin. He offered to clear the table but she shook her head and stood close to him, coiling her hands round his neck. As they kissed he wrapped his arms round her body and felt the buttons down the back of her blouse.

'That Gold Club,' he whispered. 'Something to do with gold bullion?'

'No. I told you. It's just a name. You know how wealthy the Zurich bankers are. It's a good name for them...'

He unfastened the top two buttons and slipped his hand inside, searching for the splayed strap. His exploring fingers found nothing. He undid two more buttons and realized that beneath the blouse she was naked. She had stripped herself down while he trudged through the snow from the station.

He enjoyed himself in the bedroom but when the aftermath came he began to worry like mad about what she'd said. Was Basle the worst place in the world he could have come to escape? Had he wandered into the lion's pit? He'd have to keep under cover. He'd also watch the newspapers – especially those from Geneva, Berne and Zurich, plus the locals. Something might show up in them, something which would show him the way – the way to escape the horror.

Eight

London, 13 February 1984. 6°. The atmosphere inside Tweed's office at 10 a.m. was one of appalled mystification. Besides Tweed, the other people gathered in the office included Howard, who had just returned from a weekend in the country, Monica, the middle-aged spinster of uncertain age Tweed called his 'right arm', and Mason, summoned urgently from Vienna on an apparent whim of Tweed's.

The 'object' Mason had brought with him and which he had purchased from Franz Oswald, was now locked away in Tweed's steel filing cabinet. No one had wanted to continue staring at *that* for long.

Howard, wearing the small check suit he kept for the country, was furious. He was convinced Tweed had exploited his absence to set all sorts of dangerous wheels in motion. To add insult to injury, Tweed had just returned from Downing Street where he had remained closeted with the Prime Minister for over an hour.

'Did you ask her for that document?' he enquired coldly.

Tweed glanced at the letter headed *10 Downing Street* which he had deliberately left on his desk. It gave him full powers to conduct the investigation personally. There was even a codicil promising him immediate access to her presence at any time there were developments.

'No,' replied Tweed, standing like the rest and polishing his glasses with a shabby silk handkerchief. 'It was her idea. I didn't argue, naturally...'

'Naturally,' Howard repeated sarcastically. 'So, now you've got the whole place in an uproar what's the next move?'

'I need outside help on this one.' Tweed looped his glasses over his ears and blinked at Howard. 'As you know, we're fully stretched. We have to get help where we can...'

'A name – or names – would be reassuring...'

'I'm not sure that's wise. Reliable help will only cooperate on a basis of total secrecy. If I'm the only person who knows their identity they know who to point the finger at if things go wrong. I take full responsibility...'

'You've hired an outsider already,' Howard accused.

Tweed shrugged and glanced at the letter on his desk. Howard could have killed him. It was an uncharacteristic action on the part of Tweed, but he would go to any length to protect a source. He decided he had treated Howard rather badly – especially in front of the others.

'There's already been a body,' he informed his chief. 'A man was murdered in Vienna. Mason can. tell you about it...'

'God Almighty!' Howard exploded. 'What are you letting us in for?'

'Permission to explain, sir?' the trim, erect Mason interjected. Taking Howard's curt nod for an affirmative he described in concise detail his experience with Franz Oswald. Howard listened in silence, his pursed lips expressing disapproval – and anxiety, a reaction Tweed sympathized with. He wasn't at all happy about the way the situation was developing himself.

'And did he tell you – while he was alive – how he obtained the *thing*?'

Howard nodded again, this time towards the locked drawer in the filing cabinet. He had calmed down while listening to Mason, a man he disliked but respected – they came from the same background. The trouble was he was Tweed's man. Like that bloody old spinster, Monica, who hadn't spoken a word – but Howard knew that later she could repeat the entire conversation back verbatim from memory.

'No, sir, he didn't,' Mason answered. 'I did ask but he refused point-blank to go into details. I have, however, got a photograph of the man who boarded the plane at Schwechat – that new camera is a wizard and I always carry it with me. It was a long shot, telephoto lens, but it's come out rather well.'

'Show it to me. You have got it on you?'

Mason glanced quickly at Tweed, which infuriated Howard once more. Tweed nodded acquiescence and wished Mason hadn't asked his permission. Still, Mason was being ultra-careful with this one. He watched Howard studying the photograph Mason handed to him.

'Any idea who he is?' Howard demanded.

'He's familiar,' Tweed replied. 'It will come back to me...'

'Put it through Records,' Howard suggested. 'Now, Mason, I'm going to say a word and I want you to react instantly. Give me the first association that comes into your head. Don't think about it. Ready? *Terminal...*'

'An electrical circuit,' Mason responded promptly.

'That's interesting.' Howard turned to Tweed. The Swiss are transforming their whole economy to run on electric power. New houses are heated by electricity – to avoid dependence on oil. Did you know that?'

'Yes, I knew that. You might have a shrewd point there,' he agreed.

'Supposing this whole business hinges on a massive sabotage operation?' Howard warmed to his theme. 'The enemy is planning to hit all the key points in the Swiss power system when the moment comes for them to make their move.'

'You could be right. We'll know when we find out what really is going on inside Switzerland. I need to send in someone the Swiss police and military intelligence don't know. Mason would fit. the bill. And the Ambassador in Vienna agreed to bring forward his leave – three weeks...'

'Good idea,' agreed Howard. He felt a little better about the whole thing now he was *contributing*. Time to show a modicum of goodwill. He nodded towards the letter on Tweed's desk. 'With her backing we have an open-ended call on resources. But this business still worries me. Who would imagine the Swiss getting mixed up in a situation of such international dimensions? Yes, Mason, was there something?'

'Permission to find some breakfast – if you're finished with me, sir? Airline meals turn my stomach. I haven't eaten since last night.'

'Fuel up!' Howard said breezily, still buoyant. 'That is, if Tweed has nothing more?'

'I'll be organizing your flight to Zurich,' Tweed told Mason. 'Get a train from there to Berne – it's only ninety minutes. Breakfast first though. And thank you, Mason. I'm not certain what you've triggered off yet, but it's something very big. I feel it in my arthritic bones...'

'Howard is a pain in the proverbial,' Monica remarked to Tweed when they were alone. 'Up and down like a bloody yo-yo...'

'It's his wife, Eve,' Tweed said, slumping back in his swivel-chair. 'I only met her once. Very County, very superior. She went out of her way to make me feel uncomfortable...'

'That's because she fears you,' Monica commented shrewdly.

'And that's ridiculous,' Tweed protested.

'She's ambitious, the driving force behind Howard. When he tells her the Prime Minister has given you *carte blanche* she'll really hit the roof. I know the type. On top of that she has money – a large block of ICI shares she inherited. That gives a woman a sense of power.'

'Poor Howard,' said Tweed and his sympathy was genuine. He looked at Monica, a comfortable woman whose deep loyalty to him he sometimes found worrying. Under other circumstances he might have considered marrying her, but that, of course, was quite impossible. 'I have an appointment,' he said, standing up. 'Expect me when you see me...'

'No way of getting in touching?' she enquired mischievously.

'Not this time.' He paused near the door and she was careful not to help him on with his coat. Tweed hated fuss. 'Monica, when Mason gets back, ask him to wait for me. Tell him one job will be to compile a file on Professor Armand Grange, head of the Berne Clinic...'

Lee Foley walked along Piccadilly, his expression bleak, hands thrust inside the pockets of his duffel coat. Christ, it was cold in London, a raw, damp cold. No wonder the Brits, had once conquered the world. If you could stand this climate you could stand anywhere across the face of the earth.

He checked his watch. The timing of the call was important. The contact would be expecting him at the appointed number. He glanced round casually before descending into Piccadilly underground station. No reason why anyone should be following him – which was the moment to check.

Inside the phone booth he checked his watch again, waited until his watch registered precisely 11 a.m., then dialled the London number, waited for the bleeps, inserted a tenpenny coin and heard the familiar voice. He identified himself and then listened before answering.

'Now let me do the talking. I'll catch an early flight to Geneva today. I'll wait at the Hotel des Bergues. When the time comes I'll proceed to Berne. I'll reserve a room at a hotel called the Savoy near the station – you can get the number from the Berne directory. We'll keep in close touch as the situation develops. You must keep me informed. Signing off...'

It was 12.30 p.m. when Tweed returned to his office, hung up his coat by the loop and settled himself behind his desk. Monica, checking a file with Mason, frowned. He should have put the coat on a hanger – no wonder he always had such a rumpled look. She carefully refrained from so doing. Tweed had been away for over two hours.

'I've booked Mason on Swissair Flight SR 805. Departs Heathrow fourteen forty-five, arrives Zurich seventeen twenty, local time...'

'He'll catch it easily,' Tweed agreed with an absent-minded expression. 'What are you two up to?'

'Looking through hundreds of photos. We've found the man he saw boarding that Swiss jet at Schwechat Airport. Manfred Seidler...'

'You're sure?'

'Positive,' Mason replied. 'Look for yourself.'

He handed across the desk the photo he had taken and which the photographic section in the basement of Park Crescent had developed and printed. Monica pushed Seidler's file across the desk open at the third page to which another photo was pasted.

'Poor old Manfred,' Tweed said half to himself. 'It looks as though this time he's mixed up in something he may not be able to handle.'

'You know him?' Mason queried.

55

'*Knew* him. When I was on the continent. He's on what we used to call the circuit...'

'Not an *electric* circuit?' Monica pounced. 'Remember Howard asking Mason what *Terminal* suggested to him?'

Tweed stared at her through his glasses. Monica didn't miss a trick: he would never have thought of that himself. He considered the idea. 'There could be a connection,' he conceded eventually. 'I'm not sure. Seidler is a collector – and seller – of unconsidered trifles. Sometimes not so trifling. Lives off his network of contacts. Just occasionally he comes up with the jackpot. I've no idea where he is now. Something for you to enquire about, Mason.'

'I'm going to be busy. Searching for Manfred Seidler, building up a file on this Professor Grange. We've nothing on him here.'

'The computer came up with zero,' Monica added.

'*Computer?*' An odd expression flickered behind Tweed's glasses and was then gone. He relaxed again. 'Mason, from the moment you leave this building I want you to watch your back. Especially when you've arrived in Switzerland.'

'Anything particular in mind?'

'We've already had one murder – Franz Oswald. People will kill for what I've got in that locked drawer...' He looked at Monica. 'Or has the courier from the Ministry of Defence collected it?'

'Not so far...'

'They must be mad.' Tweed drummed his thick fingers on the desk. 'The sooner their experts examine it...'

'Charlton is a careful type,' Monica reminded him. 'He's very conscious of security. My bet is the courier will arrive as soon as night has fallen.'

'You're probably right. I shan't leave my office until the thing is off our hands. Now, Mason,' he resumed, 'another unknown factor is the attitude of the Swiss authorities – the Federal police and their Military Intelligence. They could prove hostile...'

'What on earth for?' Monica protested.

'It worries me – that Lear executive jet Mason watched leaving Schwechat. The fact that it bore a flag on its side with a white cross on

56

a red ground, the Swiss flag. Don't accept anyone as a friend. Oh, one more thing. We've reserved a room at the Bellevue Palace in Berne.'

Mason whistled. 'Very nice. VIP treatment. Howard will do his nut when he finds out...'

'It's convenient,' Tweed said shortly. 'I may join you later.'

Monica had trouble keeping her face expressionless. She knew that Tweed had his own reservation at the Bellevue Palace a few days hence: she had booked the room herself. Tweed, naturally secretive, was playing this one closer to the chest than ever before. He wasn't even letting his own operative know about his movements. For God's sake, he couldn't suspect Mason?

'Why convenient?' enquired Mason.

'It's central,' Tweed said shortly and left it at that. 'We're getting things moving,' he went on with that distant look in his eyes, 'placing the pieces on the board. One thing I'd dearly like to know – where is Manfred Seidler now?'

Basle, 13 February 1984. 0°. Seidler still felt hunted. He had spent the whole weekend inside Erika Stahel's apartment and the walls were starting to close in on him. He heard a key being inserted in the. outer door and grabbed for his 9-mm. Luger, a weapon he had concealed from Erika.

When she walked in, carrying a bag of groceries, the Luger was out of sight under a cushion. She closed the door with her foot and surveyed the newspapers spread out over the table. She had dashed out first thing to get them for him. Now she had dashed back from the office – only one hour for lunch – to prepare him some food.

'Anything in the papers?' she called out from the tiny kitchen.

'Nothing. Yet. You don't have to make me a meal...'

'Won't take any time at all. We can talk while we eat...'

He looked at the newspapers on the table. The *Berner Zeitung*, the main Zurich morning, the *Journal de Genève* and the Basle locals. He lifted one of them and underneath lay the executive case. He'd made up his mind.

Since he was a youth Seidler had involved himself in unsavoury activities – always to make money. Brought up by an aunt in Vienna – his mother had been killed by the Russians, his father had died on the Eastern Front – Seidler had been one of the world's wanderers. Now, when he had the money, when he felt like settling down, the whole system was trying to locate him.

He felt a great affection for Erika because she was such a *decent* girl. He laid the table, listened to her chatting with animation while they ate, and only brought up the subject over coffee.

'Erika, if anything happens to me I want you to have this...'

He opened the executive case, revealing the neatly stacked Swiss banknotes inside. Her face, which always showed the pink flush Seidler had observed when women were pregnant, went blank as she stood up. Her deft fingers rifled through several of the stacks at random and replaced them. She stared at him.

'Manfred, there has to be half a million francs here...'

'Very close. Take them and put them into a safety deposit – not at the bank where you work. Call a cab. Don't walk through the streets with that – not even in Basle...'

'I can't take this.' She grasped his hand and he saw she was close to tears. 'I'm not interested – you're the only one I'm interested in.'

'So, bank it for both of us. Under your own name. Under no circumstances under my name,' he warned.

'Manfred...' She eased herself into his lap. 'Who are you frightened of? Did you steal this money?'

'No!' He became vehement to convince her. 'It was given to me for services rendered. Now they no longer need me. They may regard me as a menace because of what I know. I shouldn't stay here much longer...'

'Stay as long as you like. Who are these people?'

'One person in particular. Someone who wields enormous power. Someone who may be able to use even the police to do his bidding.'

'The Swiss police?' Her tone was incredulous. 'You look so tired, so worn. You're over-estimating this person's power. If it will make you

58

feel any better I will put that case in a safety deposit – providing you keep the key...'

'All right.' He knew it was the only condition under which she'd agree to do what he asked. They'd find some place inside the apartment to hide the key. 'You'd better hurry. You'll be late for work,' he told her.

She hugged him as though she'd never let go. He almost had tears in his own eyes. So decent, so nice. If only he'd met her years ago...

Inside their bedroom at the Penta Hotel, situated amid the vast enclave of Heathrow Airport, Newman checked his watch again. Nancy had gone out hours ago on her own – she knew how he hated shopping expeditions. They still had plenty of time to catch Swissair Flight SR 837 which departed 19.00 hours and reached Geneva 21.30 hours local time. The door opened and she caught him looking at his watch.

'I've been hours, I know,' she said cheerfully. 'Think we were going to miss our flight? Have I enjoyed myself...'

'You've probably bought up half Fortnum's...'

'Just about. It's a marvellous shop – and they'll post off purchases anywhere in the world.' She looked at him coyly as she hung up her sheepskin in the wardrobe. 'I'm not showing you the bills. God, I love London...'

'Then why don't we settle down here?'

'Robert, don't start that again. And you've been out. Your coat is on a different hanger...'

'For a breath of fresh air. Tinged with petrol fumes. You're cut out to be a detective.'

'Doctors have to be observant, darling.' She looked at the bed. 'Do we eat now – or later?'

'Later. We have things to do.' He wrapped his arms round her slim waist. 'Afterwards we'll just have a drink. Dinner on the plane. Swissair food is highly edible...'

Belted in his seat aboard an earlier Swissair flight, Lee Foley glanced out of the window as the aircraft left Heathrow behind and broke

59

through the overcast into a sunlit world. He was sitting at the rear of the first-class section.

Foley had reserved this particular seat because it was a good viewing point to observe his fellow passengers. Unlike them, he had refused any food or drink when the steward came to put a cloth on his fold-out table.

'Nothing,' he said abruptly.

'We have a very nice meal as you can see from the menu, sir.'

'Take the menu, keep the meal...'

'Something to drink then, sir?'

'I said nothing.'

It was still daylight when the aircraft made its descent over the Jura Mountains, heading for Cointrin Airport. Foley watched the view as the plane banked and noted Lac de Joux, nestled inside the Juras, was frozen solid. At least, he. assumed this must be the case – the lake was mantled in snow, as were the mountains. He was the first passenger to leave the plane after it landed and he carried his only luggage.

Foley always travelled light. Hanging around a carousel, waiting for your bag to appear on the moving belt, gave watchers the opportunity to observe your arrival. Foley always regarded terminals as dangerous points of entry. He showed his passport to the Swiss official seated inside his glass box, watching him out of the corner of his eye. The passport was returned and, so far as Foley could tell, no interest had been aroused.

He walked through the green Customs exit into the public concourse beyond. For strangers there was a clear sign pointing to *TAXIS*, but Foley automatically turned in the right direction. He was familiar with Cointrin.

The chill air had hit him like a knife thrust when he came down the mobile staircase from the aircraft. It hit him again when he emerged from the building and walked to the first cab. He waited until he was settled in the rear seat with the door closed before he gave the instruction to the driver.

'Hotel des Bergues...'

Foley's wariness about terminals was closer to the mark than he realized when he walked swiftly across the concourse without turning his head. Looking back drew attention to yourself – betrayed nervousness. So he had not seen a small, gnome-like figure huddled against a wall with an unlit cigarette between his thin lips.

Julius Nagy had straightened briefly when he saw Foley, then he took out a book of matches and pretended to light the cigarette without doing so – Nagy didn't smoke. His tiny, bird-like eyes sparkled with satisfaction as he watched the American pass beyond the automatic exit doors. His neat feet trotted inside the nearest phone box and closed the door.

Nagy, who had escaped from Hungary in 1956 when Soviet troops invaded his country, was fifty-two years old. Streaks of dark oily hair peeped from under the Tyrolean-style hat he wore well pulled down. His skin was wrinkled like a walnut, his long nose pinched at the nostrils.

He dialled the number he knew by heart. Nagy had a phenomenal memory for three things – people's faces, their names, and phone numbers. When the police headquarters operator answered he gave his name, asked to be put through immediately, please, to Chief Inspector Tripet. Yes, he was well-known to Tripet and he was in a hurry.

'Tripet speaking. Who is this?'

The voice, remote, careful, had spoken in French. Nagy could picture the Sûreté man sitting in his second-floor office inside the seven-storey building facing the Public Library at 24 Boulevard Carl-Vogt, at the foot of the Old City.

'Nagy here. Didn't they tell you?'

'Christian name?'

'Oh, for God's sake. Julius. Julius Nagy. I've got some information. It's worth a hundred francs...'

'Perhaps...'

'Someone who just came in from London off the flight at Cointrin. A hundred francs I want – or I'll dry up...'

'And who is this expensive someone?' asked Tripet in a bored tone of voice.

'Lee Foley, CIA man...'

'I'll meet you at the usual place. Exactly one hour from now. Eighteen hundred hours. I want to talk to you about this – see your face when I do. If it isn't genuine you're off the payroll for all time...'

Nagy heard the click and realized Tripet had broken the connection. He was puzzled. Had he asked too little? Was the information pure gold? On the other hand Tripet had sounded as though he were rebuking the little man. Nagy shrugged, left the booth, saw the airport bus for town was about to leave and started running.

At 24 Bd Carl-Vogt, Tripet, a thin-faced, serious-looking man in his late thirties, a man who had risen quickly in his chosen profession, hoped he had bluffed Nagy as his agile fingers dialled the Berne number.

'Arthur Beck, please, Assistant to the Chief of Federal Police,' he requested crisply when the operator at the Taubenhalde came on the line. 'This is Chief Inspector Tripet, Sûreté, Geneva...'

'One moment, sir...'

Beck came to the phone quickly after first dismissing from his tenth floor office his secretary, a fifty-five-year-old spinster not unlike Tweed's Monica. Settling himself comfortably in his chair, Beck spoke with calm amiability.

'Well, Leon, and how are things in Geneva? Snowing?'

'Not quite. Arthur, you asked me to report if any odd people turned up on my patch. Would Lee Foley, CIA operative, qualify?'

'Yes.' Beck gripped the receiver a shade more firmly. 'Tell me about it.' He reached for pad and pencil.

'He may have just come in on a Swissair flight from London'. I have a report from Cointrin...'

'A report from who?' The pencil poised.

'A small-time informer we call The Mongrel, sometimes The Scrounger. He'll burrow in any filthy trashcan to make himself a few francs. But he's very reliable. If Foley interests you I'm meeting Julius Nagy, The Mongrel, shortly outside. Can you give me a description of Foley so I can test Nagy's story?'

'Foley is a man you can't miss...' Beck gave from memory a detailed description of the American, including the fact that he spoke in a gravelly voice. 'That should be enough, Leon, you would agree? Good. When you've seen The Mongrel, I would appreciate another call from you. I'll wait in my office...'

Tripet went off the line quickly, an action Beck, who couldn't stand people who wasted time, appreciated. Then he sat in his chair, twiddling the pencil while he thought.

They were beginning to come in, as he had anticipated. The crisis was growing. There would be others on the way, he suspected. He had been warned about the rumours circulating among various foreign embassies. Beck, forty years old in May, was a stockily-built man with a thick head of unruly brown hair and a small brown moustache. His grey eyes had a glint of humour, a trait which often saved his sanity when the pressure was on.

He reflected that he had never known greater pressure. Thank God his chief had given him extraordinary powers to take any action he thought fit. If what he suspected was true – and he hoped with all his Catholic soul he was wrong – then he was going to need those powers. Sometimes when he thought of what he might be up against he winced. Beck, however, was a loner. *If necessary I'll fight the whole bloody system* he said to himself. He would *not* be defeated by Operation Terminal.

Unlocking a drawer while he waited for Tripet to call him back, he took out a file with the tab, *Classification One*, on the front of the folder. He turned to the first page inside and looked at the heading typed at the head of the script. *Case of Hannah Stuart, American citizen. Klinik Bern.*

Nine

Geneva, 13 February 1984. -3°. 'On duty' again at Cointrin, Julius Nagy could hardly believe his eyes. This was Jackpot Day. After meeting Chief Inspector Tripet, who had asked for a detailed description of Lee Foley, who had been sufficiently satisfied with the information to pay him his one hundred francs, Nagy had returned to meet the last flights into the airport despite the bitter cold.

Flight SR 837 – again from London – had disgorged its passengers when Nagy spotted a famous face emerging from the Customs exit. Robert Newman had a woman with him and this time Nagy followed his quarry outside. He was just behind the Englishman when he heard him instructing the driver of the cab.

'Please take us to the Hotel des Bergues,' Newman had said in French.

Nagy had decided to invest twenty or so of the francs received from Tripet to check Newman's real destination. They were tricky, these foreign correspondents. He wouldn't put it past Newman to change the destination once they were clear of the airport. As he summoned the next cab Nagy glanced over his shoulder and saw Newman, on the verge of stepping inside the rear of his cab, staring hard at him. He swore inwardly and dived inside the back of his own cab.

'Follow my friend in that cab ahead,' he told the driver.

'If you say so...'

His driver showed a little discretion, keeping another vehicle between himself and Newman's. It was only a ten-minute ride – including the final three-sided tour round the hotel to reach the main entrance because of the one-way system.

He watched the porter from the Hotel des Bergues taking their luggage and told his driver to move on and drop him round the corner.

Paying off the cabbie, he hurried to the nearest phone box, frozen by the bitter wind blowing along the lake and the Rhône which the des Bergues overlooked. He called Pierre Jaccard, senior reporter on the *Journal de Genève*. His initial reception was even more hostile than had been Tripet's.

'What are you trying to peddle this time, Nagy?'

'There are plenty of people in the market for this one,' Nagy said aggressively, deliberately adopting a different approach. You had to know your potential clients. 'You have, I presume, heard of the Kruger Affair – the German traitor who extracted information from the giant computer at Dusseldorf?'

'Yes, of course I have. But that's last year's news...'

Nagy immediately detected the change in tone from contempt to cautious interest – concealing avid interest. He played his fish.

'Two hundred francs and I'm not arguing about the price. It's entirely non-negotiable. You could still catch tomorrow's edition. And I can tell you how to check out what I may tell you – with one phone call.'

'Tell me a little more...'

'Either another Kruger case, this time nearer home, or something equally big. That's all you get until you agree terms. Is it a deal? Yes or no. And I'm putting down this phone in thirty seconds. Counting now...'

'Hold it! If you're conning me...'

'Goodbye, Jaccard...'

'Deal! Two hundred francs. God, the gambles I take. Give.'

'Robert Newman – you *have* heard of Robert Newman? I thought you probably had. He's just come in on Flight SR 837 from London. You think he arrives late in the evening anywhere without a purpose? And he looked to be in one hell of a hurry...'

'You said I could check this out,' Jaccard reminded him.

'He's staying at the Hotel des Bergues. Call the place – ask to speak to him, give a false name. Christ, Jaccard, you do know your job?'

'I know my job,' Jaccard said quietly. 'Come over to my office now and the money will be waiting...'

Arthur Beck sat behind his desk, a forgotten cup of cold coffee to his left, studying the fat file on Lee Foley. A good selection of photos – all taken without the subject's knowledge. A long note recording that he had resigned from the CIA, that he was now senior partner in the New York outfit, CIDA, the Continental International Detective Agency. 'I wonder...' Beck said aloud and the phone rang.

'I'm so sorry I didn't phone earlier...' Tripet in Geneva was full of apologies. 'An emergency was waiting for me when I got back to the office... a reported kidnapping at Cologny... it turned out to be a false alarm, thank God...'

'Not to worry. I have plenty to occupy myself with. Now, any developments?'

'The Mongrel – Julius Nagy – confirmed exactly your description of Foley. He is somewhere in Geneva – or he was when he left Cointrin at seventeen hundred hours...'

'Do something for me, will you? Check all the hotels – find out where he's staying, if he's still there. Let me give you a tip. Start with the cheaper places – two and three-star. Foley maintains a low profile.'

'A pleasure. I'll get the machinery moving immediately...'

Beck replaced the receiver. He rarely made a mistake, but on this occasion he had badly misjudged his quarry.

Foley, who had dined elsewhere, approached the entrance to the Hotel des Bergues cautiously. He peered through the revolving doors into the reception hall beyond. The doorman was talking to the night concierge. No one else about.

He pushed the door and walked inside. Checking his watch, he turned left and wandered up to the door leading into one of the hotel's two restaurants, the Pavillon which overlooks the Rhône. At a banquette window table he saw Newman and Nancy Kennedy who had reached the coffee stage.

Newman had his back to the door which had a glass panel in the upper half. Foley had a three-quarter view of Nancy. Newman suddenly looked over his shoulder, Foley moved away quickly, collected his key and headed for the elevator.

The Pavillon, a restaurant favoured by the locals as well as hotel guests, was half-empty. Newman stared out of the window as several couples hurried past, heads down against the bitter wind, the women wearing furs – sable, lynx, mink – while their men were clad mostly in sheepskins.

'There's a lot of money in this town,' Nancy observed, following his gaze. 'And Bob, that was a superb meal. The chicken was the best I've ever eaten. As good as Bewick's in Walton Street,' she teased him. 'What are you thinking about?'

'That we have to decide our next move – which doesn't mean we necessarily rush on to Berne yet...'

'Why not? I thought we were leaving tomorrow...'

'Maybe, maybe not.' Newman's tone was firm. 'When we've finished do you mind if I take a walk along the lake. Alone. I have some thinking to do.'

'You have an appointment? You've checked your watch three times since the main course...'

'I said a walk.' He grinned to soften his reply. 'Did you know that Geneva is one of the great European centres of espionage? It crawls with agents. The trouble is all the various UN outfits which are here. Half the people of this city are foreigners. The Genevoises get a bit fed up. The foreigners push up the price of apartments – unless you're very wealthy. Like you are...'

'Don't let's spoil a lovely evening.' She checked her own watch. 'You go and have your walk – I'll unpack. Whether we're leaving tomorrow or not I don't want my dresses creased.' Her chin tilted at the determined angle he knew so well. 'Go on – have your walk. Don't spend all night with her...'

'Depends on the mood she's in.' He grinned again.

Newman, his sheepskin turned up at the collar, pushed through the revolving doors and the temperature plummeted. A raw wind slashed at his face. Across the road, beyond iron railings, the Rhône chopped and surged; by daylight he guessed it would have that special greenish colour of water which was melted snow from peaks in the distant Valais.

By night the water looked black. Neon lights from buildings on the opposite shore reflected in the dark flow. Oddly British-sounding signs. The green neon of The British Bank of the Middle East. The blue neon of Kleinwort Benson. The red neon of the Hongkong Bank. Streetlamps were a zigzag reflection in the ice-cold water. Thrusting both hands inside his coat pockets he began walking east towards the Hilton.

Behind him Julius Nagy emerged, frozen stiff, from a doorway. The gnome-like figure was careful to keep a couple between himself and Newman. At least his long wait had produced some result. Where the hell could the Englishman be going at this hour, in this weather?

Sitting in Pierre Jaccard's cubby-hole office at the *Journal de Genève*, Nagy had received a pleasant shock. Jaccard had first pushed an envelope across his crowded desk and then watched as Nagy opened it. Thirty-year-old Jaccard, already senior reporter on the paper, had come a long way by taking chances, backing his intuition. Thin-faced with watchful eyes which never smiled even when his mouth registered amiability, he drank coffee from a cardboard cup.

'Count it, Nagy. It's all there. Two hundred. Like to make some more?'

'Doing what?' Nagy enquired with calculated indifference.

'You hang on to Newman's tail for dear life. You report back to me where he is, where he goes, whom he meets. I want to know everything about him – down to the colour of the pyjamas he's wearing...'

'An assignment like that costs money,' Nagy said promptly.

It was one of the favourite words in Nagy's vocabulary. He never referred to a job – he was always on an *assignment*. It was the little man's way of conferring some dignity on his way of life. A man needed to feel he had some importance in the world. Jaccard was too young to grasp the significance of the word, too cynical. Had he understood, he could have bought Nagy for less.

'There's another two hundred in this envelope,' Jaccard said, pushing it across the desk. 'A hundred for your fee, a hundred for expenses. And I'll need a receipted bill for every franc of expenses...'

Nagy shook his head, made no effort to touch the second envelope. Despite Jaccard's expression of boredom he sensed under the surface something big, maybe very big. He clasped his small hands in his lap, pursed his lips.

'Newman could take off for anywhere – Zurich, Basle, Lugano. I need the funds to follow him if I'm to carry out the assignment satisfactorily...'

'How much? And think before you reply...'

'Five hundred. Two for myself for the moment. Three for expenses. You'll get your bills. Not a franc less.'

Jaccard had sighed, reached for his wallet and counted five one-hundred franc notes. Which cleaned him out. Tomorrow he'd been on his way to Munich – but he was gambling again, gambling on Newman who had cracked the Kruger case. Christ, if he could only get on to something like that he'd be made for life.

Which was how Nagy, shivering in his shabby overcoat and Tyrolean hat, came to be following Newman who had now reached the lakeside. Earlier, just before crossing the rue du Mont Blanc, the Englishman had glanced back and Nagy thought he'd been spotted. But now Newman continued trudging along the promenade, his head bent against the wind.

As he approached the Hilton, which faces the lake, the street was so deserted that Newman heard another sound above the whine of the wind. The creaking groan of a paddle steamer moored to one of the landing stages, the noise of the hull grinding against the wood of the mooring posts. A single-funnel paddle steamer going no place: it was still out of season. Waiting for spring. Like the whole of the northern hemisphere. No more neon signs across the broadening expanse of the lake. Only cold, twinkling lights along some distant street. He stopped by the outside lift and pressed the button.

A small version of the external elevators which slide vertiginously up the sides of many American hotels, the lift arrived and Newman stepped inside, pressing another button. It occurred to him how exposed he was as the small cage ascended – the door was of glass, the lift was lit inside, a perfect target for any marksman.

Nagy timed it carefully, running up the staircase to the first floor so he saw Newman vanishing inside the restaurant. He waited, then followed. Before entering the restaurant, Nagy removed his shabby coat, stuffed his Tyrolean hat inside a pocket, smoothed his ruffled hair and walked inside. A wave of heat beat at his bloodless face.

The restaurant is a large rectangle with the long side parallel to the lake. Newman was sitting down at a window table at the far end, a table for two. The other chair was already occupied by a girl who made Nagy stare.

The little man sat at a table near the exit, ordered coffee from the English waitress who appeared promptly – the waitresses here are of various nationalities. He studied Newman's companion surreptitiously. Some people had all the luck he thought without envy.

The girl was in her late twenties, Nagy decided, memorizing her appearance for Jaccard. Thick, titian- (Nagy called it red) coloured hair with a centre parting, a fawn cashmere (at a guess) sweater which showed off her ample figure and tight black leather pants encasing her superb legs from crotch to ankle as though painted on her. Gleaming leather. The new 'wet' look. Very good bone structure – high cheekbones.

A stunner. At first Nagy thought she was a tart, then decided he was wrong. This girl had class, something the little man respected. Exceptionally animated, their conversation gradually developed so she listened intently while Newman talked, drinking his cup of coffee at occasional intervals.

At one stage she reached across to straighten his tie, a gesture Nagy duly noted. It suggested a degree of intimacy. Something else for Jaccard. Nagy had the impression Newman was instructing her, that she asked a question only to clarify a point.

When Newman paid the bill and left she remained at the table. Nagy had a moment of indecision – who to watch now? But only a moment.

Newman walked towards Nagy – and the exit, putting on his sheepskin as he walked past the little man without even a glance in his direction. Nagy, who had paid his own bill as soon as his coffee had arrived, followed.

This time Newman jibbed at the exposed elevator. He ran down the staircase and walked back briskly along the Siberian promenade. He *dived* inside the revolving doors of the Hotel des Bergues and went straight up to Room 406. Nancy, wearing a transparent nightdress, opened the door a few inches, then let him inside.

'Was she good?' was her first question.

'You think I'm some kind of stud?' he replied genially.

'I'll tell you something – when we arrived and you had to register, I was like a jelly inside with embarrassment. Mr and Mrs R. Newman...'

'The Swiss are discreet. I told you...' He had already taken off his tie. '... they only want to see the man's passport. And it's bloody freezing outside. I walked miles.'

'Come to any decisions?'

'Always sleep on decisions. See how they look in the morning.'

It was in the morning that the world blew up in Newman's face.

Ten

Geneva, 14 February 1984. -2°. The concierge called out to Newman as they made their way to the Pavillon for breakfast. Nancy had tried to persuade him to use Room Service and he had refused point-blank.

'You Americans can't think of any other way of living except Room Service...'

He excused himself, stopping at the concierge's desk. With a broad smile the concierge spread out the front page of the *Journal de Genève*. Newman's photograph stared back at him inside a box headed *Sommaire*. The text was brief, not a wasted word.

M. Robert Newman, famous foreign correspondent (author of the bestseller KRUGER: THE COMPUTER THAT FAILED) has arrived in Geneva. He is staying at the Hotel des Bergues. We have no information as to his ultimate destination or the new story he is now working on.

'It is good to be famous, yes, no?' the concierge remarked.

'Yes, no,' Newman replied and gave him a franc for the paper.

His face was grim as he pushed open the door into the restaurant. Nancy had chosen the same window table, sitting in the banquette. Newman sat in the chair opposite and stared out of the window. At eight in the morning Geneva was hurrying to work, men and girls heavily muffled against the chilling breeze.

'I've ordered coffee,' Nancy said, breaking a croissant as she studied him. 'Bob, what's wrong?'

He passed the newspaper across without a word, steepled his fingers and went on staring at the swollen Rhône. She read the news item and glowed, waiting until the waitress had. arranged their coffee pots.

'I'm going to marry a real celebrity, aren't I? Where did they get the photo? I rather like it...'

'From their files. It's appeared often enough before, God knows. This changes everything, Nancy. It could be dangerous. I think I'd better leave you here for a few days. Go on to Berne alone. I'll call you daily...'

'Like hell you will! I've come to see Jesse and I won't be left behind. Why dangerous?'

'Sixth sense...'

He paused as a small man in a shabby coat and a Tyrolean hat walked past, glancing briefly inside the restaurant and away as he caught Newman looking at him. A titian-haired girl strolled past in the same direction. She wore a short fur coat, the collar pulled up at the neck, and clean blue jeans tucked inside her leather boots. Newman winked at her and she turned her head to stare ahead.

'You're starting early today,' Nancy observed. 'I saw that...'

'Did you see the little man who was walking ahead of her?'

'No. Why?'

'Julius Nagy, a piece of Europe's drifting flotsam.'

'Flotsam?' Nancy looked puzzled.

'One of the many losers who live on their wits, by their contacts, peddling information. He was at the airport last night. He followed us here in a cab. He could be responsible for that piece of dynamite...'

His finger tapped the *Sommaire* box and then he poured coffee and broke a hard roll, covering a piece with butter and marmalade. Nancy, her mind in a whirl, kept quiet for a few minutes, knowing he was always in a better mood when he'd had his breakfast.

'You're not going off on your own,' she told him eventually. 'So, what are *we* going to do *together*?'

'Finish our breakfast. Then I'll decide...'

But by the time he'd swallowed his fourth cup of coffee, his orange juice and consumed two rolls, the decision was taken out of his hands.

Berne. Inside a large mansion in Elfenau, the district where the wealthy live, Bruno spread out the front page of the *Journal de Genève* on an antique drum table. He studied the picture of Newman carefully.

'So they have arrived,' he said in French.

'We knew they were on the way, Bruno. The question is, will they pose a problem? If so, they will have to be dealt with – you will have to deal with them.'

The large man with tinted spectacles who stood in the shadows spoke with a soft, persuasive voice. The huge living-room was dark even in the morning. Partly due to the overcast sky – and partly because heavy net curtains killed what pallid illumination filtered from the outside world.

Bruno Kobler, a hard-looking man of forty, five feet ten tall, heavily built and in the peak of physical condition, glanced towards the massive silhouette. Light from the desk lamp glinted on the dark glasses. He was trying to gauge exactly what his employer had in mind. The man in the shadows continued speaking.

'I recall so well, Bruno, that when I was building up my chemical works it looked as though a rival might upset my calculations. I didn't wait to see what he would do. I acted first. We are on the eve of a total breakthrough with Terminal. I will allow nothing to stand in my way. Remember, we now have the support of the Gold Club.'

'So, I set up close surveillance on Newman and his woman?'

'You always come to the correct conclusion, Bruno. That is why I pay you so well...'

Arthur Beck of the Federal Police sat with the receiver to his ear, waiting while the operator at Geneva police headquarters put him on to Tripet. A copy of *the Journal de Genève* lay in front of him. As he had anticipated, the momentum was accelerating. They were coming in. First Lee Foley, alleged detective with the CIDA, now Newman. Beck didn't believe in coincidences – not when events were moving towards a crisis. And this morning his chief had warned him.

'Beck, I'm not sure how much longer I'm going to be able to give you *carte blanche*. Very powerful interests are at work – trying to get me to take you off the case...'

'I'm getting to the bottom of this thing whatever happens,' Beck had replied.

'You can't fight the system...'

'You want to bet? Sir?'

Tripet came on the line and they exchanged brief courtesies. Beck then told the Geneva chief inspector what he wanted, how to handle it with *finesse*. As the conversation proceeded he detected a note of worry in Tripet's manner. He's unsure of his position, Beck judged.

'Between you and me, Tripet, this comes right from the top. And that's just between you and me. I just hope you can pick him up before he leaves town. You know where he's staying. Call him, send over a car right away if you'd sooner handle it that way. I leave it to you, but do it, Tripet...'

Beck replaced the receiver and picked up the paper, studying the photograph. He was going to need all the help he could muster – even unorthodox help. If it came to the crunch the press was one thing they couldn't muzzle. Yes, he needed allies. His face tightened. Christ! He wasn't going to let the bastards get away with it just because they had half the money in the western world.

Basle. Erika Stahel closed her apartment door and leaned her back against it for a moment, clutching the armful of newspapers. Seidler guessed she had been running as he looked up from the table. Her face was flushed an even higher colour than usual.

'We've time for another cup of coffee before I go to work,' she told him.

'That would be nice...'

She placed the papers in a neat pile on the table. She was such a tidy, orderly girl, he reflected. It would be marvellous to settle down with her for ever. She danced off into the kitchen, expressing her joy that he was back. He could hear her humming a small tune while she prepared the coffee. He opened the first paper.

'You cleared the table for me,' she called out. 'Thank you, Manfred. You're getting quite domesticated. Do you mind?'

'It could become a habit...'

'Why not?' she responded gaily.

The moment she returned to the living-room she sensed a major change in the atmosphere. Sitting in his shirtsleeves; Seidler was staring at the front page of *the Journal de Genève*. She placed his cup of black coffee within reach – he never took sugar or milk and drank litres of the stuff, another indication that he was living on his nerves. She stood close to his shoulder, peering over it.

'Something wrong?'

'My lifeline. Maybe...'

He took the gold, felt-tipped pen she had given him and used it to circle the box headed *Sommaire*. She was so generous – God knew how much of her month's salary she had squandered on the pen. He'd have liked to go out and buy her something. He had the money. But it meant *going out*...

'Robert Newman,' she read out and sipped coffee. 'The Kruger case. Newman was the reporter who tracked his bank account to Basle. We still don't know how he managed that. Why is he so important?'

'Because, Erika...' He wrapped an arm round her slim waist, 'he's such an independent bastard. No vested interest in the world can buy him once he gets his teeth into a story. No one can stop him.'

'You know this Newman?'

'Unfortunately, no. But I can reach him. You see it even says where he's staying. I'd better call him – but I'll use that public phone box just down the street...'

'You didn't want to be seen outside...'

'It's worth the risk. I have to do something. Newman might even be working on the Gold Club story. Terminal...'

'Manfred!' There was surprise, a hint of hurt in her voice. 'When I told you about that you gave me the impression you'd never heard of either the Gold Club or Terminal.'

He looked uncomfortable. Taking the cup of coffee out of her hand he hauled her on to his lap. She really weighed nothing at all. He stared straight at her. He was about to break the habit of a lifetime – to *trust* another human being.

'It was for your own protection. That's God's truth. Don't ask me any more – knowledge can kill you when such ruthless and powerful forces are involved. Whatever happens, say nothing to Nagel, your boss...'

'I wouldn't dream of it. Can't you go to the police?' she asked for the third time, then desisted as she caught his look of fear, near-desperation. She saw the time by his watch and eased herself off his lap. 'I simply have to go, Manfred. My job...'

'Don't forget to deposit that case. In your own name...'

'Only if you sign this card. I collected it yesterday. No argument, Manfred – or I won't take the case...'

'What is it?'

'A deposit receipt for a safety box. We both have to be able to get access to it. Those are the only terms on which I'll take that case.'

He sighed, signed it with his illegible but distinctive signature and gave back the card. When she had left the apartment he sat there for some time, amazed at his action. A year ago he'd have laughed in the face of anyone who told him that one day he would entrust half a million francs to a young girl. The nice thing was he felt quite contented now he had taken the plunge.

The real effort, he knew, would be to phone Newman.

They were waiting for him when Newman followed Nancy out of the Pavillon. Two men in plain clothes seated in the reception hall who stood up and walked straight over to him. A tall man with a long face, a shorter man, chubby and amiable.

'M. Newman?' the tall man enquired. 'Could you please accompany us.' It was a statement not a question. 'We are police officers...'

'Nancy, go up to our room while I sort this out,' Newman said briskly. He stared at the tall man. 'Accompany you where – and why?'

'To police headquarters...'

'Address,' Newman snapped.

'Twenty-four Boulevard Carl-Vogt...'

'Show me some identification, for Christ's sake.'

'Certainly, sir.' Ostrich, as Newman had already nicknamed the tall one, produced a folder which Newman examined carefully before handing it back. As far as he could tell it was kosher.

'You've told me where – now tell me why...'

'That will be explained by someone at headquarters...', Ostrich became a little less formal. 'Frankly, sir, I don't know the answer to that question. No, a coat isn't necessary. We have a heated car outside...'

'I'm going up to my room. I have to tell my wife where I'm going...'

He found Nancy waiting at the elevator, making no attempt to get inside. With his back to the two men, who had followed him to where they could watch from the end of the corridor, he took out his scratch pad, wrote down the address of police headquarters, and gave it to her.

'If I'm not back in an hour, call this number and set Geneva alight. That number under the address is the registration of the car they've got parked outside.'

'What is it all about, Bob? Are you worried? I am...'

'Don't be. And no, I'm not worried. I'm blazing mad. I'll tear somebody's guts out for this...'

Hidden inside the alcove of the doorway, Julius Nagy watched as Newman climbed inside the back of the waiting car with one of the men while the shorter man took the wheel. He hurried to a waiting cab and climbed inside.

'That black Saab,' he told the driver. 'I want to know where they're taking my friend...'

Newman thought Chief Inspector Leon Tripet, as he introduced himself, was young for the job. He sat down as requested, lit a cigarette without asking permission, and looked round the room, his manner expressing a mixture of irritation and impatience. He carefully said nothing.

Tripet's second-floor office, overlooking the Boulevard Carl-Vogt,

78

was the usual dreary rabbit hutch. Walls painted a pale green, illuminated by a harsh overhead neon rectangular tube. Very homely.

'I must apologize for any inconvenience we may be causing you,' Tripet began, sitting very erect in his chair. 'But it is a very serious matter we are concerned with...'

'*You* are concerned with. Not *me*,' Newman said aggressively.

'We all admired your handling of the Kruger case. I have met German colleagues who are full of praise for the way you trapped Kruger and exposed his links with the DDR...'

'You mean Soviet-occupied East Germany,' Newman commented. 'Also known as The Zone. What has this to do with my summons here?'

'Coffee, Mr Newman?' Tripet looked at the girl who had come in with a tray of cardboard cups. 'How do you like it?'

'I don't – not out of a cardboard cup. I can get that at British Rail buffets, which I don't patronize.'

'I read your book,' Tripet continued after dismissing the girl who left him one of the cardboard cups. 'One thing which really fascinated me was the way you were able to tap in to the *terminal* keyboard...'

He paused to drink some coffee and Newman had the oddest feeling Tripet was watching him with all his concentration for some reaction. Reaction to what? He remained silent.

'I refer to the keyboard at Dusseldorf where the Germans house their giant computer which has so helped them track down hostile agents. You have come to Switzerland on holiday, Mr Newman?' he added casually.

Newman stubbed out his half-smoked cigarette in the clean ashtray, watching Tripet with a bleak look as he did so. He stood up, walked over to the window behind the Swiss policeman and stared down into the street. Tripet asked was there something wrong?

Newman didn't reply. He continued staring down, being careful not to disturb the heavy net curtain. Julius Nagy was standing in the entrance to the building opposite which Newman had observed when he had arrived. *Bibliotèque Municipale.* Public Library.

'Tripet,' he said, 'could you join me for a moment, please?'

'Something is bothering you,' Tripet commented as he stood beside the Englishman.

'That man in the doorway over there. Julius Nagy. He's been following me since we arrived at Cointrin. A friend of yours?'

'I'll have him checked out,' Tripet said promptly and headed for the door out of his office. 'Give me a minute...'

'There's a phone on your desk,' Newman pointed out.

But Tripet was gone, closing the door behind him. Newman lit a fresh cigarette and waited while the comedy was played out. Within a short time he saw two policemen in their pale grey uniforms, automatic pistols sheathed in holsters on their right hips, walk briskly across the road.

There appeared to be a brief altercation, Nagy protesting as the policemen each took an arm and escorted him across the road out of sight into the building below. Newman grinned to himself and was seated in his chair when Tripet returned.

'We are questioning him,' he informed Newman. 'I have told them to concentrate on learning the identity of his employer.'

'Who do you think you're fooling?'

'Pardon?'

'Look here,' Newman rasped, leaning across the desk, 'this charade has gone on long enough...'

'Charade?'

'*Charade*, Tripet! There was a time not long ago when I was welcome in Switzerland. I helped over a certain matter which has not a damn thing to do with you. Ever since I came in this time I've been watched and harassed...'

'Harassed, Mr Newman?'

'Kindly listen and don't interrupt! I said harassed – and I meant harassed. You drag me over here for a meaningless conversation. You send two of your menials to pick me up publicly at the Hotel des Bergues like a common criminal. You don't even have the decency to phone me first...'

'We were not sure you would come...'

Newman rode over him. 'Don't interrupt, I said! Then you pretend you don't know Nagy. You go out of the room to give an order instead of using the phone in front of you – so I won't hear the order you give. "Bring in Nagy. Make it look good – he's watching from my office window." Something like that, yes, no? Well, I've had it up to here. I'm communicating with Beck of the Federal Police in Berne. Arthur Beck, Assistant to the Chief of the Federal Police...'

'It was Beck who asked me to bring you here,' Tripet informed him quietly.

Newman insisted on returning to the Hotel des Bergues, in a cab despite Tripet's efforts to provide an unmarked police car. On the way back across the river he sat thinking, his mind tangled with contradictory ideas. There was no peace for him when he'd paid off the cab and went upstairs to his room. Nancy opened the door and he knew something had happened. She grasped his arm and wrapped it round her waist.

'Bob, I thought you'd never come. Are you all right? What did they want? While you were out I had the weirdest phone call. Are you all right?' she repeated. 'Shall I get coffee? Room Service does have its uses.' All in a rush of words.

'Order three litres. No, sit down, I'll order it myself – and I'm fine. Tell me about the phone call when I've organized coffee.' He grinned. 'We have to get our priorities right...'

He refused to let her talk until the coffee had arrived. He gave her an edited version of his visit to police headquarters, conveying the impression they were intrigued by the newspaper article and wanted to know what story he was working on. And, he reflected, that might just be the real motive behind his interview with Tripet.

'Now,' he began after she had swallowed half a cup, 'tell me in your own words about this phone call.' He grinned. 'I'm not sure, of course, who else's words you would use...'

'Stop kidding. I was jumpy at the time, but I'm better now. Anyone ever tell you you're a good psychologist?'

'Nancy, do get to the point,' he urged gently.

'The phone rang and a man's voice asked to speak to you. He spoke in English but I know he wasn't English – or American. He had a thick, Middle-European accent...'

'Whatever that might be.'

'Bob! We *do* have a mixture of nationalities in the States. And I'm not bad on accents. Can I go on? Good. I told him that you weren't here, that you'd be back sometime, but I didn't know when. He was persistent. Did I have a number where he could reach you? It was urgent...'

'Urgent to him,' Newman interjected cynically.

'He *sounded* urgent,' she insisted. 'Almost close to panic. I asked him for a number where you could call him back, but he wouldn't play it that way. Eventually he said he'd call you later, but he asked me to give you a strange message, made me repeat it to make sure I'd got it...'

'What message?'

'He gave his name, too. Reluctantly and only when I said I was going to put down the receiver, that I didn't take messages from anonymous callers. A Manfred Seidler. I made him spell it. The message was that for a generous consideration he could tell you all about terminal...'

'He said what?'

'Not *a* terminal. I checked that. Just terminal...'

Newman sat staring into space. He was alone in the bedroom. Nancy had gone shopping to buy a stronger pair of boots. She'd observed that the smart girls in Geneva had a snappy line in boots, Newman suspected. She was not going to be left behind by the competition.

Terminal.

Newman was beginning to wonder whether his conversation with Chief Inspector Tripet had been as meaningless as he'd thought at the time. Correction. Beck's conversation with him by proxy via Tripet. What was it he'd said?

One thing which really fascinated me was the way you were able to tap into the terminal keyboard. And Tripet had emphasized the word *terminal* – and had watched Newman intently as he spoke.

Now this weirdo, Manfred Seidler, was offering to tell him all about – terminal. What the hell did the word signify? Tripet – Beck – had linked it to the operation of a highly sophisticated computer. Could there be any connection with the Kruger affair?

Kruger was serving a thirty-year sentence in Stuttgart for passing classified information to the East Germans. The Kruger case was over, fading into history. What signal was Beck sending him? Was he sending him any signal? More likely he was checking to see whether Newman's trip to Switzerland had anything to do with – *terminal*. Well, it hadn't. But maybe when he arrived in Berne he'd better contact his old friend, Arthur Beck, and tell him he was barking up the wrong tree. He had just reached that conclusion when the phone rang. He picked it up without thinking, assuming it was Nancy telling him she would be later than she'd expected.

'Mr Robert Newman? At last. Manfred Seidler speaking...'

Eleven

Bruno Kobler came into Geneva from Berne by express train. He paused in the booking hall, an impressive-looking man who wore an expensive dark business suit and a camel-hair overcoat. Hatless, his brown hair was streaked with grey. Clean-shaven, he had a strong nose, cold blue eyes which Lee Foley would have recognized immediately. A killer.

His right hand gripped a briefcase and he waited patiently for the two men who had travelled separately on the train from Berne. Hugo Munz, a lean man of thirty-two wearing jeans and a windcheater, approached him first.

'Hugo,' said Kobler, 'you take Cointrin. Go there at once and watch out for Newman. You've studied the newspaper photo so you will spot him easily. I doubt if he's flying anywhere but if he is, follow. Report back to Thun.' He looked directly at Munz. 'Don't lose him. Please.'

He watched Hugo walking briskly towards where the cabs parked. A moment later the second man, Emil Graf, wandered casually up to him. Graf was a very different type from Munz. Thirty-eight years old, small and stockily-built, he wore a sheepskin. A slouch hat covered most of his blond hair. Thin-lipped, he spoke on equal terms to Kobler.

'We've arrived. What do I do?'

'You wait here,' Kobler told him pleasantly. 'You also watch out for Newman. If he leaves Geneva, my guess is he'll go by train. In case I miss him, hang on to his tail. When you have news, report back to Thun.'

He watched Graf wander back inside the station, his right hand holding the carry-all bag which contained a Swiss Army repeater rifle. Kobler had made his dispositions carefully. Graf was more reliable, less impetuous than Munz. Typically, Kobler had saved for himself the most tricky assignment. He walked out of the station, got inside the back of a cab and spoke in his brisk, confident voice to the driver.

'Hotel des Bergues...'

Inside the cab as it proceeded on the short journey to the hotel Kobler dismissed both men from his mind. A first-rate business executive he was now concentrating on what lay ahead. Kobler had come a long way. The only man his chief trusted implicitly, millions of francs passed through Kobler's hands in the course of a year.

A commanding personality, a man attractive to women of all ages who sensed his dynamic energy, he could walk into the Clinic, the laboratory and the chemical works on the shores of Lake Zurich and issue any instruction. He would be obeyed as though the order had been transmitted by his chief. He was paid four hundred thousand Swiss francs a year.

Unmarried, he dedicated his life to his work. He had a string of girlfriends in different cities – chosen for two qualities. Their ability to feed him confidential information about the companies they worked for – and their skill in bed. Life was good. He wouldn't have exchanged his position for that of any other man he had ever met.

He had served his obligatory military service with the Army. He was an expert marksman and was classified to act as a sniper when they came from the north-east. Not if. *When* the Red Army moved. Still, very soon they would be ready for them – really ready. He jerked his mind into total awareness of his immediate surroundings as the cab pulled up outside the Hotel des Bergues.

'I don't know any Manfred Seidler – just assuming that's your real name,' Newman snapped back on the phone. He was sliding automatically into his role of foreign correspondent. Always put an unknown quantity on the defensive.

'Seidler is my real name,' the voice continued in German, 'and if you want to know about a very special consignment brought over an eastern border for KB then we should arrange a meeting. The information will cost a lot of money...'

'I don't deal in riddles, Seidler. Be more specific...'

'I'm talking about *Terminal*...'

The word hung in the air. Alone in the bedroom, Newman was aware of a feeling of constriction in his stomach. This had to be handled carefully.

'How much is a lot?' he asked in a bored tone.

'Ten thousand francs

'You're joking, of course. I don't pay out sums like that...'

'People are dying, Newman,' Seidler continued more vehemently, 'dying in Switzerland. Men – and women. Don't you care any more? This thing is horrific.'

'Where are you speaking from?' Newman enquired after a pause.

'We're not playing it that way, Newman...'

'Well, tell me, are you inside Switzerland. I'm not crossing any frontiers. And I'm short of time.'

'Inside Switzerland. The price is negotiable. It's urgent that we meet quickly. I decide the place...'

Newman had made up his mind, thinking swiftly while he asked questions. He was now convinced that Seidler, for some reason, was desperately anxious to meet him. He broke a golden rule – never give advance notice of future movements.

'Seidler, I'm just about to leave for Berne. I'll be staying at the Bellevue Palace. Phone me there and we'll talk some more.'

'To give you time to check me out? Come off it...'

'I'm impressed with what you've said.' Newman's voice was light and he let the irritation show. 'The Bellevue Palace or nothing. Unless you will give me a phone number?'

'The Bellevue Palace then...'

Seidler broke the connection and Newman slowly replaced the receiver. His caller had managed to disturb him on two counts. The 'eastern border' reference. Which eastern border? Newman didn't think he'd been talking about the Swiss frontier. That conferred on *Terminal* potential international dangers.

And then there had been the mention of 'KB', which Newman had deliberately not queried over the phone. KB. Klinik Bern? The talk about people dying he had dismissed as window-dressing to arouse his curiosity. Strangely enough, as he walked round the bedroom, smoking a cigarette, the words began to bother him more and more.

When the conversation opened, Newman had put Seidler in the category of a peddler of information – reporters were always being approached by these types – but later he had detected fear in Seidler's attitude, stark fear. There had been a hint of a terrible urgency – a man on the run.

'What have I walked into?' he wondered aloud.

'Tell me. Do...'

He swung round and Nancy was leaning with her back against the door she had opened and closed with extraordinary lack of noise. She moved like a cat – he'd found that out on more than one occasion.

'Seidler phoned while you were out,' he said.

'And he's worried you. What is going on, Bob?'

'He was trying to sell me a pup. Happens all the time.' He spoke in a light-hearted, dismissive tone. 'I'm glad you're back – we're catching the eleven fifty-six train to Berne. An express – non-stop...'

'I must dash out again.' She checked her watch. 'I saw some perfume. I'm packed. I have time. Be back in ten minutes...'

'You'll have to move. You're like a bloody grasshopper. In and out. Nancy, I don't want to miss that train...'

'So you can use the time settling up the bill. See you...'

'M. Kobler,' the concierge greeted the man who had just walked into the Hotel des Bergues. 'Good to see you again, sir.'

'You haven't seen me. Robert Newman is staying here.'

'He's upstairs in his room. You wish me to call him?'

'Not at the moment...'

Kobler glanced quickly inside the Pavillon before walking into the restaurant. He chose a table which gave him a good view through the glass-panelled door of the reception hall, ordered a pot of coffee, paid for it, and settled down to wait.

The cab he had travelled in from the station was parked outside. He had paid the driver a generous tip with instructions to wait for him. A titian-haired beauty wearing a short fur over her jeans tucked inside knee-length boots walked in and he stared at her.

Their eyes met and a flicker of interest showed in hers as she passed his table and chose a seat facing the reception hall. It was nice, Kobler reflected, to know that you hadn't lost your touch. She had, of course, in that long glance assessed his income group. Not a pro. Just a woman.

Half an hour later he saw a porter carrying luggage out of the reception hall, followed by an attractive woman, followed by Newman. He stood up, put on his coat and walked out of the revolving doors in time to see Newman's back disappearing inside the rear of a cab. He glanced along the pavement to his left and stiffened. Kobler missed one development as he climbed inside his own cab and told the driver to follow the cab ahead.

The titian-haired girl he had admired came out of the door leading direct on to the street. Running round the corner, she climbed on to the scooter she had left parked there, kicked the starter and followed Kobler's taxi.

Cornavin Gare, Geneva's main station, was quiet on a Tuesday in mid-February near lunchtime. Kobler paid off his cab and followed Newman and the expensively-dressed woman with him into the concourse. Standing to one side, he watched Emil Graf go into action, joining the ticket queue behind Newman. Only two people were ahead of the Englishman, so Emil, after purchasing his own tickets, soon came over to Kobler.

'He bought a one-way ticket to Berne, two tickets actually. I've bought tickets for both of us – in case you wish...'

'I do wish. Tickets to where?'

'Zurich. The eleven fifty-six goes through, of course.'

Kobler congratulated himself on his choice of Graf for the station. He took the ticket Graf handed him and put it inside his crocodile wallet.

'Why to Zurich, Emil – when Newman booked seats for Berne?'

'These foreign correspondents are tricky. His real destination could be Zurich...'

'Excellent, Emil. You see that little man with the absurd Tyrolean hat, the one buying his own ticket? That's Nagy. He is scum. The police once threw him out of Berne. He followed Newman in a cab from the hotel.' Kobler checked his watch. 'Your next job is Julius Nagy. Hang on to his tail. Wait your opportunity. Get him in the train lavatory – or some alley when he gets off. Find out who he is working for. Break a few arms, legs, if necessary. Scare the hell out of him. Then put him on our payroll. Tell him to continue following Newman, to report all his movements and contacts to you.'

'It's done.'

Kobler picked up his briefcase and watched Graf trotting away with his holdall. The contents might come in useful to persuade Nagy where survival lay. Kobler checked the departure board and headed for the platform where the Zurich Express was due to leave in five minutes.

In the far corner of the station Lee Foley watched all these developments with interest from behind the newspaper he held in front of his face. He had left the Hotel des Bergues only five minutes ahead of Newman and Nancy, anticipating this would give him a ringside seat. After buying a one-way first-class ticket to Berne he had taken up his discreet viewing point where he could watch all the ticket windows. As Kobler disappeared he folded the paper, tucked it inside the pocket of his coat, picked up his bag and made his own way towards the same platform.

The passenger everyone – including Foley – missed noticing was a titian-haired girl. A porter carried her scooter inside the luggage van. She boarded the next coach and the express bound for Berne and Zurich glided out of the station.

Twelve

Berne! A city unique not only in Switzerland but also in the whole of Western Europe. Its topography alone is weird. Wrapped inside a serpentine bend of the river Aare, it extends eastward as a long peninsula – its length stretching from the main station and the University to the distant Nydeggbrücke, the bridge where it finally crosses the Aare.

Its width is a quarter of its length. At many points you can walk across the peninsula, leaving the river behind, only to find in less than ten minutes, the far bend of the river barring your way.

Berne is a fortress. Built on a gigantic escarpment, it rears above the surrounding countryside. Below the *Terrasse* behind the Parliament building, the ground slopes steeply away. Below the *Plattform* at the side of the Munster the massive wall ramparts drop like a precipice one hundred and fifty feet to the Badgasse. Beyond, the noose of the Aare flows past from distant Lake Thun.

The escarpment is at its peak near Parliament and the station. As the parallel streets wind their way east they descend towards the Nydeggbrücke.

Berne is old, very old. The Munster goes back to 1421. And because it is centuries since it endured the curse of war, it has remained old. It is a city for human moles. The streets are lined with a labyrinth of huddled arcades like burrows. People can walk through these arcades in the worst of weathers, secure from snow and rain.

When night falls – even during heavily overcast days – there is a sinister aspect to the city. Few walk down the stone arcades of the Munstergasse, which continues east as the Junkerngasse until it reaches the Nydeggbrücke. All streets end at the bridge.

Backwards and forwards across its waist, a network of narrow alleys thread their way, alleys where you rarely meet another human being. And when the mist rolls in across the Aare, smoky coils drift down the arcades, increasing the atmosphere of menace.

Yet here in Berne are located – principally in buildings close to the Bellevue Palace – centres of power which do not always see eye to eye with the bankers. Swiss Military Intelligence, the Federal Police of which Arthur Beck is a key figure – are housed either next door to or within minutes' walk of one of the greatest hotels in Europe.

At the station a keen observer sees that Berne is where German Switzerland meets its French counterpart. The station is *Bahnhof/Gare.* At the foot of the steps leading to pairs of platforms the left-hand platform is *Voie,* the right-hand *Gleis.* The express from Geneva arrived on time at precisely 1.58 p.m.

During the journey from Geneva Newman, facing Nancy in her own window seat, had not moved. Gazing out of the window while the express sped from Geneva towards Lausanne he watched the fields covered in snow. The sun shone and frequently he had to turn away from the harshness of the sun glare.

'It's not non-stop as I thought,' he told Nancy. 'Lausanne, Fribourg and then Berne...'

'You look very serious, very concentrated. Too many things happened in Geneva?'

'Keep your voice down.' He leaned forward. 'Police headquarters for a start, then our friend on the phone. A lot to open the day...'

He was careful not to tell her he had seen Julius Nagy board the second-class coach immediately behind them. Who was Nagy really working for? The problem bothered him. At least they were heading for Berne. At the first opportunity he would go and talk to Arthur Beck. If anyone could – would – tell him what was going on, that man was Beck.

Several seats behind him Bruno Kobler sat facing Nancy, his briefcase perched on the seat beside him to keep it unoccupied. Kobler had also observed Nagy boarding the express. He hoped that Graf had accomplished his mission of persuading – forcing – the little creep to switch his allegiance.

Kobler was dressed so perfectly as the Swiss businessman that neither Newman nor Nancy had noticed him. But someone else had observed Kobler's interest in them, someone Kobler himself had overlooked.

Lee Foley had taken a seat in the non-smoking section of the coach, a section separated from the smokers by a door with a glass panel in the upper half. Twice, on the way to Lausanne, Foley had stood up and taken time extracting a magazine from the suitcase he had perched on the rack.

Foley was the only man who saw it all. Through the panel he observed Newman's grim expression as he stared out at the countryside. He also caught the fleeting glances of the Swiss business type behind the correspondent – glances always at Newman and the woman seated opposite. He would remember that hard face.

He observed more. At the far end of the smoking section Nagy appeared and looked inside. Only for a moment. A small, stocky man appeared beside him. Foley saw Nagy's startled expression. Both men disappeared inside the lavatory. Foley reacted at once.

Walking into the smoking section, staring straight ahead, he slid aside the end door, waited for it to shut automatically, and listened outside the lavatory. He heard choking noises. He reached out a hand to rattle the handle and then withdrew it. He could not afford to advertise his presence on the express. He went back to his own seat.

Inside the lavatory Graf had one hand round Nagy's throat as he extracted the Army rifle from the holdall with the other hand. Bending the little man back over the wash-basin, he put the rifle muzzle under his chin. Nagy's eyes nearly popped out of their sockets with stark terror.

'Now,' said Graf, 'you can end up being tossed off this train. People do fall off expresses. Or you can tell me – first time please, there will be no second chance – who you are working for. We know you're following Newman...'

'You can't get away with this,' Nagy gasped.

'I said first time...'

Nagy heard a click, guessed it was the safety catch coming off. He nearly filled his pants. The remote, glassy look on his attacker's face was almost more frightening than the rifle.

'Can't speak...' The vicious grip of the hand on his throat relaxed a little. 'Tripet,' he said. 'I am following Newman. For Tripet...'

'Who the hell is Tripet?' Graf asked quietly, his eyes never leaving Nagy's.

'Chief Inspector Tripet. Sûreté. Geneva. I've worked for him before. I'm his snout...'

Nagy, almost universally despised, a man you used, had guts. He was determined not to give away Pierre Jaccard of the *Journal de Genève*. There was more money there. And Jaccard had always kept his word. In Nagy's world trust was credit beyond price.

'So,' Graf told him, 'you forget this Tripet. From now on you work for me. No, shut up and listen. You carry on doing what you're doing – following Newman. You call me at this number...' Graf tucked a folded piece of paper inside Nagy's coat pocket. 'Whoever answers, give your name immediately, tell them about Newman's movements, who he meets, where he goes. You will be paid...' He tucked several folded banknotes in the same pocket. 'First, wherever Newman gets off, find out where he's staying, get a place to stay yourself. Report to the number at once where you're staying and the phone number...'

'Understood...' Nagy replied hoarsely, feeling his damaged throat when Graf removed the hand and the rifle, still aiming the muzzle point-blank. 'I'll do what you say...'

'You might be tempted to change your mind – when you think things over,' Graf went on in the same casual tone which Nagy found so disturbing. Christ! The swine had almost murdered him. 'Don't,' Graf warned. 'One of my associates will always be close to you. You won't see him. He'll simply be there. He's impetuous. Very rough. Any hint you're going independent and he'll chop you. You do understand, Nagy, I hope?'

'I understand...'

It was the contemptuous affront to his *dignity* which roused Nagy. He had been savagely assaulted in a lavatory. Graf, who would never have understood his victim's reaction, had added one further insult to intimidate the little man. Prior to leaving him in the lavatory he had stuffed a tablet of toilet soap inside Nagy's mouth.

Seated inside the second-class coach as the express left Lausanne and swung north away from the lake towards Fribourg, Nagy could still taste the soap. He was going to pay back these new employers, whoever they might be. Obstinately, he was determined about that.

The snow lay deeper on the fields – the express was climbing as it sped north. Newman was still silent, deep in thought as the train stopped at Fribourg and then proceeded on the last lap to Berne. When he stood up to lift their bags down from the rack as they pulled into Berne station Kobler had already left the coach and was waiting by the exit door. He was almost the first passenger to step down off the express.

One coach behind, Julius Nagy hurried off the train, his hat crumpled inside his coat, the coat folded over his arm. He was no longer immediately recognizable. His eyes gleamed with deep resentment as he followed Emil Graf along the platform. In his right hand he held the small Voigtlander camera he always carried.

Ahead of Graf walked Kobler, very erect and brisk, briefcase in right hand. He ran down the steps with Graf trotting behind. Outside the station where a 450 SEL Mercedes was waiting for him with a chauffeur he paused, turning up his collar against the cold. Graf caught up with him and looked around as though searching for a taxi.

'He's tamed,' he reported to Kobler. 'He's ours...'

'You're sure?'

'Certain. Scared shitless...'

Only one person noticed the brief exchange. Nagy raised his small camera and clicked it once as Kobler turned his head to catch what Graf said. Kobler walked to the Mercedes where the chauffeur held the rear door open. Nagy's camera clicked again. He then used the piece of paper Graf had stuffed in his pocket to write down the registration number. He had faded back inside the station when Graf turned round and the Mercedes was driven off.

The two plain clothes men watching the platform exit for the Zurich express missed spotting Lee Foley. The American walked past them wearing a very British-looking check overcoat he had bought in London. His distinctive white hair was concealed beneath a peaked golfing cap pulled well down. The horn-rimmed glasses he wore (with plain glass lenses) gave him a professorial appearance.

Foley walked out of the station among a crowd of passengers who had come off the same train. Ignoring the taxi rank, his case in his left hand, he continued walking down the narrow Neuengasse. Pausing to glance into a shop window in an arcade, he used the plate glass as a mirror to check the street.

Satisfied that no one was following, he resumed the short walk to the Savoy Hotel and turned inside the entrance quickly. The lobby and a sitting area were all of apiece. The girl at the reception counter looked up and Foley was already filling in the obligatory registration form in triplicate – one copy for the police who would collect it later.

'You have a room. I reserved it by phone from Geneva.'

'Room 230. It's a double...'

The girl looked round for a companion. Foley showed his passport and then pocketed it. He picked up his bag.

'I'll get a porter...'

'Don't bother. That's the elevator?' He went up inside the cage, found his room, dumped his bag on the bed and sat by the phone, waiting for the call.

Arthur Beck sat behind his desk eating the last of the English-style ham sandwiches his secretary had prepared for him. As far as Beck was concerned, the Earl of Sandwich was one of the great historical figures Britain had produced. He had acquired this liking during a stint spent with Scotland Yard in London. He was drinking coffee when the phone rang. His caller spoke in German.

'Leupin here, sir. Reporting from the station. Newman came in on the thirteen fifty-eight express from Geneva. He was accompanied by a woman. American I would guess from her clothes. Marbot tailed them to the Bellevue Palace where they booked in ten minutes ago.'

'What about Lee Foley?'

'No sign of anyone answering his description. We both watched the passengers arriving off the train...'

'Thank you, Leupin. Continue watching all trains from Geneva.'

'Marbot is on his way back here...'

Beck put down the receiver and ate the last sandwich while he thought. He had been right about one thing – that Newman would turn up in Berne. What bothered him was the earlier call from Chief Inspector Tripet. Newman, apparently, had shown no reaction to the casual reference to *Terminal*. Was it possible that the Englishman was working on an entirely different story?

Of one thing Beck was convinced – knowing Newman the way he did. The foreign correspondent wasn't visiting Berne just for a holiday. Newman was a workaholic: he never stopped looking for a fresh story.

But what really worried Beck was the non-appearance of Foley. Or should he say *disappearance?* If Lee Foley had slipped past the net Beck had a dangerous wolf stalking the streets of his city. He decided to call New York.

Lee Foley picked up the receiver on the second ring. Holding the phone to his ear he waited. The voice which spoke at the other end sounded impatient.

'Is that Mr Lee Foley?'

'Speaking. I'm in position. Listen, the first move is yours. You need to visit the place in question. Find out what the situation is. Could you please report back to me as soon as you can? No, please listen. Check out the security at the place in question. Any small item may be vital. When I'm armed with facts I can go into action. If it comes to it, I'll raise hell. I do have a talent for that, as you well know...'

Foley broke the connection and wandered over to the window of his

96

bedroom which looked down a small alley. That was the place an experienced watcher would choose to observe the Savoy. The alley was empty.

Newman put down the phone as Nancy came into the small hallway, shut the door and entered the bedroom. She had a pensive look.

'Bob, who were you calling?'

'Your beloved Room Service for a large bottle of mineral water. You know my thirst, especially at night. They must be busy – I'll call again in a minute. Incidentally, you never showed me that Gucci perfume you rushed out to buy just before we left the Hotel des Bergues.'

'*Voila!*' She produced the bottle from her handbag. 'You should have noticed I was wearing it on the express. Isn't this a lovely room?'

They had been allocated Room 428. A bathroom led off the entrance hall. There was a separate toilet. But the room itself was the cherry on the cake. Very large with a couple of comfortable armchairs, a desk in front of the spacious windows where Newman could work. Two generous single beds had been placed alongside each other to form a double. Nancy bounced her backside on one of the beds.

'Bob, this is marvellous. We could live here for weeks...'

'Maybe we will. Come and look at the. view. The porter made a big fuss about it and rightly so.'

They stood with his arm wrapped round her and she made cooing noises of sheer delight. Newman opened the first set of windows and then the outer ones a foot beyond. Chill air floated into the room which had the temperature of a sauna bath.

'That hill beyond the river with the snow is the Bantiger,' he explained. 'If this overcast clears over there to the left you'll get the most fantastic panorama of the Bernese Oberland range. Now,' he became businesslike, 'this afternoon I'm hiring a car from Hertz next door. We're driving to the Berne Clinic at Thun...'

'Just like that?' Her professional instincts surfaced. 'We should phone for an appointment to see Jesse...'

'We do nothing of the sort. We arrive unannounced. You're not only a relative, you're a doctor. With me accompanying you we can bulldoze our way in, maybe catch them on the hop...'

'You really think that's a good idea?'

'It's what we're going to do. After a quick lunch...'

'Bob, they have *three* separate restaurants. One gorgeous room overlooking the terrace down there. The Grill Room. And the coffee shop...'

'The coffee shop. It will be quick. We have to move before our arrival is reported. Don't forget that bloody newspaper article.'

'Let me just fix myself.' She left him and sat down in front of the dressing table. 'Did you notice that Englishman who was registering while you waited? I was sitting on a sofa and I saw him look back and stare at you.'

'He'd probably seen my picture in that paper...'

Newman spoke in an off-hand manner, dismissing the incident from her mind. But he knew the guest she was talking about. He even knew the man's name, but he had detected no significance in the guest until Nancy's remark.

He had waited patiently while the other Englishman filled in the registration form, ignoring the receptionist's attempt to do the job for him. A slim, erect man with a trim moustache, he wore a short camel-hair coat and would be in his early thirties.

'The porter will take your bag to your room, Mr Mason,' the receptionist had informed him, returning his passport.

'Thank you,' Mason had replied, accepting the small hotel booklet with his passport and turning away to where the porter waited.

Now he remembered Mason had glanced over his shoulder at Newman before leaving the counter. A swift, appraising glance. He frowned to himself and Nancy watched him as she combed her hair.

'That man at the reception desk. You know him?'

'Never seen him before in my life. Are you ready? It will have to be a very quick meal. I have to hire the car and it's a half hour's drive to Thun along the motorway.'

'How did you locate it so quickly?'

'By asking the concierge when you wandered off into that huge reception hall. They have a fashion show this afternoon...'

'And a medical congress reception in a few days' time...'

'So what?' he asked, catching a certain inflection in her tone.

'Nothing,' she answered. 'Let's go eat...'

Mason sat on the bed in his room, dialling the number which would put him straight through to Tweed's extension. He never ceased to be impressed with how swiftly the continental phone system worked – providing you were in Sweden, Germany or Switzerland.

'Yes,' said Tweed's voice. 'Who is it?'

'Mason. How is the weather there? We have eight degrees here...'

'Nine in London...' That established not only their identities, but also told Mason that Tweed was alone in his office – that Howard wasn't leaning over his shoulder, listening in.

'I've just booked in at the Bellevue Palace,' Mason said crisply. 'I stopped over in Zurich to gather a little information. Grange.' He said the name quickly.

'Do use the Queen's English,' Tweed complained. 'You *stayed on* in Zurich. Continue...'

'I've built up a dossier on the subject in question. Not easy. Swiss doctors close down like a shutter falling when you mention his name. I found an American doctor working in Zurich who opened up. God, the subject carries some clout. He's a real power in the land. Right at the top of the tree. You'd like a quick run-down?'

'Not over the phone,' Tweed said quickly, aware the call had to be passing through the hotel switchboard. 'I'm coming out there soon myself. Keep making discreet enquiries. Don't go near the British Embassy...'

'One more thing,' Mason added. 'Don't imagine it means anything. Robert Newman, the foreign correspondent, booked in here after me. He had his wife with him. I didn't know he was married...'

'He probably isn't. You know the bohemian life those correspondents lead...' Tweed sounded dreamy. 'Keep digging. And stay in Berne...'

Tweed put down the phone and looked at Monica who was sorting files. 'That was Mason calling from the Bellevue Palace. He has data on Professor Armand Grange of the Berne Clinic. Anything on the computer? Just supposing the damned thing is working...'

'It is working. I did check. Not a thing. I tried Medical and came up with zero. So then I tried Industrialists – because of his chemical works. Zero again. I even tried Bankers. Zero. The man is a shadow. I even wondered whether he really exists.'

'Well, at least that has decided me.' Tweed was polishing his glasses again on the worn silk handkerchief. Monica watched him. He was always fingering the lenses. 'I'm going to Berne,' Tweed told her. 'It's just a question of timing. Book me on Swissair flights for Zurich non-stop. As I miss one flight, book me on the next one. When I do leave it will be at a moment's notice.'

'What are you waiting for?' Monica asked.

'A development. A blunder on the part of the opposition. It has to come. No one is foolproof. Not even a shadow...'

Thirteen

The coffee shop at the Bellevue Palace is a large glass box-like restaurant perched above the pavement on the side overlooking the Hertz car hire office. Newman gobbled down his steak as Nancy ate her grilled sole. Swallowing his coffee in two gulps, Newman wiped his mouth with a napkin and signed the bill.

'You're going to hire the car now?' Nancy asked. 'I'll dash up to the room and get my gloves. Meet you over there?'

'Do that.'

Newman waited at the exit until she had disappeared and then retraced his steps to one of the phone booths near the *garderobe*, the cloakroom where guests left their coats. It took him one minute to make the call and then he ran back to the exit, along the pavement and into the Hertz office. Slamming down his driving licence and passport he told the girl what he wanted.

'They have a Citroën. Automatic,' he told Nancy when she came inside. 'This chap is going to take us to the car. It's on Level Three...'

In less than five minutes he was driving the car round the sharp curves up to street level. Nancy put on her wool-lined leather gloves, fastened her seat belt and relaxed. An expert driver, she still preferred to travel as a passenger.

The sky was a heavy pall hovering close to the city as they crossed one of the bridges and within a short time Newman was on the four-lane motorway which runs all the way to Lucerne via Thun. Inside forty minutes they should have arrived at the Berne Clinic.

Lee Foley paid a very generous sum in Swiss francs to borrow the red Porsche from his Berne contact. He needed a fast car although normally its conspicuousness would have worried him. But this was an emergency.

He drove just inside the speed limit through the suburbs of Berne, but as soon as he turned on to the motorway he pushed his foot down. The highway was quiet, very little other traffic in mid-afternoon. His cold blue eyes flickered from side to side as he increased speed.

'Watch it on that motorway,' his contact had informed him as he handed over the Porsche which he had brought to the Savoy. 'It's a favourite place for the police to set up speed-traps...'

Foley had driven away from the Savoy so fixed on getting to his destination in time that he for once omitted to check that no one was following him. So he completely missed noticing the helmeted figure who jumped on a scooter parked further along the pavement. The scooter was still with him, little more than a dot behind the Porsche, when he spotted the Citroën ahead.

He kept up his speed, pulling closer to the Citroën until he had a good view of the two occupants. Newman behind the wheel, his woman seated alongside him. Foley breathed a sigh of relief and reduced speed, widening the distance between the two vehicles. Behind him the scooter rider-going flat-out – also slowed down.

Foley drove under a large destination indicator board, one of several at regular intervals. The board carried the legend THUN-NORD.

Inside the Citroën the warmth from the heater had dispelled the bitter cold and Nancy removed her gloves. Her right hand played with the fingers of one glove in her lap. The motorway was in superb condition, its surface clear of snow. But as they left Berne behind, passed the turn-off to Belp, the snow in the fields on both sides lay deeper. Here and there an occasional naked tree stretched gnarled branches towards the dark grey pall overhead. The atmosphere was sullen, unwelcoming. Newman glanced at her restless hand.

'Nervous? Now we're so close?'

'Yes, I am, Bob. I keep thinking about Jesse. And I'm not at all sure they're going to let us in, just dropping on them like this...'

'Leave me to do the talking when we arrive. You're a close relative. I'm a foreign correspondent. A lethal combination for a clinic which wants to preserve its reputation. There's no publicity like bad publicity...'

'What are you going to do?' She sounded worried.

'I'm going to get inside that clinic. Now, have one of your rare cigarettes, stop fiddling with that glove, here's the pack.'

They passed under a fresh sign which indicated two different destinations. THUN-SUD, THUN-NORD. Newman signalled to the huge trailer truck coming up behind him and swung up the turn-off to Thun-Nord. Nancy lit a cigarette and took a deep drag. Now they were crossing the motorway which was below them and from this extra elevation she had a view of grim, saw-toothed mountains to the south, mountains only dimly seen in a veil of mist so for a moment she wasn't sure whether she was watching a mirage.

'Those must be pretty high,' she observed.

'They rise to the far side of Thun, to the south and the east. One of them is the Stockhorn. Probably that big brute towering above the rest...'

They were climbing a gradual but continually-ascending slope up a hillside between more fields. An isolated farm here and there, a glimpse of neatly-stacked and huge bales of hay inside barns with steep roofs. The lowering sky created an ominous sense of desolation. Over to the east a great castle perched on a hilltop with turrets capped with what looked like witches' hats.

'That's the famous Thun Schloss,' Newman remarked. 'The town is below it, out of sight...'

'You do know the way?'

'We turn off this road somewhere higher up according to that helpful concierge at the Bellevue. Check it on the map I put in the glove compartment if you like – he marked the route...'

'It's creepy up here, Bob...'

'It's just a lousy afternoon.'

But there was something in her remark. They were very close to the snow-line. Earlier sun had melted the snow blanket on the lower fields facing south. Beyond the snow line houses were dotted at intervals towards Thun. Near the top of the ridge a dense forest of dark firs huddled like an army waiting to march. Then they reached the snow-line and here no ploughs had cleared the road. Newman reduced speed, slowed even more as he saw a sign-post. The sign read *Klinik Bern*. He swung right on to a narrower road, corrected a rear-wheel skid, drove on.

'Do you think that's it?' Nancy asked.

'I imagine so...'

A large, two-storey mansion with a veranda running round the ground floor was perched in an isolated position on the wide plateau which extended to the group of private houses several kilometres to the east. The grounds, which looked extensive, were surrounded by a wire fence and ahead Newman saw a gatehouse. Close behind the mansion the forest stood, a solid wall of firs mantled with snow. He pulled up in front of the stone, single-storey gatehouse beside double wire gates which were closed. Before he could alight from the

car large, black dogs appeared and came leaping towards the gate.

'Dobermans,' Newman commented. 'Charming...'

A heavy wooden door leading from the gatehouse direct on to the road opened. A lean man in his early thirties, wearing jeans and a windcheater, walked out towards the Citroën. Glancing, over his shoulder he called out a curt order in German. The dogs stopped barking, backed away reluctantly and disappeared.

'This is private property,' the lean man began in German.

'Not where I'm standing, it isn't,' Newman snapped back. 'This is the public highway. My passenger is Nancy Kennedy. She's here to visit her grandfather, Jesse Kennedy...'

'You have an appointment?'

'She has flown from America for the precise purpose of visiting her grandfather...'.

'No admittance without an appointment...'

'You're the boss here?' Newman's tone dripped sarcasm, 'You look like paid help to me. Get on the phone and tell the Clinic we're here.

And tell them I'm a newspaper man – it would make a very good story, don't you think? Granddaughter flies all the way from America and is refused admission to see her sick grandfather. What are you running here – a concentration camp? That's the impression I'm getting – a wire fence and Dobermans...'

'And you are?'

'Robert Newman. I'm getting pretty chilled standing here yacking to you. I'll give you two minutes – then we'll drive back to Berne and I'll file my story...'

'Wait!'

'For two minutes...'

Newman made an elaborate pantomime of looking at his watch and went back to the car. The lean man disappeared inside the gatehouse while Newman settled behind the wheel and lit a cigarette. Nancy took the pack and lit one for herself.

'It might have been better to make an appointment,' she said.

'Now I've seen the set-up I think not. This place smells very peculiar. While I was talking to Lanky I saw another man peer through that open doorway, a man wearing a uniform which looked very much like the Swiss Army...'

'Bob, that's crazy! You must have been mistaken...'

'I'm only telling you what I saw. The whole goddamned place is laid out like a military encampment. Surprise, surprise – here comes Lanky, looking even more sour than before...'

'You may go up to the Clinic. Someone will meet you there...'

The lean man spoke curtly, then walked away before there was time for a reply. Newman guessed that someone inside the gatehouse had pressed a button – the double gates opened inward automatically. Remembering the dogs, he closed his window before he drove forward and up the long curving drive to the distant building. No sign of a Doberman. They had been locked inside the gatehouse until the Citroën was clear.

He drove slowly, taking in the wintry landscape, and realized the grounds were even more vast than he had first thought. The wire fence at the front ran away across the white world, disappearing down a dip in the hillside. As he approached the Clinic the whole place seemed deserted. He could now see the veranda was glassed in and six steps led up to the entrance door.

Parking the car facing the exit drive, he locked it when Nancy had alighted and they went up the steps together. Grasping the handle of the door, he opened it and they went inside on to the veranda. It stretched away in both directions, the floor tiled and spotless, a few pots with plants at intervals. The inner door led into a large tiled lobby. The smell of antiseptic hit Newman and he wrinkled his nostrils. Nancy noticed his reaction and her lips tightened.

At the back of the large lobby was a heavy, highly-polished wooden counter and behind this, sitting on a high stool with an adjustable back, was a large, fat middle-aged woman, dark hair tied at the back in a bun and with small, darting eyes. She put down the pencil she had been writing with on a printed form, clasped her pudgy hands and stared at them.

'You know who we are,' Newman said in German, 'and I want to see the man in charge of this place...'

'Please to fill in the forms,' she replied in English, her tone of voice flat as she pushed a pad across the counter.

'Maybe, after I've seen your superior. We've come to see Jesse Kennedy. You know that already from the lackey on the gate...'

'I am very much afraid that without an appointment that will not be possible...' The man who had appeared from a side door spoke quietly but firmly in excellent English. Something in the tone of voice made Newman turn quickly to study the speaker. He had an impression of authority, supreme self-confidence, a human dynamo. 'We have to consider the patient,' the voice continued. 'I also should tell you that at the moment Mr Kennedy is under sedation.'

A man almost his own height, Newman estimated. More heavily-built. A man of about forty with dark brown hair streaked with grey shafts. The eyes stared at Newman and expressed force of character. Eyes which assessed his visitor, weighing up a possible opponent. A very self-controlled, formidable man.

'I am Dr Bruno Kobler,' he added.

'And I am *Dr* Nancy Kennedy,' Nancy interjected. 'The fact that my grandfather is sedated makes no difference. I wish to see him immediately.'

'Without a doctor in attendance that would be irregular...'

'You're a doctor,' Newman snapped. 'You just told us...'

'I am the chief administrator. I have no medical qualification.'

'You're telling us,' Newman persisted, 'that at this moment you have no medical practitioner available on the premises? Is that the way you run this clinic?'

'I didn't say that.' There was an edge to Kobler's voice. 'I indicated no one was available to accompany you...'

'Then we'll drive straight back to the American Embassy,' Newman decided. 'Dr Kennedy is an American citizen. So is Jesse Kennedy. Kobler, we're going to raise hell...'

'There is no need to get excited. Bearing in mind that your companion is a doctor, I think we might make an exception. We may be able to call on Dr Novak – he is the physician in charge of Jesse Kennedy...'

He turned to the woman behind the counter and clicked his fingers as though summoning a waiter. 'See if you can locate Dr Novak, Astrid. Ask him to come here at once.'

'How is my grandfather?' Nancy enquired.

Kobler turned to her, spread his hands and gave her his whole attention, staring straight into her eyes. His manner became conciliatory but for at least half a minute he delayed his reply. She had the impression he was looking inside her. She remained silent, sensing he was hoping to make her say more.

'I am afraid I cannot answer your question, Dr Kennedy. Unlike yourself, I am not a medical doctor. My job is to administer the Clinic. I would prefer that you ask Dr Novak. I think you will find him sympathetic. You see, he is one of your countrymen.'

'Dr Novak is an American?'

'Indeed he is. A very clever man, which is why he was asked to come here. The Clinic, as you doubtless know, has a world-wide reputation...'

'I'd also like to see Professor Armand Grange.'

Kobler shook his head regretfully. 'That, I regret to say, will not be possible. He only sees visitors strictly by appointment.'

'He's on the premises at this moment?' Nancy demanded.

'I really have no idea...'

Kobler glanced over his shoulder, his attention caught by the sound of the front door opening. Newman had stepped out on to the veranda. Closing the door he walked along to his left past chairs of basketwork with cushions; presumably when the weather was good patients sat here. It was very quiet, the central heating was turned up so the enclosed corridor had the atmosphere of a hothouse.

Alongside the inner wall he passed windows at intervals, all of them with frosted glass so he could not see into the rooms beyond. At the end of the corridor he tried the door on the inner wall and found it locked. He stood gazing across the ground to the east. In a bowl stood a modern complex of single-storey buildings with tall, slim windows. The place reminded him of a chemical laboratory. A covered way, windowless, extended from the direction of the Clinic to the complex. He returned to the reception hall as Nancy was being introduced by Kohler to a tall, fair-haired man in his early thirties. He wore a white coat and a stethoscope dangled from his left hand. Kobler turned to Newman.

'This is Dr Novak, Mr Newman. I expect you will not mind sitting in the waiting room while Dr Kennedy sees her.'

'Bob is coming with me,' Nancy interrupted brusquely. 'He's my fiancé...'

Novak glanced at Kobler, as though waiting for his reaction. Kobler bent his head towards Nancy and smiled. 'Who am I to dispute the wishes of a beautiful woman? Of course Mr Newman may accompany you.'

'Waldo Novak,' the American said and held out his hand to shake Newman's. 'I've heard a lot about you. The Kruger case man. Boy, did you do a job in Germany...'

'Just a story.' Newman turned to Kobler as he shook hands with Novak. 'Why the Dobermans?' he asked abruptly. 'Plus uniformed guards and the fence. This place is like Dartmoor.'

Kobler's head, turned to one side, swivelled to Newman and his smile remained fixed. Again he took his time about replying while he studied Newman. Like Nancy, Newman said nothing, gazing back at Kobler.

'Vandals,' Kobler replied eventually. 'Even in Switzerland we have young people who have too much energy, too little respect for private property. One of my duties is to ensure that the patients endure no disturbance from the outside world. And now, if you will excuse me, I will leave you in Dr Novak's capable hands.' He spoke to Novak in a brief aside. 'I have explained the patient is under sedation. Goodbye, Mr Newman. I'm sure we shall meet again...'

'You can count on it.'

'Dr Kennedy...' Kobler bowed and left them, disappearing behind the side door he had used earlier. Newman heard the click of an automatic lock. Novak produced a computer card and ushered Nancy towards a door at the rear of the reception hall. He inserted the card in a slot and the door slid open. Newman estimated it was one-inch thick steel. The door closed behind them as the fat woman, Astrid, brought up the rear.

'You speak German fluently, Mr Newman?' Astrid enquired in a thick, throaty voice.

'No, I don't,' he lied. 'When they start to talk fast I lose it...'

He left it at that as he followed Nancy and Novak along a wide corridor which was spotless and deserted. They passed closed doors-with porthole windows. Again the glass was frosted so it was impossible to see inside. He noticed that near the end of the corridor the smooth surface began to slope downwards, then vanished found a corner. The same smell of disinfectant he associated with hospitals and so disliked pervaded the place. Novak stopped outside a door in the right-hand wall, another door with a frosted glass porthole. He had extracted another computer card from his coat pocket.'

'Dr Kennedy,' he said, 'you're accustomed to seeing patients, of course. But in my experience it's different when the patient is a relative. He won't be able to talk with you...'

'I understand.'

Inserting the card inside the slot, Novak waited while the door slid open and gestured for them to walk inside. Newman followed Nancy who stopped suddenly as Novak and Astrid joined them and the door slid shut. He took her by the arm.

'Easy does it, old girl...'

'It's not that,' she whispered. 'He's *awake*!'

In a single bed centred with its head against the far wall lay a gaunt-faced man with a hooked nose, wispy white hair, a high forehead, a firm mouth and a prominent jaw. His complexion was ruddy. For a brief moment his eyes had flickered open as Nancy walked in, then closed again like a shutter closing over a lens. Newman doubted whether either Novak or Astrid had seen the eyes open – they had been masked by his own bulk.

'You see,' Novak said gently, 'he sleeps well. He is a very strong man, a tough constitution. I was going to add, for his age – but he's one of nature's survivors...'

'You think he will survive then?' Nancy asked quietly.

'He is very sick man,' Astrid broke in. 'Very, very sick man.'

Newman stood back from the rest of them, hands in his pockets, as he watched. He had the distinct impression Novak was glad to see the two visitors. Glad? No, *relieved*. And not because one of his own kind – Nancy – had arrived. Astrid stood with tight lips and looked at her watch.

'Five minutes. Your visit. No more...'

Newman turned on her, raising his voice. 'Dr Novak, I want this woman out of the room. Who the hell is she to dictate the length of our stay? You're in charge of Jesse Kennedy's case – Dr Kobler said so in front of me. Kindly assert your authority.'

'You will see that the visit is five minutes and not one second more...' Astrid was speaking German like a machine-gun. 'I will report this outrage to Professor Grange unless you do as I say...'

'Tell her to fuck off,' Newman snapped. 'Or has this fat old bag got you by the short and curlies? Novak! Are you – or are you not – the physician in charge here?'

Waldo Novak flushed. He spoke to Astrid over his shoulder, also in rapid German. 'I suspect that the last thing Grange would be pleased to hear is that you were responsible for a scene. If these people storm out of the Clinic have you any idea of the potential consequences? Newman is a foreign correspondent of international repute, for God's sake. Kindly leave us alone...'

She was mouthing protests as he extracted the computer card key and inserted it in the slot. The door slid open. She bit her lip and shuffled out into the corridor. The closing door shut out her enraged face. Novak looked at Newman and Nancy apologetically.

'Every institution has one of them. The faithful servant who is tolerated because she has been on the staff since the dinosaurs.'

'She's a bit of an old dinosaur herself,' Nancy commented.

She had her handbag open and was using a handkerchief to dab at her eyes. Newman noticed that Jesse's gnarled hand was now lying outside the sheet. When they had entered it had been underneath. His eyes were still closed. Nancy pulled up a chair close to the bed, sat down and took his hand in hers.

'He doesn't know you're here,' Novak told her.

'What sedative are you using. Dr Novak?' she asked.

He hesitated. 'It's not normal to discuss treatment...' he began and then stopped speaking. Newman noticed he had glanced towards a porthole-shaped mirror let into the side wall. Above it was a coat-hook. Of course! The window in the door was of frosted glass. Every hospital or clinic had some technique for observing seriously ill patients.

I bet that next room is empty, he said to himself. And I bet that corpulent old pig is standing on the other side of that fake mirror. That is what is worrying Novak. He took off his jacket, walked over to the mirror and hung the jacket over it.

'Dr Novak...!' Nancy's tone was sharp-edged.

'Keep your voice down, Nancy,' Newman whispered. 'All the time.'

He looked round the room carefully, searching for a hidden microphone. Then he took a chair and placed it alongside Nancy's and gestured to Novak to sit down. The American sank into the chair and stared at Nancy who started speaking again, this time very quietly.

'I'm a doctor. I'm entitled to know the treatment...'

'Sodium Amytal,' Novak said promptly. 'He's a very vigorous man and must be kept in bed.'

He looked up over his shoulder at Newman who had rested a hand on the shoulder. Jesse's eyes flickered open, stared straight at Newman and frowned, his head jerked in a brief gesture. *Get Novak away from me and Nancy.*

'Novak,' said Newman, 'let's leave her with him. He is her grandfather. Come over with me by the window...' He waited until Novak joined him. The window, which presumably looked on the outside world from the daylight showing through, was also frosted. Which was another peculiarity of the Clinic...'

'What is it?' Novak enquired, his back to the bed.

'You and I have to meet outside. Very fast. You live on the premises?'

'Yes, I do. Why?'

'I guessed as much. This place smells of a closed community – a community locked away from the normal world. I suppose they do let you out,' he continued with a trace of sarcasm.

'During my off-duty hours I do what I like...'

'Don't sound indignant. But so far we haven't exactly felt welcome inside this place. I repeat. I insist on meeting you – so suggest somewhere. Thun would be closest?'

'I suppose it would be.' Novak sounded dubious. 'I don't see why I have to meet you anywhere...'

'Don't you?' Newman, observing what was happening behind Novak's back, kept talking fast. 'You're not compelled to, I agree. But then I could start writing articles about this place – naming you as my informant...'

'For Christ's sake, no...'

'No smart lawyer will get me for libel. I'm an expert at hinting at things and I know just how far I can go. Be honest with yourself, Novak – you're desperate to talk to someone. I sensed it within minutes of meeting you...'

'The Hotel Freienhof...' The words tumbled out. '...in Thun on the

Freienhofgasse... it overlooks the Inner Aare... a stretch of the river flowing in from the lake... the cheaper restaurant... do you know the place?'

'I'll find it. Tomorrow suit you?'

'Day after tomorrow. Thursday. Seven in the evening. It will be dark then...'

While Newman distracted Novak's attention Nancy had been talking to her grandfather, who suddenly woke up, his eyes fierce and alert. She leaned close to him so they could whisper and he spoke without any trace of being drugged.

'What are they doing to you here, Jesse?'

'It's what they're doing to the others. I never wanted to come to this place. That bastard Dr Chase shot me full of some drug in Tucson after I fell off the horse. I was hustled aboard a Lear jet and flown here...'

'What do you mean – what they're doing to the others?'

'The patients. It's got to be stopped. They're carrying out some kind of experiments. I keep my ears open and they talk when they think I'm doped out of my mind. The patients don't survive the experiments. A lot of them are dying anyway – but that's no reason for murdering them...'

'Are you sure, Jesse? How are you feeling?'

'I'm OK. As long as I'm inside here you've got a pipeline into this place. Don't worry about me...'

'I do,' she whispered.

'Nancy.' Newman had left the window and was walking round the bed. 'Maybe it would be better if we came back another day when your grandfather isn't sedated...'

She looked up at him and saw him stop suddenly. Her expression was a mixture of pathos, anxiety and puzzlement. Newman put a finger to his lips to hush both Novak and Nancy. Jesse lay inert in the bed, his eyes closed. Newman bent down close to the head of the bed and listened. No, he had not been mistaken. He had caught the sound of a whirring noise, of machinery working.

Lee Foley had followed Newman at a discreet distance until he rounded a bend on the snowbound hillside in time to see Newman turn off along the narrow road leading to the Berne Clinic. He drove the Porsche straight past the turn-off and continued up the slope towards the fir forest.

As he ascended higher and higher he looked down on the buildings of the Clinic. He continued climbing, until he reached the forest where he swung off the road, wheels skidding dangerously, heading for a narrow opening between the towering black firs. Always take the high ground.

Turning the Porsche through a hundred and eighty degrees – ready for a quick departure – he switched off the engine. On the floor of the empty seat behind him lay a pair of powerful binoculars in a leather case. He extracted them from the case, climbed out of the car and stood half-behind the erect trunk of an immensely tall tree.

Lifting the binoculars he adjusted the focus and slowly swept the lenses across the view far below. Within half an hour he had memorized the entire layout of the Clinic, the weird covered tunnel connecting it to the laboratory complex, and the laboratory itself. Then, ignoring the bitter east wind which scoured his craggy face, he settled down to wait, taking a nip of whisky from his hip flask.

Lee Foley was not the only watcher who took an interest in the Berne Clinic that wintry afternoon in mid-February. The rider on the scooter who had – by driving the machine to the limit – kept up with Foley, took a different route.

The scooter proceeded up the hillside to the point where the sign indicated the turn-off to the Clinic. Here it swung right, following the road taken earlier by Newman. Instead of stopping at the gatehouse, it went on past at full tilt, so fast that the Dobermans, again released, had no time to reach the gate.

The rider headed towards Thun, then turned off along a side track leading up the far side of the plateau. The surface of the track was diabolical but the rider continued upwards with great skill until a snow-covered knoll to the left and close to the track obscured the grounds of the Clinic. The rider stopped, perched the machine against a pile of logs and used both hands to remove the helmet.

A cascade of titian hair fell down her back in a waterfall, was caught in the wind and streamed behind her. The girl opened the carrying satchel and took out a camera with a telescopic lens. She strode up the side of the knoll, her black leather pants sheathing her long, agile legs. At the summit she peered over. The entire, huge estate comprising the grounds and the buildings of the Berne Clinic spread out below.

Crouching down, she raised the view-finder to her eyes, scanning the laboratory complex, the igloo-like tunnel linking it to the side of the Clinic, the main building of the Clinic itself. Deftly, she began taking pictures, swivelling the lens, clicking almost continuously.

Inside Jesse Kennedy's room Newman, who had acute hearing, remained stooped as he searched for the source of the continuous whirring sound. Then he saw the metal, louvred grille set low down in the wall. It looked like an air-conditioning grille.

He knelt on the floor, pressing his ear against the louvres. The sound was much louder – a whirring noise with an occasional click at regular intervals. Putting a finger to his lips again to keep them quiet, he stood up. Facing Nancy and Novak, he gestured towards the grille and mouthed the words. *Tape recorder.*

Walking a few feet away from the grille, he started talking, raising his voice. His manner was aggressive, his target Novak.

'Now listen to me, Dr Novak – and listen well. We're leaving total responsibility for Jesse Kennedy's welfare in the hands of the Berne Clinic. You understand that clearly? Answer me!'

'That has always been the situation,' Novak replied, playing along with Newman. 'Nothing will be changed by your visit – and you can rest assured Mr Kennedy will continue to receive every care and attention...'

'He'd better.' Newman stabbed a finger into Novak's chest. 'I don't know whether you're aware of the fact, but in a few days' time a major international medical congress is being held – including a reception at the Bellevue Palace. If anything happened to Jesse I'll shout my head off at that reception. We haven't exactly had the red carpet rolled out for us since we arrived at this place...'

'I do assure you...' Novak began.

'You'd better talk to Kobler and Grange and get their assurances, too. I blew the Kruger case wide open and I'm a man who can make a lot of noise. We're leaving now. Nancy...'

'Dr Novak, we'll be back – and very soon,' Nancy said firmly as Novak produced his key card.

Newman was close to the door when it slid back and he was looking beyond it. Two men in white coats walked past the opening, pushing a long trolley. Something lay on the trolley, something covered with a sheet which protruded upwards at the rear end – at the end where a patient's head would be. The silhouette was very large and shaped like a cage. From underneath the sheet a hand projected, a hand which moved in a grasping movement.

'Excuse me...'

Newman pushed in front of Nancy and Novak and turned right, away from the exit. The man behind the trolley glanced over his shoulder and the trolley began to move faster on its well-oiled wheels. Newman quickened his pace. As he had passed the door leading into the room with the mirror in the wall the door opened and behind him he heard Astrid call out. He ignored her and quickened his pace further. The two men with the trolley were almost running and had reached the point where the corridor became a downward sloping ramp. The trolley increased its momentum and Newman started running.

Reaching the corner where the corridor curved he saw ahead a steel door lifting. The trolley passed under it and the door began to descend. He arrived just as the steel plate closed with a hydraulic purr. Beyond he had caught a glimpse of the ramp descending steeply into the distance. To his right, set into the wall, was another of those infernal computer-operated slots. He heard a shuffling tread and turned to face Astrid.

'You have no business here, Mr Newman. I shall have to report this act of trespass...'

'Do that. What are you trying to hide? Report that remark too...'

He walked past her and retraced his steps rapidly along the corridor to where Nancy and Novak stood waiting for him. The American looked worried and took a step forward to speak in a whisper before Astrid reached them.

'I should leave here quickly if I were you...'

'It will be a pleasure...'

'First,' Astrid demanded, 'you must fill in the visiting forms at reception. It is the regulation...'

'It will be a pleasure,' Newman repeated.

The chill air of darkening night swept across the exposed plateau as they stood at the top of the steps outside the glassed-in veranda. But it was still daylight as Newman pulled on his gloves and Nancy shivered beside him. Novak had not come out to see them off, presumably to avoid any impression of intimacy.

'Cold?' Newman asked.

'This place gives me the creeps. My first impression – as soon as I saw the place – was right. There's something abnormal about the Clinic, Bob...'

'We'll talk about it in the car. With a bit of luck we should be back in Berne just before night...'

He drove down the curving drive slowly, again looking round to check the layout. A pallid light glowed over the stark and grim mountains on the far side of Thun. Nancy huddled herself inside her coat and turned up the heater. She looked out on both sides and then back through the rear window.

'There never seems to be anyone about – and yet I get the uncanny feeling unseen eyes are watching our every move. I'm not usually like this. Look – that's the sort of thing I mean...'

As they approached the gatehouse there were no signs of life but the gates opened. Newman drove between them, turned right and headed down the narrow road to the wider road where they had placed the sign to the Berne Clinic. She glanced at his profile.

'You've changed recently,' she remarked. 'I date it from when we'd been a few hours in Geneva.'

'Changed? In what way?'

'You used to be so light-hearted, always smiling and cracking jokes. You look so terribly serious and determined. And why did you go running after that trolley when we left Jesse's room? Novak thought you'd taken leave of your senses.'

'What do you think was lying under that sheet?'

'Some unfortunate soul who'd just passed away...'

'Do corpses normally waggle their hand? Whatever was under that sheet did just that.'

'Oh, my God. The sheet was pulled right over the body...'

'And that's only done when the patient is dead. That one was very much alive. My guess is that whoever was spread out under the sheet heard us and was trying to signal. Now you know why I ran after them. They beat me to a door which closed in my face – an automatic door, of course. That damned place is more like a giant computer than a clinic.'

'You mean they were running from you? I thought the trolley's brakes weren't working – that the momentum was carrying it down that ramp. Where does that corridor lead to?'

'A good question. There's a complex of new buildings further down the slope. I think they have a covered tunnel leading there. The corridor runs into the tunnel.'

'What kind of complex?'

'That, my dear Nancy, is one of the things I plan to ask our friend Dr Novak when I meet him in Thun on Thursday night...'

'He agreed to meet you! That's strange. Where are you seeing him? I can come, can't I?'

'The rendezvous is immaterial. It is strange that he agreed. And no, you can't come.'

'Bastard! Why do you think he did agree?' she asked as they came close to the bridge over the motorway and the slip road leading down on to the highway.

'I got the impression he's scared witless about something. I also think he's been waiting for the chance to contact someone outside that claustrophobic prison he can trust, he can confide in. And why are you so bothered about the Berne Clinic?'

'Did you notice the absence of something from Jesse's room?'

'I don't think so. I was too busy talking to Novak – to cover the fact you were talking to Jesse. What did I miss?'

'I'll tell you later,' she said, 'when we're back at the hotel. Do you think Jesse is safe in that place?'

'For the next few days, yes. Didn't you get the point of my shouting the odds about the medical reception at the Bellevue? They have a tape recorder behind that grille...'

'It really is creepy...'

'My strategy,' he continued, 'was to frighten them to ensure they don't harm him. They'll be very careful with Jesse until that medical congress is over. By then we may know what's going on at the Berne Clinic. I was buying time...'

They had turned down the slip road and were now speeding along the deserted motorway back towards Berne. It was so overcast Newman had his lights on and they were approaching the point where another slip road entered the motorway beyond a bridge. In his rear view mirror Newman saw a black Mercedes coming fast behind him. It signalled and swung out into the fast lane prior to overtaking. Then all hell broke loose on the motorway.

A helmeted figure appeared behind Newman on a scooter, sounding the horn in urgent, non-stop blasts. The Mercedes had not yet drawn alongside. Newman frowned, his eyes moving from side to side. At the exit to the slip road ahead a giant orange-coloured snowplough was moving slowly forward, its huge blade raised to its highest arc. The scooter horn continued its blasting sound.

'What's the matter with that man?' Nancy asked.

She was speaking when Newman signalled – signalled that he was turning out into the fast lane ahead of the oncoming Mercedes. The snowplough emerged from the slip road like some monstrous robot, moving straight into the path of the slow lane. Newman rammed his foot down, swinging to his left. The Mercedes began sounding its own horn. He ignored it. 'Hang on!' he warned Nancy. 'Oh, Christ!' she muttered. The snowplough was almost on top of them. Like a guillotine the massive steel blade descended. Nancy saw it coming down. She froze with horror. It was going to slice them in two. The Citroën was now moving at manic speed, way above the limit. The blade flashed past Nancy's window, missed hitting the Citroën by inches. She flinched. The Mercedes jammed on its brakes to avoid the coming collision. In the fast lane Newman accelerated. The scooter passed the Mercedes, still speeding in the slow lane, weaving past the now stationary snowplough.

Behind the wheel of the Mercedes Hugo Munz swore foully to his passenger, Emil Graf. He reduced speed, checking in his mirror for any sign of a police patrol car. The motorway was still deserted.

'You should have hit him,' said Graf.

'You're crazy! I could have bounced off, hit the steel barrier and we both end up dead. That scooter warned him...'

'So,' Graf replied in his toneless voice, 'he's better organized than we gave him credit for. We'll have to try something else.'

Fourteen

Blanche Signer sat waiting at a corner table in the ban of the Bellevue Palace while Newman fetched the drinks. She had paid a brief visit to the cloakroom to comb her titian hair, to get her centre parting straight, to freshen up generally for the Englishman after her dangerous ride back along the motorway on the scooter.

Thirty years old, the daughter of a colonel in the Swiss Army, she ran the most efficient service for tracing missing persons in western Europe. She was the girl who had secretly helped Newman to trace Kruger when the German had gone underground. She was determined to take Newman away from Nancy Kennedy.

'A double Scotch,' Newman said as he placed the glass before her and sat down alongside her on the banquette. There was not a lot of space and his legs touched hers. 'You've earned this. Cheers!'

'You know, Blanche,' he went on after swallowing half his drink, 'you took one hell of a risk back there on the motorway. I was scared stiff for you...'

'That's nice of you, Bob. Any risk of Nancy finding us here?'

'She's taking a bath. If she walks in you tried to pick me up. I think we have half an hour. What happened?'

'I waited at the Savoy as arranged. Lee Foley did follow you to the Clinic, then drove on past the turn-off and went on higher up the hill. I suspect he was doing what I did – checking out the layout of that place. It's peculiar. I've got a host of photos for you...' She squeezed her handbag. 'The film is in here. I can get it developed and printed overnight. I know someone who will do that for me. I'll get them to you tomorrow somehow...'

'Leave them in a sealed envelope addressed to me with the concierge. Now, what *did* happen? You probably saved my life.'

'It was simple, really, Bob. I took the photos, got on the scooter and started back to a place where I could wait to pick up Foley if he followed you back. I saw this car leaving the Clinic and decided to follow that. Pure hunch. The driver, a nasty-looking piece of work, knew what he was doing. He drove to where a snowplough was clearing a slip road. He got out, walked up to the snowplough operator and pointed something in his face. I'm sure it was a hair spray. The man grabbed for his eyes and Nasty hit him. It was pretty brutal. The poor devil's head came into contact with a steel bar – my guess is his skull is cracked. The driver from the clinic then put on the snowplough man's overalls and guided the machine down to the end of the slip road – just before it turns on to the motorway.'

'Waiting for me,' Newman commented. 'It was a fair assumption that when we left the Clinic I'd drive back the way I came from Berne. I blundered. I thought someone inside that place was at risk. Instead they decided to wipe me out first. But they have blundered too. Now I know something is wrong with that place. I'm not sure you ought to help me any more on this one...'

'Bob...' She took his hand and squeezed it affectionately. 'We make a good team. We did before. Remember. You don't get rid of me as easily as that. When are you coming to see me at my apartment? It's only a five-minute walk from here along the Munstergasse and into the Junkerngasse...'

'I'm involved with Nancy...'

'Officially?' she pressed.

'Well, no, not yet...'

'So you come and see me...'

'You're blackmailing my emotions...'

'And I'll go on doing it,' she assured him in her soft, appealing voice.

He studied her while he finished his drink. Her blue eyes stared back at him steadily. She had beautiful bone structure, Newman reflected. A lot of character – you could see that in her chin and high cheekbones. To say nothing of her figure which was something to knock any man out.

'What do I do next for you?' she asked.

'Go home. Relax...' He saw the look in her eyes. 'Oh, hell, Blanche, all right. You still go home and rest. Get some warmer clothes and maintain the watch on Lee Foley.' He leaned forward and grasped her upper arm. 'But you be very careful. Foley is dangerous.'

'I can handle him. Incidentally, when he's lying low at the Savoy he eats at a Hungarian place a few doors down the Neuengasse. The street is arcaded – so I can keep under cover. And it's perfect for parking the scooter. Anything else?'

She made it sound so everyday, Newman marvelled. Blanche was always very cool. She watched him over the rim of her glass; she couldn't take her eyes off him.

'There might be something else,' he decided. 'You've built up that register of people with unusual occupations. Check it and see if you have anything on a Manfred Seidler...'

'Will do. Maybe I'd better go before your pseudo-fiancée turns up. If I get something on this Seidler I'll type out a report and include it in the envelope with the photos. I'll head it MS. If there's an emergency I'll call your room number, let the phone ring three times, then disconnect. You call me back when you can. OK, Mr Newman?'

'OK, Miss Signer...'

She leaned forward, kissed him full on the mouth, stood up and walked away, her handbag looped over her shoulder. The bar at the Bellevue Palace is dimly lit, very much like many American bars. But as she walked erectly across the room men's heads turned to watch her. She stared straight ahead, apparently unaware of the impression she was creating. At the exit she passed Nancy Kennedy who was just entering.

Newman had moved Blanche's lipsticked glass on to the next table as she left. He stood up to greet Nancy. As she came closer he saw by her expression that something had disturbed her.

'That man phoned again,' she said as she sat down on the banquette. 'The same one I took the call from in Geneva. Seidler? Wasn't that his name? I told him you'd be back much later in the evening. He sounded very agitated. He put the phone down on me when I tried to get a message.'

'That's my strategy now, Nancy. Agitation. All round. By the time I talk to him he'll be going up the wall, which will make him more pliable. Same thing with the Berne Clinic. Agitation. Although there,' he said ruefully, 'it seems to have acted with a vengeance. They tried to kill us on that motorway...'

'*Us?*'

'You as well as me is my guess.' Newman's manner was forbidding. 'I'm giving it to you straight so you'll take care. You make no trips to Thun without me. Now, in the car you mentioned something missing from Jesse's room. What was it?'

'You have a good memory...'

'It's my main asset. Answer the bloody question.'

'You are in a mood. Something to tell the time by. No clock on his bedside table. No wristwatch. Jesse has no way of keeping track of the time. It's a disorientation technique. I know that from my psychiatric studies.'

'Trick-cyclists drive me round the bend...'

'You're hostile to everything medical,' she flared. 'When we were at the Clinic I saw you wrinkling your nose at the smell. They do have to keep those places hygienic. To do that they use disinfectant...'

'OK,' he said irritably. 'No clock. I've got the point. I agree it's odd.'

'And Novak told the truth when he said they used sodium amytal to sedate Jesse.' She reached into her handbag, produced a blue capsule from a zipped pocket and handed it to him. 'You can't see in here but it's a sixty-milligram dose coded F23. Jesse slipped it to me while you were talking to Novak. That's why Jesse was still awake.'

'Maybe I'm dim, but I don't follow what you've just said.'

'Jesse has become expert at palming a capsule when he's given one to swallow. He pretends to swallow it and hides it in the palm of his hand.'

'How does he get rid of it?'

124

'He drops it inside that metal grille where they've hidden the tape recorder...'

'That's a laugh,' Newman commented. 'It's also clever. It doesn't suggest a sick man who's lost most of his marbles. And one absent thing I did notice. There wasn't a single mention of the fact that Jesse is supposed to be suffering from leukaemia.'

'Soon you'll be as good as me,' she said smugly. Then her expression drooped. 'But they are sedating him heavily. He' showed me the fleshy part of his arm – it's riddled with punctures. The sods are pumping him full of the stuff with a hypodermic. We were just lucky it was capsule day. Can't you find out what's really going on when you meet Novak in Thun on Thursday night?'

'I intend to. If he turns up. He's getting very shaky about the situation there, so let's hope Kobler and Co. don't notice. I want you to stay inside this hotel the whole time I'm away at Thun. If you get any calls saying I've had an accident, ignore them. Anything that tempts you out of the Bellevue. You'll do that, won't you?'

'You have changed. You're getting very bossy...'

'I'm not asking you. I'm telling you.' His tone was bleak. 'I can no longer keep wondering what you're doing, looking over my shoulder.'

'You could ask me more nicely...'

She broke off as a waiter came to their table. He handed to Newman a folded sheet of paper. Inside was a sealed envelope. Taking the envelope, Newman looked at the waiter.

'Who gave you this?'

'A rather shabbily dressed individual, sir. He pointed you out and said would I be sure to hand this to you personally. I have never seen him before.'

'Thanks...'

Newman tore open the envelope and extracted a second, smaller sheet of folded paper which bore no clue as to its. origins. The message was brief.

Can you come to see me at seven o'clock this evening. A crisis situation. Beck.

Newman checked his watch. 6.15 p.m. He put the folded sheet back inside the envelope and slipped the envelope inside his wallet. Nancy stirred restlessly.

'What is it?'

'Things are hotting up. I have to go out. Expect me when you see me. If you're hungry start dinner without me. Choose whichever restaurant you fancy.'

'Is that all?'

'Yes. It is. Remember – stay inside this hotel...'

As he walked through the night Berne was deserted. The workers had gone home, the bright sparks hadn't come in for an evening on the town yet. He crossed over by the Casino and walked into the right-hand arcade of the Munstergasse, an arched stone tunnel with a paved walk, shop windows lit up and closed.

Newman wondered why he had been so abrupt with Nancy. A man has a habit of comparing one woman with another. Had the fact that he had been talking with Blanche so amiably before Nancy arrived influenced his attitude? Not a pleasant conclusion. But Beck's summons had decided him. With half his mind he heard the footsteps behind which synchronized with his own. He crossed the lonely street into the opposite arcade without looking back.

Yes, he had made up his mind. Before he saw Beck he was going to see Blanche – to tell her she was out of the whole business. *Crisis* was the word Beck had used. Beck didn't use words like that lightly. He was going to pull Blanche out of the firing line.

The footsteps synchronized with his own, the click-clack of a second pair of feet on the stones had followed him across the street. They were now following him down the same arcade. He didn't look back. It was an old trick – to mask your own footfall by pacing it with the man you were following.

He was nearly half-way towards the Munsterplatz when he passed a narrow alley leading through to the street beyond. The *Finstergasschen*. A spooky alley with only a single lamp which emphasized the shadows of the narrow walk. He continued towards the Munster, his right hand stiffened for a chopping blow.

'Newman! Come back here! Quick...!'

A hoarse, whispering call. He swung round on his heel. Two figures were struggling at the entrance to the *Finstergasschen*. One tall, heavily-built, wearing a cap. The second much smaller. He walked back quickly as they vanished inside the alley, slowed down near its entrance, peered round the corner.

Lee Foley had his arm round the neck of the smaller man. The American was dressed in an English check suit, a checked cap. A walking stick held in his free hand completed the outer trappings of an Englishman. The small man he held in a vice-like grip was Julius Nagy.

'This little creep has been tracking you all over town,' Foley said. 'Time we found out who his employer is, wouldn't you agree?'

Before Newman could react Foley thrust Nagy inside the alcove formed by a doorway. Shoving him back against the heavy wooden door, he suddenly lifted the stick, held it horizontally and pressed it against Nagy's throat. The little man's eyes bulged out of his head. He was terrified.

'Who is your paymaster?' rasped Foley.

'Tripet...' Nagy gasped as Foley relaxed the stick slightly.

'Who?' Foley rasped again.

'Chief Inspector Tripet. Sûreté. Geneva...'

'That came too easily,' Foley growled. 'Geneva? This happens to be Berne. You're lying. One more chance. After a little more persuasion...'

'Watch it,' Newman warned. 'You'll crush his Adam's apple.'

'That is exactly what I'm going to do if he doesn't come across.'

Nagy made a horrible choking sound. He beat his small, clenched fists against Foley's body. He might as well have hammered at the hide of an elephant. Newman glanced down the alley. Still empty. By the glow of the lamp he saw Nagy was turning purple. Foley pressed the stick harder. Feebly, Nagy's heels pattered against the base of the wooden door, making no more noise than the scutter of a mouse. Newman began to feel sick.

Foley eased the pressure of the stick. He pushed his cold face within inches of Nagy's ashen skin, his ice-blue eyes watching the little man's without pity, without any particular expression. He waited as Nagy sucked in great draughts of cold night air. It was the only sound in the stillness of the night.

'Let's start all over,' Foley suggested. 'One more chance – I simply don't have the time for lies. Who is your employer?'

'Coat pocket... phone number...... car registration... Bahnhof...'

'What the hell is the jerk talking about?' Foley asked in a remote voice as though thinking aloud.

'Wait! Wait!' Newman urged.

He plunged a hand inside Nagy's shabby coat pocket, scrabbled around. His fingers felt a piece of paper. He pulled it out urgently – Foley was not a man who bluffed. He stepped back a few paces and examined the paper under the lamp.

'There is a phone number,' he told Foley. 'And what looks like a car registration number. It *is* a car registration...' Newman had recognized the car registration. The figures were engraved on his memory. The letters too. 'Let him talk,' he told Foley. 'Ease up on him. What was that reference he made to the Bahnhof?'

'Your employer,' Foley said to Nagy. 'This time we want the truth – not some crap about the Geneva police...'

'The other coat pocket...'Nagy was looking at Newman. 'Inside it you'll find a camera. I took a shot of a man getting into that Mercedes – outside the Bahnhof. He came in off the one fifty-eight p.m. express from Geneva...'

Foley held the walking stick an inch from the little man's throat while Newman scrabbled around inside the other pocket. His hand came out holding a small, slim camera. A Voigtlander. Three shots had been taken. He looked up and caught Nagy's expression as the little man stared straight at him over the bar of the walking stick.

'I only took two shots,' Nagy croaked. 'The man getting into the car – and the Mercedes itself.' He switched his gaze to Foley. 'I think that man is the boss, my employer – and somebody important. There was a chauffeur with the car.'

'Mind if I take out the film?' Newman asked. 'I'll pay for it…'

'Jesus Christ!' Foley exploded. 'Take the film. Why pay this shit?'

Newman broke open the camera after winding the film through. Extracting the film, he dropped it inside his coat pocket, shut the camera, took a banknote from his wallet and replaced camera with banknote inside Nagy's pocket.

'I'll get it developed and printed,' he told Foley. 'Now let our friend go…'

'Break an arm – just to teach him not to follow people…'

'No!' Newman's tone was tough and he took a step towards the American. 'He was following me, so I decide. I said let him go…'

With a grimace of disgust the American released Nagy who felt his injured throat, swallowed and then straightened his rumpled tie. He seemed oddly reluctant to leave and kept eyeing Newman as though trying to transmit some message. Foley gave him a shove and he shuffled off down the alley, glancing back once and again it was Newman he stared at.

'You and I have to talk,' Foley said. It was a statement. 'I want to know what's on that film – and on that piece of paper…'

'Not now. I'm late for an appointment. Thanks for spotting my shadow, but you play pretty rough. Sometimes you get more if you coax…'

'I coax with the barrel of a gun, Newman. I'll call you at the Bellevue. Then we meet. Inside twenty-four hours. You owe me.'

'Agreed…'

Newman walked rapidly away down the Munstergasse and continued along the Junkerngasse, which is also arcaded, but without shops. Crossing the cobbled street which was now running downhill, he looked back. No sign of Foley, but that didn't surprise him. The American was too fly to follow him. He reached the closed door with three bell-pushes, a recently-installed speakphone, a name alongside each bell-push. He pressed the one lettered *B. Signer*.

Blanche had taken his advice or, woman-like, she had hoped – expected – he would turn up. Her quiet voice came to him through the speakphone grille clearly when he announced himself.

'I thought it was you; Bob. Push the door when the buzzer buzzes...'

Beyond the heavy wooden door, which closed automatically behind him on the powerful sprung-hinge, a dim light showed him the way up a flight of ancient stone steps, well-worn in the middle. On the first floor landing he noticed another new addition in the door to her apartment. A fish-eye spyhole. The door opened inward and Blanche stood there, wearing only a white bathrobe.

He sensed she had nothing on underneath as she stood aside and the bathrobe, loosely corded round her waist, parted to expose a bare, slim leg to her thigh. She closed the door, fixed the special security lock and put on the thick chain.

'Blanche, I have another film for you to develop and print.' He handed the spool to her. 'Only three shots – the third one intrigues me. The party who gave it to me said there were only two...'

'Because someone else was present? Tomorrow you have prints and negatives along with my own contribution. No, don't sit there. In here...'

Here was a tidily-furnished bedroom with one large single bed. He paused and swung round to face her. She had closed the door and stood facing him, brushing the cascade of titian hair slowly, her face expressionless.

'No, Blanche,' he said. 'I've come to tell you to forget all about the Berne Clinic. Too many pretty tough characters keep turning up. You could get hurt – that I won't risk...'

'You'll hurt me if you don't...'

She pushed him suddenly, a hard shove. The edge of the bed acted as a fulcrum against the back of his legs and he sprawled on the white duvet. She flicked the cord round her waist free, dropped the bathrobe and he had guessed right about her lack of attire. She was on top of him before he could move.

'I'm engaged,' Newman protested as she spread herself.

'Of course you are – engaged in battle...'

She giggled as her slim hands industriously burrowed, whipping, open the buttons of his coat, the buttons of his jacket underneath, unfastening his tie, his shirt buttons. He had never known a woman's hand operate with such skill and agility. He sighed. When it's inevitable... relax... enjoy...'

Julius Nagy was livid with rage and resentment. He shuffled back along the deserted *Finstergasschen*. They never expected you to come back the same way. This was twice he had been subjected to violent abuse. First the obscene experience with that thug in the lavatory aboard the express to Zurich. Now the same thing had happened again at the end of this alley.

The injury to Nagy's dignity hurt him even more than the injury to his throat. Only the Englishman, Newman, had treated him like a fellow human being. Well, he would get his revenge. He emerged from the end of the alley and peered cautiously both ways along the Munstergasse. No one in sight anywhere. Pulling up the collar of his shabby coat against the bitter cold, he turned left towards the Munster.

'Make a sound and I'll blow your spine in half...'

The violent threat, spoken in German, was accompanied by the equally violent ramming of something hard against his back. A gun barrel. Nagy froze with sheer fright, standing quite still.

'Keep walking,' the voice ordered. 'Don't look round. That would be the last mistake you'd made. Cross the street. Head for the Munsterplatz...'

There was still no one else about. It was still the interval between the workers going home and the night revellers appearing. Nagy crossed the street, the gun muzzle glued against his back, and walked down under the other arcade, praying a patrol car would drive down the street.

'Now walk round the Munsterplatz – on the pavement...'

The gunman knew what he was doing, Nagy realized with growing terror. Following this route they stayed within the dark shadows. On the far side of the square the huge bulk of the front façade of the Munster sheered up. The great tower was enclosed inside a series of builder's boards – like tiers in a theatre. Above that speared the immense spire, all knobbly and spiky.

Nagy began to suspect what was their ultimate destination – the Plattform. The large garden square alongside the Munster which overlooked the river Aare. He was pushed and prodded through the gateway and guided across the square towards the far wall. The naked trees in the garden were vague skeletal silhouettes, the only sound the crunch of two pairs of feet on the gravel. Nagy, sweat streaming down his face despite the cold, was trying to look ahead to predict the next move. His mind wouldn't function.

'I need information,' the voice growled. 'Here we can talk undisturbed...'

So that was it. The raw wind beat across the exposed heights of the Plattform, sliced at his face. No one would come out here on such a night. His attacker had worked it out well. And this was the third time! A hint of fury welled up, faded into fear again. His feet walked with leaden step. Then they reached the wall near the corner furthest from the lift which descended to the Badgasse. Nagy was pressed against the wall.

'Now I will tell you what we want to know. Then you will tell me the answers to the questions I put to you...'

Nagy stared out beyond the wall which was thigh-high, stared out at the lights of houses twinkling in the chilling night on the Bantiger, the hill which rises from the far bank of the Aare. The gun had been removed from his back. Suddenly Nagy felt two hands like steel handcuffs grasp his ankles. He was elevated bodily and projected forward over the wall. He screamed. His hands thrust out into space. The earth, one hundred and fifty feet below, rushed up to meet him. The scream faded into a wail. Then it ceased. There was a distant thud. Steps retraced their path across the gravel.

Fifteen

Newman took the devious route to the Taubenhalde (the Pigeon Hill) which houses Federal Police Headquarters in Berne.

He was becoming almost neurotically wary of shadows – and not only the shadows which cloaked the arcades. He had heard Nagy's footsteps but he had missed Lee Foley's cat-like tread. So, when he walked back up the Munstergasse from Blanche's apartment, made his way back past the Casino and crossed to the Kochergasse, he quickened his pace.

He proceeded on past the entrance to the Bellevue Palace, stopped to light a cigarette while he glanced back, checked the far pavement, and disappeared down an alley leading to the *Terrasse* in front of the Parliament. At that hour the elevated walk was deserted. Beyond the walk the ground fell away, sloping steeply towards the Aare. Ahead he saw the funicular – the Marzilibahn – which travels down the slope almost to river level. The small red car had just reached the top of the slanting rails. He broke into a run.

Sixty centimes bought him a ticket from the attendant inside the small building at the top of the funicular. The car, very new and toy-like, was empty and the door slid shut as soon as he stepped inside. It began its steeply-angled descent down a pair of ruler-straight rails.

Newman stood at the front, surrounded by windows, his hands on a rail. In the dark the lights across the river were sharp as diamonds. The descent continued and Newman felt exposed inside the illuminated car. He realized his hands were gripping the rail tightly.

The lower station came up to meet him. The car slowed, slipped inside, stopped. The moment the door opened he stepped out and left the cover of the base station. The wind blasted along the river and hit him in the face. He kept walking as he turned up his coat collar. There appeared to be no one about.

133

He passed one of the original wooden cars, preserved as a monument and perched on a tiny hill. The Taubenhalde was still some distance when he entered a modern building and presented his passport to the receptionist.

'I have an appointment with Arthur Beck,' he said. 'Seven o'clock...'

Seated behind his counter, the receptionist examined the passport, stared at Newman and then at the photo. He opened a file and took out a glossy print which Newman recognized as a photograph of himself taken the previous year during the Kruger affair. They were careful inside this place.

'You know the way to the Taubenhalde, M. Newman?' the receptionist asked as he returned the passport. 'It is a little complex...'

'I know the way. I've been here before...'

From this building a long subterranean passage leads to Pigeon Building. Newman walked along it while behind him the receptionist picked up the phone and spoke rapidly. At the end of the passage a travelator – an 80-metre-long moving staircase – ascends to the main entrance hall to the Taubenhalde. Newman stood quite still, working out what he would tell Beck, as the travelator carried him upwards.

He had come a long way round to reach this entrance hall – by doing so he avoided being recognized by any watcher checking who entered the building through the main doors. The moment Newman entered the hall he knew something was wrong. Arthur Beck was waiting for him by the reception counter where normally all visitors filled in a detailed form.

'I will deal with the formalities,' Beck told the receptionist curtly and pocketed a pad of forms. He walked to the lift without even greeting Newman. Inside the lift the policeman pressed the button for Floor 10 and stood in silence as the lift ascended. Reaching 10, the lift door remained closed until Beck inserted a key into a slot and turned it. The security inside the place, Newman recalled, was formidable.

Beck still said nothing as he unlocked the door of his office and stood aside for Newman to enter. It was unnerving – especially the business downstairs about not filling in any form. Beck explained that as he went round to the far side of his desk, sat down, and gestured for Newman to occupy the chair opposite.

'Officially, you may never have been here. We shall see...'

Beck was plump-cheeked, his most arresting feature was his alert grey eyes under thick brows. His manner was normally recessive, observant. He moved his hands and feet quickly and his complexion was ruddy. He was one of the cleverest policemen in western Europe.

Dressed in a navy blue business suit, blue-striped shirt, a blue tie which carried a kingfisher emblem woven into the fabric, he fiddled with a pencil, watching Newman. No welcoming words, nothing to indicate that they were old friends. Suddenly he threw down the pencil. His voice was abrupt.

'Can you tell me where you were this evening between six fifteen and seven o'clock?'

'Why?' Newman demanded.

'I'm asking you if you have an alibi for those forty-five minutes?'

'*Alibi*?' Newman's tone expressed astonishment, irritation. 'What the hell are you talking about?'

'You haven't answered the question.'

'Is this something to do with the crisis you mentioned in your note dragging me over here?' Newman realized his mistake. 'It can't be – I got that note earlier...'

'It is my duty to put the question to you once more formally. Think before you reply...'

Newman was thinking. There was no way he could tell Beck where he had been. That would mean dragging in Blanche. He wasn't going to do that. Not because of the possible publicity. Not because of Nancy. Because of Blanche. He was surprised by the strength of his own decision.

'I'm not prepared to answer the question until I know exactly what this is all about.'

'Very well.' Beck stood up stiffly. 'I will show you what it is all about. I think you had better wear some different clothes – to avoid the chance of recognition...'

Newman carefully said nothing as Beck opened a cupboard, took out a dark blue overcoat and handed it to Newman. 'Put that on. Leave your sheepskin here. We shall be coming back afterwards.'

'After what?' Newman enquired. 'And this coat is pretty floppy. You're fatter than I am...'

'It will do. You look fine. Now try on this hat...'

Beck slipped on a fawn raincoat he took from the cupboard as Newman put on the hat. The police chief slammed the cupboard door shut, picked up the phone and spoke rapidly.

'Be sure the car is ready. We're coming down now...'

'The hat is too big,' Newman commented. 'Your head is fatter than mine...'

'You look fine. Put on these dark glasses. Please do not argue. It is very important that you are not recognized – and God knows there will be enough people hanging around...'

'Hanging around where? I want to know where you're taking me before I move from this office.'

'Not far, Bob. This is just as unpleasant and unsettling for me as well as for you. It blew up in my face very recently. I ask you to say nothing, to talk to no one but me. If you don't do as I request you may well regret it...'

'*Request* – that's a bit more like it. Try and push me around and we won't be cooperating on anything ever again. You do know that, I hope, Beck?'

'I know that. Time is precious. The car is waiting. We have only a very short distance to go. Not five minutes' walk from the Bellevue Palace. Something terrible has happened...'

Seated in the back of an unmarked police car neither Beck nor Newman said a single word during the short journey. Newman peered out of the window and realized they were driving along the Aarstrasse in the direction of the Nydeggbrücke. In the darkness lights across the river reflected in the water.

A tram was crossing the Kirchenfeld bridge high above them just before they passed under its span. Very little traffic at that hour. Then, ahead, he saw a line of parked police cars, their blue lamps flashing on the roofs. The car slowed down at a barrier which had been erected at the entrance to the Badgasse, the street which runs immediately below the Munster Plattform.

Beck opened the window as a uniformed policeman approached and showed his identity card without saying a word. The barrier was raised and they passed up a narrow street into the ancient Badgasse. Here there was frenetic activity.

More police cars, more winking blue lamps. Flash-bulbs lighting the street in brief blazes of brilliance. Newman was reminded of the strobe lights in a disco. They drove slowly to a point near the far end of the Plattform wall on their right which faced old houses on their left. A high canvas screen had been erected around something. The car stopped. Beck grasped the door handle.

This is pretty nasty,' he warned.

Newman stepped out of the warmth of the car into the raw chill of the night. He felt slightly ridiculous in Beck's blue overcoat and the ill-fitting hat. Fortunately the glasses he wore were only lightly tinted. Police milled around. A grim-faced man in plain clothes pushed his way through to Beck.

'This is Chief Inspector Pauli of Homicide, Cantonal Police,' Beck remarked without introducing Newman. 'Pauli, would you kindly repeat the message you received over the phone?'

'The caller was anonymous,' Pauli reported in a clipped voice. 'He said we'd find a body in the Badgasse. He also said that a Robert Newman had been seen arguing with the deceased earlier this evening in the Munstergasse...'

'Pauli is from Hauptwache – police headquarters on the Waisenhausplatz,' Beck commented. 'He came at once and this is what he found...'

Behind the canvas shield a Ford station wagon was parked at a right angle to the base of the wall, facing outwards ready to be driven away. The hideous mess which was the remains of Julius Nagy lay spread all over the roof, his head twisted at an impossible angle, one eye staring at Newman like the eye of a dead fish in the beam of a searchlight mounted on top of a police car.

Newman recognized the mangled corpse as Nagy by the Tyrolean hat rammed slantwise across the crushed skull, a hat with a tiny blood-red feather. But it was not really the colour of blood – the real colour, much darker and coagulated, smeared the Ford's windscreen in snake-like streaks.

A man in civilian clothes, carrying a black bag, climbed down a ladder which had been perched against the far side of the car. Removing a pair of rubber gloves, he shook his head as he gazed at Beck.

'Dr Moser,' Beck said briefly. 'Cantonal police pathologist.'

'I'd say every other bone in his body is broken,' Moser commented. 'I can tell you more later – or will you be taking over?'

'I will be taking over,' Beck informed him.

'In that case, it's a pleasant night's work for Dr Kleist – and better her than me. I'll send over my written report...'

'Any suggestion – an educated guess – as to how it happened?' Beck enquired.

'I never guess.' Moser stared upwards at the wall towering above them. 'Of course, he'd hit the car like a cannon-ball from that height. Obviously it was either murder, suicide or an accident.' Moser paused. 'There are pleasanter ways of ending it all. And I managed to extract this envelope he had in his overcoat pocket.' He handed a crumpled envelope to Beck and glanced at Newman. 'I'll be off to start work on my report. Another late night – and my wife is already beginning to wonder why I get home so late...'

Beck produced a cellophane packet, held the envelope by one corner and slipped it inside the packet. 'Probably useless for fingerprints but one goes through the motions. What idea are you playing with now in that fertile brain of yours, Newman?'

The Englishman was staring up into the night where the massive wall sheered up. At intervals huge flying buttresses projected. It was vertiginous – even gazing up the terrifying drop. He looked at Beck as they stood alone with the pathetic and horrifying crumpled form which had once been a living, breathing man. At that moment Moser returned briefly.

'One suggestion, Beck. I'd cover the top of the Ford with a waterproof sheet and have it driven slowly to the morgue. Kleist will find she has to scrape some of the remains clear of the car. He's practically glued to the roof. Enjoy yourself...'

'I think,' Newman said after Moser had gone, 'it might be an idea to go up to the Plattform by the lift at the corner. If I remember rightly it doesn't stop working until eight thirty p.m.'

'You have a remarkable memory for details about the Plattform.'

'It's up to you...'

'I'll get the car to drive round and meet us at the exit...'

'No. Near the top of the Munstergasse...'

'If you say so...'

They emerged from the canvas shelter into hectic activity in the Badgasse. Uniformed police in leather greatcoats, 7.65-mm. automatics holstered on their right hips, walking up and down to no apparent purpose that Newman could see. Beck spoke briefly to his car driver and followed Newman who was striding to the distant corner of the wall.

The ancient lift is a small cage which ascends vertically inside an open metal shaft to the top of the Plattform. Newman had bought two 60-rappen tickets from the old boy who attended the lift when Beck arrived. They stood in silence as it made its slow ascent.

On a seat was perched a piece of newspaper with the remains of a sandwich and the interior of the lift smelt of salami. The old boy had moved from the entrance door to the exit door at the opposite end of the cage. Beck watched Newman as he stared out of the window overlooking the Aare, then switched his gaze to the facing window where he could see the slope terraced into kitchen gardens, the continuous walls of houses along the Munstergasse running into the Junkerngasse. In one of those houses Blanche would be in her apartment, probably phoning the man who would develop and print the films. At all costs he had to keep her name out of this horror.

The lift door was opened by the attendant after it reached the tiny shed at the corner of the Plattform. Newman did not make any move to get out. He spoke casually.

'You won't have many passengers at this time of night. Can you recall anyone who used the lift at about six thirty p.m.? Maybe six forty-five?'

'For sixty rappen you want me to answer foolish questions?'

Beck said nothing. He produced his identity folder and showed it to the attendant, his face expressionless. Returning it to his pocket he stared out of the open doorway.

'I am sorry...' The attendant seemed confused. 'I did not know. That awful business of the man who fell...'

'That's what I'm talking about,' Newman said amiably. 'We think he may have had a friend – or friends – who could identify him. Someone who was so shaken they took your lift down after the tragedy. Take your time. Think...'

'There was a big man by himself.' The attendant screwed up his face in his effort to concentrate. 'I didn't take all that notice of him. He carried a walking stick...'

'How was he dressed?' Beck interjected.

'I was eating my supper. I can't remember. A lot of people use this lift...'

'Not at this time of night,' Newman pointed out gently. 'I imagine you can remember the time?'

'Seven o'clock I would say. No earlier. The lift was at the bottom – he called it up – and I heard a clock chime...'

Beck walked out of the cage and Newman followed. In the distance, almost at the end of the thigh-high stone wall protecting them from the drop, uniformed policemen with torches searched the ground. A section was cordoned off by means of poles with ropes. The point, Newman guessed, where Nagy had gone over.

'Nothing, sir – at least as yet,' one of the policemen reported to Beck who shrugged.

'They're looking for signs of a struggle,' Beck remarked. 'God, the wind cuts you in two up here. And it wasn't an accident,' he continued. 'There's no ice on the stones he could have slipped on...'

Newman placed both hands on the top of the wall close to the roped-off section and peered over. Vertigo. The great wall fell into the abyss. He studied the area, looking along the wall in both directions. His hands were frozen.

'Interesting,' he commented.

'What is?' Beck asked sharply.

'Look for yourself. This is the one place where there are no buttresses to break his fall. He'd still have been seriously injured – but he might just have survived. He went over at the very place where it was certain he'd be killed...'

He looked round the great Plattform which was divided up into four large grassy beds. Stark, closely trimmed trees reared up in the night which was now lit by the moon. Behind them the huge menacing spire of the Munster stabbed at the sky. Newman thrust his hands into his pockets and began walking towards the exit he knew led into the Munsterplatz. Beck followed without comment.

Emerging from the gateway, Newman stood for a moment, staring round the cobbled square and across at the Munstergasse. The arcade on the far side was a deserted tunnel of light and shadow. He walked diagonally across the square and inside the arcade. He continued walking until he reached the *Finstergasschen*, the narrow alley leading towards the Marktgasse, one of the main streets of Berne. He checked his watch. Five minutes. That was the time it had taken for him to walk from the place where Nagy had died to the *Finstergasschen*.

The patrol car Beck had sent on ahead was parked by the kerb. Newman climbed into the rear seat without a word as Beck settled himself beside him. He gave the driver a brief instruction.

'Not the front entrance. We'll take the long way round to my office.'

'Why?' asked Newman when the policeman had closed the partition dividing them from the driver.

'Because the front entrance may well be watched. I rushed you into the car on the way out but I don't want anyone to see you come back – even in those togs...'

Togs. Newman smiled to himself. During his stint in London Beck had picked up a number of English colloquialisms. He left the talking to Beck who continued immediately.

'Do you know that pathetic crumpled wreck back there?'

'Julius Nagy,' Newman replied promptly. 'The Tyrolean hat. He was wearing it when he followed me about in Geneva...'

He had to admit that much. He had no doubt Beck had contacted Chief Inspector Tripet of the Sûreté in Geneva. Beck turned to face the Englishman.

'But how did you identify him in Geneva?'

'Because when I was last here I used him. He deserved a better death than that. He was born to a poor family, he hadn't enough brains to get far, but he was persistent and he earned his living supplying people like me with information. He had underworld contacts.'

'Here in Berne, you mean?'

'Yes. That was why I was surprised he had moved his sphere of operations to Geneva...'

'That was me,' Beck replied. 'I had him thrown out of the Berne canton as a public nuisance, an undesirable. I too felt sorry for him. Why did he risk coming back is what I would like to know...'

Again Newman refused to be drawn into conversation...' They were approaching the building close to the base of the Marzilibahn when Beck made the remark, still watching Newman.

'I am probably one of the very few people in Switzerland who knows that what you have just seen is the second murder in the past few weeks.'

'Who else knows?'

'The murderers...'

The atmosphere changed the moment they entered Beck's office from the hostility which had lingered in the air during Newman's earlier visit. A small, wiry woman whose age Newman guessed as fifty-five, a spinster from her lack of rings, followed them inside with a tray. A percolator of coffee, two Meissen cups and saucers, two balloon-shaped glasses and a bottle of Remy Martin.

'This is Gisela, my assistant,' Beck introduced. 'Also she is my closest confidante. In my absence you can pass any message to her safe in the knowledge it will reach my ears only.'

'You're looking after us well,' Newman said in German and shook hands as soon as she had placed the tray on the desk.

'It is my pleasure, Mr Newman. I will be in my office if you need me,' she told Beck.

'She works all hours,' Beck commented as he poured the coffee. 'Black, if I recall? And it is a swine of a night – on more accounts than one. So, we will treat ourselves to some cognac. I welcome you to Berne and drink your health, my friend. You must excuse my earlier reception.'

'Which was about what?'

'That bloody anonymous phone call to Pauli reporting you were seen in the vicinity. Someone wants you off the streets. We have procedures – and my immediate purpose was to close off the cantonal police. I can now tell Pauli I cross-examined you and am fully satisfied you had nothing to do with the death of our late lamented Julius Nagy. He minutes the file – sends it over to me and I lock it away for good.'

He wheeled his swivel chair round the desk to sit alongside Newman. They drank coffee and sipped their cognac in silence until Beck started talking, the words pouring out in a Niagara.

'Bob, in the last twelve hours there have been no less than five incidents all of which worry me greatly. They form no clear pattern but I am convinced all these incidents are linked. First, a mortar was stolen from the military base at Lerchenfeld near Thun-Sud. The second mortar stolen within a month...'

'Did they take any ammo – any bombs?'

'No, which in itself is peculiar. Just the weapon. The second incident also concerns the theft of a weapon. You know that all Swiss have to serve military service up to the age of forty-five, that each man keeps at his home an Army rifle and twenty-four rounds of ammunition. A house was broken into while the owner was at work and his wife was out shopping. A rifle – plus the twenty-four rounds – has disappeared. Also the sniperscope. He was a marksman...'

'Which area? Or can I guess?'

'Thun-Sud. Late this afternoon the third incident occurred on a motorway. The driver of a snowplough was viciously attacked and his machine later found on the motorway. You want to guess the area?'

'Somewhere near Thun?'

'Precisely. Always Thun! The fourth incident you know about. The murder of Julius Nagy...'

'And Number Five?'

'Lee Foley, alleged ex-CIA man, has disappeared today from the hotel we traced him to. The Savoy in the Neuengasse. Bob, this American is one of the most dangerous men in the west. I rang a friend in Washington – woke him up, but he's done the same to me. I wanted to know whether Foley really has left the CIA and he said he had. I'm still not totally convinced. If the job was big enough Foley could get cover right to the top. He's a member – a senior partner – in the Continental International Detective Agency in New York, so I'm told...'

'For argument's sake,' Newman suggested, 'let's suppose for a moment that is true. What then?'

'It does nothing to ease my anxiety. Foley is a skilled and highly-trained killer. That poses two questions. Who has the money to pay a man like that?'

'The Americans...'

'Or the Swiss,' Beck said quietly.

'What are you hinting at?'

Beck glanced at Newman and said nothing. He took out of his jacket pocket a short pipe with a thick stem and a large bowl. Newman recognized the pipe and watched as the police chief extracted tobacco from a packet labelled *Amphora*. He began packing tobacco into the bowl.

'Still wedded to the same old pipe,' Newman remarked.

'You are very observant, my friend. It's made by Cogolet, a firm near St Tropez. And the tobacco is the same – *red* Amphora. The second question Foley's presence poses is *Who is the target?* Identify his paymaster and that may point to who he has come to kill...'

144

'You're convinced that is why he is really here?'

'It is his trade,' Beck observed. 'Why have you come to Berne?'

So typical of Beck. To throw the loaded question just when you least expected it. He had his pipe alight and sat puffing at it while he watched Newman with a quizzical expression. The Englishman, who knew Beck well, realized the Swiss was in a mood he had never seen him display before. A state of fearful indecision.

'I'm here with my fiancée, Nancy Kennedy, who wanted to visit her grandfather.' Newman paused, staring straight at Beck behind the blue haze of smoke. 'He's in the Berne Clinic.'

'Ah! The Berne Clinic!' Beck sat up erect in his chair. His eyes became animated and Newman sensed a release of tension in the Swiss. 'Now everything begins to come together. You are the ally I have been seeking...'

Beck had poured more coffee, had freshened up their glasses of cognac. All traces of irresolution had vanished: he was the old, energetic, determined Beck Newman remembered from his last visit to Berne.

'I noticed something strange when we were at the Clinic this afternoon,' Newman said. 'Is that place by any chance guarded by Swiss troops?'

The atmosphere inside the bare, green-walled office illuminated by overhead neon strips changed again. Beck gazed at his cognac, swirling the liquid gently. He took a sip without looking at his guest.

'Why do you say that?' he asked eventually.

'Because I saw a man inside the gatehouse wearing the uniform of a Swiss soldier.'

'You had better address that question to Military Intelligence. You know where to go...'

Beck had withdrawn into his shell again. Newman was aware of a sense of rising frustration. What the hell was wrong with Beck? He allowed his irritation to show.

'If you want my cooperation – you mentioned the word "ally" – I need to know what I'm getting into. And how much freedom to act has the

Chief of Federal Police given you? Refuse to answer that question and I'm walking away from the whole damned business.'

'Plenipotentiary power,' Beck replied promptly. 'Incorporated in a signed directive in that locked cabinet.'

'Then what are you worrying about?'

'The Gold Club...'

Newman drank the rest of his cognac slowly to hide the shock Beck had given him. He placed the empty glass carefully back on the desktop and dabbed his lips with a handkerchief.

'You have heard of the Gold Club? Not many have...' commented Beck.

'A group of top bankers headed by the Zurcher Kredit Bank. Its base is in Zurich. The only other group capable of standing up to them are the Basle bankers. Where does the Gold Club fit in with the Berne Clinic?'

'A director on the board of the Zurcher Kredit Bank is Professor Armand Grange who, as you doubtless know, controls the Berne Clinic. He also has a chemical works on the shores of Lake Zurich near Horgen. I am under extreme pressure to drop my investigation of a project code-named *Terminal*...'

'Which is?'

'I have no idea,' Beck admitted. 'But there are rumours – unpleasant rumours which have even reached the ears of certain foreign embassies. Incidentally, a fellow-countryman of yours who is also staying at the Bellevue Palace is making enquiries about Professor Grange. A dangerous pastime – especially as news of his activities has already started circulating. Switzerland is a small country...'

'This fellow-countryman of mine – he has a name?'

'A Mr Mason. He flew in via Zurich. That is where he started his investigation – and that is where news of what he was doing leaked out. Now, as I have told you, he is here in Berne.'

'Anything else I should know?'

'Have you ever heard of a man called Manfred Seidler?'

'No, I haven't,' Newman lied. 'Where does he fit into the picture?'

146

Beck's pipe made bubbling noises. He was a wet smoker. He stirred in his chair restlessly as though bracing himself for a major decision.

'Everything about our conversation is confidential, classified. Now we are coming to the guts of the whole crisis. I have been asked by Military Intelligence to put out a dragnet for Manfred Seidler. They *say* he stole something vital from the chemical works at Horgen. Once I find him I am supposed to hand him over to Military Intelligence. Immediately! No questioning.'

'You don't like it?'

'I am *not* going to put up with it. I shall grill Seidler when we find him until I find out what is going on. There is a split between two power blocs on military policy. One group, the Gold Club, believe we should adopt more extreme measures to protect the country against the menace from the East. They even suggest we should organize guerrilla forces – that teams specially trained in sabotage should be positioned *outside* our borders. Specifically in Bavaria. That is a complete reversal of our policy of neutrality.'

'Beck, I'm not following this. Why should a group of bankers concern themselves with military strategy?'

'Because, my friend, a number of those bank directors are also officers in the Swiss Army. Not regulars. Captains, colonels. They carry a lot of clout inside the Army where the policy dispute is raging. The Gold Club, which advocates total ruthlessness, is beginning to get the upper hand. The whole thing scares me stiff. And these are the people who are trying to stop my investigation into the Berne Clinic...'

'You said the killing of Nagy was the second murder. What was the first?'

Beck walked round his desk, unlocked a drawer and brought out a file. He handed it to Newman. The file had been stamped *Classification One* on the cover. Newman opened it and read the heading at the top of the first typed page. *Case of Hannah Stuart, American citizen. Klinik Bern.*

'Who is Hannah Stuart?'

'She was an American patient at the Berne Clinic. She died at the end of last month – as you will see recorded in the file. I have a witness, a farm worker who was cycling home late near the grounds of the Clinic. He states he saw a woman running towards the fence surrounding the grounds, a woman screaming, a woman pursued by dogs...'

'They do have Dobermans prowling the place...'

'I know. That was the night Hannah Stuart died...'

'Haven't you confronted the people at the Clinic with your witness?' Newman asked.

'It would be useless – and would show my hand. The witness has a history of mental instability.' Beck leaned forward and spoke vehemently. 'But he is completely recovered. I personally interviewed him and I am convinced he is telling the truth. He had the sense to come to police headquarters in Berne with his story. Pauli phoned me and I took over the case. That woman was murdered in some way.'

'It says here she died of a heart attack. The death certificate is signed by Dr Waldo Novak...'

'Who is also American. A curious coincidence...'

'What about getting an order for an autopsy?' Newman suggested.

'The body was cremated. And that is where the trouble really started. I had an official from the American Embassy here who complained. Apparently Hannah Stuart was very wealthy – from Philadelphia. Her heirs, a son and his wife, were furious. In her original will she had made the inheritance conditional on her body being buried in Philadelphia...'

Then how the devil was the Clinic able to get away with cremation?'

'Dr Bruno Kobler, the chief administrator, produced a document signed by Hannah Stuart stating she wished to be cremated. You'll find a photocopy at the end of the file. I had the signature checked by hand-writing experts and they say it's genuine.'

'Which blocked you off. Neat, very neat...'

He broke off as someone knocked on the door. Beck called out come in, a small, myopic-looking man wearing thick glasses and a civilian suit entered. He was carrying a cellophane envelope.

'We have obtained some fingerprints,' the man informed Beck. 'All of them the same person. Probably the deceased's – but we shall only know that when the pathologist has released the body.'

'Thank you, Erich...'Beck waited until the man had gone and then handed the envelope to Newman. 'Inside is the envelope – still sealed – which Moser found inside Nagy's coat pocket...'

Newman extracted the crumpled, cheap white envelope and saw it carried a few words. *For M. Robert Newman, Bellevue Palace.* He opened it and inside there was a scrap of paper torn from a pad and a key. In the same semi-literate script as the wording on the envelope were written the words *M. Newman – Bahnhof.* He replaced the contents inside the envelope and slipped it into his wallet.

'It was addressed to you,' Beck said, 'so I gave strict orders it was not to be opened. Don't I get to see it?'

'No. Not until you tell me what you want me to do – and maybe not then.'

'I need someone I can fully trust who has access to the Berne Clinic. I have no reason to go there myself – and I don't want to tip my hand. I have not a shred of evidence – even in the case of Hannah Stuart. Only the gravest suspicions. I need to know exactly what is going on inside that place...'

'I would have thought it was the chemical works at Horgen you needed to investigate. Especially in view of this story about tracing this Seidler...'

'Hannah Stuart died at Thun,' Beck replied sombrely. 'Now, that envelope...'

'I work on my own or not at all. I'll keep the envelope for the moment...'

'I have to warn you you are up against men with unlimited power. One more thing. I have found out that the Gold Club people have secretly allocated the enormous sum of two hundred million Swiss francs for *Terminal.*' He held up a hand. 'Don't ask me how I discovered that fact, but the Americans are not the only ones who go in for what they call creative book-keeping.'

'Who controls that money?' Newman asked.

'Professor Armand Grange. Every franc of it...'

'And Grange is also a part-time member of the Swiss Army – another of those officers you mentioned?'

'At one time, yes. Not any more. You must take great care, Bob. I know you are a lone wolf, but on this one you may need help.'

'Is there anyone powerful enough, any *individual*, who can stand up to Grange and his fellow-bankers?'

'Only one man I know of. Dr Max Nagel, the Basle banker. He is also on the board of the Bank for International Settlements, so he has world-wide connections. Nagel is the main opponent of the Gold Club...'

'This Manfred Seidler – you are really looking for him?'

'I am trying to find him before the counter-espionage lot get to him. All the cantonal police forces have been alerted. I think that man could be in great danger...'

'From counter-espionage?' There was incredulity in Newman's tone. 'You really mean that?'

'I didn't say exactly that aloud...'

'And this Englishman, Mason, who is checking on Grange. Where does he come in?'

'Frankly I have no idea who he is working for. I am not sure yet *who* is working for *who*. But I also believe Mason could be at risk. Remember, we have lost track of Lee Foley, and he is a killer. Never forget, you are walking in a minefield...'

It was nine o'clock at night when Newman reached the luggage locker section at the Bahnhof. He had walked through the silent city from the Taubenhalde, doubling back through the network of arcades until he was certain no one was following him. As he had guessed, the key from Nagy's envelope fitted the numbered locker which corresponded to the number engraved on the key.

Unlocking the compartment, he stooped to see what was inside. Another envelope. Again addressed to himself at the Bellevue Palace in the scrawly hand-writing which was becoming familiar. Pocketing the envelope, he walked to the station self-service buffet. He was thirsty and famished.

He chose a corner table in the large eating place and sat with his back to the wall. As he devoured two rolls and swallowed coffee, he watched the passengers who came in through the entrance. No one took any notice of him. He took out the envelope and opened it.

M. Newman. I don't know I can last much longer. The first two photos I took outside the Bahnhof. Chief Inspector Tripet (Geneva) told me follow you. That was when I came off the Zurich train. I was beat up inside a lavatory on the train. The thug gave me money and told me follow you. The phone number on the bit of paper you took off me in the alley is the number I had to call to tell them what you was doing. The car number was a Mercedes waiting outside the Bahnhof. The man I think is the thug's boss got into the car. That's the first two photos. The third photo is the same man who got into the Mercedes. I saw him back here in Berne just before dark. Don't know the man he's talking to. I saw the first man by chance near the Bellevue Palace. Which is why I took the photo. These are very tough people M. Newman.

He felt slightly sick. He had a vivid memory flash of Julius Nagy being pinned against the wooden door by Foley's walking stick. The reaction was swiftly replaced by an emotion of cold fury. He sat working out what must have been the sequence of events after Nagy had walked away down the *Finstergasschen*.

The little man must have caught a tram – maybe even splashed out on a cab fare – to the Bahnhof. Quite possibly he had scribbled his message – Newman had had difficulty deciphering some of the words – in this very buffet. He must have then hurried to the luggage lockers, slipped the envelope inside, put the key into the second envelope with the shorter note also scribbled in the buffet – or wherever – and shoved it inside his coat pocket. The mystery was why Nagy had then hurried back to the Munstergasse.

Newman calculated the little man could have carried out these actions by 6.30 p.m. if he had hustled. By the time he arrived back at the Munstergasse someone had been waiting for him. Who lived in that district? The only person he could think of was Blanche Signer – which reminded him it might be worthwhile calling her.

He was inside one of the station phone booths when it occurred to him maybe he should first call Nancy. He dialled the Bellevue Palace with a certain reluctance. He had to wait several minutes before they located her. It was not a pleasant conversation.

'It's a bloody good job I didn't wait for you for dinner,' she greeted him. 'Where are you, for Christ's sake?'

'In a phone booth...'

'I suppose you expect me to believe that...'

'Nancy...' His tone changed. '...I came to Berne to help you find out what was happening to Jesse. The whole evening has been spent with that very objective. I have not enjoyed it overmuch.'

'Well, that makes two of us. I waited so long for dinner I was beyond enjoying it when I eventually decided I'd better eat something. May I expect to see you sometime tonight? Or will your investigations keep you out till morning?'

'Expect me when you see me...'

He put down the phone and dialled Blanche's number. She answered almost at once. When she heard his voice she sounded excited.

'Bob! I'm so glad you phoned – I've got those photos for you. My friend stayed late to develop and print them. Considering the poor light they've come out very well. All three of them. Are you coming over?'

'I'll be there in ten minutes...'

On his second visit to the apartment in the Junkerngasse she showed him straight into the sitting room, a small, comfortably-furnished place lit only by table lamps. On a low table by a large sofa two glasses stood on place mats.

Blanche was dressed in a pleated skirt and a black cashmere sweater which showed her figure without making her look tarty. It had a cowl neck, which she knew he liked. Her long mane of titian hair glistened in the half-light.

'I may have traced Manfred Seidler,' she announced, 'but more of that later. Have you eaten? I'll get the Montrachet from the fridge.'

'No food, thank you. I can't stay long...'

She vanished into the kitchen. Newman wandered over to look at a silver-framed photograph of a serious-faced officer in Swiss Army uniform. He was staring at it when she returned and filled their glasses from an opened bottle.

'Your stepfather?'

'Yes. I hardly ever see him. We're simply not on the same waveband. Cheers!'

She sat alongside him on the sofa, crossing her long shapely legs encased in sheer black nylon. Clasped under one arm was a large, cardboard-backed envelope she tucked between herself and a cushion. Newman reflected that this was only the second time in the whole ferocious day he had felt relaxed. On the first occasion they had been in another room in this same apartment.

'Manfred Seidler may be in Basle,' she said, putting down her glass on the table. 'I've been on the phone almost the whole time since you left – except for rushing out to get the photos. I'd almost given up when I phoned a girlfriend in Basle who is in banking. There's a girl called Erika Stahel who works in the same bank. Erika has let drop occasional rueful hints that she only sees her boyfriend, Manfred, when he's in town, which isn't often. This Manfred moves about a lot...'

'Manfred is a fairly common name...'

'He's quite a bit older than Erika. Recently he brought her back a present from Vienna. An owl in silver crystal. That's how my girlfriend heard of the trip. She showed the owl to her friend she was so pleased with it. Erika has a very good job,' Blanche remarked.

'What's a good job?'

'Personal assistant to Dr Max Nagel. He's chairman of the bank.'

Newman had trouble holding his glass steady. He hastily had another drink. Blanche was watching him. She tucked her legs underneath herself like a contented cat. Reaching for the envelope, she spoke again.

'It's probably the wrong Manfred. But apparently Erika is very careful

153

not to mention his second name. Mind you, that could simply mean he's married. That could be the reason this Erika is so mysterious about his background and his job. I've got Erika Stahel's phone number if you want it.'

'How did you get that?'

'I asked my friend to look it up in the directory while we were talking, of course. Here it is on this piece of paper, plus her address. She has an apartment near the Munsterplatz. I must have phoned thirty people before I came across anyone who knew someone with the name Manfred. Want to see the pics?'

'Blanche, you have done so well. I'm very grateful. God, you move...'

'You have to if you're operating a tracing service. People like quick results. They recommend you to other clients – which is the way to build up any business. The pics...'

Newman looked at the first glossy print. The rear of a Mercedes, the registration number clearly visible. The number of the car which had almost driven them under the blade of the snowplough on the motorway. Poor little Nagy might yet pay back his killers from the grave. He kept his face expressionless as he looked at the second print. Bruno Kobler. No doubt about it.

'These prints are invaluable,' he told her.

'Service with a smile – of all kinds,' she said mischievously. 'The third one any good?'

Newman felt as though he had just been hit in the solar plexus. He gazed at the last print with a funny feeling at the pit of his stomach. He recognized the building in the background. Bruno Kobler had again proved very photogenic. It was the man he was talking to who shook Newman and made his brain spin, made him start looking at everything from a new, brutally disturbing angle. The man was Arthur Beck.

Sixteen

Newman met – collided with – 'Tommy' Mason when he entered the bar at the Bellevue Palace on his way back from Blanche. It was precisely 10 p.m. Mason turned away from the bar holding a tumbler of whisky which he spilt down Newman's jacket. Newman grinned and shrugged.

'I say, I'm frightfully sorry. Waiter, a damp cloth. Quick!'

'I wouldn't lose any sleep over it...'

'Jolly careless of me. Look, the least I can do is buy you a drink. Double Scotch – or whatever...'

'You called it...'

Newman took his glass and led the way to the same corner table where he had talked with Blanche. The place was crowded. He sat with his back to the wall, raised his glass and drank as his companion eased his way on to the banquette.

'Captain Tommy Mason,' he introduced himself. The "Tommy" is purely honorary. They tacked it on when I was in the Army and the damn name stuck...'

'Bob Newman. No honorary titles...'

'I say, not the Robert Newman? The Kruger case and all that? I thought I recognized you. I'm market research. I've nearly completed my present assignment.' Mason, smiled. 'Really I'm not hurrying the job – I like this place. Marvellous hotel.'

Newman nodded agreement while he studied Mason. A military type. Early thirties. Trim moustache. Held his slim build erect. Shrewd eyes which didn't go with his general air of a man who would rise to captain and then that would be his ceiling. Mason continued chattering.

'They're all talking about some poor sod who took a dive from that square by the Castle – no, Cathedral – earlier this evening. Ended up like mashed potato on top of a car, I gather...'

'Who says he took a dive?'

Mason lowered his voice. 'You mean the old saw – did he fall or was he. pushed?'

'Something like that...'

'Well, that's a turn-up for the book. I was trotting round that square earlier today myself. Peered over the wall and nearly had a fit. Like a bloody precipice. In Berne too, of all places...'

'Berne is getting as dangerous as Beirut,' Newman remarked and drank the rest of his whisky. 'Thanks. It tastes better going down the gullet...'

'Berne you said was getting dangerous? Watch your back and all that? Don't walk down dark alleys at night. Place is full of dark alleys.'

'Something like that. A research trip, you said?' Newman probed.

'Yes. Medical. Standards of and practice in their private clinics. They rate high, the Swiss do. Their security is pretty formidable too. Here on a story?'

'Holiday. I think I'd better go. My fiancée will be going up the wall. I've been out all evening...'

'Nice of you to join me in a drink – especially considering the first one I gave you. But don't let me keep you. May see you at breakfast. Avoid the dark alleys...'

As Newman threaded his way among the packed tables Mason sat quite still, watching the Englishman until he had vanished out of the bar. Then he stood up and strolled out, his eyes flickering over the other drinkers.

'Who is this stranger I see?' Nancy enquired when Newman came into the bedroom. She raised a hand as though to shield her eyes. The gesture irritated Newman intensely. He took off his jacket and threw it on the bed along with the folded coat he had carried over his arm.

'You should keep the bedroom door locked,' he told her.

'Criticism the moment he does eventually decide to come back.'

'Look, Nancy, this is a busy hotel. If I wanted to get at you I wouldn't use the main entrance – the concierge might see me. I'd come in by the coffee shop entrance and up those stairs from the basement. The lift is then waiting for me. I'm simply thinking of your safety...'

'Have a good evening? Your jacket stinks of alcohol. Did she spill her drink in her excitement?'

'A man in the bar bumped into me. He bought me a drink to say sorry. So, before you comment on it, I also have alcohol on my breath. I've had a swine of an evening...'

'Dear me,' she said sarcastically, 'was it very rough?'

'A man who was following me earlier, a man I've used in the past for the same purpose, a nice little man, ended up spread like a goulash over the top of a car. He went over the wall behind the Munster. He was probably pushed. That sheer drop must be a hundred and fifty feet...'

'God, I've just had a very large dinner. You do have a way of putting things...'

'A large dinner. Lucky you. I've got by on a couple of bread rolls...'

'Room Service...!'

They both said it at the same time. Newman couldn't help recalling how Blanche had asked whether he had eaten. He undid his tie and loosened his collar, made no attempt to phone down for a meal. He was beyond it. She didn't press him.

'Who was killed tonight then?' she asked.

'The little man you said you didn't see passing the window of the Pavillon in Geneva when we were having breakfast...'

'Oh, I remember.' She was losing interest. 'Flotsam, you called him. One of life's losers...'

'Sympathetically I said it. You know, you should hail from New York. They divide the world there into winners and losers. He was a refugee who fled from Hungary in fifty-six. He made his living any way he could. He deserved a better epitaph.'

'I had company at dinner,' she told him, changing the subject. 'Another Englishman. Beautiful manners. I think he had been in the Army. We got on very well together...'

'Some crusty old colonel of about eighty?' he asked with deliberate indifference.

157

'No! He's very good-looking. About thirty. Very neat and with a moustache. Talks with a plum in his mouth. I found him very amusing. What time do we meet Dr Novak on Thursday?'

'*We* don't. I go alone. He won't open up in the same way if you're present. And Thun is getting a dangerous place to visit. Or have you forgotten what nearly happened to us on the motorway?'

'No, I haven't!' she burst out. 'Which is why I think you might have made more of an effort to get back earlier – to have dinner with me. I needed company. Well,' she ended savagely, 'I got company...'

The phone started ringing. Newman glanced at Nancy who shrugged her shoulders. He suddenly realized she was wearing a dress he hadn't seen before. Another black mark, he supposed. No comment. The bell went on ringing and ringing. He picked up the receiver.

'A M. Manfred Seidler to speak to you,' the operator informed him.

'Newman, we must meet tomorrow night. I will phone details for the rendezvous late tomorrow afternoon...'

Truculent. Hectoring. Was there also a hint of desperation in Seidler's tone? Newman cradled the phone on his shoulder while he lit a cigarette.

'Newman? Are you still there?'

'Yes. I'm still here,' Newman replied quietly. 'Tomorrow is out of the question...'

'Then we do not meet at all! You hear me? Other people will pay a fortune for the information I have...'

'Sell it to the other people then...'

'Newman, people are *dying*. I told you that before. Don't you even care?'

'Now you listen to me, Seidler. I can probably meet you three days from now. That's my best offer. And I need to know in advance the rendezvous...'

'You have a car?'

'I could get hold of one.' Never give out even the smallest item of information to someone who is a completely unknown quantity. 'And if you don't come to the point I'm going to put down the phone...'

'Don't do that. Please! For God's sake! Newman, I will call you again tomorrow at five o'clock. No, not tomorrow. Five o'clock on the day we meet. You must have a car. And, believe me, it is too dangerous over an open line to give you details of the rendezvous. Dangerous to you – as well as to me...'

'Five o'clock the day we meet. Good night...'

Newman replaced the phone before his caller could say one word more. He lit a cigarette and sat down on the edge of the bed, smiling at Nancy who sat watching him intently.

'You were pretty tough with him,' she said.

'In a two-way pull situation like that one participant comes out on top – dominates the other. When we do meet I'll get a lot more out of him if he's at the end of his tether. I think he's pretty near that point now. For some reason I'm his last hope. I want to keep it that way.'

'And the day after tomorrow you see Dr Novak in Thun?'

'Yes. I'm banking a lot on that meeting. I suspect we may have a similar case with Novak to the Seidler situation. Both men living on their nerves, scared witless about something. I just wonder if it's the same thing...'

'Bob, there's something I didn't tell you. But first you've got to eat. An omelette? Very digestible. Followed by fruit?'

He nodded and sat smoking while she called Room Service. The atmosphere between them had changed, had turned some kind of corner. They'd needed that phone interruption to quench their irritation with each other. Seidler had done them a favour. He waited patiently until she'd given the food order, asking also for a bottle of dry white wine and plenty of coffee. She then sat on the bed beside him.

'Bob, what do we do next? I don't know.'

For Nancy Kennedy it was a remarkable comment. She sounded bewildered, as though it was all happening too fast and she couldn't take it in. He put it down to her American background. Europe functioned differently, was infinitely complex.

'First, as I said, I see Novak. Find out what is really happening inside the Berne Clinic. That's why we are here. I'll have to find some way of putting the pressure on him, break him down. That's Item One. Next, the following day, we meet Seidler, find out what he knows. I have a feeling it's all beginning to come together. Fast. What was it you'd omitted to tell me?'

'When I was talking to Jesse at the Clinic while you occupied Novak's attention he told me they were conducting some kind of experiments...'

'*Experiments?* You're certain he used that word?'

'Quite certain. He didn't elaborate. I think he was worried Novak would hear us talking...' There was a knock on the outer door. 'I think this is your food. Eat, drink and then bed...'

Half an hour later they had undressed, turned out the lights and Newman knew from Nancy's shallow breathing that she was fast asleep. Exhausted by the day's events. He lay awake for a long time, trying to see a pattern to what he had learned.

The weird business of the rapid incidents which Beck couldn't understand. The theft of an Army mortar. The theft of one Army rifle plus twenty-four rounds of ammo. The snowplough incident he had good reason to understand, Newman thought grimly.

Then the murder – it had been murder, he was convinced – of Julius Nagy. The disappearance of Lee Foley. And Blanche had told him Foley had been in the vicinity of the Berne Clinic at the time of his visit with Nancy. So everything – excluding the Nagy killing – was happening in the Thun district.

The Gold Club business which seemed to bother Beck so much. And Seidler's reference in his Geneva phone call to bringing in a consignment across an eastern border. A consignment of what? Across which border? Newman felt certain that if only he could arrange these different factors in the right sequence a pattern would emerge.

He fell asleep with a disturbing thought. The photo showing Bruno Kobler, administrator of the Berne Clinic – again Thun – in conversation in front of the Taubenhalde with – Arthur Beck.

Seventeen

Wednesday, 15 February. Lee Foley had been sitting in the cinema for an hour when he checked his watch. He had spent most of the day inside different cinemas – there are over half-a-dozen in Berne. It had been a more restful activity compared with the previous day's-expedition to spy out the lie of the land round the Berne Clinic.

He had used this technique before when he went under cover, when an operation reached the stage of a loaded pause. After leaving the Savoy Hotel, he had parked the Porsche at different zones. He bought food he could take away and eat while he sat inside a cinema. He slept while inside a cinema. He emerged into the outside world well after dark.

Leaving the cinema, he took a roundabout route to where the car was parked. Satisfied that no one was following him, he headed straight for the Porsche. He approached the car with caution to be certain no one was watching it. He strolled past it along the deserted arcade, then swung on his heel, the ignition key in his hand. In less than thirty seconds he was behind the wheel, had started the engine and was driving away.

Tommy Mason had finished writing his report for Tweed which included details of his brief trips to Zurich by train. He was stiff from sitting in one position in his bedroom for so long and he wanted to think. Mason thought best while he was walking and wanted to ease the stiffness out of his limbs before he went to bed.

He walked out of the main entrance to the Bellevue Palace. At that time of night the huge hall and the reception area beyond – the area which within days would be used for the Medical Congress reception – were empty. The night concierge looked up from behind his counter, nodded to Mason and went back to checking his schedule for early morning calls.

Mason, protected against the freezing cold of the night with his British warm, woollen scarf and a slouch hat, made his way down to the river. He had taken the same walk the night before. It crossed his mind he was breaking a cardinal rule. Never keep to a routine. Vary your habits – daily. Worse still, he had left the Bellevue about the same time the night before. He had become so absorbed by his report he had not realized what he was doing.

Still, it was only the second night. He damned well had to get some exercise or he wouldn't sleep. His mind was active. Mason guessed that he was close to promotion. The fact that Tweed had pulled him out of Vienna and stationed him temporarily in Berne indicated that.

The wind caught him as he reached the Aarstrasse. He stepped it out, heading for the Dalmazibrücke, a much lower bridge than the Kirchenfeldbrücke he would eventually use to cross back over the river to reach the Bellevue.

Absorbed as he was by his thoughts – the report for Tweed, his coming promotion – Mason continued to look round for any sign of life. No traffic. No other pedestrians. To his left, in the dark his eyes were now accustomed to, the ancient escarpment on which Berne is built rose sheer in the night. He continued walking.

He reached the Dalmazi bridge, and still the whole city seemed to have gone to bed. The Swiss started their day early so they were rarely up late. Below him the dark, swollen flow of the water headed for the curious canal-like stretch below the Munster. At this point the Aare empties itself through a number of sluices to a lower level before continuing its curve round the medieval capital. He heard the car driving slowly behind him. It stopped. He turned round.

At the same moment the driver switched his headlights on full power. Mason was temporarily blinded. Bloody nincompoop. The headlights dipped and the car remained stationary. A courting couple, Mason guessed, oblivious to the cold of the night inside their heated love nest. The driver had probably intended to turn them off and had operated the switch the wrong way, his mind on more enticing prospects.

He was in the middle of the bridge when he resumed his walk. The lead-weighted walking stick – the most innocuous of weapons – struck him with tremendous force on the back of his skull. He was sagging to the pavement when powerful arms grasped him, hoisted him and in one swift, final movement propelled him over the rail of the bridge.

Unconscious, Mason hit the ice-cold water with a dull splash. Less than half a minute later a car's engine fired at the entrance to the bridge and was driven away. In that half-minute Mason's body had been carried close to the Kirchenfeldbrücke. Passing under the high, vaulted arch supporting the bridge, the body was suddenly swept to the right as the flow of the Aare increased in power and speed.

Caught up in a frothing whirlpool, Mason's skull hammered with brutal force against the sluice where it lay trapped. Time and again the river hurled the body into the sluice with the action of a sledgehammer. The slouch hat had gone its own way, bobbing along the surface until it, too, was swept sideways through a more distant sluice. It passed through effortlessly, soggy now with water. Somewhere before the next bend in the Aare it sank out of sight. Bernard 'Tommy' Mason would never see his cherished promotion.

Gisela, assistant to Arthur Beck, looked up from her desk as her chief came into the office, took off his overcoat and hung it by the loop. He sat down behind his own desk, unlocked a drawer and took out the file on Julius Nagy.

'It's terribly late,' Gisela chided. 'I thought you'd gone home. Where have you been?'

'Walking the arcades, trying to make some sort of sense out of this apparently disconnected series of events. One stolen mortar, one stolen rifle with its ammunition, the disappearance of Lee Foley. No news about him yet, I suppose?'

'None at all. Would you like some coffee?'

'That would be nice. Then, talking about going home, you push off to your apartment. As you said, it's very late...'

When she had left the room Beck pushed the file away. Sitting gazing blankly into the distance, he began drumming, the fingers of his right hand on the desk.

Behind the wheel of the Porsche Lee Foley was careful to keep inside the speed limit as he drove along N6, even though the motorway from Berne to Thun was deserted. He had divested himself of his English outfit and now wore jeans and a windcheater. Pulled well down over his thick thatch of white hair he wore a peaked sailor-style cap of the type favoured by Germans.

He would spend the night at a small *gasthof* outside Thun. By the time the registration form reached the local police in the morning – or maybe even twenty-four hours later as he would be registering so late – he planned to be away from Thun.

When he got up in the morning he would use a public booth to make the agreed phone call at the agreed hour. This, Foley was convinced, could be the first decisive day. And very shortly he would surface, come out into the open again. It was all a question of getting the timing right. Foley was very good at sensing timing: he had established the right contacts.

He drove on, his profile like that of a man carved in stone. Taken all round, it had been a strange day. He dismissed it from his mind. Always tomorrow – the next move – was what counted.

In Basle it was well past midnight as Seidler paced back and forth across the sitting room. On a sofa Erika Stahel stifled a yawn. She made one more effort.

'Manfred, let's go to bed. I have been working all day...'

'That bastard Newman!' Seidler burst out. 'He's playing me like a fish. People don't do that to me. If he knew what I've got in that suitcase he'd have seen me when I first called him in Geneva...'

'That *locked* suitcase. Why won't you let me see what you have got inside it?'

164

'It's a sample, a specimen...'

'A sample of what?'

'Something horrific. Best you don't know about it. And it's the key to *Terminal*. It's worth a fortune,' he ranted on, 'and I'll end up giving it to Newman for a pittance, if I'm not dead before then. A pittance,' he repeated, 'just to gain his protection...'

'I've banked a fortune for you in that safety deposit,' she reminded him. 'Surely you don't need any more. And when you talk about it being horrific you frighten me. What have you got yourself involved in?'

'It will soon be over. Newman said he'd meet me. The rendezvous will have to be a remote spot. I think I know just the place...'

Erika realized he could go on like this for hours. He was nervy, strung up, maybe even close to a breakdown. She stood up, walked into the kitchen and came back with a glass of water and a bottle of tablets.

'A sleeping tablet for you tonight. You'll need to be fresh for your meeting, all your wits about you. We're going to bed now. To *sleep*...'

Ten minutes later Seidler was sprawled beside her in a deep sleep. It was Erika who stared at the ceiling where the neon advertising sign perched on the building opposite flashed on and off despite the drawn curtains. *Horrific.* Dear God – what could the suitcase contain?

The same atmosphere of restlessness, of moody irritability which infected Basle was also apparent all day in Berne. Gisela had noticed it in her chief, Arthur Beck, and both Newman and Nancy had found the day a trial. They had felt lethargic and everything seemed such an effort they passed the whole day trying not to get on each other's nerves. Before going to bed, Newman went out for a long walk by himself.

Returning, he tapped on their bedroom door and heard Nancy unlock it. She was wearing her bathrobe. The second thing Newman noticed as he walked into the bedroom and threw his coat on the bed was a fresh pot of coffee, two cups and a jug of cream on a tray.

'I've had a bath,' Nancy said as she lit a cigarette. 'Did you enjoy your walk? You've been out ages...'

'Not especially. Enjoy your bath?'

'Not especially. Trying to bathe myself was one hell of an effort. Like paddling through treacle. What's wrong with us?'

'Two things. The concierge explained one cause – the *fohn* wind is blowing. You get edgy and tired. Yes, I know – you don't feel any sense of a wind but it drives people round the bend. And the suicide rate goes up...'

'Charming. And the other thing?'

'I sense this whole business about the Berne Clinic is moving towards a climax. That's what is getting to us...'

The unmarked police car with the two plain clothes Federal policemen drove slowly along the Aarstrasse towards the lofty span of the Kirchenfeld bridge. The river was on the far side of the road to their left. Leupin sat behind the wheel with his partner, Marbot, alongside him. They were the two men Beck had earlier in the week sent to the Bahnhof to watch for Lee Foley. It was Marbot who saw the sluice.

In the middle of the night it was freezingly cold. Because they had the heater on full blast the windscreen kept misting up with condensation. Leupin cleared it with the windscreen wipers while Marbot lowered the side window at intervals to give him a clear view.

'Slow down, Jean,' Marbot said suddenly. 'There's something odd over there by that sluice...'

'I can't see anything,' Leupin replied but he stopped the car.

'Give me the night-glasses a sec...'

Shivering, rubbing his hands as the night air flooded in through the open window, Leupin waited patiently. Marbot lowered the binoculars and turned to look at his companion.

'I think we'd better drive over there – where we can get on to the walkway to the sluices...'

As the car was driven away to cross the Aare, Mason's battered, waterlogged body continued to be churned against the sluice, a sodden wreck of a man with the head lacerated in a score of places.

Eighteen

Thursday, 16 February. The headquarters of Army Intelligence in Berne is located in the large square stone building next to the Bellevue Palace if you turn left on emerging from the hotel. This is Bundeshaus Ost.

Newman entered the large reception hall beyond glass doors, walked up to the receptionist and placed his passport on the counter. His manner was brisk, confident and he spoke while his passport was being examined.

'Please inform Captain Lachenal I have arrived. He knows me well. I am also rather short of time...'

'You are expected, M. Newman. The attendant will escort you to Captain Lachenal's office...'

Newman gave no indication of his astonishment. He followed the attendant up a large marble staircase. He was escorted to Lachenal's old office on the second floor, an office at the rear of the building with windows overlooking the Aare and the Bantiger rising beyond on the far bank of the river.

'Welcome to Berne again, Bob. You come at an interesting time – which no doubt is why you are here...'

Lachenal, thirty-five years old, tall and thin-faced with thick black hair brushed over the top of his head, exposing an impressive forehead, came round his desk to shake hands. The Swiss was an intellectual and in some ways – with his long nose, his commanding bearing, his considerable height and his aloof manner – he reminded Newman of de Gaulle. He was one of the world's greatest authorities on the Soviet Red Army.

'You expected me,' Newman remarked. 'Why, René?'

'The same old Bob – always straight to the point. Sit down and I will help you as far as I can. As to expecting you, we knew you had arrived in Berne, that you are staying at the Bellevue Palace. What could be more natural than to expect a visit from you? Does that answer your question?'

'No. I have come here with my fiancée whose grandfather is a patient in the Berne Clinic. Why should that involve a visit to you?'

'Ah! The Berne Clinic...'

Seated in a chair facing the Swiss, Newman studied his friend. Dressed in mufti, he wore a smart, blue, pin-striped business suit, a blue-striped shirt and a plain blue tie. Newman shifted his gaze to the uniform hanging on a side wall. The jacket carried three yellow bars on shoulder epaulettes, bars repeated round the peaked cap – indicating Lachenal's rank of captain.

But what interested Newman were the trousers. Down each side was a broad black strip. Lachenal was more than a captain – he was now an officer on the General Staff. The Swiss followed his gaze.

'Yes, a little promotion since last we met...'

'And you report to?'

'Again the direct question! To the chief of UNA which, as you know, is the Sub-Department Information chief and a certain two-star general, I have direct access to him at all times...'

'So you are working on a special project?'

'You will not expect me to reveal information which is not only confidential but also classified,' Lachenal replied drily.

'Why have I come at an interesting time?'

'Oh, that is simple...' Lachenal spread his long, slim-fingered hands. 'Certain military manoeuvres are taking place.'

'Military manoeuvres are always taking place,' Newman countered. 'And why did you perk up when I mentioned the Berne Clinic? Incidentally, is that place being guarded by Swiss troops?'

Lachenal shook his head, more in sorrow than anger. 'Now you know I can neither confirm nor deny what establishments in this country come under military protection. Bob, what a question!'

'It's a damned good question,' Newman persisted aggressively. 'I actually spotted a man wearing Swiss Army uniform *inside* the place...'

He watched Lachenal's dark, steady eyes for any sign of anxiety. You might just as well hope for de Gaulle himself to reveal his real feelings. There was only one tiny out of character reaction. Lachenal took a king-size cigarette from a pack on the desk and lit it, then remembered his manners.

'Sorry.' He offered the pack and lit Newman's cigarette. 'Can I talk about something for a few minutes?' he began, sitting very erect in his chair. 'As you know, we are preparing for military conflict. All able-bodied men serve specific periods annually in the forces until they are forty-five. When the war will come from the East we shall be ready to defend ourselves. What we are worried about is the enemy's massive use of helicopters. Still, that problem may soon be solved. At this very moment we are testing certain missiles in the Bernina Pass area – because in that zone we have deep snow and it is very cold. War in low temperatures, Bob...'

Newman was puzzled. At first he had thought Lachenal was skilfully guiding the conversation away from the subject of the Berne Clinic. Now he sensed the General Staff officer was telling him something quite different, something he wished to get across by subtle means.

'I do know the general attitude of the Swiss,' Newman remarked. 'I wish to God our War Office would send a team here so it could study your techniques for use in Britain...'

'Please!' Lachenal held up a slim hand. 'Let me continue so you get the complete picture. Then ask questions.' He puffed at his cigarette and continued. 'What I am about to tell you is highly confidential – on no account to be reported. You see, we have two competing military philosophies, two schools of thought, if you like. One is held by the majority – at the moment – of the regular Swiss Army. They believe we should continue to stick to orthodox strategy. But there is a second school, mostly made up of officers who spend most of the year working at their civilian jobs. Like the regulars they also subscribe to the theory of defence *tous azimuts*...'

They were conversing in French. Lachenal had an excellent command of English but when he was absorbed in what he was saying he

169

preferred to use his own language. Newman was familiar with the phrase *tous azimuts*. It expressed all-round defence – fighting to hold back the enemy on every Swiss frontier regardless of geography.

Lachenal had paused to stub out his cigarette and light a fresh one. Newman had the impression the pause was really intended to emphasize the phrase just used – as though in some way this was the key to the conversation.

'But,' Lachenal went on, 'unlike the regulars this faction, which is very influential, takes an even more ruthless view. After all, we are a small nation – but we are determined to do everything in our power to protect the few millions who make up our population. The civilian school takes *tous azimuts* very seriously. That is why I said you come at a very interesting time.'

'The civilian officers...' Newman threw the question at him. '...they are controlled largely by bankers?'

Lachenal froze. Outwardly his expression hadn't changed – it was the sudden total lack of expression. He leaned back in his chair, speaking with the cigarette in the corner of his mouth.

'What makes you say that?'

'I also have my sources. Inside and *outside* Switzerland.'

Newman emphasized the word to throw Lachenal off the track. It might be important to protect Arthur Beck. Something very strange was happening inside Switzerland.

'I can't imagine why you say that,' Lachenal commented eventually.

'It's obvious,' Newman rapped back quickly. 'You referred to the civilian group being very influential – your own words. Influence suggests power, power suggests money, money suggests bankers.'

'Theories are abstract, abstractions are misleading,' Lachenal said brusquely.

Newman stood up to leave and slipped on his coat. He chose the moment deliberately. Lachenal was a brave, very able man but he was also sensitive. He had just spoken almost rudely and Newman knew he would regret it. Lachenal followed his visitor as the latter put his hand on the door-handle.

'You must realize, Bob, that none of us really believe you are here on holiday. You have to be working on a story...'

'I am here with my fiancée for the reason I gave,' Newman said coldly. 'Check up on me, if you wish to...'

'Instead of that, let us have dinner together one evening. I am truly glad to see you again. But you must admit that your reason for being here would make an excellent cover story...'

Newman paused in the act of turning the handle, looking back at Lachenal. The Swiss was one of the shrewdest, most intuitive men he knew. He took the hand Lachenal had extended and shook it.

'I accept your invitation with pleasure. René, take care of yourself...'

Tous azimuts. That had been the key phrase, Newman felt sure as he descended the marble steps and walked out of Bundeshaus Ost. And Lachenal was genuinely deeply worried about something. Newman had the strongest hunch that if he knew what that worry concerned it might unlock the whole strange business.

Nancy came running towards him as he pushed his way through the revolving doors inside the Bellevue Palace. She had been sitting where she could watch the entrance. Looping an arm through his, she guided him quickly to an obscure corner table.

'Now we have the Swiss Army on our backs,' he told her. 'I don't like the way things are developing...'

'I've got something to tell you, but what are you talking about. Who have you seen?'

'A high-ranking Swiss Army officer, an old friend. We had coffee at that restaurant across the street. Don't ask me his name. I think he was warning me off the Berne Clinic...'

'You said an old friend. If he's that he should know the one way to encourage you to go on is to threaten you...'

'That occurred to me. Curious, isn't it? Now, I can see you're agog to tell me some news...'

'There's been a phone call from a man called Beck. He says will you go and see him at once. He said it was very urgent.'

Nineteen

'Newman, do you know this man?'

Beck was hostile again. His manner was stiff. His voice was flat, toneless. His official voice. Three people stood in the morgue. The room was cold. The floor and walls were tiled. The place had all the comfort and cheerful atmosphere of a public lavatory, a spotless public lavatory.

The third person was Dr Anna Kleist, Federal Police pathologist. A tall, dark-haired woman in her late thirties, she wore a white gown and watched Newman through tinted glasses with interest and a sympathetic expression. He had felt she liked him from the moment they had been introduced.

Newman gazed down at the body lying on the huge metal drawer Dr Kleist had hauled out for his inspection. The sheet covering the corpse had been partly pulled back to expose the head and shoulders. The head was horribly battered but still recognizable – mainly from the sodden moustache. Newman suddenly felt very angry. He turned on Beck.

'Am I the first person you have asked to identify him?'

'Yes...'

'Well, Beck, you had better know I am getting fed up. Why choose me? This is the second time you've dragged me to view the wreck of a corpse...'

'Just answer the question. Do you know this man?'

'He told me his name was Tommy Mason. That he was engaged on market research. Medical. Something to do with clinics-Swiss clinics...'

'You do know this man then? You were using him as a contact?'

'For Christ's sake, Beck, shove it. I was brought here without a hint as to what was waiting for me. I've answered your question. If you want to ask me anything else we'll go straight back to the Taubenhalde...'.

'As you wish...'

Beck turned away to leave the room but Newman lingered. Dr Kleist had considerately closed the drawer. A tag was attached to the handle by a piece of string, a tag bearing a number. Tommy Mason was no longer a person, only a number.

'Dr Kleist,' Newman requested in a normal voice, 'have you any idea how he died – or is it too early?'

'He was found floating...'

'Anna!' Beck broke in. 'No information...'

'And why not, Arthur?' She removed her glasses and Newman saw she had large pale blue eyes with a hint of humour. 'Mr Newman has answered your question. And remember, I am in control here. I intend to answer Mr Newman...'

'You have the independence of the devil,' Beck grumbled.

'Which is why you had me appointed to this position.' She turned her attention to Newman. 'The body was found in the river. His injuries are due in part to the fact that for some time before he was found he was caught in one of the sluices below the Munster.'

'Thank you, Dr Kleist.'

As he left the room Newman hoped she would get married and leave this place before her emotions became as dead as the body she had just shown him.

He said nothing to Beck during the drive back to the Taubenhalde. Inside the building the same routine. The ascent to the tenth floor. Beck producing the key which unlocked the lift. Outside Newman gestured towards a punch-time clock on the wall.

'Do you still clock in and out morning and night? The Assistant to the Chief of Police?'

'Every time. It is the regulation. I am not exempt...'

Beck was still stiff and unbending but once inside the office he did ask Gisela to make them coffee and then please leave them on their own. Newman, his mind still focused on his interview with Captain Lachenal, made a great effort to push that into the past. He needed all his concentration on this new development. Beck stared out of the window, hands clasped behind his back, until Gisela brought the coffee on a tray and left the office.

'I'm sorry, Bob,' he said, walking wearily round his desk and sagging into his chair before attending to the coffee. 'You see, this is the second body you have been directly linked with. First, Julius Nagy...'

'You said that was an anonymous phone call to Pauli...'

'This was an anonymous phone call to Gisela. A man. Someone who spoke in broken German – or pretended to. Last night you were seen with Bernard Mason, or so the caller alleged...'

'*Bernard?*'

'Yes, I noticed you called him Tommy in the morgue. When we fished him out we found he carried his passport in a cellophane folder which protected it to some extent against the water. He is – was – Bernard Mason. How did you come to know him, Bob?'

'In the bar at the Bellevue Palace. I went in for a drink and he turned round with his glass in his hand and bumped into me. The contents of the glass spilt over my jacket and he insisted on buying me one to compensate. We sat talking for maybe five minutes. That's how I know him. It's also how I know the data I gave you on him back at the morgue. He told me. A chance acquaintance...'

'I wonder...'

'And what do you mean by that?'

'Could he have spilt his drink over you deliberately – to contrive this chance acquaintance? Chance always worries me.'

'How could he have contrived anything?' Newman demanded. 'I only decided to pop in there for a drink at the last moment. Any more questions?'

'I'm only doing my job, Bob. And I'm getting a lot of flak from the British Embassy. A chap called Wiley. He's a British citizen and was apparently an influential businessman. First, this Wiley wants to know exactly how he died...'

'How did he die?'

'I think it was murder. I called the Embassy to see if they had any information on him. Wiley asks a lot of questions – then he puts in an urgent request for the minimum of publicity. So who was Mason is what I keep asking myself. And, like it or not, two men have now died in peculiar circumstances – both less than a kilometre from the Bellevue Palace, both who had links, however tenuous, with you...'

Newman emptied his coffee cup and stood up. Beck watched while he slipped on his coat, buttoned it up. The Swiss also stood up.

'You haven't asked me why I think this Mason was murdered.'

'That's your job...'

'He's number two. Julius Nagy ends up at the bottom of the Plattform wall which faces the sluice where Mason was found floating. Mason was thirty-three – I got that from the passport. He ends up in the river. You think he stumbled into the Aare? Two very convenient accidents. Were you outside the Bellevue late last night?'

'Yes, as a matter of fact I was. I went for a walk along the arcades. I couldn't sleep' And no one saw me. May I go now?'

'Gisela, what is it?' Beck asked his assistant who had opened the door to the connecting office where she worked most of the day.

'He's on the phone. Would you like to take it in here?'

Newman waited while Beck disappeared into the next room. *He* would be the Chief of Police, he imagined. Gisela asked if he would like more coffee but he refused and asked her a question, keeping his voice low.

'Mr Beck tells me you took that mysterious call reporting that I knew Mason, the man they dragged out of the river. I gather the caller spoke in broken German?'

'Yes, I had only just arrived. I ran to the phone, expecting it to stop ringing before I got there. The voice sounded muffled – like someone talking through a handkerchief. I had to make him repeat what he said, then he rang off. I've just realized something – I think I detected a trace of an American accent.'

'I should tell your boss that,' Newman suggested. 'Had Beck arrived in the building when the call came through?'

'No. He came in about a quarter of an hour later...'

'Thanks. Don't forget that bit about an American accent. I was leaving – tell Beck I couldn't wait any longer. I'm in a rush...'

Lee Foley was humming Glenn Miller's *In the Mood* as he drove the Porsche back along the motorway towards Berne. He had spent the night in a *gasthof,* had breakfasted in Thun, made the agreed call to Berne, and now he was coming into the open.

Despite his almost infinite capacity for patience, he found it highly stimulating that the time for action had arrived. He had most of the data he needed, the equipment, he thought he knew at long last what was going on. The moment had come to stir things up, to raise a little hell. He pushed his fool down on the accelerator and let the Porsche rip.

'Who was that on the phone?' Newman asked as he came into the bedroom. 'And you left the door unlocked again...'

'A wrong number.' Nancy had replaced the Receiver. She came towards him with an anxious expression. 'Forget about the door – I've been worried sick. What did the police want?'

'Pour some of that coffee. Sit down. And *listen*!'

'Something is wrong,' she said as she handed him his cup and sat down, crossing her legs.

'Everything is wrong,' he told her. 'On no account are you to take the car and visit the Berne Clinic on your own...'

'I'll do so if I want to. And I do want to see Jesse today. You have your date with Dr Novak tonight in Thun. You won't want two trips...'

'Nancy, listen, for God's sake. There's been another killing. At least, that's the theory the police are working on. This time some Englishman – and he was staying at this hotel. They hauled his drowned body out of the river in the middle of the night. A man called Mason. There's something odd about him – the British Embassy is making too much fuss.'

'That's dreadful. But that is a problem for the police...'

'Nancy! We can no longer trust the Swiss police. I have also visited an old friend in Swiss Army Intelligence – counter-espionage – it comes to the same thing. We can no longer trust Army Intelligence. They're both trying to manipulate me. I'm almost certain they're using me as a stalking horse-and that is very dangerous. For you as well as for me.'

'A stalking horse?' She wrinkled her smooth brow. Nancy really did have a superb complexion Newman thought. He had a vivid recall of the state of Tommy Mason's complexion in the morgue. 'I don't understand,' Nancy said.

'Then I'll try and explain it, so you'll understand, so maybe just for once you'll listen to me. And – no maybe – do as I tell you...'

'Give me one good reason.'

She annoyed him by standing up and walking over to gaze out of the window. It was another overcast day. A cloud bank like a grey sea pressed down on Berne. A white mist drifted closer along the river, heading in towards the city off the Bantiger.

'There's some kind of conspiracy,' Newman began. 'It's very widespread. I'm still vague on the details but I sense that it affects the whole of Switzerland – what you'd call in America the industrial-military complex. The police – the Federal lot – may be mixed up in it. Do you realize what that means?'

'I'm sure you're going to tell me...'

'I'm sure as hell going to do just that. You didn't understand my reference to a stalking horse. I happen to be a well-known foreign correspondent. I can't convince anyone I'm not here after another big story. The Kruger thing has caused them to think like that. So if we make one wrong move, take one step that disturbs them, the whole Military Intelligence and police machine will crash down on our heads. Are you with me so far?'

'I think so. The weather is beginning to look fantastic...'

'Bugger the weather. There appear to be two rival power groups fighting each other for supremacy. One group may be trying to use me to break the other – by exploding the whole conspiracy in a sensational expose story in *Der Spiegel*. The group working underground is very powerful – I think it may have millions of Swiss francs at its disposal. Money means power – power to infiltrate the security organs of the state...'

Newman stopped in mid-sentence. When she turned round he was staring at the bottom of his cup. She went to him and placed her arm round his neck.

'What is it, Bob?'

'I may have missed something. What if we are dealing with patriots? Not villains in the normal sense of the word – men who sincerely believe they are protecting their country, who will go to any lengths to achieve their purpose?'

'And if that is the case?'

'It makes things far worse, more dangerous.' Newman put the cup on the tray and started pacing the room, hands clasped behind his back. 'I'm right, Nancy. There is no one we can trust. We're on our own. There are only two men who could crack this thing wide open...'

'Waldo Novak?'

'Yes. And Manfred Seidler. The police have put out a dragnet for Seidler. I have to reach him first. You make no trips to the Berne Clinic on your own. A certain Army officer went cold on me when I mentioned the place. So, we only visit the Clinic together. And when I'm out on my own – as I will be tonight when I see Novak – you stay in this hotel. Preferably in one of the public rooms...'

'You make me feel like a prisoner,' she objected.

He grabbed her by both arms and pulled her close to him. She stood quite still when she saw his expression.

'One more thing you'd better prepare yourself for. We might have to make a run for the border. I know places where it's possible to slip across quietly...'

'I won't go without Jesse...'

'Then we may have to take him with us. I don't like that remark he made to you about "experiments". God knows what is happening inside that place. Swiss Army guards. Dobermans. It's abnormal.'

'Bob, listen to me. In two days' time they're holding a reception here for that medical congress. I made some enquiries on my own from the concierge. He has a list of guests expected. One of them is Professor Armand Grange. Why don't we wait for him to come to us?'

He released his grip and she rubbed her upper arm. He had held her so tightly she felt bruised. She had never known him so alarmed and yet so determined at the same time. He went to the window. She had

178

been right about the view. It was fantastic. The drifting wall of white mist now blotted out the lower slopes of the Bantiger so the flat summit appeared to be an island floating on a white sea.

'You could have an idea there,' he said slowly. 'So tonight it's Novak. Seidler as soon as we can arrange a rendezvous. Then I believe we shall know...'

A heavy grey overcast also shrouded lunchtime London, but here there was no mist creeping in. Inside the Park Crescent office Monica inserted the documents into the folder and handed it to Tweed who was checking the small suitcase he always kept packed ready for instant departure.

'Here are your air tickets for Geneva,' she said. 'A return flight booked for tomorrow. If anybody is checking at Cointrin they'll assume it's an overnight visit. You have that note with the train times to Berne?'

'In my wallet...'

Tweed looked up as Howard strolled into the office, again without knocking on the door first. He snapped the catches on his case shut and dumped it on the floor. Howard stared at it as Tweed, taking no notice of him, put a file in a drawer and locked it.

'I've just heard the appalling news,' Howard said gravely, 'Are you off somewhere?'

'Berne, of course.'

'Because of Mason? The decoded telex from the Embassy refers to an accident...'

'Accident my foot!' Tweed allowed the contempt he felt to show in his tone. 'I talked to Wiley on the phone. Mason goes for a walk late at night, then falls into the river. Does it sound likely? Look at his age, his track record. Mason was murdered and I'm going to find out who did it.'

'Isn't that a job for the Swiss police?'

Howard brushed an imaginary speck from his sleeve, shot his cuffs and strolled round the office, glancing at the papers on Tweed's desk. Tweed sat in his chair and adjusted his glasses. He said nothing, waiting for Howard to go.

'The Swiss police,' Howard repeated somewhat peevishly.

'Have you forgotten what Mason brought back from Vienna? I gather you read the Ministry of Defence report on the object. I find the implications quite terrifying. I think that is why they killed Mason.'

'And who might be "they",' Howard enquired with characteristic pedantry.

'I have no idea,' Tweed confessed.

'You're going alone? No back-up?'

'I told you earlier I might have to call in outside help – that we're fully stretched with Martel being away. I've had someone out there for some time.'

'Who?' Howard pounced.

'The helper's safety – survival – may depend on secrecy, total secrecy. The person concerned knows Switzerland well.'

'You're being very coy about their sex,' Howard observed.

Coy. Tweed winced inwardly at the use of the word. Taking off his glasses, he polished them with his handkerchief until Monica gave him a paper tissue. Howard stared at Monica.

'Does she know?' he snapped.

'She does not. You can leave the whole matter in my hands.'

'I don't seem to have much choice. When do you leave?'

'This evening...' Tweed decided he had been very cavalier with Howard. 'I'm catching the nineteen hundred hours flight to Geneva. It arrives twenty-one thirty local time. Then the express on to Berne. At that hour anyone watching the airport is likely to be less alert.'

'You'll contact Beck, I suppose?'

'Frankly, I have no idea what I'm going to do.'

Howard gave it up as a bad job. He walked stiffly to the door and then paused. It occurred to him that if Mason had been murdered this could be a dangerous one. If anything did happen to Tweed he'd regret an abrupt departure.

'I suppose I'd better wish you luck.'

'Thank you,' Tweed replied politely. 'I think I'm going to need a lot of that commodity...'

On the first floor of the Berne Clinic Dr Bruno Kobler had finished checking the medical files when the door to his office opened. A large shadow entered the room which was lit only by the desk lamp despite the darkness of the afternoon. Kobler immediately rose to his feet.

'Everything is ready for tonight,' he informed his visitor.

'We are nearly there,' the huge man wearing tinted glasses commented in his soft, soothing voice. 'One more experiment tonight and then we shall be sure. Any other problems?'

'There may be several. Newman for one...'

'We can deal with extraneous matters after the medical congress and the reception at the Bellevue Palace,' the large man remarked as though referring to a minor administrative detail.

His bulk seemed to fill the room. His head was large. He was plump-faced and had a powerful jaw. His complexion was pallid, bloodless. He stood with his long arms close to his sides. He created the impression of a human Buddha. He had a capacity for total immobility.

He wore a dark business suit which merged with the shadows. The huge picture windows were smoked plate glass, which deepened the gloom. He wore tinted glasses because strong light bothered his eyes. He was a man who would dominate every room he entered without speaking a word. And his powers of concentration were phenomenal.

'Once the medical reception at the Bellevue is over they will all go home,' he observed to Kobler. 'Then will be the time to clear up loose ends. Then we shall present *Terminal* as a fait accompli. *Tous azimuts,*' he concluded. 'The dream of a generation of the General Staff will be reality.'

He stared out of the window at the distant mountains. The massive butte, rugged and brutal, rearing above the low cloud bank. The Stockhorn. There was a similarity between the rock which had dominated Thun for eons and the man who stood, still quite immobile, staring at it.

'This is the subject I have chosen for tonight's experiment,' Kobler said, walking round his desk to show the open file, the photo of the patient attached to the first page. 'You approve, Professor?'

Twenty

For the rest of the day Newman encouraged Nancy to explore Berne with him. Anything to get her outside the hotel. He had not forgotten her remark, *You make me feel like a prisoner*. He expected to be away for a long time in the evening, interviewing Dr Novak in Thun. He wanted to be sure she did stay inside the Bellevue Palace.

Their exploration was also therapy for himself. He needed to clear his mind of two tense interviews which had already taken place. The trip to the morgue with Arthur Beck, followed by their conversation in his office. And his encounter – it had seemed like that – with René Lachenal kept running through his mind. Why was the normally cool Lachenal worried? Something, Newman was convinced, was preying on the Intelligence man's mind.

It was bitterly cold as they wandered along the arcades, stopping while Nancy gazed in shop windows. He took her the full length of the main street, the cobbled Marktgasse with an ancient tower at either end, continued along the Kramgasse and the Gerechtigkeits-gasse.

They were walking down the centre of the peninsula towards its tip at the Nydegg bridge where the Aare swings in a huge hairpin bend and sweeps on parallel with its earlier course on the other side of the city. Gradually the streets began descending until the arcaded walks were elevated above the street below. Slim, pointy-nosed green trams rumbled past but otherwise there was little traffic.

They reached the approach to the Nydeggbrücke and Newman peered over a wall down at a huddle of weird old houses that fronted on a street at a lower level. Nancy stared down with him.

'They must have been here for centuries...'

'It's the Matte district. No wars, you see. So the past is preserved.

Let's hope to God it continues that way – it would be a crime for this lovely old city to be touched...'

He vetoed her suggestion that they should visit Jesse. She didn't argue the point when he explained.

'It could scare off Novak from coming to meet me this evening. I sensed he was nervous enough about the whole idea as it is...'

'I wonder why?'

'I think he's a frightened man. Frightened but at the same time desperate to talk to someone he can trust.'

'There seem to be a lot of frightened men. Manfred Seidler is another. What do I do if he calls while you're out?'

'Tell him I'm sticking to the arrangement we made. If he'll call me tomorrow, I'll meet him tomorrow...'

They had lunch at the Restaurant Zum Ausseren Stand inside the heated Zeughauspassage off the Marktgasse. First, they walked through the snack place which was full of people eating and watching the Winter Olympics at Sarajevo on a colour television set.

The restaurant was comfortably furnished with heavily-upholstered green arm chairs, the walls covered with posters of Yugoslavia. Again, Sarajevo. They had an excellent soup, a plate of superbly-cooked chicken and finished the meal with ice cream which Nancy pronounced 'Gorgeous. And even the coffee is first-rate.'

'It has to be good, if an American approves...'

He watched her glowing eyes and didn't want the evening to come. For almost the first time since they had landed in Geneva there was a carefree atmosphere. Cynically, he hoped it wasn't the prelude to something quite different.

Newman timed it so they arrived back at the Bellevue Palace at 6.15 p.m. Dusk had crept in over the city. The lights had come on in the streets and on the bridges. He wanted her to be alone for the shortest possible period. Following her into the entrance hall where people were circulating back and forth, he paused.

'I'm off to Thun,' he told her. 'I suggest a leisurely dinner, a good

183

bottle of wine. Expect me when you see me – I've no idea how long this will take. The longer I'm away the more information I'll be getting...'

He stopped speaking, staring over her shoulder. Lee Foley had just stepped out of the lift. The American appeared not to have seen him, turning right and disappearing down the staircase in the direction of the bar. Nancy also had turned to see what he was looking at.

'Is something wrong, Bob?'

'No. I was just making up my mind about something. You'd better know now I'm meeting Novak at a hotel called the Freienhof in Thun...'He spelt it out for her. 'The phone number will be in the directory. Just in case you have to reach me urgently. I'm off now...'

'Take care...'

The tall thin man hurried across the Kochergasse to one of the phone booths near the Hertz car hire offices. He had been waiting inside the café opposite the Bellevue for ages, pretending to read the *Berner Zeitung*, ordering three separate pots of coffee and making each last while he watched both the main entrance and the way in to the coffee shop. He dialled a number and spoke rapidly when he heard the voice at the other end.

'Newman has just got back. He's gone inside the hotel with a woman. About two minutes ago. Hold on. I think he's come out again. By himself? Yes. He's walking towards me. Now he's crossed the street. He's heading for a silver Citroën parked by a meter. He's opening the door. I can't do a thing about it. He's driving off any second...'

'I can,' the voice replied. 'We have cars waiting for just such a development. I must go. And thank you...'

Driving down the N6 motorway to Thun, Newman felt tired. It had been a full day and it was only just starting. A lot of enjoyable walking round Berne, but still tiring.

He switched off the heater, lowered his window. Icy night air flooded in. He welcomed it. He had to be alert when helmet Novak. The four-lane highway – two lanes in either direction separated by a central island – swept towards him in the beams of his headlights. He immediately began to feel better, sharper.

The red Porsche appeared from a slip road, headlights dipped as it followed him at a proper distance. He idly noticed it in his wing mirror. No attempt to overtake. Newman was driving close to the limit. The Porsche was behaving itself.

Bridge spans flashed past overhead. Occasional twin eyes of other headlights came towards him in the lanes heading back towards Berne. He checked his watch. As planned, he should arrive at the Freienhof before 7 p.m. Ahead of Waldo Novak. He drove on. He would know about the Porsche when he reached Thun. If it was still with him...

Behind the wheel of the Porsche, Lee Foley had two problems to concentrate on. The Citroën ahead. The black Audi behind his car. He had first noticed the Audi as two specks of light a long way back. It attracted his attention because the two specks swiftly became large headlamps. It was coming up like a bat out of hell.

Then it lost a lot of speed, began to cruise, keeping an interval of about a hundred yards between itself and his tail-lights. Foley swivelled his eyes alternately between the Citroën and the Audi in his rear-view mirror.

Why break all records – and the speed limit – and then go quiet? He came to a point where the normally level motorway, reached a gentle ascent at the very point where it curved. A car heading for Berne beyond the central island came over the brow of the rise. Headlights full on.

Foley blinked, looked quickly again in the rear-view mirror as the other vehicle's undipped lamps hit the Audi like a searchlight. Two men in the front. He thought there were two more in the back. Full house.

Turning off the motorway, Foley came into Thun behind the Citroën along the Bernstrasse, then turned down the Grabenstrasse as Newman continued along the Hauptgasse. He pulled in to a parking slot almost at once, switched off his motor and watched his rear-view mirror.

The Audi paused at the corner turn, as though its driver was unsure of his bearings. Two men got out of the rear of the car which then drove on quickly along the Hauptgasse, the route the Citroën had taken. Foley still waited, hands on the wheel.

One of the men – something about his manner, a man in his forties with a moustache, suggested he was in charge – let an object slip from his right hand. His reflexes were very good. He caught the object in mid-air before it hit the cobbles. An object which looked exactly like a walkie-talkie.

Foley smiled to himself as he climbed out of his car and locked it. He thought he knew their profession.

Unlike Berne, the town of Thun is as Germanic as it sounds. The river Aare, flowing in from Thunersee – Lake Thun, too far from the town to be seen – bisects it. The river also isolates the central section on an island linked to both banks by a series of bridges.

Arriving in Thun, as with Berne, is an excursion back to the Middle Ages. Ancient buildings hover at the water's edge. Old covered bridges, roofed with wood, span stretches of the Aare which, leaving Thun behind, flows on to distant Berne.

Driving along the Hauptgasse, Newman saw the red Porsche as it turned down the Grabenstrasse and decided his suspicions were groundless. He drove on, turned right on to the island over the Sinnebrücke and parked the Citroën in the Balliz. He then walked back through the quiet of the dark streets to the Freienhof Hotel which overlooks a stretch of the Aare. The first surprise was Waldo Novak had got there before him.

Taking off his coat and hanging it on a hook in the lobby, he studied the American who sat at a corner table in the public restaurant. Two empty glasses on the table told Newman that Novak had arrived early to tank up, to brace himself to face the Englishman, which suited Newman very nicely.

'Another Canadian Club,' Novak ordered from the waiter and then saw Newman.

'I'll have the same...'

'Don't forget – doubles,' Novak called out to the waiter's back. 'Okay, Newman, so you made it. Where do we go from here?'

'Why did you take that job at the Berne Clinic?' Newman enquired casually.

He sat waiting while Novak downed half his fresh glass and sipped at his own. The American wore a loud check sports jacket and grey flannel slacks. His face was flushed and he fiddled with the glass he had banged down on the table.

'For money. Why does anyone take any job?' he demanded.

'Sometimes because they're... dedicated is the word I'm seeking, I think.'

'Well, you found it – the word! Found anything else recently I should know about?'

'A couple of bodies.'

Novak stiffened. The high colour left his young-looking face. He gripped his glass so tightly, the knuckles whitened, that Newman thought he was going to crush it. Although the tables close to them were unoccupied he stared round the restaurant like a hunted man.

'What bodies?' he said eventually.

'First a little man called Julius Nagy. There's an ironclad link between him and Dr Kobler. Someone shoved Nagy off the Munster Plattform in Berne the other night. It's a drop of at least a hundred feet, probably more. He ended up on top of a car. Mashed potato.'

'You trying to frighten me?'

'Just keeping you informed of developments. Don't you want to know about the second body?'

'Go ahead, Newman. You're not scaring me...'

'An Englishman called Bernard Mason. He had been investigating Swiss clinics – which I'm sure we'll find was a cover for checking on the Berne Clinic. He ended up in the river – his body pounded to pulp by a sluice. It doesn't seem to be too healthy an occupation – taking an interest in the Berne Clinic. Waiter, another two doubles. We like reserves...'

'I don't think I want to talk to you, Newman.'

'You have someone else you can trust? What makes it worth your while to work for Professor Armand Grange?'

'Two hundred thousand bucks a year...'

He said it with an air of drunken bravado, to show Newman he counted for something, that even at his comparatively early age he was a winner. Newman discounted the enormous salary – Novak had to be exaggerating. Wildly. He paid the waiter for the fresh round of drinks and Novak grabbed for his glass, almost spilling it in the process.

'What kind of a boss is Grange to work for?' Newman enquired.

'I've come to a decision, Newman.' He made it sound like Napoleon about to issue orders for the battle of Austerlitz. 'I'm not talking to you any more. So why don't you just piss off?'

That was the moment Newman knew he had lost him. It was also the moment Lee Foley chose to walk in and sit down in the chair facing Novak.

'I'm Lee Foley. You are Dr Waldo Novak of New York. You are at present assigned to the Berne Clinic. Correct?'

Bare-headed, Foley wore slacks and a windcheater. His blue eyes stared fixedly at the doctor. He had not even glanced in Newman's direction. There was something about Foley's manner which caused Novak to make a tremendous effort to sober up.

'So what if I am?' he asked with an attempt at truculence.

'We are worried about you, Novak.' Foley spoke in a calm, flat tone but his voice still had a gravelly timbre. 'The fact is, we are growing more worried about you day by day,' he added.

'Who the hell is "we"? Who the hell are you?'

'CIA...'

Foley flipped open a folder and pushed it across the table. Novak put down his glass without drinking. He picked up the folder and stared at it, looked at Foley, then back at the folder. Foley reached across and wrenched it out of his hand, slipped it back inside his breast pocket and the blue eyes held Novak's as he went on talking quietly.

'I'll tell you what you're going to do. You're going to give Newman answers to any and all questions he may ask. Do I make myself clear?'

'And if I don't?'

'Nothing to drink, thank you,' Foley said, refusing Newman's offer, his eyes still holding Novak's. 'If you don't. I think you should know we are already considering withdrawing your passport. And I understand the Justice Department has gone further. Discussions are under way on the possibility of revoking your American citizenship...'

Foley still spoke in a cool, offhand manner. He glanced at Newman and said yes, he would have a drink, just some Perrier water. His throat was rather dry. It must be the low temperatures. He checked his watch.

'I'm short of time, Novak. And don't approach the American Embassy in Berne. That will only make matters worse for you. This comes direct from Washington. Make up your mind. Are you – or are you not – going to cooperate with Newman?'

'I'd like a little time to consider...'

'No time! Now! Yes. Or no.'

Foley drank his Perrier and stared away from Novak, gazing out of the window. Beyond a narrow road was an arm of the river. Beyond that were old buildings whose lights reflected in the dark water. He finished his Perrier, checked his watch again and looked direct at Novak.

'And you haven't met me. I don't exist. That is, if you value your health. Now, which is it to be?'

'I'll cooperate. This will be kept confidential, I hope?'

Foley stood up without replying, a very big man, nodded to Newman and walked out into the night. Novak gestured to the waiter who brought two more glasses. Newman waited until he had downed more Canadian Club and left his own glass on the table.

'What do you want to know?' Novak asked in a tone of resignation.

'What is the nationality of the patients in the Berne Clinic? Mixed?'

'It's odd. No Swiss. They're all American – with a few from South America when they can afford it. Grange charges enormous fees. Most of them come to him as a result of his lecture tours in the States. He's into cellular rejuvenation in a big way. So, it's a two-way pull.'

'What does that mean?'

'Look, Newman...' Novak, 'ashen-faced from his encounter with Foley, turned to look at the Englishman. '... this isn't an ideal world we live in. There are a lot of American families reeking with money, often new money. Oil tycoons in Texas, men who have made millions in Silicon Valley out of the electronics boom. Others, too. Grange has a sharp eye for a set-up where the money is controlled by some elderly man or woman whose nearest and dearest are panting to take that control away. They send the head of the family to the Berne Clinic for this so-called cellular rejuvenation. That gets them out of the way. They apply for a court order to administer the estate. You get the picture?'

'Go on...'

Novak's voice changed and he mimicked a man making out a case to a judge. 'Your Honour, the business is in danger of going bankrupt unless we have the power to keep things running. The owner is in a Swiss Clinic. I don't like to use the word "senile" but...' He swallowed more of his drink. 'Now do you get the picture? Grange offers the patient, who *is* seriously ill, the hope of a new lease of life. He offers the dependants the chance to get their hands on a fortune. At a price. It's a brilliant formula based on a *need*. Professor Grange is a brilliant man. Has a hypnotic effect on people, especially women.'

'In what way – hypnotic?'

'He makes the relatives feel what they want to feel – that they're doing the right thing in exiling to Switzerland the man or woman who stands in their way. Loving care and the best attention.' Novak's voice changed. 'When all the bastards want to do is to get their hands on the money. Grange has worked out a perfect formula based on human nature.'

'There's nothing specifically criminal so far,' Newman commented.

'*Criminal?*'

Novak spilt some of his drink on the table. The watchful waiter, ready for a fresh order, appeared with a cloth and wiped the table. Novak, shaken, waited until they were alone.

'Who said anything about criminal activities?'

'Why is the Swiss Army guarding the Clinic?' Newman threw at him.

'That's a peculiar business I don't want to know about. I do my job and don't ask questions. This is Switzerland. The whole place is an armed camp. Did you know there is a military training base at Lerchenfeld? That's at the other side of the town. In Thun-Sud...'

'But you have seen men in Swiss Army uniform inside the Berne Clinic?' Newman persisted. 'Don't forget what Foley said.'

'I've been here a year. In all that time I've only seen men in some kind of uniform. Once inside the main gatehouse, once patrolling the grounds near the laboratory...'

'Ah, the laboratory. What goes on inside that place?'

'I have no idea. I've never been allowed there. But I have heard that's where the experiments with cellular rejuvenation are carried out. I gather the Swiss are very advanced with the technique of halting the onset of age.' Novak warmed to his theme, relaxing for the first time. 'The technique goes back before the war. In nineteen-thirty-eight Somerset Maugham, the writer, first underwent treatment. He was attended by the famous Dr Niehans who injected him with cells scraped from the foetus of unborn lambs. Timing was all-important. No more than an hour had to elapse between the slaughter of the pregnant ewe and the injection of the cells into the human – patient. Niehans first ground up the cells obtained from the foetus and made them soluble in a saline solution. The solution was then injected into the patient's buttocks...'

'It all sounds a bit macabre,' Newman remarked.

'Somerset Maugham lived to be ninety-one...'

'And Grange has a similar successful track record?'

'That is Grange's secret. His technique, apparently, is a great advance on Niehans'. I do know he keeps a variety of animals in that laboratory – but what I don't know. There's also another clinic which goes in for the same sort of treatment near Montreux. They call it *Cellvital.*'

Newman quietly refilled his glass with Perrier from the bottle Foley had left. He found the information Novak had just given him interesting. It could explain Jesse Kennedy's reference to 'experiments' – an activity no more sinister than the fact that it was not yet accepted by the medical profession everywhere.

'You've told me the nationality of the patients,' he said after a short pause. 'You're American. What about the other doctors?'

'They're Swiss. Grange asked me to come during one of his American tours...'

'And you came for a very normal reason – the money?'

'Like I told you, two hundred thousand dollars a year. I make a fortune – at my age...'

So, Novak hadn't been clutching a figure out of the air to impress him, Newman reflected. He felt he still wasn't asking the right questions. He flicked Novak on the raw to get a reaction, posing the query casually.

'What do you do for that? Sign a few dummy death certificates?'

'You go to hell!'

'I get the impression there may be some kind of hell up at that Clinic – and that you suspect more than you're telling. You live on the premises?'

'Yes.' Novak had gone sullen. 'That was part of my contract.'

'And the Swiss doctors?'

'They go home. Look, Newman, I work very long hours for my money. I'm on call most of the year...'

'Calm down. Have another drink. What about the staff – the guards, cleaners, receptionists. Where do they come from?'

'That's a bit odd,' Novak admitted. 'Grange won't employ anyone local – who lives in Thun. They also live on the premises. Most of them are from other parts of Switzerland. All except Willy Schaub. He goes to his home in Matte – that's a district of Berne near the Nydeggbrücke. Goes home every night.'

'What job has he got?' Newman asked, taking out his notebook.

'Head porter. He's been there forever, I gather. The odd job man. Turns his hand to anything. Very reliable...'

'I'll take his address...'

Novak hesitated until Newman simply said, 'Foley,' then he changed his mind. 'I do happen to know where he lives. Once I needed some drugs urgently and since I was in Berne I picked them up from his house. Funny old shanty. Gerberngasse 498. It's practically under the bridge. There's a covered staircase runs down from the end of the bridge into the Gerberngasse. He probably knows as much about the Clinic as anyone – except for Grange and Kobler…'

'Thank you, Novak, you've been very accommodating. One more thing before I go. I'll need to see you again. Will you be attending the medical reception at the Bellevue Palace?'

'The Professor has asked me to be there. Most unusual…'

'Why unusual?'

'It will be the first public function I've been to since I came out here.'

'So you'll be able to slip away for a short time. Then we can talk in my bedroom. I may have thought of some other questions. Why are you looking so dubious? Does Grange keep you on a collar and chain?'

'Of course not. I don't think we ought to be seen together much longer…'

'You could have been followed?' Newman asked quickly.

He looked round the restaurant which was filling up. They appeared, from snatches of conversation, to be farmers and local businessmen. The farmers were complaining about the bad weather, as though this was unique in history.

'No,' Novak replied. 'I took precautions. Drove around a bit before I parked my car. Then I walked the rest of the way here. Is that all?'

'That laboratory you've never been inside. It has a covered passage leading to it from the Clinic. You must have heard some gossip about the place.'

'Only about the *atombunker*. You probably know that the Swiss now have a regulation that any new building erected, including private houses, has to incorporate an *atombunker*. Well, the one under the laboratory is enormous, I gather. A huge door made of solid steel and six inches thick – the way it was described to me made it sound like the entrance to a bank vault in Zurich. It has to accommodate all the patients and the staff in case of emergency…'

So that could explain something else innocently which Newman had thought sinister – the covered passage to the laboratory also led to the *atombunker*. Despite all his questions, there was still nothing positively wrong on the surface about the Berne Clinic. It was an afterthought: he asked the question as he was slipping on his coat.

'You thought then that you might have been followed?'

'Not really. Kobler said he had been going to suggest I took the evening off. He urged me to spend the night out if I felt like it...' Novak paused and Newman waited, guessing that the American had made a mental connection. 'Funny thing,' Novak said slowly, 'but the last time he did that was the night when Hannah Stuart died...'

Twenty-One

Newman walked into a silent, freezing cold night. Deserted streets. He waited until his eyes became accustomed to the dark. He was about to light a cigarette when he changed his mind. Nothing pinpoints a target more clearly than the flare of a lighter. And he had not forgotten that one of the weapons Beck had reported stolen was a sniperscope Army rifle – from the Thun district.

Checking for watchers, he strolled to the Sinnebrücke. He was still not convinced that Novak had told him everything. The American could have been sent by Kobler – to lure Newman to Thun. Later, after too much drinking, Novak might have decided to take out insurance by talking to him. Newman was convinced of one fact – he could trust no one.

Water coming in from the lake lapped against the wall below the bridge. Then he heard the sound of an approaching outboard motor chugging slowly. The small craft was flat-bottomed. As it passed under a streetlamp he saw it was powered by a Yamaha outboard. One man crouched by the stern.

Newman stepped back into the shadows, unsure whether he had been seen. The man lifted a slim, box-like object to his mouth. A walkie-talkie. They had been watching him from the one area he had overlooked – the river. It would have been easy to observe Newman and Novak sitting at the window table inside the illuminated restaurant. Was he reporting that Newman had just left the restaurant?

Berne is like a colossal ocean liner built of rock and stone, rearing up above the surrounding countryside. Thun's centre lies on the island in a basin. Newman glanced up at the northern bank where the forested hillside climbed steeply, a hillside where the lights of houses glittered like jewels. He left the bridge, crossed the street in the shelter of one of the numerous smaller arcades – smaller than Berne's.

He followed a roundabout route to where he had left his car parked in the Balliz. He was looking for a red Porsche, any sign of Lee Foley, any sign of more watchers. With its network of waterways Thun is like a tiny Venice or Stockholm.

Looking south, at the end of a street he saw the vague outline of a monster mountain, its upper slopes white with snow. He continued walking slowly, listening. He passed one of the old covered bridges on his right and had a view to the north. On the highest point immediately above the town reared the great walls and turrets of the ages-old Schloss, a sinister, half-seen silhouette in the starlit night. The only sound was the slosh and gush of the river flow. He made up his mind.

Newman had not only been checking for watchers: he had taken his lonely stroll while he wrestled with a decision. He could not get out of his mind something Novak had said. *Kobler said he had been going to suggest I took the evening off... the last time he did that was the night when Hannah Stuart died.*

He walked swiftly back to where the Citroën was parked, got behind the wheel, fired the motor and drove off through the empty streets uphill towards Thun-Nord, towards the Berne Clinic.

The horrific scene jumped towards Newman's headlights as he came over the brow of a hill. He had followed a route which would take him to the main gatehouse of the Berne Clinic – coming in from the north-west. To his right alongside the narrow road was the wire fence guarding the Clinic's extensive grounds which, at this point, included some rough country. He had crossed the snow-line some time earlier and he knew the laboratory was beyond the fence, hidden by a fold in the landscape.

In his headlights he saw a gate in the wire fence wide open. Two police cars, the blue lights on their roofs flashing and revolving, were parked in the road by the gateway. A woman inside the grounds was running up the rocky slope towards the gateway, a woman wearing some kind of robe. Behind her in the gloom a vague shape bounded after her. One of the bloody Dobermans. The woman ran on, a stumbling run. In front of one of the police car's lights stood two people. Beck and, Oh, Christ! Nancy...

The Doberman was going to get her, the running woman. She was just too far from the open gateway. Jesus! It was a nightmare. Newman pulled up near the gateway as Beck raised both hands and stood very still. He was gripping a gun. Behind him a third car appeared. Not a police car. It braked savagely and someone jumped out. That was the moment when Beck fired. The dog leapt vertically into the night, seemed to stay there in suspension, then flopped to the ground. So much was happening it was difficult to take it all in.

Newman left his car. The man who had just arrived was Captain René Lachenal. In full uniform. The running woman staggered through the gateway and collapsed on the road. Her robe fell open and Newman saw she was wearing pyjamas underneath a thick dressing gown and sensible shoes caked with snow.

Nancy was already bending over the inert form. Beck was using his walkie-talkie. Newman counted six uniformed policemen, all wearing leather overcoats and automatics holstered on their right hips. Beck slipped his weapon into his pocket and put on gloves. He closed the gate and stooped over it, fiddling with something. Newman couldn't see what he was doing.

'You are trespassing inside a military zone,' Lachenal called out angrily. 'We will look after this woman...'

'Military zone?' Beck straightened up and walked away from the gate which Newman saw was now padlocked. 'What the hell are you talking about? And I have summoned an ambulance for this woman. It will be here very shortly...'

'We are conducting military manoeuvres,' Lachenal insisted. 'There was a barrier at the entrance to this road...'

His tall, gaunt-faced figure towered over Beck who was staring in the direction of Berne where an approaching siren could be heard, growing louder every second.

'Yes, we saw the barrier,' Beck told him. 'We drove through it. And, it appears, a good job we did. In any case, there was no formal notification beforehand of any manoeuvres. And, we have saved this woman. You saw that dog...'

Newman had a series of vivid impressions he recalled later like pictures taken by flash-bulbs. An armoured personnel carrier pulling up behind Lachenal's car. Troops jumping out clad in battle gear – helmets, camouflage jackets and trousers and carrying automatic weapons – who spread out in a circle. Lachenal lifting a pair of field glasses looped round his neck and briefly scanning the grounds beyond the wire fence, lowering them with a grave expression. Nancy, who was close to Newman, standing up slowly and whispering to Beck so the only other person who heard her was Newman.

'We haven't saved her, I'm afraid. She's dead. I don't like the look of her. I can't be sure, of course, but all the signs are she died of asphyxiation. More serious still, I detect distinct signs of some form of poisoning. If you asked me to guess – it could be no more than that – I diagnose cyanosis...'

'Say no more,' Beck suggested. 'I have all I need.'

The ambulance had arrived. The determined driver eased his vehicle past the personnel carrier and Lachenal's car, drove on until his bonnet almost touched Newman's Citroën, backed into the gateway area, turned so the ambulance faced back towards Berne, and stopped it alongside the woman's body in the road. The rear doors opened, two men in white emerged carrying a stretcher, and this was the moment when Lachenal intervened.

'What are you doing?' he demanded. 'I can have her taken for immediate attention to a military hospital...'

'She's dead, Lachenal,' Beck told him in a cold voice.

It was extraordinary. The lofty figure of the Intelligence captain, a member of the General Staff, was dominated by the much smaller figure of Beck by sheer force of personality. The policeman took out his automatic again and held it so the muzzle pointed at the ground.

'We can still take her,' Lachenal said after an interval. 'This may be a matter for counter-espionage...'

'Forget it, Lachenal. I'm taking over jurisdiction. And I am treating this as a case of suspected homicide. It is a matter entirely for the. Federal Police. Incidentally, if you do not immediately order your men to lower their weapons I'll bring a charge against you for obstructing the course of justice the moment I arrive back in Berne...'

'They are not threatening anyone...'

'I am waiting.'

Lachenal gave a quick order to the officer in charge of the detachment. The troops boarded the personnel carrier which was then, with some difficulty, reversed before it was driven off towards Berne. Beck watched these proceedings with an icy expression, the gun still by his side. Lachenal turned and stared down at him.

'Homicide? I don't understand...'

'Neither shall I – until after the autopsy has been performed. One more thing, I have a fully-qualified doctor here who has examined the body. She states the dead woman shows clear signs of having died from cyanosis or some other form of poisoning. Just in case you have second thoughts. You have your own walkie-talkie, I imagine, to keep in touch with these manoeuvres which sprung up so suddenly? Good. Let us synchronize wavebands. I wish to keep in direct touch with you until we reach Berne safely. Perhaps you would be so good as to follow in your car?'

'I find the implications behind that request outrageous...'

'But you will comply,' Beck told him grimly. 'Homicide was the word I used. That takes precedence over everything with the sole exception of a state of war. Agreed?'

'I will accompany you in my car to the outskirts of Berne. Perhaps you would like to drive off first, then the ambulance, and I bring up the rear?'

Beck nodded, still in full psychological command of the situation. The bearers had carried the woman's body inside the ambulance and closed the doors. At Newman's request Beck had agreed one of his own men should drive the Citroën back to the Bellevue so Newman could travel in Beck's car with Nancy.

Before leaving, Beck gave the remaining policemen orders to pile into the other car and patrol the entire perimeter of the Berne Clinic. Passing the ambulance, he clapped a gloved hand on to the edge of the driver's window to indicate he should follow him. As they left, he exchanged not one more word with Lachenal, maintaining his total control of the situation to the last.

He opened the rear door of his car, ushered Nancy inside and introduced her to his subordinate, Leupin, who joined her on the other side. He made the remark as he climbed behind the wheel and Newman settled himself alongside.

'I'm not too happy yet about Lachenal. He seems to have so many troops at the snap of a finger. You do realize that he must have called up that armoured personnel carrier when he'd arrived but *before* he got out of his car?'

Beck had started driving when Newman pointed to the walkie-talkie lying in Beck's lap. The communication switch was turned to *off*.

'You can keep tabs on him with that, can't you?' Newman observed.

'But who is he calling at this moment – on a different waveband? I simply don't know. Certainly, Lachenal looked very worried and uncertain about the whole business. He's a very complex character, our René Lachenal – but basically a man of integrity. His one concern is Switzerland's security...'

'And how far would he go to protect that? The military do live in a world all their own.'

'A great deal may depend on how he reacts during the next few minutes – before we reach the motorway to Berne...My God! I think he's gone over the top. Look at that...'

Ahead of them as they went downhill, blocking the road like a wall, was a gigantic tank with a gun barrel like a telegraph pole. Newman went cold. It was a German Leopard 11.

The tracked monster was stationary. Except for one moving part. The immense gun barrel, with a massive bulge of a nozzle at its tip, was elevated at a high angle. Slowly it began to drop. In the rear of the car Nancy, stiffened with fear, bit her knuckles, unable to take her eyes off the muzzle which was being lowered. Soon it would be aimed at them point-blank.

Beck had stopped the car. Newman had an awful premonition. He knew the capacity of the Leopard. One shell could blow them into fragments. The car would disappear. The ambulance on their tail would disintegrate. They would have to scrape the remnants of the two vehicles – and their occupants – off the road. The elevation continued to fall.

'They must have gone mad,' Beck said hoarsely.

He reached for the walkie-talkie to contact Lachenal, then dropped the instrument back in his lap. Newman shook his head in agreement. There simply wasn't time to reach Lachenal. Always supposing the officer was tuned in to the agreed waveband.

'No time for Lachenal,' Newman warned.

'I know...'

The gun barrel seemed to move in slow motion, remorselessly. Originally it had pointed at the sky. Now it had lost half that elevation. Now it only had a few more degrees to lose before they would be staring straight at that diabolical nozzle.

Nancy glanced at Leupin, a tall, thin-faced man. His face was moist with sweat. He seemed hypnotized by the inevitable descent of the huge tube. Still gazing ahead, he reached out his left hand and grasped her arm, an attempt to bring her a little comfort.

'Hold on tight!' Beck shouted suddenly.

He released the brake and rammed down his foot on the accelerator. The Audi shot forward down the icy road, skidded, recovered its equilibrium under Beck's iron control as they went on speeding towards the tank which was growing enormously in size as it rushed towards them through the windscreen. The gun tip was almost facing them. Newman had a horrible preview of the huge shell hitting. A fraction of a second and the explosion would be ripping through metal, tearing apart flesh, incinerating it in one horrendous inferno under the hammer blow force of the detonation.

Beck, facial muscles tensed, drove on – passed *underneath* the gun

201

barrel extending far beyond the tank's chassis. He jammed on the brakes. Although braced, everyone inside the car jerked forward. Beck had stopped within inches of the massive caterpillar tracks. It was no longer possible to fire the cannon. He snatched up the walkie-talkie.

'Lachenal! Are you there? Good. What the fucking hell are you trying to do. There's a bloody great tank which aimed its gun at us. I'm in direct radio communication with Berne. They've heard it all. Get this piece of scrap metal out of my way. Tell it to back off, clear the road... Do you read me...?'

'I've been trying to call you...' The strain in Lachenal's voice came clearly over the walkie-talkie. 'You kept talking. It's all a mistake. Kobler is waiting in a car to speak to you. The tank was to stop you driving past him. He caught me at. the main exit from the Clinic...'

'Tell Kobler to go jump off a cliff,' Beck rapped back as he reversed the car a few inches, using one hand to drive. 'I'm telling you just once more. Tell that tank commander to back off. There will be an enquiry...'

'I've already given the order,' Lachenal reported when he came back on the walkie-talkie. 'You must understand there are manoeuvres...'

'Dr Bruno Kobler's manoeuvres?'

That silenced Lachenal. They sat without speaking as the Leopard began its reverse movement, its tracks grinding ponderously as the commander backed it and turned it up a fork road just behind him. Beck glanced in the rear view mirror and briefly saluted the driver of the ambulance to show him the crisis was over. As soon as the road was open he shot forward, turning left away from the Leopard and downhill on the road which led to the motorway.

Twenty-Two

'I think, Bob, I should explain Dr Kennedy's presence,' Beck said as he drove along the motorway. 'One of my men – Leupin, in fact, who is sitting behind me – was watching the Bellevue Palace when he saw her leaving. He asked her to wait and called me. It is only two minutes by car from my office – using the siren,' he added with a ghost of a smile.

'I told you on no account to go anywhere, Nancy...' Newman began.

'Please!' Beck interjected. 'Let me finish. Her help back there at the gateway was invaluable. She told me she had received an urgent phone call from the Berne Clinic. Her grandfather had taken a turn for the worse. I persuaded her to come back with me to the hotel and I called Dr Kobler. He said they had made no such call, that Jesse Kennedy was fast asleep. We still don't know who tried to lure her out. I was on the way to the Clinic myself and she agreed to come with me in the police car. I thought it best to keep an eye on her...'

'What took you to the Clinic tonight of all nights?'

'I have someone inside,' Beck replied cryptically.

'Who?'

'You, as a foreign correspondent, are in the habit of revealing your sources?' Beck enquired in a mocking tone. 'We drove past the main gateway to that second gate...'

'Which was open,' Newman commented.

'I opened it myself. In the boot is a pair of strong wire-clippers I used on the padlock chain. Quite illegal, of course, but we could see that poor woman fleeing for the gate. Afterwards, I locked it again with an identical padlock I had taken the precaution of bringing with me.'

'You seem amazingly well-organized,' Newman remarked.

'I know the file on Hannah Stuart backwards. I told you of a certain witness I can't use. Afterwards, I paid a visit to that gate from the laboratory and noticed the type of padlock used. I was banking on a second opportunity – although I did not foresee the consequences would be so tragic.'

'What are you going to do?'

'First, you must realize everything I have told you has to be in the strictest confidence. I am walking a tight-rope – I explained that to you also. Now, we are proceeding with the ambulance to the morgue. I have already alerted poor Anna Kleist who will lose yet another night's sleep. But I wish her to hear Dr Kennedy's diagnosis. And you should be thanking her for being there – not chastising her!'

'You are grateful for her help?'

'Yes!' Beck settled himself more comfortably behind the wheel. They had passed the turn-off to Belp and would soon be approaching the outskirts of Berne. He glanced in his rear-view mirror before continuing. 'Dr Kennedy completely neutralized any authority Lachenal might have asserted by her diagnosis of asphyxiation and possible cyanosis. That made it potential homicide. That put it in my court. That check-mated Lachenal...'

'There is some borderline between yourself and Military Intelligence, I gather?'

'Yes. Tricky on occasion. Officially we always cooperate. We are both concerned with the security of the state. A very flexible phrase. If Lachenal could have made out a case that it concerned counter-espionage the dead woman would have been his. Once it became homicide, even suspected, I had him.'

'I suppose as regards Nancy I should really thank you...'

'You really should!'

Newman glanced in his own wing mirror and then turned as though to speak to Nancy. The ambulance had dropped back to give reasonable clearance. Some distance behind it was a red streak, a Porsche. He wondered whether Beck had seen it.

'I hate the stink of these places,' Newman remarked without thinking as they sat round a table drinking coffee. 'And an empty stomach doesn't help...'

'There you go again!' Nancy flared in a sudden rage. 'Anything to do with a medical atmosphere and you're off – and maybe that includes doctors, too?' she ended savagely.

'We are all tired,' Beck intervened. He clasped Nancy's hand affectionately. 'And we have all had a series of most unnerving shocks.' He glanced at Newman. 'Maybe the best solution would be not to take him with you when you visit patients,' he suggested humorously.

They were sitting in the ante-room of the morgue and they had been quarantined there for a long time. At least, that was how Newman termed it to himself. There was the usual smell of strong disinfectant. The walls, painted white, were bare. There was the minimum of furniture. The single window was frosted glass so there was nothing to look out at in the street beyond.

'Anna does a thorough job,' Beck remarked to break the new silence which had descended on their conversation. 'I am sure she will be here soon...'

Dr Anna Kleist, the pathologist, had been waiting to examine the body of the unknown woman as soon as they arrived. Beck had made brief introductions between Nancy and Kleist, who had asked no questions before she disappeared. Newman had just stood up to stretch his legs when the door opened and Anna Kleist appeared. She addressed herself to Nancy.

'I'm so sorry to keep you waiting so long. I think I am now in a position to have a preliminary discussion as to how this unfortunate woman died...'

Tweed came into Geneva on Flight SR 837 which landed him at Cointrin at 21.30 hours. He moved swiftly through Passport Control and Customs, ran across the reception hall, clutching his small suitcase, and hailed a cab. Fie gave the driver a good tip and he was lucky. Green lights all the way along empty streets to Cornavin Gare.

He caught the 21.45 express by the skin of his teeth, panting as he sank into his first-class seat and the train glided out of the station. His short legs were not built for such sprints. Reaching Bern Bahnhof – or

Berne Gare – at 23.34, he took another cab to the Bellevue Palace and registered.

'Take my bag up to the room for me,' he told the porter and turned back to the receptionist, speaking in French. 'I am the executor of the estate of the late M. Bernard Mason who, you doubtless know, was drowned in the Aare. My London office phoned you about this...'

'Yes, sir, we have a note...'

'Thank God for that.' He paused. 'M. Mason was also one of my closest friends. Can I see any papers he left in the safety deposit? I don't want to take them away – you can watch me while I scan them briefly. Something to do with his estate...'

'M. Mason did not have a safety deposit box...'

'I see.' Tweed looked nonplussed. 'Could I make a rather unusual request? I would like to look at the room he occupied. That is, if it is still vacant...'

'I do understand, sir. And it will be quite possible.' The receptionist produced a key. 'The room has been cleaned and all his personal effects impounded by the Federal Police...'

'Naturally. May I go Up alone? Just to look...'

'Certainly, sir. The lift...'

'I know where the lift is. I have stayed here before on several occasions.'

Tweed took the lift to the fourth floor and stepped out. The mention of the Federal Police worried Tweed as he inserted the key, opened the bedroom door, went inside and closed and locked the door. That suggested Arthur Beck. Still, they had no reason to suspect Mason had been anything but the market researcher he had registered as under the heading *Occupation*.

He stood for a moment just beyond the threshold, a mark of respect, and then the inhuman emptiness of the room hit him and he muttered, 'Sentimental old fool...' The thing now was where would Mason have hidden his report?

Tweed had no doubt Mason had compiled a written report on Professor Armand Grange – for just the appalling eventuality which had overtaken him. Mason was a professional to his fingertips. *Had been*, Tweed corrected his mental comment.

First, he checked the bathroom and the separate lavatory – without much hope. Chambermaids, especially Swiss chambermaids, were notoriously proficient in their cleanliness. He found nothing in either place.

So, that left the bedroom – and very little scope. Which was the same problem Mason must have faced. How had he solved it? Tweed climbed on a chair and searched behind the curtains at the top near the runners for an envelope attached with adhesive surgical tape. Nothing. Wardrobe empty.

He peered underneath two tables, getting down on his hands and knees. Standing up, he stood with his back to a wall and coolly surveyed the room. The only thing left was a small chest of drawers. He opened the top one. Lined with paper, it was impeccably clean – and empty. He ran his hand along the inner surface of the drawer. Zilch – awful word – as the Americans would say.

The notebook was attached with surgical tape to the lower surface of the third drawer down at the back. He found it when he was checking the bottom drawer. Even Swiss chambermaids could hardly be expected to dust this area.

It was a cheap, lined notebook measuring approximately three-and-a-half inches wide by five-and-a-half inches deep. Comparatively cheap. On the cover it still carried the tiny white sticker which gave the price. 2.20 francs. Also the shop where it had been purchased. *Paputik*. Am Waisenhausplatz Bern. Near Cantonal police headquarters. Which told Tweed nothing.

The neat script – a fine Italianate hand – inside the notebook, which was so familiar it gave him a pang, told him a great deal. The first page began, *Professor Armand Grange, age: sixty...* Standing by the chest of drawers, Tweed rapidly read everything in the notebook and then placed it in an inside pocket.

Tweed had exceptional powers of concentration – and total recall. In future, if it should be necessary, he would be able to recite Mason's last will and testament – because for Tweed that was what it amounted to – word for word.

He left the bedroom, locked the door and went down in the lift to the ground floor. He handed back the key and pushed his way through the revolving doors. He hardly noticed the cold night air as he turned right, hands thrust inside the pockets of his worn, patched sheepskin.

He covered the ground at surprising speed, his legs moving like stubby pistons. Crossing the road in front of the Casino, he walked on down the right-hand arcade of the Munstergasse, deep in thought. Another part of his brain kept an eye on the tunnel of the arcade ahead, the arcade across the street.

Reaching the large square in front of the Munster, he walked round rather than across it. A car could drive you down crossing wide open spaces. He entered the Plattform through the open gateway and between the bare trees the wind scoured his face as his feet crunched gravel.

He walked on to the low wall and stopped, staring down at the Aare far below. Tweed didn't realize at the time, but he was standing at almost the exact point where Julius Nagy had been tipped into the depths. Nor was he making a pilgrimage to look down where Mason had died. Such an idea would have made the dead man snort.

Tweed was trying to work out how they had killed him. It was the work of a professional, of course. A trained assassin, a commando-type soldier-or a policeman. No one else could have got close enough to Mason to do the job. His eyes scanned the river from the Dalmazi bridge to the Kirchenfeld.

Wiley, 'commercial attaché' at the British Embassy, had given him sufficient details when he phoned him in London for Tweed to work it out. He started from the premise as to how he would have planned the killing.

Dropping the body into the river so it would be battered by one of the sluices had been deliberate, he felt sure. It was a brutal warning, an intended deterrent. No good pushing Mason over the railings lining the Aarstrasse below – the body might easily have simply drifted into the backwater near the Primarschule in the Matte district.

The Kirchenfeld bridge was out – too great a danger of traffic. No, it must have been the small and much lower Dalmazi bridge he decided. A body – Mason must have been unconscious because he was a strong swimmer – dropped from the centre of that bridge would inevitably be carried by the river's natural flow until it was hurled against one of the sluices.

Satisfied that he knew now how it had been done, Tweed walked back to the exit from the Plattform and continued along the Munstergasse. It was very quiet. No sound except his own footsteps. He walked on into the Junkerngasse and the pavement was sloping downwards now. He paused just before he reached his destination, listening. He was very concerned to protect her.

He resumed his walk a short distance and stopped outside a doorway with three bell-pushes. He approved the sight of the newly-installed speakphone. He pressed the bell-push alongside the name, *B. Signer*.

'Who is it?' Blanche's voice twanged through the metal grille.

'Tweed...'

'Come on up...'

Twenty-Three

Anna Kleist pulled up a chair to the table and sat down facing Nancy. The two doctors, Newman had already noticed, were on the same waveband. Kleist removed her tinted spectacles, clasped her hands on the table and began speaking.

'Now, this could be important to me, Dr Kennedy. I was told by Mr Beck you were the first person to examine the body of the unfortunate woman who was brought here. You may like to know I have phoned Dr Kobler of the Berne Clinic. He informs me the patient was called Holly Laird from Houston, Texas. According to his version she was suffering from a state of mental imbalance. She overpowered one of the staff, a woman called Astrid, stole her keys to their poisons cupboard and made off with a quantity of potassium cyanide. Although outwardly calm, I detected in Kobler a state of agitation. He qualified every statement he made. "Subject to further verification", was the phrase he used. Could you please tell me your impression after you examined Mrs Laird?'

'It was not a proper diagnosis, of course,' Nancy replied promptly. 'It was carried out under the least ideal conditions. I was surrounded with not only policemen but also armed soldiers. It was dark. I used a torch borrowed from one of the police. You understand?'

'Perfectly...'

'One factor I had to take into consideration was exposure. It was a bitterly cold night. The temperature was sub-zero. Mrs Laird was wearing only a pair of pyjamas and a thick dressing-gown. She may have run quite some distance before she reached the road.'

'Death due to exposure?' Kleist asked. 'That was what you concluded?'

'No!' Nancy began talking more rapidly. 'I had the strong impression she died from some form of asphyxiation. And the complexion of the face showed distinct traces of cyanosis. Her mouth was twisted in the most horrible grimace – a grimace consistent with cyanosis.'

'May I ask, Anna,' Beck intervened, 'what is your reaction to Dr Kennedy's on the spot conclusions?'

When she sat at the table Kleist had taken a scratch pad from a pocket of her pale green gown and she now produced a ball-point pen and began doodling on the pad. Newman guessed it helped to concentrate her thinking. She continued her doodling as she replied in her soft voice.

'My examination so far confirms precisely Dr Kennedy's impression. We have taken blood samples and they, in time, may tell us more...'

'How much time?' Newman demanded. 'That may be a commodity we are very short of – time.'

'A week. Possibly only a few days. Another pathologist is dealing with that aspect. I have requested that he give the matter the most urgent priority...'

'So we just have to wait,' Newman commented.

'I did find something else, something which puzzles me greatly,' Kleist went on. 'There are unexplained lacerations round the neck and over the crown of the skull...'

'You mean she could have been strangled?' Beck probed.

'Nothing like that. It is almost as though her neck and head had been bound in cloth straps...' She was still drawing something on her notepad. 'One explanation – although it seems bizarre to say the least – is that shortly before she died she was wearing some kind of headgear...'

'Some kind of mask?' Beck queried.

'Possibly,' she agreed, with no certainty in her tone. 'I can only be positive at this stage about the asphyxiation...'

'An oxygen mask?' Beck persisted. 'That would fit in with the equipment you'd expect to be available in a clinic. Maybe the oxygen supply was turned off, causing asphyxiation?'

Kleist shook her head. 'No. You have forgotten – she was seen running some considerable distance according to what you told me. It is the *agent* which caused death we have to isolate and identify. There we have to wait for the results of the blood tests.' She frowned. 'It is those lacerations which I find so strange. Still, I am probably saying far too much at this early stage. After all, I have not yet completed the examination.'

'You said she was a Mrs Holly Laird from Houston,' Newman remarked. 'Did you get any further information from Kobler about this woman's background? How old was she, by the way?'

'Fifty-five. And yes, I did press Kobler for more details. He. was reluctant to say much but also, I sensed, wary of not appearing to cooperate fully. Mrs Laird is the nominal head of a very large oil combine. She was brought to the Berne Clinic by her step-daughter in one of the company's executive jets...'

'Any information on her husband?' Newman said quickly.

'He's dead. I couldn't obtain any further details.' She glanced at Beck. 'I had to use your name to get that much out of him...'

'Another similar case,' Newman commented.

'And what might that mean?' Beck enquired.

'I'll tell you later.' Newman stood up. 'And now I think we have taken up more than enough of Dr Kleist's time. I appreciate her frankness at this early stage...'

'My pleasure...' Kleist hesitated, staring at Newman. 'It is just possible I may be able to tell you more by morning.'

'You're working through the night?' Newman asked with a note of incredulity.

'This man...' Kleist also stood up and linked her arm in Beck's, '... is the most unfeeling taskmaster in Switzerland. You do realize that, Arthur?' she added mischievously.

Beck shrugged and smiled. 'You would do the job, anyway, but I appreciate your dedication. And I have the same premonition as Newman – time is what we don't have...'

'Dr Kleist,' Newman said as they were about to leave, 'I wonder if you would mind if I took your doodle? I collect them...'

'Of course.'

She tore off the sheet, folded it and handed it to him. He slipped it inside his wallet and she watched him with a quirkish smile.

Beck drove them back to the Bellevue Palace in a police car and in silence. Nancy had the impression the experiences of the night had exhausted everyone. She waited until they were inside their bedroom before she asked the question.

'What is on that sheet of paper you took off her?'

'Exhibit A. When they doodle, clever people sometimes reveal what is in their subconscious. Prepare yourself for a shock. The Kleist is very clever. Here you are...'

'Oh, my God!'

Nancy sank on to the bed as she stared at the doodle the Swiss pathologist had drawn while she talked. It showed a picture of a sinister-looking gas-mask.

Twenty-Four

Tweed sat down on the sofa and Blanche Signer arranged a cushion behind him, treating him like a favourite uncle. She was very fond of Tweed. He was a nice man, a kindly man. He watched her as she disappeared inside the kitchen, walking with agile grace.

Settling himself against the cushion, he looked round the sitting-room to see if anything had changed since his previous visit. Then he spotted the silver-framed portrait of a late middle-aged man in the uniform of a colonel in the Swiss Army. He blinked, got up and moved swiftly across to examine it more closely.

'That's my stepfather,' Blanche called out as she returned and flourished a bottle behind his back. 'He adopted me when my mother – who died recently – remarried.'

'I don't think I've ever seen him before,' Tweed remarked slowly. 'He's a handsome-looking man.' He made a great effort to speak casually.

'Look!' she said exuberantly. 'Montrachet. Especially for you, this one. See!' She held out the bottle for his inspection, so he could note the year. He felt it and the bottle was as chilled as the waters of the Aare.

'I was going to ask for coffee...'

'No,' she told him firmly, 'you've had a beastly journey. All the way from Geneva – from London, in fact. And it's well after midnight. You need something relaxing.'

'I'm sorry to be so late...'

'But you phoned me first...' She was pouring wine into the two elegant glasses already waiting on a low table. '... and like you, I'm an owl, a creature who prefers the night, who perches on branches and hoots a mournful sound!'

'I think I'd have trouble getting up a tree these days,' he observed. 'Cheers! And this *is* very welcome. Do you see your stepfather often?'

'Hardly ever. We don't see eye to eye on anything. He goes his way, I go mine. He doesn't even know what I do to earn my living – at least I don't think so. He *is* the sort of man who seems to know about almost everything that's happening in Switzerland. He's not regular Army.'

'I see,' said Tweed, and left it at that. 'I imagine it's far too early for you to have found out anything about the man whose name I gave you?'

Shoeless, she was wearing her black leather pants with a white blouse which, even in the dim light of shaded table lamps, displayed in all its glory her cascade of titian hair. She had perched herself next to him on the arm of the sofa, her long legs crossed. He suspected she was capable of teasing him and for a moment wished he had such a daughter, a lively, mischievous girl you could carry on an intelligent conversation with for hours.

'I do already have some possible information about Manfred Seidler,' she said. 'The trouble is ethics are involved – and you were cryptic on the phone. Could I trace a man who had flown in from Vienna very recently on a private Swiss jet. And could I also get any info, on this Seidler type. Are they the same person?'

'Frankly, I don't know,' Tweed replied evasively. 'The man who flew in from Vienna is important. Seidler is purely an inspired guess on my part. I know a lot about him and his activities. Always close to the borderline of legality and, sometimes, probably over the edge.' He drank more of his wine and she refilled his glass. 'This is really excellent. What's your problem about ethics? Not another client?'

'You cunning old serpent...' She ruffled his hair. He couldn't remember when he had last let a woman do that to him but Blanche made it seem the most natural, affectionate gesture in the world. 'Yes, another client,' she said.

'It's important – to my country,' he said, gazing at the photo. 'So probably to yours. We're all in the same boat.'

'You know, I'd hate to be interrogated by you. You're too damned persuasive by half.'

He waited, sipping his wine. She had dropped her hand so it rested on his shoulder. He glanced up from behind his glasses and she was staring into space. He still kept quiet.

'All right,' she said. 'It means breaking a confidence with a client for the first time, but I'm assuming you wouldn't let me do that unless it was something very serious. I'm placing all my integrity in your hands. For me,' she continued on a lighter note, 'that's equivalent to entrusting you with my one-time virginity...'

'That's safe enough with me,' he said drily.

'Bob Newman, foreign correspondent. He asked me only this week to trace a Manfred Seidler. I may have got lucky – but I'm not sure. I have an address – and a phone number – for a Manfred. No guarantees issued that he's Seidler, but he does sound like him...'

'Address, phone number...'

Tweed had his small notebook on his lap, his old-fashioned fountain pen in his hand. She gave him both items of information out of her head. He knew that both would be correct. Like himself she only had to see a face once, hear a name, read an address or phone number, and it was registered on her brain for ever.

'What I've given you,' she went on, 'are the details of a girl called Erika Stahel. She may be Seidler's girlfriend. Incidentally, Stahel is spelt...'

'It sounds as though he may be holed up in Basle,' Tweed suggested. 'If it is Seidler...'

'I've no idea. I have an idea I'm going to regret giving you this information.'

'You expect to see this foreign correspondent, Newman, again soon?'

'Why?' she asked sharply.

'Just that I wondered whether you had any idea what story he is working on...'

'You're going too far!' The annoyance showed in her tone and she didn't care. She stood up from the sofa arm, walked across to a chair and sat facing him, crossing her legs again. He gazed into her startling blue eyes and thought how many men would be clay in her slim hands, clay to mould into any shape she wished. She spoke angrily.

'Again you ask me to betray a confidence. Are you really working for the Ministry of Defence in London? I keep your secrets. If I give away other people's, you should cease trusting me!'

'I spend most of my life in a thoroughly boring way – reading files...'

'Files on people I have helped you track across Europe...'

'Files on people who are dangerous to the West. Switzerland is now part of the West in a way it never has been before. No longer is neutrality enough...'

He took off his glasses and started polishing them on his pocket handkerchief. Blanche reacted instantly, tossing her mane of hair as she clicked her fingers. He paused, holding the glasses in his lap.

'You're up to something!' she told him. 'I always can tell when you're plotting some devious ploy. You take off those glasses and start cleaning them!'

He blinked, thrown off balance for a moment. She was getting to know him too well. He put away the handkerchief and looped the glasses behind his ears, sighing deeply.

'Is Newman interested in the Berne Clinic at Thun?' he asked quietly.

'Supposing he was?' she challenged him.

'I might be able to help him.' He reached inside his pocket, brought out Mason's notebook and handed it to her. 'In there is information he might find invaluable. You type, of course? I suggest you type out every word inside that notebook. He must not see the notebook itself. Give him your typed report without revealing your source. Make up some plausible story – you are perfectly capable of doing that, I know. I'll collect the notebook when next I see you.'

'Tweed, what exactly are you up to? I need to know before I agree. I like Newman...'

'The data from that notebook will keep him running.'

'Oh, I see.' She ran a hand through her hair. 'You're using him. You use people, don't you?'

'Yes.' He thought it best not to hesitate. 'Isn't it always the way,' he commented sadly. 'We use people. We all use each other.'

Reaching inside his breast pocket he brought out an envelope containing Swiss banknotes. He was careful to hand it to her with formal courtesy. She took it and dropped it on the floor beside her chair, a sign that she was still annoyed.

'I expect it's too much for what I've done,' she remarked. Her mood changed as the blue eyes watched him. Uncrossing her legs, she pressed her knees together, clasped her hands so the fingers pointed at him and leaned forward. 'What is it? Something is worrying you.'

'Blanche, I want you to take great care during the next week or two. There have been two killings, probably three. What I am going to say is in the greatest confidence. I think someone may be eliminating anyone who knows what is going on inside the Berne Clinic...'

'Will Newman know?' she asked quickly.

'He is one of the world's top foreign correspondents. He will know. Providing him with that typed report may well be a form of protection. What I am getting at is this – no one must connect you even remotely with that Clinic. I am staying at the Bellevue Palace. Room 312. Do not hesitate to call me if anything happens that worries you. And use the name Rosa – not your own.'

She was astonished and perturbed. It was out of character for Tweed to reveal his whereabouts, let alone to suggest that she could call him. Always before he had called her. She gave a little shiver as he stood up to go and then ran to help him on with his coat.

'It's time you bought yourself a new sheepskin. I know a shop...'

'Thank you, but this is like an old friend. I hate breaking in new things – coats, shoes. I will be in touch. Don't you forget to call me. Anything unusual. An odd phone call. Anything. If I'm out leave a message. "Rosa called..."'

'And you take care, too.' She kissed him on the cheek and he squeezed her forearm. He was glad to see that before opening the door she peered through the fish-eye spyglass. 'All clear,' she announced briskly.

As he trudged homeward up the Junkerngasse through the silent tunnel Tweed's mind was a kaleidoscope of conflicting and disturbing impressions. Berne was like a rabbit warren, a warren of stone.

As the raw wind fleeced the back of his head exposed above his woollen scarf he remembered standing by the Plattform wall, staring down at the frothing sluices where poor Mason had been found. Mason had done his job so well – the notebook was a mine of suggestive information.

But the image which kept thrusting into his mind was that silver-framed portrait of Colonel Signer in Blanche's sitting-room. That had been the greatest shock of all. Victor Signer who was now president of the Zurcher Kredit Bank, the driving force behind the Gold Club.

Twenty-Five

Friday, 17 February. Kobler stood behind the desk in his first floor office at the Berne Clinic, his back to the huge smoked glass picture window overlooking the mountains beyond Thun. It was ten o'clock in the morning and he was staring at the large man with the tinted glasses who again remained in the shadows. The soft voice spoke with a hint of venom.

'Bruno, you do realize that last night's experiment was a disaster.' It was a statement, not a question. 'How could the Laird woman possibly have left the grounds? Now we have no way of knowing whether the experiment succeeded or not...'

Kobler never ceased to be astounded by the Professor's colossal self-confidence, by the way he could focus his mind like a burning-glass on a single objective. Wasn't it Einstein who had said, 'Clear your mind of all thoughts except the problem you are working on' – or something like that? And Einstein had been another genius.

Kobler's mind was full of the problem of the police holding the Laird woman's body and the dangerous developments that could lead to. All of this seemed to pass the Professor by. As though reading his thoughts, the soft voice continued.

'I leave to you, Bruno, of course, the measures which may be necessary to deal with those tiresome people who had the impertinence to interfere last night.'

'It will be attended to,' Kobler assured him. 'I may have more positive news – about Manfred Seidler...'

'Well, go on. God knows you've been searching for him for long enough. Another tiresome distraction.'

'I concentrated men in Zurich, Geneva – and Basle,' Kobler explained. 'Knowing Seidler, I felt sure he would hide himself in a large city – one not too far from the border. The most likely, I decided, was Basle. Not Zurich – because of the works at nearby Horgen he is too well-known there. Not Geneva because the place crawls with agents of all kinds who spend their lives looking for people. So, the largest number of men I put on the ground in Basle – and it paid off...'

'Do tell me how.'

The flat, bored tone warned Kobler he was talking too much. The events of the previous night had imposed an enormous strain on him. He came to the point.

'We got lucky. One of our people spotted Seidler walking into the rail terminal. He bought a return ticket to Le Pont up in the Jura mountains. It's a nowhere place, a dot on the map. The interesting thing is he didn't use the ticket right away. He just bought his ticket and left the station. We are covering that station with a blanket. When he does use that ticket we'll be right behind him. I'm flying Graf and Munz to Basle Airport from the airstrip at Lerchenfeld...'

'They leave when?'

'They are on their way now.' Kobler checked his watch. 'I expect them to be at Basle Hauptbahnhof within the hour. And Le Pont would be an excellent place to deal with the final solution to the Seidler problem. Everything is under control,' he ended crisply.

'Not everything,' the voice corrected him. 'My intuition tells me the main danger is Robert Newman. You will yourself delete that debit item from the ledger...'

Having gone to bed in the middle of the night Newman and Nancy slept until the middle of the following morning. Newman, for once, agreed without protest to the suggestion that they use Room Service for a late breakfast.

They ate in exhausted silence after dressing. The weather had not improved: another pall of dense cloud pressed down on the city. Nancy was in the bathroom when the phone rang and Newman answered it.

'Who was that?' she asked when she came back into the bedroom.

'It was for you.' Newman grinned. 'Another wrong number...'

'That's supposed to be funny?'

'It's the best I can do just after breakfast. And I'm going out to see someone about what happened last night. Don't ask me who. The less you know the better the way things are turning out...'

'Give her my love...'

Which, Newman reflected, as he walked down the Munstergasse, had been a shrewder thrust than Nancy probably realized. The brief call had been from Blanche Signer. The photographs she had taken of the Berne Clinic from the snow-covered knoll were developed and printed. The surprise, when he arrived at her apartment, was that she was not alone. Carefully not revealing his name, she introduced a studious-looking girl who wore glasses and would be, Newman judged, in her late twenties.

'This is Lisbeth Dubach,' Blanche explained. 'She's an expert on interpreting photographs – normally aerial photos. I've shown her those I took of the Fribourg complex. She's found something very odd...'

The Fribourg complex. Blanche, Newman realized, was showing great discretion. First, no mention of his name. Now she was disguising the fact that the photos were taken at the Berne Clinic. On a corner table where a lamp was switched on stood an instrument Newman recognized in the middle of a collection of glossy prints.

The instrument was a stereoscope used for viewing a pair of photographs taken of the same object at slightly different angles. The overall effect obtained by looking through the lenses of the instrument conjured up a three-dimensional image. Newman recalled reading somewhere that during World War Two a certain Flight Officer Babington-Smith had – by using a similar device – detected from aerial photos the first solid evidence that the Nazis had created successfully their secret weapon, the flying bomb. Now another woman, Lisbeth Dubach, years later, was going to show him she had discovered what? As he approached the table he was aware of a tingling sensation at the base of his neck.

'This building,' Dubach began, 'is very strange. I have only once before seen anything similar. Take a look through the lenses, please...'

The laboratory! The building jumped up at Newman in all its three-dimensional solidity as though he were staring down at it from a very low-flying aircraft. He studied the photos and then stood upright and shook his head.

'I'm sorry, I don't see what you're driving at...'

'Look again, please! Those chimneys – their tips. You see the weird bulges perched on top – almost like huge hats perched on top?'

'Yes, I see them now...' Newman was stooped again gazing through the lenses, trying to guess what he was looking at could mean. Once again he gave it up and shook his head.

'I must be thick,' he decided. 'I do now see what you've spotted but I can't detect anything sinister...'

'Once while visiting England,' Dubach explained, 'I made a trip to your nuclear plant at Windscale, the plant where Sir John Cockcroft insisted during its design that they had to install special filters on the chimneys...'

'Oh, Christ!' Newman muttered to himself.

'There was a near-disaster at Windscale later,' Dubach continued. 'Only the filters stopped a vast radiation cloud escaping. The filters you are looking at now at the Fribourg complex are very similar...'

'But one thing we can tell you,' Newman objected, 'is that this building has nothing whatever to do with nuclear power.'

'There is something there they are making which needs the protection of similar filters,' Dubach asserted.

Newman, still absorbing the appalling implications of what Lisbeth Dubach had detected in the photos, now found himself subjected to a fresh shock.

As soon as they were alone, Blanche produced a sheaf of papers from an envelope and placed them on the sofa between them. They were, Newman observed, photocopies of typed originals. He had no suspicion that – by making photocopies of the sheets she had typed from the notebook – Blanche was protecting her source, Tweed.

She had gone to the length of typing them single-spaced, whereas her normal typing method was double-spacing, as Newman was well aware. She was careful with her explanation.

'Bob, I can't possibly tell you the identity of the client concerned. I'm breaking my iron-clad rule as it is – never to show information obtained for one client to another...'

'Why?' Newman demanded. 'Why are you doing it now?'

'Bob, *don't push* me! *The* only reason I'm showing you this data is because I happen to be very fond of you. I know you are investigating the Berne Clinic. What worries me is you may not realize what – who – you are up against. If you read these photocopies it might put you more on your guard. The power wielded by this man is quite terrifying...'

'So I read these and give them back to you?'

'No, you can take them with you. But for God's sake, you don't know where they came from. They were delivered to you at the Bellevue Palace. See, I've typed an envelope addressed to you at the Bellevue Palace. They were left with the concierge at the hotel...'

'If that's the way you want to play it...'

'I'll make you coffee while you're reading them. I could do with some myself. What Lisbeth Dubach told us has scared the wits out of me. What have we got into?'

Newman didn't reply as he picked up the photocopies and started reading. The report on Professor Armand Grange had, he realized quickly, been prepared by an experienced investigator who wasted no words. There were also signs that he – or she – had been working under pressure.

SUBJECT: Professor Armand Grange. Born 1924 at Laupen, near Berne. Family wealthy – owners of watchmaking works. Subject educated University of Lausanne. Brief period military service with Swiss Army near end World War Two.

Rumoured to be member of specialist team sent secretly into Germany to obtain quantity of the nerve gas, TABUN, ahead of advancing Red Army. Note: Repeat, rumour – not confirmed.

After war trained as doctor at Lausanne Medical School, followed by post-graduate work at Guy's Hospital, London, and Johns Hopkins Memorial Hospital, Baltimore, Maryland, USA. Brilliant student, always top of his class.

Military service not continued due to eye defect. After qualifying as lung consultant, trained as accountant. He proved to be as brilliant in this field as in the medical.

1954. Due to financial flair became director of Zurcher Kredit Bank at early age of 30. 1955. Founded Chemiekonzern Grange AG with factory at Horgen on shores of Lake Zurich. Chemiekonzern manufactures commercial gases, including oxygen, nitrous oxide, carbon dioxide and cyclopropane, a gas used in medical practice.

Rumoured finance for foundation of Chemiekonzern provided by Zurcher Kredit Bank. Note: Repeat, rumour – not confirmed.

1964. Subject bought controlling interest in Berne Clinic. This establishment reported engaged in practice of cellular rejuvenation since subject took over.

General comment: subject speaks fluent German, French, English and Spanish. Has made frequent visits to USA and South America. Believed to be millionaire.

I was told by reliable contact no decision affecting Swiss military policy taken without reference to subject. One of the most influential voices in Swiss industrial-military complex. This comprises preliminary report based on sources in Zurich and Berne.

Newman read through the report twice and his expression was grim as he inserted the sheets inside the addressed envelope. Recent incidents flashed into his mind, triggered off by the report.

The doodle he had been given by Anna Kleist, a doodle of a gas-mask. Arthur Beck's comment about Hannah Stuart. 'The body was cremated...' The photograph Julius Nagy had taken of Beck outside the Taubenhalde – talking to Dr Bruno Kobler, chief administrator of the Berne Clinic.

Col Lachenal's reference to *tous azimuts* – all-round defence of Switzerland. And, most recent of all, Lisbeth Dubach's interpretation of the photos Blanche had taken of the laboratory at the Berne Clinic – '... something there they are making which needs the protection of similar filters.'

Another aspect of the report intrigued Newman: it bore all the hallmarks of a military appreciation with its terse, precise phraseology. That took his mind back to his meeting in the bar at the Bellevue Palace with Captain Tommy Mason. What was it the Englishman had said during their conversation when Newman had queried his research trip?

'Yes. Medical. Standards of and practice in their private clinics...'

Newman had little doubt he had just read a report drawn up by Mason – Mason who had 'accidentally' bumped into him in that bar, who was now dead. He asked Blanche the question, feeling pretty sure he already knew the answer.

'At the end of the report the word "preliminary" is used. That suggests more to come. Did you get the impression from your other client this would be the case?'

'No, I didn't.' Blanche paused. 'Nothing was said about any further data coming from the same source.' She perched on the arm of the sofa next to him. 'Bob, that report is frightening. Where is all this leading to? There is a mention of the Zurcher Kredit Bank – my stepfather is president of that bank...'

'There really isn't a close relationship between you two?'

'If you don't do exactly what my stepfather wants you to – and I didn't – he just forgets all about you. He's very much the military man. Obey orders – or else...'

'Blanche...' He took her hand. '... this whole business is beginning to look far more dangerous than I ever suspected. Is there any way your father could know that we are friends?'

'Our lives have gone separate ways. He doesn't know who my friends are – and doesn't want to know. And he *is* my stepfather. My mother divorced my real father who is now dead. You see now why we're so far apart...'

'I'd like you to keep it that way.' Newman kissed her and walked across the room to collect his coat. 'I'm off now – and thanks for this report...'

'Take care, Bob. Please. Where are you going now?'

'To blow someone up with verbal gelignite...'

Lachenal agreed to see Newman as soon as he arrived. It is only a ten-minute walk from the upper Junkerngasse to the Bundeshaus Ost. On that morning it had been a freezingly cold walk through the warren-like arcades and on the way Newman had taken the precaution of slipping into the Bellevue Palace to leave the report on Grange in a safety deposit box at the hotel.

Coming out of the safety-deposit room, he bumped into a small, plump-faced man who had turned away from the reception counter, a man who blinked at him through his glasses before he spoke.

'I'm sorry,' Tweed said. 'I didn't see you coming...'

'No harm done,' Newman assured him.

'I haven't been here long,' Tweed rambled on as though pleased to encounter a fellow-countryman. 'Has the weather been as beastly as this recently?'

'For days – and I think we're due for snow. Best thing is to stay indoors if you can. The wind out there cuts you in two...'

'I think I'll take your advice. This is a marvellous hotel to take refuge in....'

Tweed wandered off across the inner reception hall and Newman paused by the door, taking his time putting on his gloves. Sitting in a corner with her back to him was Nancy and the plump Englishman was heading straight towards her table followed by a waiter carrying a tray of coffee – coffee for two.

Newman waited just long enough to see the Englishman sit down opposite her while the waiter served them with coffee. They were talking together when Newman walked out and turned left to the Bundeshaus Ost.

'Lachenal,' Newman began savagely in the Intelligence chief's office as he sat facing the Swiss across his desk, 'what was all that bloody nonsense out at the Berne Clinic? I'm referring to that Leopard tank – for a moment it looked as though it was going to blow us to kingdom come. My fiancée nearly had a fit. I didn't enjoy the experience too much myself. And what is a German Leopard 11 tank doing in Switzerland? If I don't get some answers I'm going to file a story...'

'Permission to reply?' Lachenal's tone was cold, hostile. Even seated he seemed a very tall man, his back erect, his expression mournful. He's not a very happy man, Newman was thinking as he remained silent and the Swiss continued.

'First, I must apologize for the most unfortunate incident due entirely to a brief lack of communication. It was a simple but unforgivable misunderstanding. The people responsible have been severely reprimanded...'

'What's a Leopard 11, the new German tank, maybe the most advanced tank in the world, doing in Switzerland...'

'Please! Do let me continue. That is not classified. As you know, we manufacture certain military equipment but we buy a lot abroad – including tanks. We are in the process of re-equipping our armoured divisions. We have just decided to buy the Leopard 11 after thorough testing at Lerchenfeld. It is no secret...'

'Tabun. Is that a secret? The special team sent into Germany near the end of the war to bring back Tabun gas. Is that a secret?' Newman enquired more calmly.

'No comment!'

Lachenal stood up abruptly and went over to the window where he stood gazing at the view. Even dressed in mufti, as he was that morning, Lachenal reminded Newman of de Gaulle more than ever. The same distant aloofness at a moment of crisis.

'You know the *fohn* wind has been blowing,' Lachenal remarked after a pause. 'That probably contributed to the incident outside the Berne Clinic. It plays on the nerves, it affects men's judgement. It is no longer blowing. Soon we shall have snow. Always after the *fohn*...'

'I didn't come here for a weather forecast,' Newman interjected sarcastically.

'I can tell you this,' Lachenal went on, thrusting his hands into his pockets and turning to face Newman, 'it is true that the Germans had a large quantity of Tabun, the nerve gas, near the end of the war. Twelve thousand tons of the stuff, for God's sake. They thought the Soviets were going to resort to chemical warfare. The Red Army captured most of it. They've now drawn level with the West in a more sinister area – in the development of organo-phosphorous compounds. They have perfected their toxicity...'

'I do know that, René,' Newman said quietly.

'But do you also know the Soviets have perfected far more deadly toxic gases – especially those highly lethal irritants which they have adapted for use by their chemical battalions? I am referring, Bob, specifically, to hydrogen cyanide...'

Hydrogen cyanide...

The two words rang through Newman's head like the clang of a giant hammer hitting a mighty anvil. Lachenal continued talking in a level voice devoid of emotion.

'This substance is regarded in the West as being too volatile. Not so by the Soviets. They have equipped their special chemical warfare sections with frog rockets and stud missiles. Artillery shells filled with this diabolical agent are also part of their armoury. Did you say something, Bob?'

'No. Maybe I grunted. Please go on...'

'The Soviets have further equipped aircraft with sophisticated spray tanks containing this advanced form of hydrogen cyanide gas. We have calculated that a single shell fired through the vehicle of a missile, an artillery shell or from a spray tank – aimed by a low-flying aircraft – would destroy all life over an area of one square kilometre. Just a single shell,' Lachenal repeated.

Newman heard him but he also heard Nancy's diagnosis of how Mrs Holly Laird had died. *And the complexion of the face showed distinct traces of cyanosis.* What was it Anna Kleist had replied? *My examination so far confirms precisely Dr Kennedy's impression...*

Lachenal walked back from the window and again sat behind his desk, clasping his hands as he stared at his visitor who sat motionless. Newman shook his head slightly, brought himself back into the present. He had the distinct conviction that the Swiss was labouring under enormous tension, that he was concealing that tension with a tremendous effort of will.

'And so,' Lachenal concluded, 'all that started with Tabun. Which was what you came here to talk about – not the Leopard.'

'If you say so, René.' Newman heaved himself to his feet and reached for his coat. 'I'd better be going now...'

'One more thing, Bob.' Lachenal had stood up and he spoke with great earnestness. 'We all have to be the final judge of our own conduct in this world. No hiding behind the order of a so-called superior...'

'I would say you're right there,' Newman replied slowly.

It was this conversation which decided Newman as he left the Bundeshaus Ost – decided him that at the very first opportunity he would get Nancy out of Switzerland – even if it meant he had to crash the border.

Twenty-Six

'I'm going to visit Jesse – with or without you,' Nancy announced when Newman returned to their bedroom. 'They're holding that Medical Congress reception here tomorrow evening. Are you, or are you not, coming with me?'

'I agree – and I'm coming with you.'

Newman dragged a chair over to the window and sank into it, staring at the view. The dark grey sea of cloud was lower than ever. He thought Lachenal had been right: they would have snow in Berne within the next twenty-four hours. Nancy came up behind him and wrapped her arms round his neck.

'I expected an argument. You're looking terribly serious. God, you've changed since we started out on this trip. Has something upset you?'

'Nancy, I want you to listen to me carefully. Most people think of Switzerland as a country of cuckoo clocks, Suchard chocolate and skiing. In one of his novels a famous writer made a wisecrack about the cuckoo clocks. There's another side to Switzerland most tourists never even dream exists.'

'Go on. I'm listening...'

'That makes a change. The Swiss are probably the toughest, most sturdy nation in Western Europe. They are ruthless realists – in a way I sometimes wish we were in Britain. They'll go a long way to ensure their survival. You know about their military service. This country has been on a wartime footing ever since nineteen thirty-nine. They still are. From now on we have to move like people walking through a minefield – because that's what lies in our path. A minefield...'

'Bob, you've found out something new since you left the hotel. Where have you been? And why the sudden turnabout as regards visiting the Berne Clinic?'

Newman stood up and began pacing the large room while he lit a cigarette and talked. He punctuated each remark with a chopping gesture of his left hand.

'We started out with four people who might have told us what is really going on. Julius Nagy, Mason – the Englishman I met briefly in the bar – together with Dr Waldo Novak and Manfred Seidler. The first two have been murdered – the police are convinced of that although they can't prove a thing. That leaves us Novak and Seidler...'

'You want to see Novak again? That's why you agreed to go back to the Berne Clinic?'

'One reason. If I can get Novak on his own for a short time I think he will tell me more – especially after that appalling episode over the death of Mrs Laird. He's very close to cracking, I'm convinced. Incidentally, you mentioned the Medical Congress reception. Why do you want to see Jesse before that takes place?'

'To get more information from him, if I can. To find out, again if I can, what his real condition is. Then at that reception I'm going to confront Professor Grange. We know he's going to be there. Don't try and stop me, Bob – I've made up my mind. Now,' she continued briskly, 'what about Seidler?'

'He could be the key to the whole labyrinthine business. He's phoning me here at five and we'll meet him this evening. Better pack a small case for both of us – essentials for an overnight stay...'

'Why?' she asked suspiciously.

'Seidler sounds even more trigger-happy than Novak. My guess is he'll fix a rendezvous point a long way off – some place we can just reach in time after his call by driving like hell. That way he'll hope we won't have time to alert anyone else. He smells like a man who trusts no one.'

'Oh, by the way, Bob,' she said casually, 'Novak knows I'm visiting the Clinic today. I phoned him while you were out. I got lucky. That creepy old bitch, Astrid, must be off duty. A man answered the phone and put me straight through to Novak. And he told me Kobler is away some place.'

'Kobler's not at the Clinic?' Newman asked quickly.

'That's right. Neither is Grange. Novak did ask me if you would be coming. He sounded anxious that you would be. Can we leave soon?'

'After I've kept a brief appointment with someone in the bar. I met him on my way in. One of your own countrymen – a Lee Foley...'

'And who might he be?'

'A killer...'

He left her on that note, driving home again that she had better watch her step if she wanted to live.

The tall American with the thatch of white hair stood up courteously as Newman came across to his table inside the bar. He already had a drink in a tall glass crammed with ice. Newman said he would have a large Scotch and sat down on the banquette alongside Lee Foley who wore an expensive blue business suit, a cream shirt and a smart blue tie with small white checks. Gold links dangled from his cuffs.

'You're staying at the Bellevue, Lee?' Newman enquired.

'For the moment, yes. Unfinished business.' He raised his glass. 'Cheers! I've just had a visit from that bastard Federal policeman, Beck. I could feel sorry for the gentleman – he can't find a reason to throw me out of the country...'

'Not yet...'

'By then I'll be gone...'

'You still keep up your flying – piloting a plane?'

'Just light aircraft. Pipers, stuff like that...'

'What about a Lear executive jet?' Newman suggested.

'Now you're reaching.' Foley smiled his dry smile which was not reflected in the ice-blue eyes. 'Beck,' he continued, 'is concerned with the way the body count is rising. Two so far. The little man you and I talked with – and now some Englishman...'

'*Three*,' Newman amended. 'An American woman has just died outside the Berne Clinic...'

'I know. Just goes on climbing, doesn't it?'

'I get the impression,' Newman ruminated, 'that Clinic is a place needing a lot of protection. They could afford someone expensive...'

233

'You'd better apply for the job...'

'More your line of country, I'd have thought...'

Foley put down his glass and stared at it. 'Remember that night we took the town apart on the Reeperbahn in Hamburg? You're the only man who ever drank me under the table...'

'The night *you* took the town apart,' Newman amended. 'Do you still speak good German?'

'I get by. You know something, Bob? The West is getting too civilized. There was a time when the Brits, stopped at nothing when survival was at stake. I'm thinking of Churchill ordering the sinking of the whole goddamned French fleet at Oran – to stop the Nazis getting their hands on some real sea-power. Ruthless. He was right, of course...'

'You're trying to tell me something, Lee?'

'Just having a drink with an old friend, making a few random observations...'

'You never made one of those in your life. I have to go now. See you around, Lee...'

Newman let Nancy take the wheel of the Citroën for the drive to the Clinic. She handled the car with the confident ease of an expert driver along the motorway. In his wing mirror Newman kept an eye on the black Audi behind them which maintained its distance. Beck's minions were on the job.

'We're approaching the turn-off,' he warned.

'And who is driving this goddamn car?'

'You are, I hope – otherwise we're in trouble...'

'How did you get on with that man you went to meet in the bar? What was his name?'

'Lee Foley. I'm still trying to work out why he wanted to see me. He's a cold-blooded sod. As much a killing machine as that Leopard 11 we met. What I can't yet decide is who he is working for. If I knew that I might have the final piece of this enormous jigsaw in my hand.'

'We're both meeting some interesting people,' she observed as she turned off the motorway. He checked the mirror. Yes, the Audi kept on coming. 'This morning while you were out doing God knows what,' Nancy went on, 'I was having coffee in the reception hall with an intriguing little man, another Englishman. He seemed so mild and yet I sensed, under the surface, a very determined personality. Tweed, his name is.'

'What did you talk about?'

'I told him about the Berne Clinic...' There was a touch of defiance in her tone, challenging him to criticize her indiscretion. He said nothing as she chattered on. 'He's a very sympathetic type – easy to talk with. He advised me to be very careful...'

'He did what!'

'I've just told you. He explained that as I was a foreigner I ought to tread carefully...' She glanced at Newman. '... that I should stick close to you from now on...'

'And just how did the Berne Clinic subject crop up?'

'No need to get piqued. He's a claims investigator for a big insurance company. It's weird, Bob – last month another American woman, a Hannah Stuart, died under similar circumstances to Mrs Laird. Why always women?'

'I've wondered that myself. Too many unanswered questions. And here we are. Brace yourself...'

They had arrived at the gatehouse to the Berne Clinic. But this time their reception was in surprising contrast to their previous visit. A man they had never seen before came out of the gatehouse, checked their passports, gestured towards the gatehouse and the automatic gates opened.

No sign of a guard, a Doberman, as they proceeded up the drive across the bleak plateau. It always seemed more overcast, more oppressive at Thun than in Berne. Newman thought it could have something to do with the big mountains holding the cloud bank.

'Novak told me to park the car in the lot at the side of the main building,' Nancy remarked. 'And I don't get the same feeling of being watched this time...'

'Maybe with both Grange and Kohler being away the hired help has gone slack. Or maybe they just want to give us that impression. Nancy, park the car in fresh snow...'

'Anything you say. I'm only the bloody chauffeur...'

'And when you get out disturb the snow as little as possible.'

'Christ! Any more instructions?'

'I'll let you know when I think of some...'

Waldo Novak, his fair hair blowing in the wind, came out of the glassed-in veranda entrance and down the six steps to meet them. Alone. No sign of the come-hither Astrid.

'I'll take you straight in to see him,' Novak told Nancy as he shook her hand. He stepped back alongside Newman to let her go first and dropped his voice to a whisper. 'Newman, on your way out, ask Mrs Kennedy to go to the powder room. That will give me the chance to tell you something.'

There was a male receptionist behind the counter, a man who took no interest in them. No nonsense about filling in visitors' forms. The same business with Novak's computer card keys to let them into the corridor and then inside the room where Jesse Kennedy sat propped up in bed against several pillows.

'Hold everything a minute,' Newman warned.

Taking off his coat he hung it from the hook, sealing off the mirror window. From his jacket pocket he extracted a compact transistor radio he had purchased for the purpose. He switched it on low power to some music, bent down and placed it next to the wall grille. That neutralized the hidden tape-recorder. He straightened up.

'Go ahead...'

'I have not followed my instructions,' Novak informed them. 'Mr Kennedy is not sedated – but to cover me I'd appreciate it if he'd take this capsule just before you leave...'

'We do understand – and thank you,' replied Nancy before she pulled up a chair and sat close to her grandfather. 'How are they treating you, Jesse?' She hugged him warmly, kissed him on both cheeks. 'Now tell me, do you really have leukaemia?'

'So they keep telling me. Including Novak here. Jesus H. Christ! I don't believe a word of it. You know some other poor woman was killed the other night? The cellular rejuvenation treatment didn't work is the story. She'd have died anyway they say. Poppycock! But I'm going to get to the guts of what's going on here – just like I did with that spy in Arizona ten years ago.' He chuckled. 'That CIA operative sure cleaned up that mess of...'

'You mean you want to stay here a while longer?' Nancy asked.

'Sure do. Didn't want to come in the first place – but now I'm here I'm going to clean up *this* mess. Just see if I don't. No need to worry about Novak. He's feeding everyone information so fast he's practically running his own wire service. Ain't that the truth, Novak? See, he's shy – don't like talking in front of strangers...'

It went on for another fifteen minutes. Nancy trying to persuade him to leave the Clinic. Jesse insisting he had to stay on to clean up the mess. Novak, clad in his uniform of white coat with stethoscope dangling from one hand, and Newman, listening in silence.

Suddenly Jesse, tired out by his unaccustomed burst of conversation, said he'd like to get some sleep. He took his capsule of sodium amytal, swallowed, opened his hand to show it was empty, winked at Newman and fell fast asleep.

Novak stood outside the Clinic in the snow, alone with Newman. Nancy had agreed to Newman's suggestion without a word of protest, asking the receptionist to show her the way to the powder room.

'Now,' Newman said, 'what is it you wanted to tell me? We'd better be quick – we may not have much time...'

'Willy Schaub, the head porter I told you about back in Thun. He's agreed to talk with you. I gave you his address in the Matte district. He'll see you at three in the afternoon tomorrow. He's got the day off and he knows more about this place than anyone...'

'Why has he agreed?'

'Money. Two thousand francs should turn the trick. Maybe a little less. He'll want cash – cheques can be traced through a bank. It's up to you, Newman. I've done my best. And I am leaving when I can. What do I tell Schaub?'

237

'That I'll meet him. One more question before Nancy arrives. All the patients in this place – just how ill are they?'

'We've got leukaemia, multiple sclerosis. You name it, we've got it. All the patients are – terminal...'

Twenty-Seven

Basle. About the same time when Newman and Nancy ended their second visit to the Berne Clinic, Bruno Kobler was sitting in his bedroom at the Hotel Terminus which faces the Hauptbahnhof at Basle. Kobler had flown to Basle and this hotel had been chosen because of its strategic position.

Manfred Seidler had been seen purchasing a ticket to Le Pont, the tiny town close to the edge of Lac de Joux in the Jura Mountains. Since then they had lost track of Seidler, which was unfortunate, but Kobler possessed almost the calm patience of Lee Foley when it came to waiting. He spoke to the short, stocky Emil Graf who stood by the window, waiting for a signal from Hugo Munz who was in charge of the team inside the Hauptbahnhof.

'Seidler has to show,' Kobler observed. 'I'm sure he has a rendezvous with someone at Le Pont. And we have more men waiting at the Hotel de la Truite...'

'I don't know Le Pont,' Graf replied. 'From the map it looks a godforsaken place...'

'It is – just the remote spot where Seidler will feel safe to meet whoever he's going to sell the sample he stole from us. And the Hotel de la Truite is near the station...'

'He must have arrived! Munz has just signalled...'

Kobler was already opening the bedroom door, slipping into his astrakhan coat. He gestured towards the holdall bag on the bed to remind Graf not to forget it. Kobler had no intention of carrying the holdall, considering what it contained. Hired lackeys were paid to take such risks. Kobler would only lay his hands on the weapon when the time came to use it. He might not even have to use it at all – not when he had hired backup.

239

'He's boarded the two o'clock train,' Munz informed them as they hurried inside the huge station. 'Here are your tickets – and you'd better move...'

'It's Lausanne first,' Kobler guessed as he settled himself in his first-class seat alongside Munz. Graf had boarded the coach where Seidler was seated.

Kobler studied the rail timetable he had brought with him. He nodded his head as the train glided out of the station, turning the pages as he checked connections, then he glanced at Munz who sat in a rigid posture.

'Relax. We have to wait until we get him on his own. It may be hours yet. We're doing a simple job – like cleaning up some garbage...'

He looked out of the window as the train picked up speed, moving through the suburbs. He was not sorry to leave – the city of Basle was hostile territory, the home base of Dr Max Nagel, the main opponent of the Gold Club. Kobler need not have worried. At that moment Nagel was aboard another train – bound for Berne.

Five coaches ahead Manfred Seidler was a bundle of nerves. He broke open a fresh pack, lit his forty-first cigarette of the day as he thought of the scene back in the flat before he had left.

Erika had rushed back from the office to make him a meal during her lunchtime break. It was during the meal that he had told her he was leaving. She had looked appalled.

'Do you have to? I could take a long lunch hour. Nagel has gone to Berne...'

'What for?' Not that he was really interested.

'It's queer. I had to make him a reservation at the Bellevue Palace: He's attending some Medical Congress reception. He's not even a doctor. And I've never seen him look grimmer – he's up to something...'

'Probably to tie up some deal which will net him another million or two. Erika, I may not be back till tomorrow – so don't start worrying...'

'You know I will – until I see you safe and sound again. Where are you going? What is it all about? I'm entitled to know something, surely?'

'Where doesn't matter,' he had told her. 'I'm going to meet that British foreign correspondent, Robert Newman. He can give me protection – by blowing Terminal wide open. No, don't ask me any more. And thanks for the meal...'

Seated in the train he wished he had said more. He looked up at the rack where he had stored his two suitcases. One contained some of the newspapers Erika had brought him, the other the sample. It would be difficult for anyone to snatch *two* suitcases off him when he was walking along a platform. And they wouldn't know which case contained the sample. You had to think of little things like that.

Seidler stirred restlessly and took a deep drag on the cigarette. They had turned up the heating and he would dearly have liked to take off his jacket. But that was impossible. He was too aware of the 9-mm. Luger inside the spring-loaded holster under his left armpit.

Berne. Beck sat behind his desk in his office and looked at Gisela who had just taken the call. She put down the receiver and turned to speak to her chief.

'That was Leupin. Newman and Dr Kennedy are just leaving the Berne Clinic. He spotted them through his binoculars and radioed in the information...'

'Thank you. Gisela, I want you to make reservations at the Bellevue Palace for three of our men. I want them there during that Medical Congress reception tomorrow. Professor Grange will be there. I may put in an appearance myself.'

'Things are coming to a head, aren't they?'

'Your instincts are usually good, Gisela. The one piece still missing is Manfred Seidler. The fox has gone to cover, but he has to surface. When he does I want to be there – before the military get him. Send out a fresh alert. Seidler must be found at all costs...'

Newman infuriated Nancy when they had left Novak and were approaching the parked Citroën. She just wanted to get away from the place – she was so depressed by Jesse's attitude.

'Let me check the car,' Newman warned. 'Wait here...'

'Why in God's name!'

'To make sure no one has tampered with it.'

He looked for fresh footprints, for any sign that Someone had been clever, using their own footprints still sculpted in the hard snow. He checked the bonnet where he had pressed a small amount of snow on arrival, snow which had frozen immediately at the point where the bonnet lifted. The snow was undisturbed. He unlocked the car and waved to Nancy to get into the passenger seat.

'I'm driving this time,' he informed her as he got behind the wheel and she flopped beside him.

'You don't like my driving?' she flared.

'Remember last time – the snowplough?'

'Maybe you're right. Why all the fuss about someone tampering with it?'

'In case they'd placed a bomb,' he told her brutally as he continued his policy of unnerving her.

'Jesus! You want a nervous wreck on your hands?'

They said nothing more to each other during the drive back to Berne which was uneventful. At the Bellevue Palace they had a late lunch in the coffee shop which was quiet so it was safe to talk freely. Nancy brought up the subject over their coffee.

'The next thing is Seidler?'

'That's right. Don't forget to pack the two overnight cases. I have an idea we're going to need them...'

'Which was the first thing I was going to do. At least this time I'm permitted to accompany you...'

'Nancy, do shut up...'

They spent the whole of the rest of the afternoon inside the bedroom in case Seidler phoned early. Newman had purchased a road map the previous day and he studied this while Nancy kicked off her shoes, lay on the bed and tried to sleep. She was certain she'd stay awake and the ringing of the phone jerked her back into consciousness with a start. Newman grabbed for the instrument, the map spread out on the other bed.

242

'Newman speaking...'

'This is Manfred Seidler. I am only going to say this one time...'

'You'll repeat it if I don't get it. Go on...'

'Le Pont, in the Juras, near Lac de Joux. You know it?'

'Yes...'

'We rendezvous at exactly nineteen twenty-eight hours. At the station. I will be on the train which arrives at nineteen twenty-eight...'

'For Christ's sake, I'll never make it. Don't you realize it's five o'clock now?'

'If you are interested in the information I can provide – no details over the phone – bring two thousand Swiss francs in cash. Park your car a very short distance from the station – but out of sight. I shall be carrying two suitcases.'

'I need more time. There's snow in the Juras. The roads will be hell...'

'Nineteen twenty-eight hours. And I won't wait. Are you coming or not?'

'I'm coming...'

There was a click at the other end of the line. Seidler had broken the connection. Newman replaced the receiver and checked his watch again. He examined the map quickly while Nancy leaned over his shoulder.

'Can we make it?' she asked.

'If we go this way we just might. He's cutting it bloody fine...'

His finger traced a route from Berne along motorway N12 down to Lake Geneva. The finger turned on to motorway N9 – roughly running parallel westward to the lake until it joined the third motorway, N1. At a place called Rolle, between Lausanne and Geneva, on the shore of the lake, Newman traced a route along a road winding up over the Juras and stopped at Le Pont.

'That's a long way round,' Nancy objected. 'It's two sides of a triangle...'

'It's also the only way we'll get there in time – by using the motorways. And I've driven up the section from Rolle, so I know the road. It will be diabolical when we get above the snow line. Come on, girl. I'll take the cases. Thank God I had the tank refilled on the way back from Thun...'

They were waiting for the lift when Nancy told Newman to go ahead to the car and she'd follow. 'I've forgotten my purse,' she explained as the lift arrived and Newman, swearing, stepped inside.

Lausanne Gare. Seidler lugged the two suitcases out of the phone booth back on to the platform. He felt a sense of relief: Newman was coming. He hurriedly made his way to the restaurant where there would be plenty of people while he waited for his next train.

He was deliberately taking a roundabout route – to make sure he was not being followed. Now he had to wait for the *Cisalpin*, the Paris express which travelled non-stop to the frontier station at Vallorbe. From there he would back-track on the small local leaving Vallorbe at 19.09 and reaching Le Pont at 19.28.

Berne. 'Leupin calling, Chief. Newman has just left the hotel carrying two cases. He's putting them in the back of his car, the Citroën. Hold on, his fiancée has dashed out to join him...'

'It's all right, Leupin,' Beck reassured his subordinate. 'I have allocated another six men to the job – as a contingency measure. Six men with three more cars. They can leapfrog to make sure he doesn't know what we're doing. You and Marbot tail him for the first lap. Good luck...'

Beck put down the phone and sighed as he looked across at Gisela. She brought over the fresh cup of coffee she had poured for him. It looked as though it was going to be quite a night: Beck was in his shirtsleeves, the sure sign of a long siege.

'Newman and his girl just left the Bellevue with two cases,' he told her. 'They're getting into that hired car...'

'They're trying to leave the country?'

'That would be out of character for Newman at this stage of the game. You have laid on that other facility I requested?'

'The machine is already standing by...'

It was very dark that night. It was very cold. Newman almost made the Citroën fly, moving well over the limit when he felt he could risk it on the motorways. At that, they were overtaken several times, twin headlights turned full on, flashing past them at God knew what speed.

'That couldn't be the police, could it?' Nancy wondered aloud when the second car sped past.

'Hardly. The first was a Saab, that was a Volvo...'

'I keep thinking about Jesse. I don't see what we can do about him.'

'Nothing. I can see where you get your stubborn streak from.'

'We can't just do nothing....'

'Leave him to me...'

'And what does that mean?' she asked.

'I'll think of something...'

He slowed down on the way to Geneva. A few minutes later the route sign appeared indicating a turn-off. *Rolle VD* – Rolle, Canton of the Vaud. Newman swung away from the lake, away from the N1 on to the side road north which immediately began to climb. In the distance the Juras loomed like a giant white tidal wave arrested in mid-motion. Then they were above the snow line.

In their headlights the narrow road ahead was like a mirror, a mirror of ice. The road turned and twisted, climbing steeper and steeper. The danger signs began to appear, signs with a sinister zigzag. *Risque de Verglas*. Skid. Ice. Now the road really began the ascent. Newman's arms ached with the strain of holding the wheel, keeping the car on the road. Nancy glanced at him. His lips were compressed, eyes narrowed. She lit a cigarette, glanced in the wing mirror. The lights of the black Audi were still there. A long way back on an unusually straight section. First the Saab, then the Volvo, now the Audi. She looked ahead and stiffened.

'Oh, Christ!'

The wave of the Juras hung above them. *Verglas*. The zigzags were incredible. Newman was constantly turning the wheel. And now they had entered a narrow gulch. Snow banked high on both sides. Beyond reared dark walls of dense fir forest, the branches of trees sagging under the weight of the snow. She reached to turn up the heater and found it already full on. They went on climbing, twisting inside the gulch. The clock on the dashboard registered 19.20 hours. Eight minutes to rendezvous time. They'd never make it.

They went over the top without warning. Swinging round a particularly suicidal bend, the road suddenly levelled out. They started to descend. Lights appeared in the distance.

'Le Pont,' Newman said.

A cluster of houses, steep-roofed, spilling down a hillside. The roofs heavy with snow. Wooden balconies at first-floor level. Hardly more than a hamlet. Newman nudged the car past a hotel ablaze with lights. Hotel de la Truite.

'Look!'

Newman pointed up at the hotel. Under the eaves shards of ice a foot long projected downwards. A palisade of icicles. Inverted. The station was little more than a one-storey hut, an isolated building with no one about. The dashboard clock registered 19.26 hours. Newman parked the car beside the building, out of sight of the exit. First, he had swung it through one hundred and eighty degrees – involving a major rear-wheel skid which made Nancy clench her hands. Ready for a swift departure. He left the engine ticking over.

'I want you to take over the wheel,' he told Nancy. 'I'm going to stand near the exit when the train comes in. This could be a trap. If I come running move like a bird when I dive inside – back the way we came. I'm leaving you now – look, the train is coming...'

The train, three small coaches, an abbreviated caterpillar of lights, stopped behind the station – no more than a wayside halt. Newman heard the distinctive sound of a door slamming. A gaunt-faced man, hatless, carrying two suitcases, appeared under the pallid light over the exit. He had a haunted look, calling out in German.

'Newman! Where is the car... I am being followed...'

Two men appeared behind him in the exit. A car driven at high speed came up the road from the direction of Neuchatel – and Berne. Its headlamps swept like searchlights over the station exit. Newman caught a flash of red – red like the Porsche he had seen on the Thun motorway. There was a scream of brakes applied savagely. The barrel of a rifle projected from the driver's window. At the same moment Nancy drove the Citroën round from the side of the station, pulled up, threw open the doors.

'Inside the car, Seidler!' Newman yelled.

He grabbed one suitcase, hurled it on the rear seat, shoved Seidler after it, shut the door and dived into the front passenger seat. The other car was still moving, slithering in a skid on ice as the rifle barrel moved further out of the window. One of the two men following Seidler was pulling something out from inside his coat.

'Move!' Newman shouted at Nancy. 'Back the way we came...'

The rifle was fired, a detonating report above the sounds of both cars' engines. The man hauling something out from inside his coat pocket was thrown backwards as though kicked by an elephant. The rifle spoke a second time. The other man performed a weird pirouette, clutching his chest, then sagging into the snow...'

It was incredible marksmanship. Two bullets fired by a man who had to be driving with one hand, operating the rifle with the other, all while his car was recovering from a skid. Two men died. Newman had no doubt that neither had survived the impact of what had sounded like a high-velocity rifle.

Nancy was driving the Citroën across the beam of the other vehicle's headlights, speeding beyond them as she pressed her foot down regardless of the treachery of the ground beneath their wheels. Then the station was behind them and they were going back over their previous route.

'That man behind him pulled out a gun,' Seidler croaked hoarsely.

'I saw it,' Newman replied tersely.

They were approaching the Hotel de la Truite when a black Mercedes swung out from the drive straight across the path of the Citroën. Nancy jammed on the brakes, the car slithered, then stopped. The Mercedes drove on past towards the station.

'Bastard!' Nancy snapped between clenched teeth.

'Maybe he's on his way to meet two bodies,' Newman speculated.

Nancy glared at him and started the car moving again. Outside the hotel a pair of skis had been rammed vertically into the ground. During their brief stop Newman had heard singing with a drunken cadence coming from inside the hotel. Death at the station, revelry at the inn. *Après-ski* in full swing.

Seidler leaned forward, grasping the backs of their seats. He stared through the windscreen as though getting his bearings. He spoke suddenly, this time in English for Nancy's benefit.

'Not the left turn to Rolle! Bear right. Take the lakeside road...'

'Do as he says,' Newman said quietly. 'Why, Seidler? I'd have thought this was a good place to leave fast...'

'There is a house on the left-hand side of this road at the foot of the mountain. We talk there... *Mein Gott,* what was that?'

'It's that helicopter again,' Nancy said, glancing out of her side window. 'If it *is* the same one. I first heard it when we turned off at Rolle...'

'So did I,' agreed Newman. 'It followed us up the mountain. There are a lot of military choppers floating around...'

'*Military?*' Seidler sounded alarmed. 'You were followed?'

'Shut up!' Newman told him. 'Just warn us before we reach this house...'

'Keep to the road round the lake before I tell you to stop. Keep the very fast speed...'

'I need directions as to the route, not how to drive,' Nancy replied coldly.

At about three thousand feet the Vallée de Joux nestles inside folds of the Jura Mountains. To their right the lake was a bed of solid ice covered with a counterpane of snow. To the left the mountain slopes were scarred with the graffiti of daytime skiers propelling themselves across the snow. Here and there loomed the silhouettes of two-storey houses constructed of shiny new wood. As a winter ski resort Le Pont was prospering.

'This is it,' Seidler called out, 'just before we arrive in the L'Abbaye village...' He leaned forward again. 'Place the car in the garage...'

'Don't,' Newman interjected. 'Drive it under that copse of firs. Back it in if you can – facing the way we're going now.'

'You know something? I might just manage that, Robert...'

Newman's mind was galloping. He had just seen his opportunity. L'Abbaye. Beyond the far end of the lake was Le Brassus. Only a few kilometres beyond Le Brassus was a tiny *Douane*, a Customs post, thinly manned. And beyond that the road passed into *France*. The road continued over French soil for another twenty kilometres or so to La Cure. He could even remember the Hotel Franco-Suisse where he had once stayed the night – the strange hotel where you went through the front door still in France and out of the back door into Switzerland! At La Cure they could turn north, continuing into France. That was how he was going to get Nancy out of Switzerland – to safety – tonight.

'Why not the garage?' Seidler complained.

'With the car left outside we can escape quickly – or have you not noticed that chopper is still with us?'

'You have brought the two thousand Swiss francs?' demanded Seidler.

'No. You just put that in because people don't value something they can get for nothing.' Newman turned to face Seidler. 'If you don't want to talk we'll drop you here and drive away. Make up your mind...'

'We go into the house...'

Seidler looked to be near the end of his tether. Haunted eyes, deep in their sockets, stared back at Newman as Nancy skilfully backed the Citroën off the road a short distance up the slope under the firs. She switched off the engine and Newman got out of the car, standing for a moment to stretch his aching limbs.

The two-storey house stood a few yards back from the road on the lower slope. It was old, decrepit and a veranda ran the full length of the ground floor. A short flight of wooden steps led up to the front door and there were balconies in front of the shuttered windows on the first floor.

The downstairs windows were also shuttered. Nancy thought it was a grim, eerie-looking place.

The beat of the chopper's motor was louder now the Citroën was silent. Newman craned his neck but it was somewhere behind the copse and going away from them. He slapped his gloved hands round his forearms.

'God, it's freezing,' commented Nancy.

At that height it was Arctic. No wind. Just a sub-zero temperature which was already penetrating Newman's shoes and gloves. Another row of stiletto-like icicles was suspended from the house's gutter. Newman made no effort to help with the two suitcases Seidler carried up the steps.

'Whose place is this?' he asked as Seidler took a key out of his pocket.

'A friend's. He dwells here only in the summertime...'

'Sensible chap...'

To Newman's surprise, the key turned in the lock first time. They entered a huge room which seemed to occupy most of the ground floor. At the far end on the left-hand side a wooden staircase led up to a minstrel's gallery overlooking the room below.

The floor, made of wooden planks, was varnished and decorated with worn rugs scattered at intervals. The furniture was heavy and traditional; old chairs, tables, sideboards and bookcases. Nancy noticed a film of dust lay over everything.

Along the right-hand wall was the only modern innovation – a kitchen galley with formica worktops. She ran a finger along them and it came away black with dust. Opening a cupboard she found it well-stocked with canned food and jars of coffee.

'I will demonstrate at once what this is all about,' Seidler informed Newman in German. 'Please wait here...'

He disappeared through a doorway in the rear wall, dumping one suitcase on the floor and carrying the other. Newman turned to Nancy and shrugged. She asked him what Seidler had said and he told her. Even inside the house with the front door closed it was icy – and they could still hear the chopper in the distance as though it were circling.

Nancy opened her mouth and screamed at the top of her voice. Newman swung round and stared at the back of the room.

A hideous apparition had appeared in the doorway through which Seidler had disappeared. Newman understood the scream as he gazed at the man with no head standing there, the man with the blank goggle-eyes of an octopus. Seidler was wearing a gas mask, a mask with strange letters stencilled above the frightening goggle-eyes. *CCCP*. USSR.

Twenty-Eight

'I brought half-a-dozen consignments of these gas masks over the border... smuggled them across the Austrian frontier from the Soviet depot inside Czechoslovakia... I speak Czech fluently which helped...'

The words tumbled out of Seidler – like a man who has carried too much locked away in his mind for too long. After the macabre demonstration he had removed the mask and Nancy was now making coffee. She had broken the seal on one of the jars of instant coffee, found a saucepan inside a cupboard and had boiled a pan of water on the electric cooker. Pouring the water into each of three chunky mugs containing some of the coffee, she stirred and then handed them round.

'We need some internal central heating in this ice-box,' she observed. 'And I do wish that bloody chopper would go away...'

Newman heard a car approaching along the icy lakeside road from the direction of Le Pont. The shuttered windows made it impossible to see outside. He ran to the front door and heaved it open – just in time to see the tail-lights of the car vanishing towards Le Brassus. A red car. It was moving like a bat out of hell despite the icy surface. He closed the door again.

'Who employed you for this job, Seidler?'

'You'll write a big story – get it in the international press, expose them... otherwise I'm finished... I'm giving you the scoop of a lifetime...'

Seidler was badly rattled, self-control gone, almost on the verge of hysteria as he rambled on in German. He wore an expensive camel-hair coat, a silk scarf, hand-made shoes. Newman drank some of the scalding coffee before he replied.

'Answer my question – I'll decide how to handle it later. Keep to the point. I think we have very little time left,' he warned in English for Nancy's benefit.

'That car which shot past worries you?' she asked.

'Everything worries me. That car, yes. Plus the Audi, the Saab and the Volvo which kept passing us on our way up here. And that military chopper up there. Add the carnage back at the station and we all have a great deal to worry about. So, Seidler, who employed you? One question at a time...'

'The Berne Clinic. Professor Grange – although mostly I dealt with that brute, Kobler. Grange used me because of my connections inside Czechoslovakia...'

'And how did you obtain these consignments? You can't just walk in and out of a Soviet military depot.'

For the first time a bleak smile appeared on Seidler's cadaverous face. He sat down gingerly on the arm of a large chair as though it might blow up under him. He gulped down some of his coffee, wiped his mouth with the back of his hand.

'You've heard of the honey-traps the Russian secret police use? They get a girl to compromise someone, take photos...'

'I know all about honey-traps. I told you to keep to the point! Any moment now this house may become one of the most dangerous places in Switzerland...'

'This honey-trap worked in reverse. By pure chance. The brilliant Czech they use to operate the computer for stock control at the depot met an Austrian girl on holiday while he was in Prague. He's crazy over her. She's waiting for him in Munich – waiting for him to get out. For that you need money, a lot of it. I provided that money. He provided the gas masks and fiddled the computer...'

'Why does Grange want this supply of Soviet gas masks?'

'To defend Switzerland, of course – and to make another fortune. Seventy per cent of the Swiss population have *atom-bunkers* they can go to in case of nuclear war. Imagine how many gas masks it would take to equip the same number of people to protect them against Soviet chemical warfare.'

'But why have them delivered to the Berne Clinic? The place isn't a factory. I still don't get it...'

'He *tests* the gas masks there...'

'He does what!'

'Bob,' Nancy interrupted, 'do we have to talk to him here? There's something about this place I don't like...'

The wind had started to rise in the Juras. The timbers of the ancient house began to creak and groan. The place seemed to *tremble* like a ship in a choppy sea. Newman guessed it was the low temperature – the wood was contracting. During their brief drive from Le Pont he had noticed in the glare of the headlights places on the verge of the road where the snow had melted. The sun must have shone down on the Vallée de Joux; hence the criss-cross of ski-tracks on the slopes. It was the extreme change in temperature which was affecting the old building – plus the onset of the wind.

'We have to talk here,' he said rapidly in English, hoping Seidler would miss his meaning. 'I told you, I think we have very little time. God knows what's waiting for us outside when we do leave...'

'Thank you. You are *so* reassuring...'

Newman's callousness was deliberate. He was preparing Nancy psychologically for the dash to the French frontier. He continued questioning Seidler.

'How does Grange test the gas masks?'

'He started using animals. I once saw an obscene sight – a chimpanzee escaped. It was wearing a gas mask, clawing at it to try and get it off its head...'.

'And then?'

'He decided he had to progress to testing the masks on human beings. He uses the patients – they're terminal, anyway. I arrived late in the Lear jet from Vienna a few weeks ago with the previous consignment. A cock-up at Schwechat Airport outside Vienna. The driver of the van waiting for me at Belp was ill – food-poisoning, he said. I had to take over the wheel and drive to the Clinic well after dark. I saw a woman – one of the patients she must have been – running in the grounds wearing a gas mask and a bathrobe. She was trying to tear off the mask while she ran. They were firing canisters from something at her – the canisters burst in front of her...'

'So where do they get the gas from?' Newman demanded.

'How the hell do I know? I certainly never brought any gas out of Czechoslovakia. Luckily they didn't see the van – so I turned it round and arrived at the Clinic later. The Swiss Army is guarding that place...'

'How do you know that?'

'I've caught glimpses of men in Swiss uniform – inside that gatehouse and patrolling the grounds at a distance. We're in real trouble, Newman, the worst kind...'

'What goes on inside that laboratory – and inside the *atombunker*?'

'No idea. I've never been there...

'I'm still not convinced. Give me your full name...'

'Gustav Manfred Seidler...'

'And you brought these gas masks on the orders of Dr Bruno Kobler of the Berne Clinic?'

'I told you that. Yes. He takes his orders from Grange...'

'Seidler, why did you do this?'

'For money, a lot of money. One other thing, I have a girlfriend in...'

'That's enough!' Newman rapped out.

He walked over to a large armchair which stood with its tall back to Seidler who suddenly frowned and crossed the room to stare at the miniature tape-recorder Newman had placed there and turned on during Seidler's brief absence when they first arrived. The German grabbed for it but Newman grasped his arm and shoved him away. Seidler's expression was livid.

'You bastard!' Seidler exploded.

'Part of any self-respecting newspaper man's equipment,' Newman lied as he pressed a button and ran the tape to the end. 'Some take notes, but I thought that might inhibit you...'

'So that was what you bought today in that shop in the Marktgasse,' Nancy commented as she peered over the back of the armchair.

'I want you to find somewhere to hide this, Nancy...'

Newman had extracted the small tape and he handed her the machine. He next took the gas mask Seidler had left on a table and placed it on the working top in the kitchen under the glare of the spotlights which illuminated the galley. Standing back a few feet, he took from his pocket Nagy's small Voigtlander *Vitoret 110* camera and attached one of the flash-bulbs he had purchased from the same shop. He took four pictures of the mask with flashes and then excused himself, asking Seidler to guide him to the lavatory.

'Through that door where I went when we arrived,' Seidler told him sullenly. 'You'll find it on your right when you get inside...'

Hidden in the lavatory, Newman pulled up his trouser legs and concealed the miniature tape inside the thick sock on his left foot. The film from the camera he shoved down inside his other sock. When he came out Seidler was putting the gas mask into one of the suitcases and snapping the catches shut.

'I'll keep this if you don't mind...'

'It's your property. Why the sudden desire for cleanliness, Nancy? We've got to get out of here fast before something unfortunate happens.'

She was crouched by the huge open fireplace filled with logs, using a dustpan and brush to sweep up the hearth. She stood up, put the pan and brush back inside a cupboard and rubbed her hands clean of dust.

'You wanted the tape-recorder hidden. It's underneath the logs,' she snapped.

'That's a good place. Thanks, Nancy.' Newman turned towards Seidler. 'You were saying something about a girlfriend – I didn't think you'd want her details on record...'

'I am grateful...' Seidler swallowed and showed signs of emotion. 'If anything happens to me I would like her to know. She had nothing to do with Terminal. Will you take down her address and phone number? Erika Stahel...'

Newman wrote the details in his notebook with a wooden expression as though he had never heard of her. He went on writing and then froze for a second at Seidler's next words.

'She works for Dr Max Nagel, the big Basle banker. Nagel is the only man powerful enough to oppose Grange. He has just left Basle for Berne to attend some medical reception at the Bellevue Palace...'

'The reception tomorrow?' Nancy asked sharply.

'I don't know when. Hadn't we better leave this place?'

'Immediately,' responded Newman. 'And prepare yourself for a rough ride. I'm driving like hell along the road to Le Brassus...'

'Why Le Brassus?' Seidler queried, picking up the suitcase containing the gas mask.

'Because we want to avoid Le Pont – after what happened at the station. God knows what could be waiting for us there.'

Nancy had washed up the pan, their mugs and replaced them where she had found them. She was carrying the opened jar of coffee which she said ought to be taken away. No trace of their visit remained when Seidler, still nervy and anxious to leave, opened the front door. There was a score of questions Newman would have liked to ask him but the priority was to move, to get over the border into France. Newman held the front door key Seidler had handed him. The first shot was fired as Newman locked the door while Seidler and Nancy were heading for the Citroën parked under the trees. In the cold silence of the night the report was a loud *Crack!*

'Run!' Newman yelled. 'Crouch down! Get into the car for Christ's sake!'

The second shot – Newman now realized it was a rifle – was fired in rapid succession. Stumbling down the icy steps, holding the second suitcase Seidler had left behind in his left hand, Newman saw the case Seidler had taken jerk out of his hand. The shot had passed through the case. Seidler picked it up and continued his shambling trot towards the car which Nancy had already reached, unlocked and opened the doors.

A third shot was fired, a fourth – neither came anywhere near them. That was when Newman realized there was a second rifleman – firing at the first. The night reverberated with a fusillade of shots.

The wind blew and there was a strange weather phenomenon Newman had never seen before. A wave of snow dust, as fine as salt particles, cruised a foot high across the lower slopes, swirling round his ankles as he reached the car. Seidler had dived into the rear seat, Nancy was in the front passenger seat. She had inserted one of the keys

257

Newman had given her on their arrival while he studied the old house, in the ignition. He slid in behind the wheel, slammed the door, drove out from under the trees and a rifle shot grazed the bonnet.

'Oh, Jesus!' said Nancy. 'What's happening?'

'It's weird – there are two of them. One firing at us, the other firing at the first marksman. Christ, how many people know we're up here?'

The sound of the shots faded as he drove as fast as he dare. In their headlights the road was gleaming like a skating rink. He passed through the main street of L'Abbaye and the village seemed deserted. Now for Le Brassus – and the French border. That was when he heard again the sound of the chopper coming closer.

Le Brassus VD – the road sign said – was a village of ancient villas, stark trees and gardens fronted with beech hedges half-buried under a coating of snow. Again deserted. They had left the lake behind. Newman pulled out of a skid and drove on.

'The second case I threw in the back,' he called out. 'It contains what, Seidler?'

'Old newspapers. Where are you taking me?'

'To safety. The French frontier is just ahead. If I have to, I'll crash the border to get through...'

'We're leaving Switzerland?' Nancy asked.

'You'll be safer in France, so will Seidler. And I may be able to operate more freely outside Switzerland. I plan to phone Beck, tell him we have Seidler's evidence, see if he'll raid the Berne Clinic...'

The sign came up in their headlights. *Zoll-Douane. 2 km.* They were within a couple of kilometres of escape. Newman pressed his foot down, at times gliding over the ice shining threateningly in the beams. He glanced at Nancy and she nodded her approval of the course he was taking. She had been badly shaken by the violence at Le Pont station, by the shooting outside the old house.

'Oh, God! No!' she exclaimed.

Something else was showing up in the headlights and Newman slowed down. The black Audi had been positioned at right-angles, acting as a road-block. To one side a second car, a Saab, was parked on the verge. Uniformed policemen stood waving torches frantically. Newman stopped the car, sagged behind the wheel. They were trapped.

The first sound he heard as he stepped out on to the slippery road was the roar of the chopper's rotors as it landed, a large, dark silhouette, in a nearby field. He told Nancy and Seidler to stay in the car and went to meet the nearest policeman.

'What the devil do you think you're doing?' he asked in French.

'Instructions, sir. Someone is coming...'

The policeman gestured towards the field where the chopper had landed. A compact figure came out of the darkness, hatless and wearing an overcoat. Arthur Beck. Of course. The Federal police chief trod his way carefully across the road and peered inside the Citroën.

'You've no reason to stop us,' Newman snapped.

'You were thinking of leaving the country?' Beck enquired.

'What concern is it of yours?'

'Every concern, my friend. You are a material witness in my investigation into the deaths of Julius Nagy and Bernard Mason...'

Another man had emerged from the helicopter and was walking towards Beck. A man of medium height, well-built, who walked with a deliberate tread. As he passed in front of the headlights of the Citroën Newman saw he was dressed in the uniform of a colonel in the Swiss Army. Under his peaked cap, beneath his thick eyebrows, motionless eyes stared at Newman. Clean-shaven, he had a strong nose, a thin-lipped mouth and he carried himself with an air of confidence verging on arrogance. Newman recognized him before Beck made his introduction.

'This is Colonel Victor Signer, president of the Zurcher Kredit Bank. He called on me just before I was leaving – he expressed a wish to accompany me. This is Robert Newman...'

No handshake. Signer half-smiled, not pleasantly, dipped his head in acknowledgement. The blank eyes, still studying Newman, reminded him of films he had seen of sharks, which was fanciful, he told himself. Of one thing he was sure. God had just arrived.

'I hear you have been causing us some trouble, Newman,' Signer remarked.

He spoke through his nose, like a man with adenoids and he looked at the ground as though addressing a subordinate.

'You are speaking personally?' Newman suggested.

'I didn't come here to fence with you...'

'Why did you come here, Signer?'

The eyes snapped up and there was a brief flicker of fury. He would be a bastard to serve under. Autocratic, callous, sarcastic. The original martinet. Newman understood now why Blanche disliked her stepfather so much. The colonel clasped his hands which, despite the cold, were clad in fine suede gloves. A very tough baby, Victor Signer. Beck intervened, as though afraid things were getting out of control.

'Newman, I have to ask you to return with me to Berne – together with your two companions...'

Signer walked slowly round the Citroën and peered in at the rear seat. Seidler shrank back from his gaze, clutching his suitcase.

'Not Dr Kennedy,' Newman said firmly. 'You have no grounds for detaining her...'

'She witnessed the death of Mrs Laird. Until that case is resolved I must insist that she remains on Swiss territory...'

'You bastard,' Newman whispered.

'And the man in the rear of the car. He wouldn't by chance be Manfred Seidler?' Beck opened the rear door. 'Please step out Mr Seidler-we have been searching everywhere for you.'

'Grab his case,' Newman whispered again. 'Don't open it – and don't let Signer get his hands on it...'

Seidler emerged shakily from the car, releasing the suitcase Beck reached for without protest. Signer wandered round the Citroën to join them, flexing his gloved hands. Then he stood waiting. He would be about five feet ten tall, Newman guessed, but the controlled force of his personality made him seem taller. This was a man who dealt in millions at his bank.

'I would like to see the contents of that suitcase,' he remarked.

'No! Colonel,' Beck replied. 'I am investigating three potential homicides, two positive ones. Not an hour ago a couple of men arriving at Le Pont station were murdered. This case may well contain evidence. It goes straight to our forensic people unopened. It is not a matter I care to debate...'

'As you wish...'

Signer half-smiled again and walked across to stand in front of the headlight beams of the Saab parked on the verge. He removed his left glove and clenched his hand. Beck, still holding on to the suitcase, gestured for Seidler to follow him. Newman sensed that something was wrong but couldn't immediately put his finger on it. Signer had given up too easily...

'Seidler! Get away from those headlights!' he shouted.

Following Beck, Seidler was illuminated by the headlamps of the Citroën – illuminated like a target on a firing range at night. There was a loud report and Seidler leapt forward, vaulted clear off the ground and sprawled over the bonnet of the Audi. A second rifle report shattered the night. The sprawled body coughed, a convulsive movement, then flopped back over the bonnet. In the headlights a patch of dampness – blood – began to spread midway down the centre of Seidler's back. The second shot had fractured his spine. He was dead twice over.

Twenty-Nine

Chaos. Beck shouting, 'Douse those bloody lights...' An order hardly necessary – the drivers inside the Audi and the Saab turned them off while he was shouting the order. No one wanted to be a target for the marksman. Policemen running all over the place. Newman had turned off his own lights.

It was Beck who regained control of the situation, issuing terse commands through his walkie-talkie. Policemen crouched under cover of the vehicles. Nancy was crouched over Seidler's spread-eagled body, checking his pulse. She turned to Beck who gently pressed her down by the car as Newman joined them.

'He's dead,' Nancy told them. 'Half his head was shot away by the first bullet...'

'My commiserations, madame,' said Beck.

'Why?'

'For your most unfortunate experiences in my country. This is the second time this week you have been present to confirm a violent death. If I may offer my services? We can fly you back to Berne in the helicopter. A policeman can drive your Citroën back to the Bellevue Palace.' He looked up. 'There is something wrong, Newman?'

'Signer. Look at him. He's the only man who didn't move...'

The colonel was still standing motionless in front of the Saab where he, also, had been silhouetted in the glare of the beams of headlights. He stood with his hands clasped over his lower abdomen. Newman noticed he had now replaced the suede glove on his left hand.

'He is a soldier,' Beck commented, 'a man accustomed to the experience of being under fire. Here he comes...'

Signer walked slowly towards the crouched trio and remained standing as he stared down at them. His tone was remote and calm when he spoke.

'He missed me. You realize I was the target?'

Newman stood up slowly. He shook his head, staring direct at the colonel. Signer made an irritable gesture with one hand. When he spoke his tone suggested he was addressing a corporal he had decided to demote.

'Why are you shaking your head? Of course I was the target. I was standing still. Doubtless one of these crazy terrorists.'

'The killer was a marksman,' Newman replied. 'Maybe if there had been only one bullet the target would have been disputable. There was a second – which also hit Seidler straight on. That means a marksman. How many marksmen do you have under your command, Signer?'

'You are implying... what?'

'Gentlemen!' Beck had also stood up, retaining his hand on Nancy's shoulder to keep her under cover. 'Gentlemen,' he repeated, 'we have another murder on our hands. Many here are still in a stale of shock. No arguments, no quarrels. That is final. Colonel, you wish to accompany us back to Berne in the helicopter?'

'Give me a car, a driver. I will go on to Geneva now we are so close. And I understood Military Intelligence wished to interview this man Seidler...'

'They might have some difficulty doing that now,' Beck 'observed. 'I will deal with the body – and you may have both a car and a driver to take you to Geneva. The Saab, I suggest. If you could leave at once, Colonel, it will help me to go about my duties.'

It was a dismissal and Signer knew it. He didn't like it. He turned on his heel without a word of thanks and climbed inside the rear of the Saab. Within a minute the tail-lights of the Saab were vanishing towards the French frontier.

'I thought that was the way to France,' Nancy said to Beck.

'Madame, it is a most curious road. You cross the border into France, drive fifteen to twenty kilometres over French soil to La Cure, and there the road forks. One way north to the French hinterland, the other way down a devilish road to Geneva – after re-crossing the border into Switzerland.' He glanced towards Seidler's crumpled form. 'And now some unknown marksman has eliminated our only surviving witness.'

'There may be someone still left,' Newman replied.

'The name, please,' Beck demanded.

'I think the person I'm thinking of may be safer if for the moment I keep that information to myself. Incidentally, Beck, I noticed you led Seidler in front of those headlights.'

'I have never claimed papal infallibility,' Beck responded stiffly. 'Shall we all board the helicopter and return to Berne...' He reached inside the rear of the Citroën. 'And I think we will take this second suitcase with us...'

'Beck, I'm asking you one more time. Let Dr Kennedy go. She can drive this car into France...'

'Out of the question. It is regrettable, madame, but you are a vital witness...'

'Then you'll get the minimum of cooperation from me,' Newman told him.

'Again regrettably, if necessary I shall have to soldier on by myself. May we now depart? I insist...'

'What about that poor sod's body?'

'I have already summoned an ambulance to take him to the morgue in Berne. More work for the unfortunate Dr Kleist. And there are two more bodies at Le Pont station. Which route did you take to arrive here? And where did you pick up Manfred Seidler?'

Newman spoke quickly before Nancy could say anything. 'I drove up from Rolle. Seidler had phoned me earlier this evening to make the arrangement. He was waiting for us outside the Hotel de la Truite. I turned the car round and we drove for the French border. Seidler wanted to get out of Switzerland before he'd talk...'

'You did not go on to the station? Are you certain?'

'I was driving the bloody car. When we'd collected Seidler the job was done. The next objective was the French border. How many times do I have to tell you? And these bodies at the station. Whose bodies?'

'That we do not know. One of my patrol cars – I have them covering the whole Jura – reported finding the corpses over the radio. A message reached me aboard the helicopter. Two men – carrying no means of identification. Both armed with 9-mm. Lugers. One man was clasping his weapon when they discovered them.' He turned to Nancy. 'Tomorrow there is to be a large medical reception held at the Bellevue. Will you be attending that?'

'Yes. Since we have to go back I'll take the opportunity to talk with Professor Grange. There are a few questions I want to ask him...'

'That reception may be an explosive affair,' Beck commented. 'Before I flew here I heard that Dr Max Nagel had just arrived from Basle – Professor Grange's most bitter enemy. There maybe more than one confrontation. Something tells me this affair is coming to a head...'

'I'm frozen,' Nancy protested. 'Can we get moving...'

'Of course. My apologies. Let me lead the way. It is a large machine so you should have a comfortable flight...'

'Don't expect much conversation,' Newman rapped back.

The helicopter was a French Alouette. As it lifted off and gained height Newman looked down on the white wasteland below, the graveyard of three men in one night. There were two incidents during the flight to Belp.

Beck opened each suitcase, raising the lids so no one else could see the contents. Newman saw him freeze for a moment when he saw the gas mask. Beck leaned over in his seat and he spoke with his mouth close to Newman's ear.

'Did you have a chance to open these cases?'

Newman shook his head, making no verbal response above the roar of the rotors. A short while later Beck received a message over the radio. He made no reference to it as the chopper flew on to Belp.

Another black Audi was waiting for them when they landed at Belp. Beck took the wheel after placing both suitcases in the boot, inviting Nancy to sit in the back while Newman sat alongside him. They drove in silence along the motorway to Berne. Newman was determined to give the police chief no conversational opening. His only comment was to insist that Beck drove them to the Bellevue Palace. No more interviews at the Taubenhalde: Nancy was exhausted with her ordeal and he was pretty tired himself.

265

'That radio message I received aboard the Alouette,' Beck began as they approached the outskirts of Berne. 'One of the patrols stopped a red Mercedes for checking near Neuchatel, a car driven by a chauffeur with one passenger in the back.'

'That concerns me?'

'It might concern us both. The passenger was Dr Bruno Kobler. He said he was on his way to Geneva from Berne. A curious route to take. He brushed aside any suggestion he had been anywhere in the vicinity of the Juras. One of the patrol car men noticed the car's tyres had faint traces of snow crust embedded in the treads. There is no snow at that level...'

'I see. Why didn't they search the car?'

'On what grounds? And I have to be careful. Very powerful men are waiting for me to make one false move – so I can be removed from the case. I found his destination interesting – recalling that Colonel Signer said he also was heading for Geneva.'

'You did say a *red* Mercedes?' Newman enquired. He said no more when Beck confirmed the colour of the car.

'God! I feel *trapped*, Bob,' Nancy said as they settled down in their bedroom. She kept walking about restlessly. 'One part of me wants to stay – to be near Jesse, to try and haul him out of that place. Another part wants to get away – yet I like Berne, I like the people. Do I have to go to Beck's office with you in the morning?'

'Stop pacing round like a tigress. Sit down and have something to drink. It will relax you...'

They had used Room Service to send up plates of smoked salmon and a bottle of Yvorne, a dry Swiss white wine. Newman filled their glasses and sipped at the wine as Nancy flopped in a chair beside him.

'Beck needs affidavits from both of us. We witnessed the murder of Seidler...'

'We witnessed two more murders. You were quick with your reply when he asked you about the station at Le Pont. Can we get away with that? Is it wise?'

'It's self-preservation. Beck has enough ammunition to hold us here already. Why give him more? Aren't you curious as to who the marksman was?'

'I'm more concerned about challenging Grange face to face at the reception – now we have to stay. What are you going to do about all this, Bob? You said there was another witness. Who is it?'

Newman shook his head and drank more wine before he replied. 'I'm meeting the witness tomorrow afternoon. Better you don't know who or where. And don't forget we still have Novak. He is coming to that reception. Explosive was the word which Beck used. I think he could be right – especially if Nagel from Basle turns up. Beck is stage-managing something, I'm sure. The trouble is, I'm not sure about Beck.'

'We can't trust anyone then?'

'I've tried to hammer that into you. It was a natural route towards the chopper when Beck led Seidler past those headlights but, as I said, I wonder. Then Signer cleverly placed himself in front of the Saab's headlights. I suspect he signalled to the marksman...'

'That I *could* believe. He's a creepy, cold-blooded swine. But how did he do it?'

'You didn't notice? He took off one of his suede gloves and clenched his fist. *Kill him!* I think that was the way it was done.'

'You mean Beck and Signer worked as a team?'

'Nancy! I don't *know* yet!'

'Is that why you didn't give Beck that tape of your conversation with Seidler in the house – or the photographs you took of that hideous gas mask? That's vital evidence...'

'It is, but Beck gets it only when I decide I can fully trust him – if ever. That would be the time for another sworn affidavit from you – that you witnessed the recorded conversation.'

'I'm flaked out.' She drank her glass of wine, slipped off her skirt and sprawled on the bed, her raven hair spread out on the pillow. 'So what do you plan on doing next?' she asked sleepily.

'First, see my final witness tomorrow. He may just blow the whole thing wide open. Second, accompany you to the reception so I can get a good look at Grange, maybe Max Nagel, too – the leaders of the two opposing power blocs. Third, if nothing else has worked, I'm going to try and break in to the Berne Clinic – with Novak's help. I want to see inside the laboratory – and their *atombunker*...'

He stopped speaking. Nancy had fallen fast asleep, leaving her smoked salmon untouched. Newman swallowed his own food, drank some more of the wine, put on his coat and slipped out of the bedroom, locking the door behind him. As soon as he had left the room Nancy opened her eyes, sat up and reached for the phone.

Newman stepped inside the lift and pressed the button for the lowest level, the floor below the main entrance hall. Using this route he hoped to leave the hotel unseen. When the doors opened he turned right past the *garderobe* which was now closed. It was 10 p.m.

Climbing a flight of steps into the deserted hall below the coffee shop, he walked out into the street, pausing to turn up his collar and glance in both directions. Then he walked rapidly to the public phone box, glancing all round again before he went inside. He dialled the number from memory. The familiar voice answered immediately.

Inside Room 214 at the Bellevue Palace, seated on the bed. Lee Foley picked up the phone on the second ring. He had been expecting the call for the past half hour. He listened for several minutes, then interrupted his caller and spoke rapidly.

'I know about Le Pont. I think from now on you're going to have to let me operate on my own. Goddamnit, we do have enough information at this stage in the game to guess at what is going on. It's going to get pretty tough. Playing tough games is what I'm trained for. Just go on keeping me informed...'

Inside Room 312 at the Bellevue Tweed perched on a chair, crouched forward, his expression intent as he held the phone to his ear. When the conversation ended he replaced the receiver and walked over to his bed where he had spread out two maps.

268

One map, large-scale, showed the Canton of Berne. The second was a road and rail map of the whole of Switzerland. Polishing his glasses on the silk handkerchief, he looped the handles over his ears and stopped to examine closely the map of Berne.

Reaching for a ruler lying on the bed, he measured roughly the distance between Berne and Thun along the motorway. He'd have to hire a car in the morning – although he knew Blanche would have been happy to act as *chauffeuse*. Tweed hated driving; perhaps he should have asked Blanche who, he knew, had a car as well as her scooter. He decided he would sleep on the decision. Tomorrow promised to be D-Day.

'And who was that calling at this hour?' asked Gisela. 'It is after ten o'clock. Time you went home...'

'An informant,' Beck replied. He felt depressed. On his desk lay the new file Gisela had opened. *Case of Manfred Seidler*. He turned to the first page she had typed from his dictation and his eyes wandered to the neat stack of other files to his right. Hannah Stuart, Julius Nagy, Bernard Mason. To say nothing of the files which would need to be opened on the two bodies found at Le Pont station as soon as some sort of identification had been established. It was becoming a massacre.

'Things will look better in the morning,' Gisela said gently. 'You're tired and in a black mood...'

'Not really. All the players in this terrible drama have – or soon will be – assembled under one roof. The Bellevue Palace. Tweed, Newman, Dr Kennedy, Lee Foley. Tomorrow we'll have under that same roof Armand Grange – doubtless accompanied by his hatchet man, Bruno Kobler. Also Dr Max Nagel is there already. Very satisfactory that to a policeman – to know the location of all concerned. Our people are already inside the Bellevue, I take it? With my trip to the Juras I've not been in touch...'

'Three of our men – all unknown to the Bellevue staff – booked in at the hotel at different times. Their names are on the pad by your left elbow.'

'So, as the august Colonel Signer would say, we have made our dispositions. The Bellevue will be our battlefield...'

It was close to midnight when Bruno Kobler arrived back at the Berne Clinic and hurried inside to his office on the first floor while his chauffeur parked the red Mercedes in the garage. His employer was waiting for him.

Huge curtains were drawn over the smoked glass picture window. The office was illuminated by shaded lamps which threw dark shadows. The Professor stood listening while Kobler reported on the evening's events in terse sentences.

'Very good, Bruno,' he commented, 'that solves one outstanding problem very satisfactorily. All other discordant elements can be dealt with after the dispersal of the doctors attending the Congress. I have decided to bring forward our final experiment. Once that is confirmed as successful, *Terminal* becomes a *fait accompli*.'

'Bring it forward?' Kobler sounded puzzled. 'To when?'

'Tomorrow evening.'

'While the reception is taking place at the Bellevue Palace?'

'Exactly.' There was a note of contentment in the soft voice. 'It occurred to me the opportunity was too good to overlook. You see, Bruno, everyone will have their eyes focused on the reception. It has become known that I shall put in an appearance.'

'But you will not be present to witness the results...'

'You are perfectly capable of supervising the experiment. As to the results, I can examine the body when I return from the reception. We chose female patients for the previous trials because – as you know – they are biologically stronger than men. This time, as I mentioned earlier, we will use a male patient.'

'I may have the perfect subject, Professor. Also, we know now this patient has been playing tricks on us. We moved him to another room for a few hours to clean out his permanent quarters. While removing the grille to feed a fresh reel on to the tape-recorder we discovered a quantity of sodium amytal capsules. This patient has not been sedated when it was assumed he was. He may have overheard anything.'

Kobler took a file from his drawer, opened it to the first page, which carried a photo and the name of the patient, and placed it under his desk-lamp for the Professor's inspection.

'Excellent, I agree.'

The photograph showed a man with strongly-defined features and a hooked nose. The name at the top of the page typed in red and underlined was Jesse Kennedy.

Thirty

Saturday, 18 February. Newman himself used Room Service to order breakfast – the complete works. He did this from sympathy with Nancy's ordeal the previous day; also because he wanted to talk in privacy. And this was Confrontation Day.

Nancy climbed out of bed and pulled back the curtains. She stared at the view, slipping on her dressing-gown. Standing there, she crossed her arms, deep in thought as he came up behind her and grasped her round the waist.

'Look at it, Bob. Not a good omen?'

The mist had returned, a sea of dirty cottonwool, blotting out the Bantiger and rolling slowly along the straight stretch of the Aare to envelop the city. Soon it would be drifting into the arcades, creating an eerie silence.

'Come and have breakfast, an American breakfast,' Newman said, pulling her away from the window. 'Bacon, eggs, croissants, rolls – the lot. How did you sleep?' he asked as they faced each other across the table.

'I didn't – but I'm ravenous...'

'You ate nothing last night. What especially kept you awake?'

'Your conversation with Seidler inside that house. You translated some of it – but considerately not all. What you didn't realize was I know German rather well. It was my second language at high school. Then, a few weeks before I left St Thomas's – when we first met at Bewick's – I'd come back from Germany where I spent time with a German medical family. Do you really think they're using patients at the Clinic to test those gas masks, Bob?'

'I'm convinced we still don't know the whole story. I'm not sure Grange's ultimate purpose ends with the testing of those Soviet masks.' He continued quickly. 'Let's not talk about it until I've seen Grange, had

272

a chance to weigh him up. Maybe we ought to take Jesse out of that place today. We could drive there immediately after breakfast if you agree...'

'I don't think it will do any good. Jesse will refuse – and without his consent we've no authority to force the issue. I want to talk to Grange myself first. And I'm sure Grange will play it cool until the reception is over...'

'It's your decision. I'm not too happy about it,' Newman said and drank more coffee. 'You seem very confident about this reception. You wouldn't know something you haven't told me?'

'And what might that be, I'd like to know? You always want to do things your way,' she bridled.

'You're tired. Forget it!'

Tweed was on the warpath. After an early breakfast in the dining-room – he couldn't be fussed with Room Service – he left the hotel without delay to keep his appointment with Arthur Beck. He walked into the main entrance of the Taubenhalde, placed his passport on the receptionist's counter. At that moment Beck emerged from the lift.

'Let's go straight up,' he invited Tweed. 'Don't fill in a form...'

Anyone who knew Tweed well would have recognized the danger signs. There was an intent expression in the eyes behind his spectacles. He crossed the hall to the lift with a brisk stride and the look on his face was forbidding as he stared at Beck.

They travelled up to the tenth floor in silence, Beck unlocked the door with his key. In the hall beyond he took out a card and inserted it in the time clock before opening the door to his office. Tweed took off his coat and sat facing Beck across his desk.

'Welcome to Berne once more,' Beck began.

'I hope you will still think me welcome when we have ended this conversation,' Tweed warned. 'I have come here because we are very worried about the Berne Clinic – and the experiments which are being carried out there, possibly under military supervision...'

'I don't like your tone,' Beck replied stiffly.

'I don't like the reason for my visit...'

'You are talking nonsense: Where have you picked up this nonsense about a Swiss clinic?'

'From various sources.' Tweed dropped his bomb. 'We know about Manfred Seidler. We have in London one of the gas masks he has supplied to the Berne Clinic. Our Ministry of Defence experts have examined it and confirmed it is the sophisticated type now issued to the Soviet chemical battalions...'

Beck stood up, his expression frozen. He stood behind the desk, his hands thrust inside his jacket pockets, studying his visitor who gazed back at him.

'Just supposing I found there was even one iota of truth in this extraordinary story, how would it concern you?'

'It concerns the President of the United States, the Prime Minister of Britain – both of whom are fighting to conclude a new treaty with Moscow, a treaty effectively banning the use of chemical warfare in Europe. You read the papers, don't you? Can you imagine the propaganda advantage Moscow would have if they could point to one single country in Western Europe – a country outside NATO at that – which was equipping its forces with chemical warfare units? It would give them just the excuse they need to continue building up their own resources in this diabolical field. That, Beck, is why I am here. That is why it concerns London. That is why I take such an interest in the Berne Clinic.'

'Quite a speech,' Beck commented. He sat down again. 'I take your point. May we speak in confidence? Good. Manfred Seidler was murdered last night in the Juras...'

'My God! He was a vital witness...'

'Agreed. It doesn't make my job any easier, Tweed. Can I ask you how you know so much?'

'An associate of Seidler's sold one of the gas masks from the latest consignment to someone at the British Embassy. Our agent followed Seidler to the airport outside Vienna – and saw him board a Swiss jet. I alerted our people here to watch your airports. We had a piece of luck at Belp. My man saw the consignment from Vienna being taken away in a van – that van carried the legend *Klinik Bern* on the outside. The van proceeded in the direction of the Clinic after leaving the airport at Belp...'

'You have been very busy in our country.' Beck smiled, a smile of resignation. 'Under other circumstances I might be angry.' He pressed the switch on his intercom. 'Gisela, coffee for two, please. Black without sugar for my guest... just a moment.' He looked at his visitor. 'A little cognac in your coffee?'

'Not at this hour, thank you.'

'That is all, Gisela.' He switched off. 'Anything else you know, my friend?'

'We know,' Tweed continued in the same flat tone, 'you are under great pressure to drop your investigation – pressure from the Gold Club. I come here to help you resist the pressure at all costs. You are at full liberty to disclose what I have said – what I am going to say. As a last resort – I emphasize that – we might feel compelled to leak the news of what we believe is going on at the Berne Clinic...'

'To some foreign correspondent like Robert Newman?'

Tweed looked surprised. 'He is investigating the same subject?'

'I don't know,' Beck admitted. 'He is here with his fiancée, an American. Her grandfather is a patient in the Clinic.'

'May I suggest how we should proceed?' Tweed requested with a hint of urgency.

'I am open to any suggestion. You seem to have established a network inside Switzerland. You may know more than me.'

'We put the Berne Clinic under total surveillance – round the clock. Specifically, smuggle a film unit into the area, choosing a strategic position where you can survey and photograph not only the Clinic but also the laboratory and their very extensive grounds. There is a dense forest behind the Clinic on high ground...'

'You have been out there?'

'I have studied a map.'

'I know the forest you mean and it would be the best point of vantage.

The film unit will be inside a plain van with porthole windows which open – but I cannot send it to take up position until well after dark, late tonight. Otherwise it would be spotted...'

'By Military Intelligence?' Tweed interjected.

'You *have* been busy...'

Beck paused at a knock on the door, called out to Gisela to come in and played with a pencil while she served coffee. When she had gone Tweed leant forward to emphasize his words.

'Please use one of your sophisticated, infra-red cine cameras. The danger – the evidence to be obtained – probably is during the night. Hannah Stuart died after dark. So did Mrs Holly Laird...'

'I have kept all reference to Mrs Laird out of the papers,' Beck said sharply.

'Certain individuals inside Military Intelligence are as uneasy about this business as we are,' Tweed observed and sat back to drink his coffee.

'Who are you going to see?' Nancy asked as Newman put down the phone inside their bedroom. 'You didn't mention a name.'

'I'm stirring the pot to boiling point before that reception tonight – hoping to break someone's nerve. Then they may make a mistake. I'm on my way now to start the process. You wait here till I get back...'

Two minutes later he walked out of the main entrance of the Bellevue. There was the smell of fog in the heavy air. The clammy damp of mist caressed his cheeks. He went straight inside the Bundeshaus Ost and was taken to Captain Lachenal's second-floor office. When the attendant closed the door and Lachenal, dark circles under his eyes, rose from behind his desk, Newman unbuttoned his coat but made no attempt to take it off.

'Manfred Seidler is dead,' was his opening shot.

'My God! I didn't know, I swear to you...'

'He was murdered up in the Juras. You were looking for him. I was there when a marksman blew off half his head – and so was Colonel Signer. Do you take orders from Signer?'

'Have you gone crazy? Of course not...'

'Maybe indirectly – through a complex chain of command whose ultimate origin even you don't know...'

'That's impossible. Bob, you don't know what you're saying...'

'That rifle with a sniperscope that was stolen from the Thun district was probably the murder weapon. Who are the marksmen in Thun? There can't be too many of them – and you hold a record of such things. Care to let me look at that record? Or are you going to try and cover up? We are talking about cold-blooded murder, Lachenal.'

'Two such rifles have been stolen – both from the Thun district,' Lachenal said quietly. 'We tried to keep the second theft quiet. It reflects on the Swiss Army...'

'So you will have consulted that record of marksmen very recently – probably still have it in this office,' Newman pounded on. 'May I see it? I might believe in you if you show it to me.'

'You are telling me the truth about Seidler?'

'You really didn't know? There's the phone. Call Beck and ask him...'

'There is a temporary hitch in liaison.'

Which, Newman thought, was a neat way of saying they were no longer speaking to each other. Lachenal looked worried sick, close to the end of his tether. Without another word he went over to a steel filing cabinet, produced a ring of keys, unlocked the cabinet, took out a red file and brought it back to his desk.

'This is classified information...'

'Since when did brutal assassination become classified?'

Lachenal rifled through the typed sheets inside the file. He stopped at a page near the end and Newman guessed it was arranged alphabetically by district. 'T' for 'Thun'.

The Intelligence chief gestured for Newman to join him on his side of the desk. He used the flat of both hands to prevent Newman flipping over to another page. There were five marksmen in Thun, a high proportion, Newman guessed. Alongside one was an asterisk. He pointed to this name. Bruno Kobler.

'What's the asterisk for? Or is that top secret?'

'Expert with both rifle and handgun. A crack shot...'

'Get the link?' Newman queried. 'Kobler, deputy to Professor Grange. And Grange's closest financial supporter is Victor Signer – present at the execution of Manfred Seidler...'

'Execution?' Lachenal was shocked.

'By a one-man firing squad, a marksman. And Signer may have given the order. Think about it, check it, Lachenal. And I'm leaving now...'

'There are questions I would like to ask...'

Newman shook his head. He buttoned up his coat. He had turned the handle of the door when he fired his closing shot over his shoulder.

'And at long last I know what *Terminal* means – yesterday in conversation with someone they told me by chance.'

Thirty-One

'I'll be there if I'm needed,' Lee Foley said, gripping the phone with his left hand while he reached for the lighted cigarette with his other hand. 'All those people at that reception means something's going to break. I'll be there like I said – to watch it happen...'

Inside Room 214 the American replaced the receiver, checked his watch and stretched out on the bed. 11.30 a.m. Today he was staying in the bedroom which had already been cleaned. On the outside door handle a notice hung. *Please Do Not Disturb.*

He had used Room Service to order lunch. The fox was in its hole – and would remain there until the moment came to act. Closing his eyes, he fell fast asleep.

Newman walked out of the phone booth and headed along the familiar route to the Junkerngasse. Blanche was waiting for him, clad in a beige sweater and her wet-look black pants, the outfit she wore when she thought she might need to ride her scooter.

'I have a big favour to ask,' Newman told her, 'and very little time to spare. Would you be willing to evacuate your flat for a day or two – I've provisionally booked you a room at the Bellevue. I may need a hideaway – this would be ideal geographically...'

'Of course you can have it...'

'Not for myself. If you agree, lock up any valuables or confidential papers. Your temporary lodger might be nosy. I just don't know...'

'When do I move to the Bellevue? And here is a spare key.'

'By one o'clock. About clothes, pack what you're wearing. And something dressy – for a reception. This has two plusses for me. I have what the pros call a safe house. And I have you where I can keep an eye on you. People are getting killed. A lot of people.'

Inside the Bellevue Tweed knocked gently on the door after first making sure the corridor was deserted. The door to the suite was opened by a small, very broad-shouldered man with a large head, thick black hair and a wide, firm mouth. He was smoking a Havana cigar and he wore an expensive and conservative dark grey business suit.

'Come in, Tweed,' said Dr Max Nagel. 'On time to the minute, as always.'

'We may be getting somewhere,' Tweed replied as Nagel shut the door and ushered him to a deep armchair which enveloped the small Englishman.

'Tell me,' Nagel continued in English, drawing up a similar chair to join his guest. 'You saved me a lot of embarrassment over that Kruger affair when you traced the funds he'd embezzled to my bank.'

'That was only achieved by keeping track of that newspaperman, Newman's, activities. I've manoeuvred all the pieces on the *Terminal* board as best I could. Now we hope and we pray...'

'Maybe not.' Nagel, who spoke in a hoarse growl, reached for his briefcase, unlocked it and handed a file to Tweed. 'Those are photocopies of highly intricate banking transactions covering the movement of no less than two hundred million Swiss francs. At one stage they went out of the country to a company in Liechtenstein – then, hey presto! they come back again and end up, guess where?'

'In a bank account accessible to Professor Armand Grange?'

'Where else? You can keep that set of accounts. What is your strategy? When you phoned me before you left London telling me you were coming here you didn't say too much...'

'Not over an open line...'

Tweed then told Nagel all he had discovered – including the gas mask 'an emissary' had brought from Vienna and Manfred Seidler's involvement. Nagel listened in silence, smoking his cigar. His appearance reminded Tweed of a gorilla in repose; an amiable, determined and highly intelligent gorilla. Great force of character emanated from the man and his energy was proverbial.

'So,' he declared when Tweed had finished, 'I repeat, what is your strategy?'

280

'To squeeze Grange from every possible quarter – to exert such psychological pressure he miscalculates. I don't think we have much time left, Max. And have you another spare set of those accounts?'

'Certainly. Here you are. May I ask who they are for?'

'Newman, the foreign correspondent – passed to him through an intermediary so he doesn't know their source. I can't believe he's here simply to pay a visit with his American fiancée who, incidentally, has a grandfather as a patient at the Berne Clinic. Max, as the Americans say, we may have to go public as a final resort.'

'That I'd like to avoid. This Newman, can you trust him?'

'When these documents are handed over it will be conditional on his not publishing them. Yes, he lives on trust. But if Grange knows he's got them it will unnerve him...'

'I hope so.' There was a hint of doubt in Nagel's voice. 'Grange is a fanatic – you do know that? He'll go to any length to achieve his objective – which is to change, the whole military policy of this country. Tread carefully – Grange is a very dangerous and unpredictable man. Like a cobra he strikes when you least expect it...'

Half an hour later Newman, who had phoned from Blanche's flat, walked into Beck's office. The police chief began to feel he was under bombardment when Newman started speaking.

'I don't see any reason why you shouldn't take a full team including Forensic to the Berne Clinic today with a warrant to examine not only the Clinic but also the laboratory...'

'You are trying to rush me? On what grounds could I furnish myself with a warrant?'

'On the basis of the findings of Dr Kleist concerning the death of their patient, Mrs Holly Laird. Cyanosis poisoning was the diagnosis, for God's sake...'

'Please!' Beck held up a defensive hand. 'And won't you sit down. All right, stay on your feet! Dr Kleist has not yet produced her final report. There are aspects about Mrs Laird's demise which still puzzle her. Until

I do receive her report I cannot – will not – obtain a warrant. Haven't I already explained I have to move cautiously – that there are powerful forces trying to have me taken off the case?'

'Then I'll give you my affidavit about the events in the Juras last night and go...'

'I also need a statement from Dr Kennedy...'

'She is waiting downstairs. I insist on being present when you take her statement...'

'That I cannot permit...'

'Then you only get her statement in the presence of the most high-powered lawyer in Berne. Take your choice...'

'You give me one?' Beck spread his hands. 'You are in a ferocious mood, Bob. I will ask them to send Dr Kennedy up now and we will take both statements and get the damned paperwork out of the way. What frightens me is that you are going to do something independent – and highly dangerous...'

Their statements had been taken, signed and witnessed by Gisela. Beck had courteously asked Nancy whether he could have a few words in private with Newman and she had been taken to another room. It was Beck's turn to startle Newman. Opening a drawer he brought out a shoulder holster, a 7.65-mm. police automatic and six magazines which he pushed across the desk.

'Bob, I am not convinced Seidler was the target last night. I also believe you were earlier at Le Pont station when two hired gunmen were killed. No, please don't interrupt. I think you were the target. I recall you are familiar with the use of firearms?'

'What are you proposing?'

'Take this automatic for your protection...'

'So you can have me picked up, searched and found to be in possession of a deadly weapon? No thanks. I happen to know the Swiss penalties for carrying firearms...'

'Then for the protection of Dr Kennedy...'

Beck produced from the same drawer a permit to carry the weapon

– which he again pushed across the desk. Newman read the document upside down without touching it.

'I will sign the permit personally,' Beck continued, 'and Gisela – or a policeman chosen at random – will witness my signature. I am pleading with you. For old times' sake...'

Newman agreed to take the weapon.

The day was moving fast. It was 1 p.m. when Tweed, seated in a chair in the reception hall, saw Blanche Signer arrive with a case. He waited until she had registered, then stood up and strolled over to join her by the lift. He spoke only when the lift doors had closed, holding his briefcase in his left hand.

'Come to my room, Blanche. We have to talk...'

She slipped inside his room unseen by anyone and dropped her case on the floor. In her concise manner she explained why she had booked in at the hotel – that Newman needed her flat for a purpose unknown to her.

Tweed listened and nodded his head in approval. He should have thought of this precaution himself – Blanche would be safer inside the Bellevue until they had brought this matter to a successful conclusion – if that were possible. Taking a set of the accounts he had received from Dr Nagel and which he had put inside a sealed envelope, he handed the envelope to her.

'Can you get this into Newman's hands very urgently? And he must have no inkling as to where you obtained it...'

'I'm sure I can manage that. I'm just not sure when. He may be staying here but I don't want his fiancée to see me.'

Tweed smiled sympathetically. 'I understand. But as soon as possible. Any moment now everything may blow up in our faces...'

Newman had strapped on the shoulder holster, slipped the automatic inside it and dropped the magazines inside his coat pocket before he joined Nancy and they left the building. He made no mention of the weapon to her.

He insisted that they had a leisurely lunch in the Grill Room and, because he sensed she was jumpy, steered the conversation away from recent events. Occasionally he checked his watch.

'You're going to meet that last witness this afternoon,' she observed quietly, watching him over the rim of her glass. 'Isn't that why you keep checking your watch?'

'I looked at it twice...'

'Three times...'

Oh, Jesus! he thought. He smiled. 'Yes, I am. It may take me a couple of hours – I can't tell. I'd appreciate it if you would stay inside the hotel...'

'After last night wild horses wouldn't drag me out...'

'You wanted to see me, Bruno?'

Kobler stood up behind his desk and closed the file he had been checking, the file on Jesse Kennedy. He walked round the desk and hesitated, unsure of his employer's reaction.

'If something is worrying you, Bruno, tell me. So far I have found your instinct for problems infallible. Do we have a problem?'

'It's Willy Schaub, the head porter. I saw him carrying on a long conversation with Dr Novak before he went off duty. And Schaub is greedy for money,' added Kobler who was paid an enormous salary.

'So?'

'It's Schaub's day off. He lives in the Matte district in 276 in Berne. I really think it might be worth checking him out.'

'Do it,' said the Professor.

Lee Foley's plans for a quiet afternoon inside the hotel were changed by the phone call. Wasting no time, he put on his jeans and windcheater and left the hotel, carrying the holdall in his right hand.

Like Newman, he had also realized that the way to leave unseen was by descending in the lift to the lowest level, walking past the *garderobe* and emerging by the exit from the coffee shop. He crossed the road, went inside the café facing the Bellevue and ordered coffee. He was careful to pay as soon as the beverage was served. The Porsche was parked round the corner so there was nothing more he could do. Except to sip at his coffee and wait – and watch.

Newman drove a long way round to reach Gerberngasse 498, the home of Willy Schaub. Novak had made the appointment for three in the afternoon so he left the Bellevue in the Citroën half an hour earlier.

One of the great advantages of Berne, he reflected, was that it was not to difficult to throw off a tail. The place was such an intricate network of streets – and with a little audacious driving the trams could be exploited.

At 2.50 p.m. he was driving along the Aarstrasse with the river on his right. He drove on past the sluices into the Schifflaube which brought him deep into Matte where everything was centuries-old. Continuing on into the Gerberngasse, he slowed down as he approached the Nydegg bridge and slid into an empty parking slot.

On both sides of the street ancient houses formed a continuous wall, a huddle of misshapen edifices – several storeys high – which protruded at intervals. The street was deserted in mid-afternoon and the mist, which had withdrawn earlier, was coming back. It was very silent in the canyon and Willy Schaub's place was on the left, overshadowed by the bridge high up. 2.55 p.m. Newman peered up a covered wooden flight of steps which ran up to the bridge alongside it and went back to Schaub's house. He pressed the bell alongside Schaub's name and wriggled his shoulders. He was still very much aware of the automatic nestling inside the holster under his left armpit.

A short barrel-shaped man, late middle-aged and holding a bottle of beer in his left hand which, Newman reflected, explained his large belly, opened the creaking door and stared suspiciously at his visitor. Wisps of white hair stuck out from his turnip-like head and his only small feature was the wary eyes peering at Newman.

'Willy Schaub?'

'Who wants to know?' the man asked truculently in German.

'Robert Newman. You're expecting me. Three o'clock...'

'Got some identification?'

Newman sighed audibly. 'It might not be too bright keeping me out here on view, you know.' He produced his passport, opening it at the page which showed his photograph, closing it again and holding up the cover which bore his name.

'You'd better come inside, I suppose.'

The interior was gloomy and strangely constructed, stepped up on different levels because it climbed the steep hillside on which it was built. Newman followed the wheezing barrel up three twisting staircases and the place had a musty smell. He wondered whether Schaub lived on his own and they entered a weird, box-like room with the far wall occupied almost entirely by a grimy window broken up into large panes of glass. A decrepit roller blind ran across the top of the window.

'We'll sit here and talk,' Schaub announced. 'Beer?'

'Not just now, thank you,' Newman replied, noticing the grubby glass on the table.

It was only when he walked over to the window and gazed up the slope of terraced garden that he realized he was inside one of the old houses he had looked down on with Nancy the previous Thursday when he had walked her to the Nydegg bridge and told her this was the Matte district. When he turned round Schaub was seated at the table in the middle of the room, guzzling beer from the upturned bottle. He reached up and pulled the roller blind down to cover the upper half of the window.

'What you do that for?' Schaub demanded. 'I like to look at the view...'

'This room is very exposed.' Newman took a folded five-hundred franc note from his pocket and placed it on the table. 'That's for answering questions about the Berne Clinic. You've worked there long enough – you have to know just about everything that goes on there...'

'Novak said you'd pay more...'

Newman produced a second five-hundred franc note and sat down alongside Schaub. facing the window. The porter was wearing a baggy pair of stained corduroy trousers, an open-necked shirt and shoes which hadn't seen polish in months. He shook his head at the second note.

'More...'

'This is the lot. No more haggling...' Newman produced a third note and placed it with the others. 'What goes on inside that laboratory for starters...'

'More...'

'Forget it!' Newman reached slowly for the notes but Schaub beat him to it, grabbing all three in one scoop and thrusting them inside his trouser pocket. 'All right, answer the question...'

'Never been inside the lab...'

The bullet shattered a pane in the window and blew the beer bottle Schaub had left on the table into small pieces. Newman put his hand against Schaub's shoulder and shoved the porter's considerable weight off the chair, toppling him onto the wooden planks of the uneven floor.

'Keep down you fat slob or they'll kill you!' he yelled.

Newman had dropped to the floor as he shouted. His shout synchronized with the second bullet which shattered two more panes and thudded into the rear wall. Newman could never recall how the automatic found its way into his right hand but he realized he was holding it as he scrambled low down across the floor to the window – just in time to see the muzzle of a rifle disappearing over the top of the wall on the street leading to the bridge.

'Get behind that cupboard! Stay behind it! I'll be back in a minute...'

He rushed, stumbled, half-fell down the bloody staircases, threw open the front door, the automatic inside his pocket now. Running along the empty street, he turned up the covered steps leading to the bridge. There were a hell of a lot of steps, treads worn in the centre by the feet of ages. Why do people always walk straight up the middle? The useless question flashed through his mind as, panting, he reached the top and came out on to the street.

He glanced in both directions. Nothing. Not even a pedestrian. He walked a few paces towards the centre of Berne, then scooped up off the pavement an ejected cartridge which he pocketed. No sign of the other one. The killer must have collected one and departed in a hurry.

Newman leaned over the wall at the point where the cartridge had fallen and stared down direct into Schaub's living-room. If he hadn't lowered the blind the porter would now be a bloated corpse. He looked towards the city centre again and saw a man standing outside a shop who was watching him.

'Thought I heard something,' Newman remarked in German as he joined the portly man who wore no overcoat.

'Sounded like a shot, two shots...'

'Or a couple of backfires.' Newman smiled. 'I arranged to meet a girl at the top of the staircase. A brunette – a slim girl in a pant suit, maybe wearing a windcheater. I wondered whether you'd seen her?'

'That description fits half the girls in Berne. I only came out to check this window I'm dressing. No, I haven't seen your girl. All I saw after the backfires was the red car...'

'Red? What make? A Porsche? A Mercedes?'

'Couldn't say – I just saw the flash of red as it roared out of sight across the bridge. Exceeding the speed limit, too...'

Returning to the house, Newman found Schaub still crouched behind the cupboard, a shivering jelly of a man. He looked up, his beady little eyes terrified.

'Have they gone?'

'Yes. I'll give you two minutes to pack a small bag – just your pyjamas and shaving kit. I'm taking you where no one will dream of looking for you. Hurry it up...'

'But my job at the Clinic...'

Newman looked at him with a stare of sheer amazement. 'I thought you'd have grasped it by now. The people at your Clinic are out to kill you...'

Newman drove the Citroën up to Schaub's front door and the porter did what he had been told to do. Running in a crouch, he dived inside the rear of the car through the door Newman had opened, hauled the door shut and pressed his bulk close to the floor. To all outward appearances the Citroën was occupied only by the driver.

In the centre of Berne Leupin, behind the wheel of a Fiat, a car

Newman had not seen in the Juras, followed one car behind the Citroën. Marbot sat alongside him.

'I wish we could have got closer to that house in Gerberngasse,' Leupin remarked.

'Then he would have spotted us. We'll have to find out who lives there,' Marbot replied. 'Beck will want to know that – but first let's find out where Newman is going. He seems to be leading us round the houses...'

'My thought, too...'

Newman glanced in his rear-view mirror again. The Fiat was still there. He timed it carefully, slowing down as he came up to the intersection. The tram which had stopped in the main street to his right began to move forward again. Newman accelerated, sweeping forward and missing the nose of the on-coming tram by inches. The tram made a rude noise. Behind him Leupin jammed on the brakes.

'The clever bastard! We've lost him...'

Five minutes later Newman led Schaub inside Blanche's flat and showed him how to operate the special security lock. He also gave the porter a lecture on keeping the place clean, although to be fair, despite his clothes, Schaub had the appearance of a man who bathed regularly and his jowly chin was well-shaven.

'Now,' Newman said, 'you stay here until I come for you. No answering the door or the phone. No calls to anyone – it could be the last call you ever made. There's food in the fridge – to go on living, stay here. And I have fifteen minutes before I must go. For starters, what goes on inside that laboratory? Talk...'

Schaub talked.

Thirty-Two

Nancy took trouble over her battle gear for the Medical Congress reception. Coming out of the bathroom, swearing at having to wear a dinner jacket, Newman stopped and stared. She was clad in a long, form-fitting dress of red taffeta. Round her slim neck glittered a pearl choker.

'Well, will I do?' she enquired. 'I'm out to kill the competition...'

'You'll slay them. You look terrific. And isn't that the outfit you were wearing that first night we met in London – when by chance I was also at Bewick's?'

'By chance?' She was amused. 'Half London knew you took your latest fling to that place. It's seven – shouldn't we be getting downstairs? I *am* completely ready and rarin' to go

'Give me a minute to fix this bloody tie. You're nervous, aren't you? I can tell.'

'So are a lot of doctors before a tricky case – if they're not they're probably no good. But I can tell you one thing, Bob. When I walk into that reception I'll go cold as ice. I don't care how much clout Grange carries – he's going to hear from me...'

'Pioneer stock,' Newman joked as he finished fixing the tie. 'There's still some of it left in Arizona. I'm ready. Are you?'

She thumped his arm and they made their way to the bank of lifts. The celebration was being held in the large reception room between the lobby and the terrace restaurant. The floor was covered with priceless carpets, including one huge Persian hunting carpet. A large buffet table had been furnished with champagne glasses and a selection of food. There were a lot of people there already. Newman held Nancy back by the arm.

'Let's just see who is here and where they are. Tonight could be very decisive...'

Blanche Signer was talking to Beck. She wore an emerald green dress with a mandarin collar which showed off her superb figure to full advantage. Her small feet were sheathed in gold shoes.

'Your next conquest?' Nancy enquired.

'I was wondering what Beck is doing here...'

In a chair offside with his back to the wall sat Lee Foley, holding his glass as his cold eyes studied each person in the room. Tweed, looking uncomfortable in his dinner jacket, sat near Foley, watching the room with no particular expression.

'I think that must be Grange over there, holding court,' Nancy whispered.

At the back of the room, surrounded by half-a-dozen men, a tall, very heavily-built man wearing tinted glasses was talking while others listened. His left hand was close to his side, the fingers stretched downwards while his right hand held a glass. There was a gap in the crowd and Newman had a good view of him. A large head, his complexion pale, his lips appeared hardly to move as he spoke. The feature about him which intrigued Newman was his sheer immobility.

'Is that Professor Grange over there in the corner?' Nancy asked a passing waiter with a tray of glasses.

'Yes, it is, madame. May I offer you champagne?'

They both took a glass for appearance's sake. Newman sipped at his champagne, listening to the babble of voices, the clink of glasses. Another large man brushed past him without apology and made his way, very erect and confident, over to join Grange's group. Victor Signer had arrived.

'I can't see Kobler,' Newman whispered. That worries me...'

'Someone has to mind the store back at the Clinic, I suppose...'

'You're probably right. Let's circulate – horrible word. When are you going to challenge Grange...'

'Bob!' She grabbed his arm. 'Wait! Look at that...'

Newman was looking at the weird incident. Grange had just greeted Signer when a waiter tipped a full glass of champagne off his tray. The liquid spilt down the lower half of Grange's dinner jacket and the upper half of his trousers. The waiter, obviously appalled, took the napkin folded over his sleeve, ran to the buffet, dipped it in a jug of water, returned to Grange and began to sponge the damp material.

The uncanny aspect of the incident was that as the waiter sponged and dabbed at the damp cloth Grange remained totally motionless, his left arm still close to his side, his large figure more Buddha-like than ever as he listened to Signer, ignoring the waiter as though nothing had happened. It was abnormal, unnatural. Newman stared incredulously as Nancy spoke in a low, tense tone.

'My God! No sane man has that amount of self-control. I think he's unbalanced – and I've had psychiatric training...'

It was the first doubt raised in Newman's mind as to Professor Grange's *sanity*.

Thirty-Three

Jesse Kennedy opened his eyes and blinked. What the hell was going on? He was lying full-length on a trolley which was being wheeled somewhere. He couldn't see properly – a mask of some sort had been placed over his head and face. He was gazing through eyepieces up at a white sheet pulled over the mask thing. The trolley was moving downhill now.

He tried to move his hands and realized both were strapped down by the wrists. He attempted to shift the position of his legs and found they too were strapped down round the ankles. He was completely immobilized. What was happening to him?

Then he recalled his last memory. They had injected him with a sedative. Not Novak. That bitch, Astrid, had done the job. He fought down a feeling of panic, of claustrophobia, and began to flex his fingers to get some strength back into them. The same with his feet – but cautiously. He sensed that the orderlies pushing the trolley, which was now tilted at an angle as it moved down a steep slope, must not know he was preparing himself for escape.

The sound of hydraulically-operated doors closing. The angle of the decline increased. He blinked again. It was more difficult to see even the sheet: the eyepieces were steaming up. He was suddenly wide awake and became aware of other sensations and sounds. The squeak of the trolley's wheels, the dryness in his throat, the circulation returning to his arms and legs. Another door opened and they moved on to a level surface. Weird, animal-like sounds – was he going out of his mind? He closed his eyes when the trolley stopped moving.

The sheet was whipped off him. There should be voices, the voices of the orderlies. Why weren't they talking to each other? The absence of voices got on his nerves, was frightening – together with the continuous

293

animal-like gibbering. It recalled monkeys chattering inside cages in a zoo. Ridiculous...

They were removing the straps now. One near the head of the trolley taking off the straps binding his wrists, the other unfastening the ankle straps. Then he was free. He remained inert, eyes closed. Hands grasped both his forearms, jerked him upright. In a sitting position he was swivelled round until his legs dangled over the edge of the trolley. He let his head flop, still keeping his eyes shut. Holding him by both arms, they hauled him off the trolley and held him upright. They shook him roughly. He opened his eyes and gasped in horror.

He was wearing a heavy dressing gown over his pyjamas, the cord round his waist tied firmly. He was inside the laboratory, he was convinced of it. It was colder. The steam cleared completely from the eyepieces. Plastic green curtains were closed over long narrow windows. The huge room was filled with large benches. The tops of the benches were crowded with cages – wire cages. Inside the cages, which varied in size, were the animals he had heard. It was a nightmare.

The two orderlies wore gas masks. Soulless eyes stared at him. From their height, their build, he guessed they were the two men he had heard called Graf and Munz. A third man stood further back, also wearing a mask, pacing among the cages. His way of moving told Jesse this was Bruno Kobler. Jesse pretended to sway unsteadily on his feet as Munz and Graf approached him.

A variety of animals occupied the cages: mice, rats and a lot of chimpanzees which chattered incessantly, their faces grinning hideously at him seen through the Plexiglas of the eyepieces. This section of the laboratory was dimly lit by low-power neon strips which cast an eerie light over the horrific scene.

Still swaying, stooping, Jesse noticed a giant door which was open, the door to the *atombunker*. A fourth man appeared from inside, a man carrying a metal cylinder in each hand, cylinders which reminded Jesse of mortar bombs he had once seen in a war film. Graf took hold of the side of Jesse's mask and eased it upwards so he could speak.

'This is the final stage of treatment, a revolutionary technique invented by Professor Grange. It may cure you – but you must follow instructions. When we take you outside you run *down* the slope – *down*. I will point the way...'

Could the chimpanzees sense that something evil was about to be perpetrated, Jesse wondered. They were going wild, their chattering increasing in volume as they scrambled up and down inside their cages, clutching at the wires, staring at Jesse as the two men grasped him firmly by both arms and led him to a door Kobler had opened. Icy cold night air flooded into the laboratory and Jesse shivered. They had slipped walking shoes on to his feet, his own shoes, while he had lain unconscious.

He dragged his feet, slumped, a dead weight between the two masked men. They went outside into the bitter night. Jesse shook his head slowly, glancing all round. On top of a small rocky hill men in uniform crouched round a squat barrel like a piece of sawn-off drainpipe, a barrel aimed at a trajectory across a declining slope. A mortar. Jesse again recognized the weapon from a war film. And Christ! It was manned by men in uniform, army uniform. Grange was a puppet of the Swiss Army...

'You run *down* that slope,' Munz yelled in his ear. 'Go!'

They released his arms and Jesse stood swaying. Beside the mortar was a neat pile of bombs, bombs like those carried by the man who had emerged from the *atombunker*. Behind the mortar a windsock billowed from a small mast, a windsock like those seen on small airstrips. The windsock was whipping parallel to the ground showing the direction the wind was blowing. Down the slope. *Away from* the mortar position.

Jesse staggered towards the edge of the slope. Masked figures like robots watched him. One man held a bomb over the mouth of the mortar. Ready to open fire as the target moved on to the range. The target. Himself...

Bastards! The adrenalin was flowing fast through Jesse. He paused at the edge of the slope and stared down it to check for obstacles, to accustom his eyes to the darkness. The slope was blind territory, could not be seen from the road, was concealed under a fold in the ground.

They were waiting for him now. He thought he heard Munz shout again. He took a step forward, stumbled like a man on the verge of collapse. They couldn't fire their infernal machine yet. Suddenly he took off, running like mad.

He caught them off balance. As he ran with long strides, stretching his legs, increasing speed, he heard the thump of a bomb exploding *behind* him. A long way off the clouds parted briefly and he caught a glimpse of a huge mountain, a flat-topped butte, like the buttes of Utah. He was heading for the distant road. That butte was the Stockhorn. He had watched it when they had let him sit for brief periods inside the enclosed veranda.

Despite his age he was a virile man, strong from so many hours of riding in the saddle. His legs were gaining power, flexibility. He paced himself like a professional runner, knowing he would cover the ground faster that way. He wished Nancy could see him – he was giving the swine one hell of a surprise. He heard a thud. The ground quavered under his feet. Closer, that one.

He made no attempt to tear off the mask. He could feel the tightness of the straps round his neck, over his head. Stopping to attempt that would be fatal. And they had made another mistake. By tying the cord tightly round his waist they had obviated the danger that he might be slowed down by the flapping of the dressing gown. He ran on.

The bomb landed ten feet in front of him. It burst. A cloud of mist-like vapour drifted across his face as he ran through it. Too late to run round it. He began coughing, choking. Another bomb landed ahead of him, another cloud spread. He was choking horribly, his eyes trying to force themselves through the Plexiglas. He reached out with both hands and crashed to the ground. His gnarled hands scrabbled, twitched once more and then he lay still.

Five minutes later the stretcher bearers took him away.

Thirty-Four

By 7.30 p.m. there was a mellow, relaxed atmosphere at the reception. Over a hundred people were present and the room was crowded, shoulder to shoulder. With Newman following her, Nancy threaded her way through the mob to where Professor Grange stood in deep conversation with Victor Signer. She walked straight up to Grange.

'I'm Dr Nancy Kennedy. My grandfather is a patient at the Berne Clinic...'

'If you care to make an appointment, my dear,' the soft voice intoned. Blank eyes stared down at her from behind the tinted glasses. 'This is hardly the moment...'

'And this is an intrusion on a private conversation,' Victor Signer informed her in a tone which suggested women were an inferior species.

'Really?' Nancy turned on him, raising her voice so that people nearby stopped talking to listen, which made their conversation carry an even greater distance. 'Maybe *you* would like to talk about the convenient execution of Manfred Seidler up in the Juras last night? After all, Colonel, you were there. Alternatively, perhaps you could kindly shut up while I talk to Professor Grange...'

'Gross impertinence...' Signer began.

'Watch it,' Newman warned. 'Remember me? Let her talk.'

'Your suggested appointment is not helpful,' Nancy continued in the same clear, carrying voice, staring straight at the tinted glasses. 'You hide behind Bruno Kobler at the Clinic. You are never available. Just exactly what is it you fear, Professor?'

An expression of fury flickered behind the glasses. The hand holding the champagne glass shook. Grange tightened his pouched lips, struggling for control while Nancy waited. The silence was spreading right across the room as people realized something unusual was happening: a woman was confronting the eminent Professor Armand Grange.

'I fear nothing,' he said eventually. 'What exactly is it you want, Dr Kennedy?'

'Since I have no confidence in your Clinic and the secretive way it is run, I wish to transfer my grandfather, Jesse, to a clinic near Montreux. I wish to arrange this transfer within the next twenty-four hours. That is what I want, what I am going to get. You have no objection, I assume?'

'You question my competence?'

Nancy sidestepped the trap. 'Who was mentioning your competence – except yourself?' Nancy's voice rose and now every person in the room could hear her loud and clear. 'Are you saying it is against the law – or even medical etiquette – in this country to ask for a second opinion?'

Possibly for the first time in his life – and in public – the head of the Berne Clinic was checkmated. Newman could see it in the rigid way he held himself. There were even beads of moisture on his high-domed forehead and the tinted glasses stared round at the silent assembly which stood gazing at him.

'Of course,' Grange replied eventually, 'I agree to your request. May I, with the greatest possible courtesy, remind you that we are here to enjoy ourselves tonight?'

'Then start enjoying yourself. Professor...'

On this exit line Nancy turned and made her way between the crowd which parted to let her through. Watched by Grange and Signer she went straight up to Beck and started talking to the police chief, giving the impression she was seeking further backing for the decision she had prised out of the Professor. Newman seized his opportunity, guessing that Grange would not welcome a fresh public row.

'I'm glad to meet you at last.' He smiled amiably without offering to shake hands. 'I'm writing a series of articles on Swiss industry and I understand you have at Horgen one of the most advanced factories in the world for the production of commercial gases?'

'That is so, Mr Newman... Grange seemed relieved at the change of subject, by the prospect of conversing with someone in normal tones. 'Horgen is totally automated, the only type of plant in that field in the whole world...'

'Except that, naturally, the containers are supplied from outside...'

'But they are not, Mr Newman. We manufacture our own cylinders.'

'Some photographs would help...'

'I will send some to you here by special courier. It will be a pleasure...'

'Thank you so much. And now I had better... circulate.'

Newman smiled and withdrew. He joined Nancy who was still chatting with Beck. The police chief looked quizzically at Newman and then glanced across the room to where Signer was talking rapidly to Grange.

'You had a pleasant conversation?' he enquired.

'Grange just made one of his rare – and possibly fatal – mistakes. He gave me the last piece of information I was seeking...'

'You know Dr Novak has arrived?' Nancy said to Newman as soon as they were alone. 'I think he tanked up in the bar before he decided to join us...'

She stopped speaking as a hush fell on the guests. The silence was so pronounced that Newman turned towards the entrance to see what had caused every head to turn in that direction. A short man with a large head and a wide mouth, smoking a cigar, stood surveying the assembly.

'My God!' he heard someone behind him say in French. 'Dr Max Nagel has arrived. Now we'll see some real fireworks.'

Nagel, whose dinner jacket emphasized the great width of his shoulders, carried two large envelopes tucked under his arm. He dipped his head, acknowledging a waiter and taking a glass of champagne from the proffered tray, then walked across the room slowly, his mouth tightly clamped on the cigar.

There was a feeling of tension, hardly anyone was talking as Grange and Signer watched him coming. Nagel paused, thanked another waiter who held a tray with an ashtray for him. He carefully dropped the ash from his cigar, increasing the tension. The man was a superb actor, Newman reflected. He held the entire gathering in the palm of his large hand.

'Good evening, Grange. Colonel Signer. I have something for you both...'

'This is a medical reception,' Grange said coldly. 'I was not aware you had joined the profession...'

'Signer is a doctor?' Nagel's voice was a rumbling growl.

Newman glanced over his shoulder. Signer had switched his gaze to someone behind him. Blanche was watching the scene with a frown. Not Blanche. Lee Foley, one of the few men present not in evening dress, who was wearing a dark blue business suit with matching tie, a cream shirt and gold links fastening his cuffs, was now standing, staring at Signer. Close to him stood the small Englishman, Tweed, who was gazing intently through his spectacles. Newman had the impression of a stage manager studying the actors performing in a play he had rehearsed. Newman heard the growl continuing and faced the other way.

'I think we're near the end of the line,' Nagel pronounced. 'It has taken two months for the most brilliant accountants to trace the movement of two hundred million francs to its ultimate destination. A copy of the report for you, Professor Grange, one for you Colonel Signer. *Terminal* is terminated...'

'What is this to do with me?' Signer asked with a sneer as he took the sheaf of stapled papers from the envelope and gave them a mere glance.

'They are photocopies,' Nagel rumbled on, 'the original is in my vault. And I expect you're capable of recognizing your own signature, Colonel. It appears three times on those documents. And you might care to know, Grange, I have called a meeting of bankers to take place in Zurich. We will travel to meet you from Basle. The main item on the agenda? Those complex transactions. I bid you good night. Enjoy your medical ruminations, gentlemen...'

Newman turned round again as the banker left, smoking his cigar. He saw Dr Novak leaning up against a wall, holding a glass at a precarious angle. Novak was watching the drama like a man

300

hypnotized. It seemed a good moment to persuade the American to fall in with his plans. He excused himself and the buzz of many voices talking started up as Nagel let himself out through the revolving doors and climbed into the rear of a waiting limousine.

'Novak,' Newman said, 'they're all watching Grange and Signer. Go to the lift – I'll join you there in a second. We have to talk. Don't argue – the whole thing is collapsing and they'll be looking for scapegoats. You could fit the part beautifully. And dump that glass on the table...'

He walked out into the main hall, asked the concierge to have two pots of black coffee sent up to his room, and went along to the lift where Novak was waiting.

'Novak, tomorrow night I'm going to break in to the Berne Clinic and you're going to help me...'

'You crazy, Newman?'

The American was sagged on the bed in Room 428, his shirt collar open at the neck, his tie loose. He also wore a business suit and Newman had emptied one jug of black coffee inside him. Novak was sober, reasonably so.

'You saw Lee Foley tonight at the reception?' Newman asked. 'One word from me and he'll put in motion the revoking of your passport. You have access to those computer key cards which open the outer doors. I'm going inside that laboratory...'

'Those keys I don't have...'

'But I do. I got them off Willy Schaub this afternoon – they're so important he carries them with him everywhere. He talked, Novak. And he won't be coming back to the Clinic. I imagine Sunday is quiet at the Clinic?'

'Yes, it is. The only day both Grange and Kobler are away from the place. Grange spends the night at his large house in Elfenau – that's a suburb of Berne. Kobler spends the night with a girl somewhere. But there are a whole posse of guards left...'

'So I'll have to evade them. We meet after dark. The only problem I haven't solved is the Dobermans...'

'They're keeping them indoors. They don't patrol at the moment – not since that business with Mrs Laird. Grange has said he wants the place to look normal. I go off duty myself Sunday night at nine in the evening.'

'I'll be there before then. About eight o'clock. Just be waiting for me inside that lobby. And Novak, I'd pack a bag and clear out yourself. I've booked a room for you here at the Bellevue. Stay inside it. Use Room Service for food until I arrive back. You'll do what I'm telling you?'

'I want out. I'll do it. It sounded downstairs like Nagel is going to blow the whole thing wide open...'

Newman escorted him to the door. 'If you think of changing your mind, just say two words to yourself. Lee Foley.'

He was closing the door when someone pushed against it from the outside. He eased it open a few inches, then opened it wide. Blanche walked into the room carrying an envelope similar to those Nagel had handed to Grange and Signer. She pirouetted in the middle of the bedroom.

'Like my dress, Bob? If you come closer you'll be able to appreciate my perfume...'

'You've the nerve of the devil. Nancy could arrive at any moment...'

'When I slipped up to my room and then along here she was deeply involved in conversation with a doctor from Phoenix...'

'Blanche, I think your dress is out of this world, to say nothing of what's inside it. By the way, how did you manage to arrive just after Novak left?'

'By waiting on one of those seats in the corridor. Bob, I don't like the look in your eye, the set of your mouth. You aren't planning on doing something foolish, I hope? Watch your answer – I know you...'

'I have no intention of bedding you here...'

'That's not what I meant.' She held out the envelope. 'I was asked to give this to you by Mr X. No probing trying to get his identity out of me. Maybe I had letter leave now.'

Newman slipped the envelope inside a drawer. 'Your stepfather is at the reception. Have you talked to him?'

'You must be joking. He walked straight past me as though I didn't exist. I was rather glad. I look a good long look at him and I didn't like what I saw. He's grown even harder. I'll go now.' She kissed him full on the mouth, then gave him a tissue from her handbag. 'You're wearing the wrong shade of lipstick. Bob, for God's sake don't do anything I would worry about. Promise?'

'I'll bear your affectionate request in mind...'

It was midnight when the unmarked van carrying Beck's film unit arrived at the forest above the Berne Clinic. Leupin was behind the wheel with Marbot alongside him. In the back of the van was the cine camera technician, Rolf Fischer, and his equipment.

Leupin stopped the van and then backed it off the snowbound road into a clearing under the trees. He had no way of knowing he was choosing the same vantage point Lee Foley had selected to observe the Clinic on the previous Tuesday. Leupin, having tested the firmness of the ground, now swung the vehicle through a hundred and eighty degrees so the rear of the van faced the panoramic view of the Clinic and its grounds.

In each rear door of the van was a round window of frosted glass, a hinged window which could be opened so Fischer's telephoto lens could be aimed at any required area of the Clinic, a lens which could see what was happening as clearly in the darkness as in broad daylight. Leupin got out, treading carefully in the snow, and made his way to the back where Fischer had already opened one of the windows.

'This suit you?' Leupin called out.

'Perfect. I can see everything – the Clinic, the laboratory, the grounds, even that deep slope near the lab.'

'And they won't see us in the daytime – not a white van against the snow. Just a moment, something's moving beyond the Clinic...'

Leupin raised the night-glasses looped round his neck and focused them on the drive curving down to the gatehouse. A black, six-seater Mercedes was driving away from the Clinic. Leupin lowered his glasses, calling out again to Fischer.

'That's funny. I'm sure that car is Grange's. He's not supposed to be here tonight...'

It was Beck who had vetoed the suggestion that they should arrive earlier. He was determined the van should not be spotted. And, as he had remarked, nothing would happen that evening with Grange at the reception and later spending the night at Elfenau.

Thirty-Five

Sunday, 19 February. The call came late in the morning just after Newman and Nancy had got out of bed. They had slept in late and Nancy drew back the curtains as Newman reached for his wristwatch on the bedside table. 11.45 a.m. He threw back the bedclothes and hoped no one would make a loud noise.

'Bob! Just come and look at this...'

He blinked at the unusually strong light. The sun was shining brilliantly. Slipping into his dressing-gown, he yawned and joined Nancy at the window. No more mist. No traffic on the Sunday roads. Nancy gripped him by the arm and pointed to the left.

'Isn't it just magnificent? And we might never have seen it if the weather hadn't cleared.'

In the near distance – or so it seemed – they were gazing at the vast panorama of the Bernese Oberland range, a wall of mighty snowbound peaks silhouetted against a background of an azure sky. Newman wrapped an arm round her waist, squeezing her. The long night's sleep, the dream-like view, had relaxed her.

'I think that big job is the Jungfrau,' he commented. 'It's the right shape...'

'Isn't it just wonderful? We can have breakfast up here, can't we?'

'Probably the only way we'll get some at this hour...'

That was when the phone started ringing. Nancy danced to the phone, picked up the receiver and announced herself in a lilting tone.

Newman realized something was very wrong from the change in her expression, in her tone of voice, in the way the conversation turned. She was standing very erect now, her complexion drained of all its natural colour and she began to argue, her voice harsh and aggressive.

'You can't do that! I forbid it! You bastard! I'll call you a bastard any time I want to – because that's what you are... I don't believe any of it...

305

I'm going to raise bloody hell! Don't interrupt... You murdering swine...'
Her voice suddenly went strangely quiet. 'You'll pay for this – that I promise you...'

'Get them to hold on,' Newman called out. 'Tell me what it's about. I'll talk to them...'

She had slammed down the receiver. She turned to look at Newman and he stared back at her. Her face had closed up. She began to walk slowly round the room, sucking her thumb, which Newman guessed was reversion to a childhood habit.

Tell me,' he said quietly.

She went into the bathroom and closed the door. He tore off his night clothes, slipped into vest and pants and pulled on a pair of slacks, his shirt and shoes. At that stage she emerged from the bathroom where he had heard the tap running. She had washed and applied her makeup. She moved like a sleepwalker.

'Do as I tell you,' he snapped. 'Sit down in that chair. Talk.'

'They've killed Jesse...' She spoke in a flat monotone. 'That was Kobler. He said Jesse had had a heart attack – that he died almost immediately. They've already cremated him...'

'They can't do that. Who signed the death certificate? Did Kobler say?'

'Yes, he said that Grange signed the certificate. He said they have a sworn document signed by Jesse requesting cremation...'

'They can't get away with that. It's too quick. Christ, this is Sunday...'

'They covered themselves on that one, too. Kobler said Grange found Jesse was infected with cholera. That could justify immediate cremation. I think it could. I'm not familiar with Swiss law...'

She was talking like the playback of a slow-running tape-recorder. She sat quite still, her hands slack in her lap as she looked up and Newman was startled by the coldness in her eyes.

'We'll get them to send up some coffee...'

'That would be nice. Just coffee, no food. You order for yourself. You must be hungry...' She waited while he gave Room Service the order and then asked the question. 'Bob – can you tell me something? Is

Signer really mixed up in this Terminal thing Dr Nagel mentioned last night?'

'Yes, I'm sure now. I'll show you something while we're waiting for the coffee.' He was glad to get her mind moving on another track – any other track. He produced the report Blanche had brought him. She remarked wasn't that what he had been reading when she'd fallen asleep? He said it was and showed her three pages where he had turned down the corners.

'His signature confirming the transfer of these huge sums of money is clear enough. Victor Signer. He's president of the Zurcher Kredit Bank, the outfit which dominates the Gold Club which backs Grange. After breakfast,' he went on, 'I suggest we go and see Beck if he's in his office – which I'm sure he will be. He's practically sleeping on the job...'

'So,' she said, ignoring his last suggestion, 'Grange and Signer and Kobler are the mainspring behind the Terminal thing?'

'It's beginning to look very much like that. Did you hear what I said about Beck? That we go and see him after we've eaten?'

'I think I'd like that...'

Beck, clean-shaven and spruce, sat behind his desk listening while Nancy repeated the gist of her phone call from Kobler. As she talked he glanced at Newman once or twice, raising an eyebrow to indicate he was disturbed by the calm, detached way she spoke. At the end of her story he used the intercom to call in Gisela and was waiting by the door when she came in.

'Stay with Dr Kennedy until we come back,' he whispered. 'On no account leave her alone – not for a moment. I think she is in a state of severe shock.' He raised his voice. 'Bob, could you come with me, please? There's someone you will want to meet.'

When they were outside in the corridor he closed the door and folded his arms. He pursed his lips as though uncertain how to phrase what he was going to say.

'Ever since you arrived I have sensed you found it difficult to trust anyone – probably for very good reasons. That included myself. We are now going to the radio room. You have met Leupin, you know his voice. Since about midnight I have had a film unit van in position watching the Berne Clinic from the edge of the forest above it. When we reach the radio room you can ask Leupin any question you like – bearing in mind security – including checking his position. Now, let's get this poison of mistrust out of your system. I need all the help I can get...'

It took less than five minutes inside the radio room and Newman immediately recognized Leupin's voice. The policeman confirmed that they were in position 'by the forest'. He further mentioned that they had watched 'a certain eminent personage's well-known car leave the place in question about midnight...'

And that, thought Newman, unfortunately would fit in with the story that Grange had diagnosed cholera, had signed the death certificate, had been present at the Clinic after leaving the Bellevue reception to carry out these actions. He asked Beck if they could have a few minutes alone where they could talk privately. Beck led him inside an interrogation room and closed the door.

'This tape,' said Newman, placing the spool on a table, 'is the recorded interview I had with Manfred Seidler when he admitted bringing in Soviet gas masks on the instructions of Professor Grange. Nancy will give you a sworn statement confirming she witnessed the interview – but not today, if you don't mind. And this is the film of several shots I took of the gas mask Seidler handed to you when you grabbed his suitcase...'

'I am grateful,' Beck replied.

'And this cartridge is from a rifle fired at a certain member of Grange's staff at the Clinic. I'm talking about Willy Schaub, head porter. You'll find him at this address. When you pick him up include a man who speaks good English. Tell him to knock on the door of the first-class flat and call out, "Newman here". He'll tell you a lot. Keep him in a safe – very safe – place. Don't be worried by the name alongside the bell-push, B. Signer. She's Victor Signer's daughter and I don't want her bothered. Signer has no time for her. May I rely on you?'

'For every request, yes.'

'You can bring in Grange now?' Newman asked.

'Not yet. That cholera nonsense is clever. He will have put the Clinic in a state of quarantine...'

'So we still haven't got him?'

'Not yet. He is very powerful.'

It was 6 p.m. Soon it would be dark. Blanche sat at a window table in the Bellevue coffee shop, eating a leisurely meal which she had paid for in advance. Earlier, she had watched Newman's parked Citroën from her bedroom window at this side of the hotel. Now she watched it from the table. Her scooter was parked against the wall of the Hertz offices and she was dressed in her riding gear. The wet-look pants, a thick woollen sweater – and her windcheater was thrown over the back of her chair.

Pausing before dessert, she glanced round the empty room and opened her handbag. The hand grenade she had brought from her flat bulged in the side compartment. Strange how she had acquired it – going back to the days when her stepfather had tried to mould her to his will.

He had taken her with him to a grenade practice range and, she had suspected, only his rank had permitted her to accompany him. He had thrown several grenades himself, then asked her to follow his example, watching her for any sign of nerves. That was when she had pocketed this grenade while he watched the previous one explode behind the concrete barrier. She had already escaped being raped in a dark alley by producing the egg-shaped weapon and threatening to blow herself and her attacker to pieces. She zipped up the compartment, looked out at the Citroën again and continued her meal. She was convinced Newman was going to make some reckless move before the evening was out. And to reach the Berne Clinic he had to use that Citroën.

Thirty-Six

It was that intense dark which only comes on a cold, starlit night when Newman parked the Citroën within inches of the wire fence surrounding the Clinic. Switching off the motor, he got out and his feet ground into crusted snow. This part of the fence was a long way from the gatehouse.

He climbed on to the bonnet, heaved himself up on to the roof of the car, and he was within six inches of the top of the fence. He flexed his legs, crouched down and jumped up and over. He landed the way he had seen paratroopers land, rolling over, and when he stood up his only memento of the leap was a bruised shoulder. He walked briskly across hard snow towards the Clinic entrance at a diagonal angle, his ears attuned for the slightest warning that Dobermans were on the prowl despite Novak's assurance to the contrary.

He reached the entrance without seeing anyone, frozen by the wind blowing from the north. Without hesitation he mounted the steps, opened the first door, strode across the deserted veranda, threw open the inner door and two people turned to stare at him.

Astrid was seated behind the counter. Novak, wearing a business suit ready for departure, was checking a file which lay open on the counter-top. Astrid stood up, astounded, then she recovered her poise and grabbed for the phone. Newman leaned over the counter and smashed his fist against her full, fleshy chin. She reeled over backwards, caught her head against the rear wall and sagged out of sight.

'My God! You could have killed her...'

'No such luck. Let's move, Novak. Open that door into the corridor. Come on! Is that your car outside?'

'Yes, I...'

'When you've opened the door, get behind the wheel and pretend it's Indianapolis...'

Novak produced his card, inserted it inside the slot and the door slid back. Newman snatched the key card out of Novak's hand and walked into the deserted corridor. The door closed behind him. He was wearing a dark padded windcheater and a pair of jeans – clothes he rarely used – and his tough walking shoes were rubber-soled.

The only sound in the eerily silent corridor was the muted hum of the air-conditioning. He walked on rapidly, moving down the slope now. He paused where the corridor turned and the angle of descent increased, peering round the corner. A further stretch of empty corridor illuminated by overhead neon strips until it reached the hydraulically-operated steel door which was closed.

As he walked up to the door he extracted from his pocket the six key cards Willy Schaub had handed to him. The first three cards he tried didn't work. He inserted the fourth card and there was a sound of whirring machinery as the steel slab elevated. He walked through quickly and again heard the door closing behind him.

This section was different. At intervals in the green walls on both sides were windows. He paused to glance through one and there was something about the surface of the glass which suggested this was one-way glass – you could see outside but no one would be able to look inside from the grounds.

He guessed he was very close to the laboratory – it was probably behind the closed door at the end of the passage. He was looking uphill towards the wall of dark fir forest which overlooked the Clinic. On top of a small mound uniformed figures moved slowly round some device perched on top of the mound. He couldn't see too clearly.

By the side of the door at the end of this passage was a box with a slot exactly like the previous lock. The first card he chose operated the door which slid up, revealing what lay beyond. A dimly-lit chamber, very large and crammed with tables which supported wire cages. Inside these cages were housed animals. The chimpanzees turned round to stare silently at the intruder.

The room was not only occupied by animals. At the rear of the chamber behind the cages stood Professor Armand Grange. Two figures wearing the weird gas masks stepped forward, grabbed Newman by the arms as the door closed. A fourth man stood near Grange. Bruno Kobler. Newman ground his shoe down on the instep of the man on his left who grunted in pain but retained his grip. Kobler walked over, staring at the prisoner, not hurrying, and while the two men held Newman he searched him, running his hands over his padded windcheater, under his armpits and down the sides of his arms and legs.

'He is carrying no weapon,' he reported.

'But why should he carry a weapon, Bruno?' Grange asked as he padded closer. The poor lighting had the effect of blanking out the tinted glasses so he seemed eyeless. 'He is a reporter,' Grange continued. 'He works on the basis that the pen – the typewriter – is mightier than the sword. This may be an occasion when the old adage is proved wrong...'

'How the hell did you know I was coming?' Newman enquired. His lone expressed disgust, his expression showed a hint of fear.

'Through the medium of radar, of course! Also we have concealed television cameras sweeping the approaches. The security here has been brought to a fine art, Mr Newman...'

'Along with gassing people to test those Soviet masks...'

'A well-informed reporter, Bruno,' Grange commented, his tone mocking.

'Except that isn't the real object – it's the *gas* which you're testing, the gas you manufacture at Horgen. You made a slip when you told me you manufacture your own cylinders at Horgen – you have the facilities to make the bombs which contain the gas you test here. *Tous azimuts.* All-round defence of Switzerland, isn't that it, Professor?'

'Oh dear, he is *too* well-informed, Bruno...'

'You *have* developed a new gas, haven't you?' Newman persisted. 'A gas which will penetrate the latest Soviet masks. Hence *tous azimuts*, *t*he new strategy. If the Red Army does come you plan to encircle the whole of Switzerland with this wall of gas they will never get through – alive. But you had to be sure the latest Soviet masks were useless against it – so you used patients to test it...'

'But Mr Newman, these patients are terminal...'

'Hence the name of the operation which has puzzled so many people – because the word has different meanings. What kind of gas, Grange? Something developed from Tabun, the gas you grabbed out of Germany when you were a member of the special team sent in at the end of the war?'

'Worse and worse, Bruno. So *very* well-informed. I repeat, the patients are terminal, so what difference does it make? We have a population of millions to defend. It is a question of numbers, Mr Newman. As to the gas, we have come a long way from Tabun. We now have the most advanced form of hydrogen cyanide in the world – and we have found a way to control its volatility. We can distribute belts of the gas as we wish – in the face of an advancing armoured division. They will be dead within thirty seconds, their tanks useless scrap metal. But the gas, Mr Newman, disperses very quickly – swiftly loses its toxicity...'

'You think you'll get away with murder?'

'We have triumphed...' Grange's voice rose to a pitch of ecstasy. Newman realized finally he was faced by a megalomaniac – Grange *was* a madman. He went on in the same tone of exhilaration. 'Signer has called a meeting of the General Staff for Wednesday night. The new policy will be adopted – with the aid of what we call the irregulars – those officers who support our determination to defend our country at all costs...'

'And Nagel's conference of the bankers?'

'It is scheduled for Thursday morning. The meeting will be cancelled. A matter of military security. And now, since you know it all, we will convince you I am right. You will be our final experiment – a more virile specimen than those who went before you. Bruno! Proceed...!'

'You dare not let me see inside the *atombunker* then?'

'Of course you may see. Bring him inside...'

Grange led the way, a massive figure in the gloom. Newman estimated the half-open door to the *atombunker* was at least six inches of solid steel. They paused as a man wearing one of the masks emerged.

He carried in each hand a small blue cylinder with a flow meter attached to its head. Stencilled along each cylinder were the words *Achtung! Giftgas!* Beware! Poison gas!

Inside the vast windowless bunker piles of the blue cylinders were stacked against a wall. The man who had walked out wore a uniform which Newman briefly mistook for a Swiss Army uniform. Then he realized it *was similar* in appearance – but not the same. It was the outfit of a security unit designed to look superficially like the military version. The Swiss Army was *not* guarding the Clinic. Grange had been diabolically clever – he had given the impression he was being protected by the military.

'The filters on top of the chimneys,' Newman asked Grange as they stood staring round the place. 'Why do you need them?'

'He knows everything, Bruno. The filters, Mr Newman, were designed by my top chemist at Horgen in case of an accident here – in case the gas escaped. It would not do to exterminate a dozen patients wandering round the grounds in summer. Those filters render the gas harmless. On the basis of that design we shall develop a mask to protect ourselves against a change in wind direction in wartime. But the gas comes first. Now, Bruno, time for Mr Newman to leave us...'

Bruno Kobler supervised the operation. They held his arms by his sides and Kobler himself fastened the mask over Newman's head and face. He struggled but they held him firmly. Through the Plexiglas eyepieces he saw the tinted glasses of Professor Grange staring at him with no expression at all. It was a scientific experiment he was engaged on.

Kobler led the way out of the *atombunker* across the laboratory chamber to a door one of the other masked figures had opened. Icy air crawled over Newman's hands. The straps round his neck chafed the skin. Kobler paused at the doorway, lifted the mask over one ear and gave instructions.

'You run *down* the slope. It is your only chance of survival. Who knows? You are a fit man – you might just make it to the road. Not that anyone will believe what you have seen here. I will point the way you go...'

The two men held Newman in a vice-like grip as Kobler slipped on an overcoat. Then they led him into the night. He looked round quickly through the eyepieces, checking where everyone was positioned. The nearby mound overlooking the downward slope, the mound where the mortar was mounted, a stock of bombs by its side. The men grouped round it – one holding a bomb near the mouth of the barrel. The slope behind them, climbing up towards the forest.

Hannah Stuart and Holly Laird had died running *down* that slope, doubtless hoping to reach the road they would have seen earlier while sitting inside the enclosed veranda – Mrs Laird had even reached the road, but had then died.

Kohler was pointing down the slope. On top of the mound a few yards away half-a-dozen masked figures watched him, watched their target. The two men on either side released him. Kobler gestured impatiently down the slope. Newman flexed his stiff arms, nodded his head to show he understood and walked slowly forward to the edge of where the slope started downhill. Kobler, wearing no mask, retreated inside the laboratory.

Newman flexed each leg, easing the stiffness, then bent down to rub his left ankle. He jerked upright, the automatic Beck had given him, the weapon he had concealed behind his sock, gripped in his right hand. He aimed it at the men grouped round the mortar, firing over their heads.

They scattered, abandoned the mound as Newman ran straight for it, kicking over the mortar barrel, running on *uphill*. The wind blew in his face. He knew they dare not fire the mortar even if they remounted it successfully. The gas would blow back in *their* faces. They could only pursue him up the steep incline on foot. He doubted they would risk the sound of any more shots. But he was handicapped by the bloody mask which was constricting his neck. No time to stop and try to tear it off – they'd be on top of him. God, the ascent was steep, the forest seemed so very far away.

Blanche stood on the knoll above the Clinic, the knoll she had used when she had photographed the Clinic and its grounds. She had followed Newman's Citroën on her scooter along the motorway. She had watched through her pair of night-glasses from a distance when he

315

vaulted the fence. She had ridden on to the knoll, the only point from where she might see what was happening.

She had the night-glasses pressed to her eyes now, watching in horror as Newman kicked over something after scattering the men in Swiss uniform. She knew the running figure was Newman – his movements were familiar enough for her to be quite certain.

The swine had recovered from their surprise, men who wore horror film masks, and they were running after Newman, gaining on him as, bunched together, they took the same route up a gulch below where she stood. Her mouth was tight as she bent down to pick up her helmet. Her hair was blowing in her face, confusing her vision. She rammed the helmet over her head. Reaching into her pocket, she brought out an egg-shaped object. The hand grenade.

Blanche removed the glove from her right hand. At the Gstaad finishing school she had been a top-flight player of tennis with a vicious backhand. She hesitated, gauging the distance between Newman, who was slowing down, and his pursuers. Newman reached a point where the defile turned at an angle. He ran round the corner. She took out the pin and counted, her hand held behind her. It was ironic that Victor Signer had furnished her with the opportunity to obtain the grenade.

Her hand came up in a powerful, controlled swing. She lobbed the grenade and held her breath. It landed a few feet in front of the group of men hurrying up the defile, detonated. The lead pursuer threw up both arms in a wild gesture and fell. The men behind sagged to the ground, some of them crawling on all fours before they, too, collapsed.

Newman heard the explosion. It gave him the strength for one final burst up to the end of the defile – he thought they were using grenades to stop him. He came out on top of the hill and the wire fence – with the road beyond in front of the forest – was a few yards away.

To his right there was a gate in the fence. He found it was padlocked when he reached it. Hauling out the automatic from his pocket, he shot off the padlock, pulled the gate open and staggered along the road. He was still wearing the gas mask when Leupin came to meet him.

Thirty-Seven

Monday, 20 February. Snow came to Berne in the middle of the night. Newman, who had spent half that night with Beck at the Taubenhalde, dragged himself out of bed, grabbed his wristwatch and went over to the window to pull back the curtains. 7.30 a.m. He looked over his shoulder at Nancy who was lying on her back with her eyes open.

'Come and look at this,' he said.

Without a word she got out of bed and joined him, pulling on her dressing gown. For the first time since their arrival it was a white world. Rooftops heavy with snow across the river. The twin headlights of cars crawled along the snowbound Aarstrasse. A tram, its lights blurred, crept over the Kirchenfeldbrücke. Large snowflakes drifted down past their window.

'What will happen to Grange and Signer and Kohler?' she asked. 'You flopped out when you got back from seeing Beck. I guess that experience at the Clinic must have been pretty horrible. I appreciate your calling in here first...'

'Beck was vague. They have the film they took from the van they'd parked in the forest of my being chased. They have the gas mask I was wearing. They have my statement – but I'll be required to stay on for the inquiry...'

'Inquiry?'

'The Swiss don't like washing dirty linen in public. What country does? And there's military security involved. They also have the sworn statement of Willy Schaub, the head porter who knows a lot...'

'They haven't arrested Grange yet?'

'They have to handle it carefully. They won't want the fact that the most deadly poison gas in the world was being made and tested to hit the world's press if they can avoid it...'

'But if Grange is still at the Clinic won't he destroy the evidence – those cylinders you saw in that *atombunker*?'

'Oddly enough, no. He's arrogant enough – mad enough – to feel confident he can bluff his way through. He's proud of the fact that he's produced that gas. These men think they are patriots. And it's complicated by Grange's tactic saying Jesse had suspected cholera. Note the word "suspected". He can always say it was a wrong diagnosis later – meantime he has the place under quarantine. It's a kind of stalemate...'

'Jesse raised me.' Her voice was suddenly harsh. 'He was the only father I ever had.' He glanced at her. Her posture was rigid and she stared at the drifting snowflakes as though looking at something way beyond them. 'He deserved a better way to go,' she continued in the same disturbing tone of voice.

'I'm sure they'll eventually get the lot,' he said.

'I'm going to bathe. Order me a full breakfast...'

He dressed quickly in a troubled frame of mind. He had a feeling this thing wasn't over yet. When she emerged from the bathroom she was wearing a cashmere sweater and slacks tucked inside short leather boots, the kind of outfit she wore in Arizona. Over breakfast he realized her mood had changed. Her speech was brisk, her chin tilted at an aggressive angle.

'I'm leaving for Tucson on Wednesday,' she announced. 'I shall catch the three o'clock Dan-Air flight to Gatwick, then on to Dallas by American Airlines...'

'I told you, I have to stay on for the inquiry...'

'I don't like being used, Bob. You've used me from that very first evening we met in London. You needed someone who could get you inside the Berne Clinic. I fitted the role perfectly. My birthday party at Bewick's that night was well-advertised in advance. Enough people knew about it at St Thomas's. And there was that patient they kept under armed guard – men in civilian clothes everyone knew were Secret Service. One of those guards tipped you off about my party. You turn up at the table next to mine. Really it was very neat. I first began to

318

wonder about you in Geneva. You changed, you turned into a hunter. Since then there have been a whole series of odd incidents. Phone calls you said were wrong numbers. Trips off without me to see people you never told me about when you got back. I don't know who you're working for, but by Christ, I know you've used me. I am right, aren't I?'

'Up to a point, yes...'

'Jesus! Why qualify it?'

'Because later I became genuinely very fond of you...'

'Shit!'

'If you say so...'

'And now I'd like the room to myself for a while. I have to call Tucson to warn Linda I'm coming home...'

'She'll be asleep,' Newman pointed out. 'They're eight hours behind us in Arizona...'

'Linda is never in bed before two in the morning – and it's only midnight now in Tucson. So, maybe you could go downstairs and read a paper – or find a girl to screw...'

Lee Foley called the Berne Clinic from his room and asked to speak to Dr Bruno Kobler. When Kobler came on the line Foley continued speaking in German, giving his name as Lou Schwarz and explaining that his wife was seriously ill. He asked for details of fees and carried on a conversation for five minutes, studying Kobler's voice, before ending the call.

He then went down to reception for his case, which he had kept packed – as always – ready for a speedy departure. He paid his bill after questioning the amount they were charging for phone calls, which involved a lengthy conversation. As he left the hotel Leupin, who had been sitting nearby, pretending to read a newspaper, stood up and walked to the Taubenhalde to report on this development to Beck.

Foley next drove the Porsche to the friend he had hired it from and gave him precise instructions. Foley was keeping the Porsche a little longer. At one o'clock the following day the friend must phone the cantonal police headquarters in Berne to report the theft of the Porsche.

He further arranged for the friend to have ready for him a Volvo – any colour except red. He would collect the Volvo the following morning. He paid over a large sum of money in Swiss banknotes and asked permission to use the phone in privacy. As soon as he was alone in the office he called a private airfield near Paris and gave further instructions. He thanked his friend and left.

Climbing behind the wheel of the Porsche, he drove out of Berne and took the motorway north. He was careful to keep inside the speed limit. His next destination was Zurich.

Epitaph

Tuesday, 21 February. At 1 p.m. Victor Signer, wearing his uniform, sat in the back of the Mercedes while his chauffeur drove up to the entrance of the Berne Clinic. He was puzzled by the urgent summons but assumed some crisis had arisen.

Bruno Kohler had phoned him at his office inside the Zurcher Kredit Bank in Zurich. Kobler had sounded agitated. A fresh development had taken place at the Clinic. No, it was not something he could discuss over the phone. Professor Grange wished to see him urgently.

The car swung in a half-circle as it reached the entrance to the Clinic and pulled up. Signer did not bother to wait for the chauffeur to open the door. He was an impatient man who did not stand on ceremony except for the purposes of intimidating someone.

He stood for a moment in the sunshine, straightening his tunic. The first bullet slammed square into the centre of his broad chest. He stood quite still for a fraction of a second as the red patch spread, staining his immaculate uniform. The second bullet whipped his cap off, skimming the top of his head away. He sagged to the ground. The third bullet hammered into his abdomen.

Armand Grange, who had been talking to Astrid, her chin bandaged where Newman had hit her, heard the shots and came out to the top of the steps. He stared at the crumpled form of Signer like a man who cannot credit what lies before him.

The fourth bullet penetrated his neck. As he staggered under the impact blood gushed from an artery. The fifth bullet slammed into the huge body as it sprawled at the foot of the steps. Grange jerked convulsively and then he also lay still.

Bruno Kobler reacted with greater decision. Looking out of his office window at the scene beyond the veranda, he ran to a cupboard, opened it, grabbed his repeater rifle and ran downstairs. Both doors were open and his military training asserted itself. He looked for cover. The parked Mercedes, inside which the chauffeur was crouched behind the wheel, terrified.

Kobler went out through both doors at a rush and dived behind the car. A bullet ricocheted close to his right heel as he crouched at the rear of the vehicle. He peered through the rear window and caught a brief movement at the top of the knoll perched near the forest. The marksman was up there.

As he ducked his head a bullet smashed through the rear window. Kobler recognized this was first-rate shooting. A professional marksman. He poked the barrel of the rifle round the right-hand side of the car and loosed off a shot. There was a puff of dust at the top of the knoll. He had the range.

Put yourself in the other bastard's shoes. He would expect Kobler to appear next on the left-hand side of the car. Kobler thrust the barrel close to the right-hand side, moved out to get a clear shot and an express train crashed into his chest, throwing him clear of the car and into the open. The next shot smashed his throat, the final shot shattered what was left of his chest. He lay in a spreading pool of blood and it was very silent in the sunlight.

'Grange, Kobler and Victor Signer were shot dead this morning at the Clinic,' Newman said as he shut the bedroom door and came into the room. 'It's in the stop press in the *Berner Zeitung*...'

'I know,' said Nancy, staring out of the window without turning round.

'You can't know – it's not in the paper. Too early. I've just heard from Beck. So how do you know? You had advance knowledge – that's how you know...'

'What do you mean?' She had swung round and her expression was bleak. She wore the same outfit as the previous day, her Arizona outfit. Newman recalled some remark he had made that she was the last of the pioneer stock.

'Yesterday you lashed me for using *you*,' he said, walking towards her. 'You omitted to say *you used me*...'

'Just what the hell are you talking about?'

'You felt you needed back-up when you came to Switzerland – someone who spoke the languages, who knew people in high places. I qualified. In the beginning you got to know me, used your feminine wiles so I'd make the trip with you...'

'I'm glad you said "in the beginning",' she replied quietly. 'Yes, I did feel I needed someone. Then gradually I became very fond of you...'

'If that was all, I might accept it. But it wasn't all...'

'I don't know what you're talking about,' she flared.

'I'm talking about Lee Foley. You're ruthless. Maybe it's that pioneer stock. You could be right, but I can't take being tricked *twice* over. That first night we had dinner in Geneva I spotted Foley outside the Pavillon. I spotted him again in the next coach on the train from Geneva to Berne. Then I met him in the bar downstairs one evening and he made a rare slip. I referred to the death of Mrs Laird – Foley replied, "I know." But Beck kept the news out of the papers. The only people who witnessed Mrs Laird's death were Beck, myself, Lachenal, Dr Kleist later – and *you*. The only possible candidate for passing that information to Foley is yourself...'

'You're crazy...'

'There's a whole lot more. Foley kept following us – in a red Porsche, for God's sake. He'd never normally use such an easily recognizable car – he used it so you would know he was on the job, to reassure you...'

'What job?' she demanded.

'First, you hired him as extra – and very tough – back-up to supplement me. Remember over ten years ago in Tucson they sent a CIA operative to cooperate with Jesse? I think we'll find that operative was Lee Foley. You'd be about seventeen or eighteen then. That was when you first met Foley...'

'You're reaching...'

'We wondered about. Foley for quite a while – was he ex-CIA, a real detective? I'm sure now he was. I think you phoned him in New York from Tucson – when we decided to come to Berne – and hired him. You phoned him again while we waited at Heathrow-when you went into

323

the West End to shop at Fortnums. How else would he know we'd be at the Hotel des Bergues? Before we left Geneva you rushed out to get some Gucci perfume, and to phone the news to Foley we were leaving. How else would he know we'd be aboard that express?'

'You're even brighter than I thought...'

'It doesn't end there. He became protection. He shot those gunmen at Le Pont station. Only someone with Foley's skill with a rifle could gun down both men from a moving car...'

'Have you finished?' She was tense. 'I've had enough...'

'No! Beck and I puzzled quite a bit over who could afford to hire Foley...'

'I could afford him?'

'You could borrow whatever it took from any USA bank on the basis of your four million dollar expectations from Jesse's will. Everyone knew about it. You must have paid him a packet for his final mission...'

'Final mission?'

'For shooting down Grange, Signer and Kobler. And Kobler was a marksman – it would take a Foley to pull that off. I gather Beck has a dragnet out for him now...'

The phone rang. Nancy moved to reach it but Newman grabbed the instrument first. It was Beck. The time was 5 p.m.

'We've traced his Porsche,' Beck said. 'Left in the car park at Kloten, the airport for Zurich, as you know. He has a first-class reservation on Flight SR 808 out of Zurich for London. I've flooded Kloten with men. Wish me luck...'

'Good luck...'

And you're going to need it he thought as he replaced the receiver. He told Nancy who had called, the gist of their brief conversation. Then the phone rang a second time. Newman lifted the receiver, asked who it was and a familiar gravelly voice replied.

'Thought I'd just say goodbye for now, Newman,' Foley opened. 'Save Beck a little time. He found the Porsche? Good. Did he find the Volvo I stole and left at Belp? I had a Cessna waiting for me there. I warned you the body count would go on rising. The finish reminded me of

They had found the other stolen Army rifle on top of the knoll from where the marksman had killed three men in thirty seconds, Beck had reported earlier in the conversation. And Ballistics had confirmed this was the same weapon which had eliminated two men at Le Pont station.

It was close to dusk as Newman wandered through the arcades, the only sign of life a single tram rumbling past in the slushy snow. It would take years to explore every arcade and alley, he thought. He really liked Berne. It had a unique quality he had never encountered in any other city during his worldwide travels.

He had one more job to do. Someone had to tell Blanche her stepfather was dead. He had no idea what her reaction would be – but the job had to be done. His footsteps trailed in the relics of slush other feet had brought inside the arcade. He stopped outside the door with the bell-push and a name alongside it. *B. Signer*. He pressed the bell and braced himself.

'Who is it?' her voice called through the speakphone.

'Bob. Blanche, I have a single, one-way ticket for a flight to London...'

'I see...'

'I thought you'd like to watch me tear the ticket into a thousand pieces...'

Milton Keynes UK
Ingram Content Group UK Ltd.
UKHW040739111223
434160UK00004B/484